DANGEROUS

By Jessie Keane

JESSIE KEANE

DANGEROUS

MACMILLAN

First published 2015 by Macmillan
an imprint of Pan Macmillan, a division of Macmillan Publishers Limited
Pan Macmillan, 20 New Wharf Road, London N1 9RR
Basingstoke and Oxford
Associated companies throughout the world
www.panmacmillan.com

ISBN 978-1-4472-5426-3

3 5 7 9 8 6 4

A CIP catalogue record for this book is available from the British Library.

Typeset by Ellipsis Digital Limited, Glasgow
Printed and bound by CPI Group (UK) Ltd, Croydon, CR0 4YY

Visit **www.panmacmillan.com** to read more about all our books
and to buy them. You will also find features, author interviews and
news of any author events, and you can sign up for e-newsletters
so that you're always first to hear about our new releases.

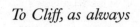

To Cliff, as always

ACKNOWLEDGEMENTS

To my friends, old and new, to my contacts (you know who you are), to the team at Pan Macmillan, to all my Facebook and Twitter followers – a huge thanks, guys. Onward and upward . . .

For the love of money is the root of all evil.
Some have wandered away from the faith and
impaled themselves with a lot of pain
because they made money their goal.

1 Timothy 6:10
Common English Bible

PROLOGUE

Soho, London, February 1962

It happened on a Saturday night. She was at the Carmelo, working in the office over the club, when there was a commotion downstairs and Mitch the barman burst through the door, wild-eyed, dishevelled, and so scared it was all he could do to breathe.

'It's fucking Sears!'

The words came out as a strangled yelp, and then he was gone as quickly as he'd appeared, leaving the door swinging on its hinges behind him.

For a moment she was so stunned by Mitch's sudden entrance that all she could do was sit there, immobile, the pen poised over the accounts, listening. When she'd passed through the club earlier, it had been packed with a typical Saturday-night crowd, out for a good time. With the door closed and her mind on the accounts, she'd barely registered the disturbance until Mitch came up to give her the glad tidings.

Now, above the sudden mad pounding of her own heart, she could hear glasses smashing, tables being overturned, women screaming and a man's voice roaring threats.

Oh shit. It was happening, just as Marcus Redmayne had

1

said it would when he came into another of her clubs two weeks earlier, trying to scare the arse off her.

She was scared now all right. Her legs felt weak underneath her as she forced herself out of the chair and hurried to close the door. For a moment she stood with her ear pressed to the wood, listening to the pandemonium downstairs.

Oh fuck oh God oh help . . .

Trembling, she turned the handle, stepped out onto the landing and peered over the banisters. There was a fight going on, people with baseball bats and bike chains striking out at anyone who got in their way, and women were running, shrieking in fear.

Clara's heart was beating so hard she was afraid it would tear its way through her chest wall and thump to the carpet in a bloody heap.

Fulton Sears.

There he was, in the centre of the room, huge and bald and ugly as sin, swinging left and right with brass knuckledusters, his hands red with blood all the way up to the wrists, wallowing in this bloodbath like a hippo in the mud. Limp with fright, Clara edged backward, trying to be invisible – but before she could make it back to the office he looked up and saw her there.

She froze.

His face split in a wide grin. She saw him knock one of the waiters to the floor and then glance up again, up to where she stood on the landing, and . . .

Shit! He was coming up!

He was surging through the fight, barging people out of the way. Clara raced into the office and slammed the door closed. Instinctively she fumbled for a bolt or latch, but there was no lock on the inside of the door – why would there be?

2

Improvising, she jammed one of the chairs under the handle and stood there, watching it, panting with terror. Then she lunged for the desk, snatched up the phone and dialled 999, her eyes never leaving the door, the handle, all the time waiting for it to turn, waiting for that monster to try to get in at her.

As she was dialling, she could hear Toby's voice in her head: *Whatever happens in the clubs, we don't ever call the police. We never involve the Bill, not even the ones on the pay-roll. We sort things out ourselves.*

Clara paused for a long moment. Then she slammed the phone back down onto its cradle. Looked around for a weapon, anything, to defend herself.

There was nothing.

Sweating, trembling, all she could do was stand there, listening to the chaos downstairs and waiting for the handle to turn. How long would a chair hold him? About two seconds. Unable to look away, she carried on staring at it.

Oh God, please help me, she thought, her pulse deafening in her ears. She felt she was going to pass out or throw up, sickened by the images flashing through her mind of what he'd do when he got his hands on her.

The noise downstairs seemed to be fading. She could hear only men's voices now, shouting, no more screams. Groaning, did she hear groaning? She thought she did. And . . . oh sweet Jesus, she could hear someone coming up the stairs. She could hear *him,* moving stealthily, creeping up the stairs. Her eyes were riveted to the handle. To the door. To the chair. She couldn't move, she couldn't even breathe.

The handle was turning.

Slowly, excruciatingly slowly, it was starting to turn.

With a desperate cry Clara flung herself forward, put her full weight against the flimsy barrier of the chair. Her chest was tight with fear. She was right up against the door, she could almost *feel* him there, right there, on the other side of it.

The handle continued to turn. She could feel his weight go against it, felt it shuddering through the wood. The chair bucked beneath her. He was going to get in here. He was going to get her.

She waited, sweat trickling down her temples, sliding down her back. She could smell her own fear. If he got in here . . .

There was no *if* about it.

He was going to.

And then . . . oh God, what was going to happen to her?

A faint, deep-throated chuckle came from the other side of the door.

The hairs on the nape of her neck stood on end. He was laughing at her. He knew she was here, she was trapped, and he was mocking her. Any moment now he would burst in here and hurt her, kill her. She could almost see him on the other side of the door, barrel-chested, bloodstained, sadistic and out for revenge.

God, please help me, she thought. *I'll do better. I'll be good, I promise, just help me right now, will you?*

God wasn't listening.

Was it any surprise? Would anyone, God included, actually care if she came to grief? Not her family, that was for sure, and she had no friends.

The only thing she had left was a reputation – and it wasn't a good one.

She was Black Clara – twenty-four years old, twice married and twice widowed, a hard-hearted gold-digger, a cold-blooded chaser of men and their money. Clara Dolan, the hopeful young girl she had once been, hadn't survived the move from the slums of Houndsditch. But all she'd ever done was what she *had* to do. Wasn't that the truth?

Suddenly the door buckled as he launched a ferocious kick. Jarred by the impact, her teeth snapped together so that she bit her tongue and made it bleed.

Clara flinched and let out a hopeless yell.

Then another.

Jesus, oh please, please . . .

Another kick. Clara was thrown backward against the desk, floundering. Then the door and the chair flew inward, and Sears burst into the room.

1

Houndsditch, London, 1953

Clara was fifteen when she found out that love is dangerous, that it will destroy you. It was a lesson she learned at
her mother's side, when Kathleen Dolan went into labour
for the fifth time.

Kathleen's first pregnancy had brought Clara into the
world; then came a stillbirth, followed five years later by
Bernadette, or Bernie as she was always known; and then,
two years after that, came Henry. Now there would be
another baby and it was the last thing they needed, any of
them, because Dad had run off to avoid a prison sentence,
leaving them with nothing.

So here they were, what was left of the Dolan family:
Kathleen, Clara, Bernie and Henry, living in a hellhole, with
barely enough money to feed themselves on post-war
rations and a constant struggle to find the rent, which was
so high – six pounds a week! – that Clara thought Frank
Hatton the rent man ought to be wearing a fucking mask,
since he was committing daylight robbery.

Clara still couldn't believe that Dad had left them. Night
after night, she dreamed that he would come back to tell
them it was all a joke, a mistake, they were going home. It
was eight months since he'd abandoned them. Not long

after, Kathleen his pregnant wife learned that he'd been fiddling the books on his business and she had confided as much, amid floods of tears, to her eldest daughter Clara.

It all came out then, as disgusting and unsightly as spilled entrails unravelling. Tom Dolan's engineering firm was deeply in debt, while all the money he'd scraped off the top had been squandered on living like a lord. The firm – which had been a successful growing concern employing two hundred and fifty people – was in ruins. And there was worse to come. Without telling Kathleen, Tom had taken out a raft of huge loans from the bank and put their home up as security.

'It's going to be fine, Mum,' said Clara, sitting on the bed, which was soaked with her mother's sweat, and dabbing gently at her feverish brow with a cool flannel. Kathleen moved fitfully, and the old newspapers they'd put under her to save soaking the mattress crackled.

Oh, is it?

Clara was trying hard not to let her fear show in her face. She kept glancing nervously at the hugely swollen belly straining beneath her mother's sweat-stained nightdress. She knew nothing of childbirth. All she knew was that her mother had been lying here in agony all night. Now, morning was nudging at the curtains, sending strands of light through, and the daylight made her more anxious than ever. Was this right, for the labour to go on so long?

Against her better judgement, she'd sent Bernie out in the small hours to fetch the district nurse. They all hated being in the flat, but venturing outside it was even worse. The Dolans occupied the attic, but on the floors below them there were other families, some packed in ten to a room, and often they spilled out onto the communal stairs, blocking access to and from the top floor.

Hatton the rent man had told Kathleen that their landlord Lenny Lynch had 'put the schwartzers in to de-stat',

7

and Kathleen had to explain to Clara what that meant – that since the 1952 McCarran–Walter provisions blocked the Caribbean's emigration outlet to America, West Indians had been pouring into Britain and landlords had seen this as a golden opportunity.

People like Lenny Lynch had lost no time in packing the immigrants into places previously occupied by white families, and had ruthlessly encouraged them to do their worst: to piss in doorways, leave rubbish up and down the pavements, play jazz at all hours, install white prostitutes to pimp off, behave in a threatening manner toward the whites so that they would move out . . . and then landlords could move the more profitable, more easily exploited blacks in.

So Clara spent a long, anxious time waiting for Bernie's return. When she eventually made it home in one piece Clara was relieved. But the news wasn't good. The district nurse was off across town attending some other poor bitch who couldn't afford the ten shillings a proper midwife would cost.

'But her husband said she'd come straight over as soon as she got back,' said Bernie, who was now hovering, fidgeting, her pixie face screwed up with worry, in the bedroom doorway. Little Henry was clinging on to Bernie like she was a life raft in a sea of doubt.

Hours crept by.

'Should I go over again and see if she's back yet?' asked Bernie finally, her face wet with tears of terror at the sight of her mother in such pain.

'Yeah,' said Clara. She thought of the doctor's place, several streets away, but they didn't open until nine, that was *hours* off, and anyway the doctor was never there, he hadn't been there yesterday because it was Sunday and no one worked on a Sunday, it was a Holy day. Still, they had to try. This couldn't be right, not this long. 'And I'll write you a note for the doctor – you can drop it through his letterbox too. And for God's sake, be careful. Don't talk to anyone.'

They could only hope. They could only *try*.

Bernie charged off down the stairs and at the noise of the door slamming behind her Kathleen's eyes fluttered open. She let out another deep, growling moan. Then, pitifully, she tried to give Clara a reassuring smile. Clara thought her heart would break, to see that smile. A bleak bitterness gripped her. *Fucking men*. There had been a time when she believed her father could do no wrong – not any more. There he was, swanning about who knew where, having ducked his creditors, and a jail term too, and here was poor Mum, who was worth ten of him, no *twenty*, suffering because of what he'd done to her.

'Mum, I think we're going to have to try and get you over to the hospital,' said Clara.

'Oh yeah? What we gonna do then? Fly? Or walk?' Kathleen smiled and then winced as a fresh contraction hit her.

Clara winced too as Kathleen gripped her hand and let out another one of those gut-wrenching moans.

She could die, thought Clara with a thrill of real horror. *Oh, Dad, why did you do it? How could you leave us like this?*

They'd lost their lovely house, their precious home, when he'd done a runner. Clara felt ready to puke her guts up when she thought of their house; it had been so beautiful, with its manicured lawns. They'd had a gardener then, and a cleaning lady who came in once a week, and there was a fish pond with a fountain shooting up to the sky. There was an elegant top-of-the-range Jaguar on the drive that Dad liked to use as a runabout, and a Rolls-Royce in the garage for family outings.

Clara would never forget that life, their other life, their *real* life. There were trips out to the races, expensive holidays at the seaside. She could still see him in her mind's eye,

9

Tom Dolan, her father, that bastard, laughing and flicking his silver monogrammed Ronson lighter, the flame flaring as he lit another Havana cigar. His gold tie-pin and matching cufflinks would glint in the sunlight. His black hair – like Clara's own – was thick and glossy, and his eyes – also like hers – were the striking violet-blue of an English bluebell wood, always shining with confidence.

And Mum, she'd looked so different then! Mum in designer dresses, her copper-brown hair swept up, styled by the hairdresser at a costly salon up West. Five pounds a week each – a bloody fortune! – for Clara and Bernie, and Henry, the apple of his dad's eye, indulged so much. *Too* much, maybe. No expense spared, not then. The sky was the limit. But suddenly it had ended, it had all come unwound, the threads of their once-gilded lives. Clara had been vaguely aware that creditors were queuing up, staff were being laid off, suppliers who hadn't been paid in a long while were baying for blood and demanding money that was no longer there.

And then the biggest shock of all.

The money was no longer there because Dad had been systematically robbing the company. He'd creamed off sixty thousand pounds to live a lavish lifestyle way beyond his means, all so that he could impress his friends, play the big I-am, buy Rollers and spend days out at Ascot and mix with the nobs he so admired, so wanted to *be* like; pretending he wasn't an ordinary working-class bloke who'd made good, pretending he was something he wasn't.

But what use was it, thinking about that now? Kathleen had rented this flat. They were here. They *had* to cope.

'I'll get hold of a copper, see if he can't whistle up an ambulance,' said Clara. She knew this was like wishing for gold bars down a sewer. The coppers never came round this area if they could avoid it; and on the rare occasions they did, they came in twos and threes, never alone.

They didn't have a phone here – a *phone*, what a bloody joke! – and no one else who lived in these rat-hole flats did either. The telephone box out in the road had been vandalized months back and no PO engineers had proved brave enough to venture into this warren of thieves to fix it.

'We could get a taxi,' gasped Kathleen, still trying to smile through the agony.

This too was a joke. They couldn't afford a taxi. A taxi was the stuff of dreams. They couldn't afford fuck-all. Not any more.

So this is what they mean by being up shit creek, thought Clara.

They had no money and they were three weeks behind with the rent. One of the few things they'd hung on to from their old life was Mum's battered Singer sewing machine, and for the first few months Kathleen had got by taking in dressmaking work, never bringing her clients here – of course not – but going out to do fittings and deliveries. The last few weeks, however, Kathleen had been too ill to even lift a needle.

They couldn't turn to the neighbours for help, either.

'You mustn't talk to anyone,' Kathleen had told her children when they'd moved in here.

Clara had been mystified by this to begin with. It took her a while to understand that all the big terraced houses along this street and the adjacent ones had been greedily parcelled up into flats and let out by uncaring landlords, mostly to migrants and their white 'girlfriends', who were prostitutes whose wages the men lived off. Late into the night there were fights, music played full-volume, people loitering in groups, smoking and grinning on the stinking stairs as they tried to pass, watching the family who occupied the top floor as though they were prey.

This, truly, was a nightmare. Clara had heard of such

things, but she had never dreamed she'd see them close-up. This place – the furnished flat Kathleen had assured her eldest daughter would be the answer to their newly homeless state – was hell: red-hot in summer, freezing in winter, and there was never any peace. The basement of their building had been turned into an illegal cellar-club where people could gather to smoke marijuana and gamble day and night. The Dolans had to share a squalid, filthy toilet two floors down with everyone else in the block, and it was a battle just to get down there and back without being stopped or asked for cash or manhandled.

And the flat itself was no haven from the squalor. The walls were green with damp, old wallpaper peeling off and hanging in brown mouldering strips from every corner, cockroaches scuttling around in the rotting floorboards beside the skirting board. All the Dolans' own beautiful furniture had been seized by bailiffs before the eviction order was served, so they had to make do with the stuff that came with this 'furnished' sweatbox. The stained mattresses reeked of piss and were crawling with bugs. The bedside cabinets were empty orange boxes with bits of fabric tacked onto them. The previous occupants must have had a dog or a cat, because soon after they moved in Henry developed fleabites all round his ankles.

Kathleen had rented this flat because she'd had no choice: it was the only one they could afford. Now, they couldn't even afford this. It had got to the stage where they kept the front door firmly locked at night and daren't answer it by day, knowing it would either be someone wanting to rob them of what little they had, or the never-never man wanting payment for items Kathleen had bought on tick. Or, worst of the lot, Frank Hatton.

Clara shuddered. *Hatton.* Last week Kathleen had been too sick to deal with the repulsive, bristle-chinned old thug when he showed up at their front door to collect the rent money, so Clara had reluctantly answered the door and told him that they had a few problems but would pay him in full next week.

'Promise?' leered Hatton. He wore a battered brown leather coat and he had an Alsatian, mad-eyed and with thick black-and-tan fur, on a stout lead at his side. Round here, Clara reckoned he daren't go out without the damned thing or else someone would rip his teeth out and sell them for dentures. The dog was snarling. It looked like it wanted to tear Clara's throat out. She thought that if Hatton let it go for a second, it would do just that.

Clara hated the way Hatton's eyes roamed over her; it felt disgusting, like having a slug crawling over your skin.

'A pretty girl like you need never starve, you know,' he'd said. 'Well, I suppose you do know. You must.'

Clara felt her face stiffen with distaste. She knew she was a striking girl, with her black hair, white skin and violet-blue eyes. Men had propositioned her before. But he was old enough to be her *granddad*.

'Tuesday,' she said, and shut the door in his face.

'Three o'clock, I'll be here!' he shouted.

Clara leaned against the door, feeling sick, her heart hammering, her mind chasing around in never-ending circles. They were trapped here and they would all die here, in poverty and in fear. They were in hell, and there was no way out.

2

Soho, 1953

Lenny Lynch looked at his flashy gold watch as he stood at the bar in the Blue Banana club. The place was packed, everyone having a good time, playing chemmy and poker. Eartha Kitt was pouring out sultry vocals on the turntable, singing '*C'est Si Bon*'; Lenny didn't know what that meant, but he guessed it was something sexual, something hot.

It was almost time.

Pet an animal too much, feed it too well, and eventually, the thing's going to turn and bite you on the arse. Simple common sense. Dogs, women, men – they were all the same in this respect, Lenny knew it for a fact. But . . . what could you do? He'd always had a soft spot for Marcus Redmayne.

Lenny studied his reflection in the mirrors behind the optics. *Poor old cunt*, he thought, half-laughing to himself – or trying to, anyway. All the Brylcreem in the world couldn't hide his thinning hair, all the costly wet shaves and hot-towel head massages at Trumper's couldn't disguise the fleshy pouches around his bloodshot blue eyes, or the way gravity and time were pulling the sides of his mouth down. His shirt was expensive, his suit bespoke, Savile Row, the best. *But, come on, let's face the music and dance, shall we? I'm old*, he thought. And now he felt tired and sad, too, because

14

it had reached the point where something had to be done about Marcus, something drastic.

And it would be done tonight. He'd already arranged it.

'Put me another one in there, would you, sweetheart?' He handed his empty glass to Delilah, a statuesque Nigerian beauty in her forties who for years had managed this Soho basement bar for him. She tended the bar naked but for a pair of thigh-high black leather boots, as was her usual rather startling practice.

Lenny looked around. The place was busy for a Monday, full of English, Americans and Italians – all sorts of scum in here since the war – most of them playing at the gaming tables, and he'd take a cut from every winning pot. The tarty-looking hostesses with their hard acquisitive eyes and ready smiles were giggling and flirting while serving the punters overpriced drinks and anything else they fancied.

'You a bit down, m'boy,' Delilah purred, eyeing him up. 'Troubles?'

Lenny thought about confiding in her, then bit his tongue. Delilah was one of the people, his old trusted people, who had put the finger on Marcus, saying he'd been coming in here with that scrawny sidekick of his, checking out the books, acting like she was scooping off some of the honey for herself, which of course she would never do. Delilah had been outraged by this implication, by the mere suggestion that she would ever take from Lenny Lynch. And Lenny was, too. There were lots of complaints coming in about Marcus now, half of Soho was in uproar.

'You know what, Lenny boy? You want to sort that pup Marcus out afore he bite you,' said Delilah, reading his thoughts.

Lenny looked at her, startled. But she was right. Delilah was a wise woman. Lenny watched her swagger away to the optics at the back of the bar. Once upon a time, that black arse jiggling around the place would have excited him. In the past, he'd romped happily with Delilah in the back room. Now? Forget it. He was limp as a windsock on a dull day.

Delilah refilled Lenny's glass and turned back to the bar with a broad smile, but inside she was furious. Fucking Marcus Redmayne, sticking his nose in things that didn't concern him, coming in here like a frigging accountant, checking the stock, examining the books, asking questions like she was a damned criminal. She'd run this bar for Lenny ten years now, right through the war and everything – of *course* she dipped in now and then, didn't everyone? Lenny wouldn't mind, even if he knew; she was sure of that. Not that he did know, and she was never going to tell him, but if Marcus would only back off and let well alone, everything would go on as normal and things would be just fine.

She had put the word out around Lenny's other clubs, and sure enough Marcus had been in most of them, checking over things, asking questions. He was all over the place like a fucking rash, she was sick of that boy. Hiding her irritation, she sauntered back to the bar, working it hard, doing her utmost to make ol' Lenny's cock stand up – if it still could, which she very much doubted. All the same, she had to try, because that was the way she'd always kept Lenny off-balance in the past, using sex to keep him sweet. But it was obvious he wasn't up for it tonight. He was too busy staring at his watch. In fact he'd been flicking glances at it all evening.

'Something going down?' she asked him.

Startled, Lenny looked up. He seemed almost surprised to see her there.

'Eleven o'clock,' he sighed. 'Got some boys doin' a job.'

Delilah's attention sharpened. 'Would that something involve Marcus?'

Lenny nodded.

Well, thank fuck for that, thought Delilah.

Lenny could tell that Delilah was happy Marcus was going to get it in the neck. No doubt about it, she was a gorgeous girl. But right now . . . not even Delilah's prodigious big-nippled tits, swaying teasingly in front of him like two over-filled balloons, were doing it for him. Smirking, she placed his drink on the bar. He downed it in one, just as he had the one before. He knew he'd pay for it later. Once he'd been a ten pints a night boy, but he was too long in the tooth for all that shit now. One whisky was his limit. Two gave him heartburn. Three had him up and down to the bog the whole night long.

He looked around. The Blue Banana was an important part of his little empire. No one owned all of Soho, but he prided himself that a good portion of it belonged to him. In addition to the Blue Banana, he had the Blue Heaven, the Blue Bird, and the Calypso. And then there was the property he had dotted about London: flats in Notting Hill and Houndsditch, stuffed with all sorts, most of them running prossies. Since he'd edged out all the decent working-class families that used to live there, he was pulling in a fucking fortune.

As for Soho, it had been a battleground since the war, with the whites, the Maltese and a few Italians all wrestling for control. So far, Lenny had come out on top. He had the best troops, the best men. And Marcus was the best of the lot, his right hand, his wingman. Or at least he had been, until the rumours started up, until it all began to turn sour.

Lenny hadn't wanted to believe any of it. At first, he'd refused to. He was the one who'd taken the boy off the

17

streets, groomed him, made him into a man. They'd grown close. He'd spent a fortune on Marcus, sorted him out with a house, a wardrobe of decent suits, all the whores he could fuck. They'd drunk together, fought together, and slowly, inch by inch, Lenny had sat back, relaxed a little, let Marcus take the reins.

You fucking fool, he told himself.

Truth was, he was getting tired. Truth was, he was getting bloody *old*. He was sixty-eight now, past retirement age, and sometimes it seemed easier to let Marcus take the strain off, let him handle the active stuff. Marcus was a young blood of twenty-two, sharp as a tack and handy in a fight, he could take it.

Oh yeah, he can take it, he's taken you for a cunt, *after all.*

Lenny sighed and drained his glass. He looked around at the punters, the girls, and felt weariness overwhelm him. He'd put things in motion, and he felt sad to the depths of his soul about it.

Why'd you do it, Marcus? Wasn't I always good to you?

But Lenny was no fool. He knew this was the natural order of things. It was inevitable that a leader of men, growing into his strength, would try to take over. It was the same in the animal kingdom. Like those stags he'd seen when he was up in Scotland that time, doing a bit of business: the old ones got pushed out to die alone, the younger, stronger ones became the new rulers. It was nature.

Once, he and Marcus had practically been mates. Buddies. But no more. The young whelp had turned on its master, trying to drive a wedge between Lenny and his old and trusted friends, accusing them of cheating him. Lenny had confronted one or two of them, asked was there any truth in it. Wounded by these groundless accusations, they'd asked him, was he blind? Couldn't he see what that fucker was up to? Couldn't he see that the cunt was trying to push him over the edge? It was all a ploy to isolate him so that he could shove him out of the way and take over.

Lenny Lynch knew they were telling the truth. But he was a fighter, always had been. He looked at his watch again. It was time. Eleven o'clock, and goodbye Marcus. It was all set up. Old he might be, but Lenny wasn't ready to retire from the game just yet, he wasn't ready to give in and get out. He was going to fight, and fight dirty, to keep his place at the top of the heap. And Marcus was about to learn that Lenny Lynch still had teeth. Bloody great sharp ones.

3

Monday lunchtime, and the doctor still hadn't come and neither had the district nurse. Leaving Clara with no choice but to go out.

'Don't,' begged Bernie, afraid of being left in the flat without Clara to take charge. Clara was *always* in charge. In any emergency, they all turned to her, even Mum; they all turned to cool, level-headed Clara.

'You'll be fine,' said Clara, and hoped it was true. With Hatton due to call at three o'clock tomorrow, she had to find the money to pay him, else they would be thrown out onto the streets and then what would become of them?

'Don't open the door to anyone except me, the doctor or the nurse,' ordered Clara.

'Please don't be long,' pleaded Bernie, eyes wide, teeth chattering with fright.

Poor Bernie, thought Clara. Her little sister had delicate nerves, and it was easy to see that the poor kid was in shreds. The slightest thing sent her into a panic – a sudden noise downstairs, the rent man's heavy knock at the door.

'I won't.' Clara patted her sister's shoulder reassuringly, feeling wretched. At nine years old, Bernie shouldn't have to go through all this. And then there was little Henry, holding on to Bernie as he always seemed to since Dad had run out on them – only seven, and abandoned by his father and with his mother in labour. Poor little bastard.

Clara took Dad's Hunter watch – one of the few things he'd left behind – and hurried down to 'Loot Alley'. For over an hour she stood there on the pavement outside the Exchange Buildings in Cutler Street, shivering and stamping her feet against the freezing cold and drizzling rain, holding out the watch hopefully to anyone who passed by, but no one seemed to be interested in buying watches. They were buying Voigtlander cameras, nylons, cosmetics – anything but watches. Not even one with a handsome brass Prince Albert chain attached to it, not even for a few measly shillings.

'Well, it ain't the real thing, is it, dearie?' one elderly man said to her with a condescending smile. 'That chain's not gold – not even nine carat.'

People glanced at her standing there, then looked away, walked on. Plenty of other, better things to see. She shivered, hugging herself to keep warm, hunching her head down into her shoulders.

'Little Clara Dolan ain't it?' said a voice.

Clara looked up and her heart sank to her boots; it was Frank Hatton the rent collector, his Alsatian on its stout leash at his side.

Shit, she thought.

'Just selling off a few things,' she said, as casually as she could. 'Old things, things we don't want.'

He nodded, half-smiling. Clara stepped away from that horrible great dog, which was straining against its leash, lunging at her with its massive fangs.

'Shut up, Attila, you berk,' Hatton snapped, jerking its chain. He looked at Clara. 'What's that – a watch? Your dad's, is it?' He reached out, touched it. Clara flinched. He saw her reaction, and frowned. 'Don't look worth much.

21

Your mum's getting the rent money together, right? She'll have it, as promised? Tomorrow, like we said? Three o'clock – I'll be there to collect.'

'She will,' said Clara stiffly. *She won't.*

'Lenny Lynch don't like late payers.'

'He'll have his money,' said Clara.

'Good.' He stood there a moment longer, staring at her. *Go on, just bugger off will you?*

'Look . . . ' There was a flush of colour in his cheeks as he fished in the pocket of his grubby leather coat, pulled out a stub of pencil and a scrap of paper. He scrawled something, held it out to her. 'I've been meaning to say . . . Take this.'

'What is it?' She looked down at the paper, back up at his face. There was an address written on it.

'That's where I live. If you . . . Well, it's got to be paid, ain't it? One way or the other.'

Clara's face was stiff with disgust and dislike as she shoved the paper into her pocket. She felt like chucking it onto the muddy pavement and stomping it underfoot. The urge to do so was almost overwhelming, but she fought it. She might be only fifteen, but she knew Hatton's game. He'd always fancied her – that was the only reason her family weren't out on the street already. If the rent couldn't be paid in cash, he was suggesting she do it in kind. Clara gagged at the thought.

'Yeah,' she muttered, though it choked her.

Finally he moved on, dragging the Alsatian with him. A shuddering gust of a breath escaped Clara as she allowed herself to relax. She held the watch out to the milling crowds, even more determined now to sell it, to fetch *some* money in. Even if she didn't get the full amount for the rent, it would be something to appease Frank Hatton and his boss, that bastard Lenny Lynch, a little sweetener that might make them think again about chucking the Dolans into the gutter.

She tried to smile, to catch the eye of a punter willing to part with a bob or two. And as she did so, a young boy in short trousers with a cap pulled down over his ears ran by and snatched the Hunter straight out of her hand.

'Hey!' she shouted, taking off after him, but he was too fast, weaving through the crowds with ease while she collided with passers-by. Within seconds he was lost to sight.

Clara could only stand there, her shoulders slumped in defeat.

The watch was gone.

It had been the last item they had of any value – apart from Mum's old Singer sewing machine, and they daren't sell that, it was their only means of income.

Now, they had nothing.

4

'Fuckin' things have been doped, if you ask me,' said the red-faced man standing alongside Marcus Redmayne, shouting to be heard above the roar of the crowd. The cheers echoed all around White City Stadium as the five greyhounds raced around the track after the rabbit. Number one – a pure-black dog – was steadily pulling away from the other four. 'You see that? They been got at, I'm tellin' ya.'

Marcus didn't reply; he was already making his way through the packed stadium to collect his loot. When the black dog shot past the winning post the crowd went mad: the cheers from the handful of winners drowned out by the hundreds of losers baying their displeasure as they tore up their betting slips and hurled them to the concrete floor. Too right the other dogs had been doped; Marcus had personally slipped the kennel lads a hefty bung apiece and told them to mix a dose of chloretone in with their food before the race.

A cure for travel-sickness in humans, chloretone sent a dog's blood pressure sky-high the minute he started to run, so he 'faded' fast. Best of all, it was damned near impossible for a vet to trace.

The bookie gave Marcus a surly look as he collected his winnings. With a smirk of satisfaction he made a show of counting the money, then he moved along to the next bookie, and the next – collecting all the while.

DANGEROUS

Satisfied with his evening's takings, he made his way out of the ground and strolled, deep in thought, toward his motor. He was justifiably proud of his car. A few years ago he'd been a half-starved kid with his arse hanging out of his trousers, not a pot to piss in; now he was minted – and his choice of motor reflected that. It was a sporty racing-green Jaguar XK120, newly imported from California, left-hand drive, soft top. An expensive beauty – and he had earned it by the sweat of his brow. First thing he'd done when he got it was drive over to his mum's place so he could show it off. And his mum had taken one look and said, 'It's just a car,' before going back inside.

As chief enforcer for Lenny Lynch, Marcus worked hard for his money. He expected others to do the same, but it turned out a lot of Lenny's so-called friends had cottoned on to the fact he was getting soft in his old age and they were ripping him off left, right and centre. Take the Blue Banana, for instance. That mouthy cunt Delilah was slicing a big hit off the top every month, doctoring the books and thinking nobody was ever going to notice. Well, he had. And he'd got his old pal Gordon to do an audit.

Delilah had shrieked and complained and moaned to Lenny about it, but what could she do? Marcus was Lenny's number one. She had to soak it up.

Her accounts might have got past Lenny, but Gordon was a different prospect entirely. Soon as he put the books under the microscope he uncovered all her little tricks: crates of drinks going 'missing' and being sold on, all sorts of stuff being left off the accounts. Marcus had told Lenny about it, but did Lenny believe him? He did not.

'Delilah – do a thing like that?' Lenny had shaken his head and laughed when Marcus told him. 'She been with me for years, that girl.'

'Yeah, and that's why she's doing it,' Marcus had argued.

25

'She knows you won't come down on her, check the books over. When'd you last check them? Seriously?'

'Marcus,' Lenny had said, almost sadly, 'I don't have to check. Delilah's straight as a die.'

'Len—'

'No.' Lenny's pouchy eyes had sharpened in their folds of fat, grown mean and threatening. He'd raised a stubby, nicotine-stained finger, waved it under Marcus's nose. 'Leave it right there, or we're gonna fall out, I'm telling you.'

So Marcus had left it. But he'd done so reluctantly, and deep down he was still seething. Unlike some, he appreciated what Lenny Lynch had done for him.

When they first met, he'd been living on the streets, running wild. He had no home to go to; after his dad died, his mum had found herself a new bloke – a good earner, with his own joinery business, and he treated her like a queen, which was all Lulu Redmayne cared about – and she'd been only too happy to defer to her new husband's wishes and kick her tearaway teenage son's backside out the door.

Relations had remained strained between Lulu and Marcus, but after his stepdad had departed for that great workshop in the sky he'd started visiting home again. So long as he showered her with gifts, he could be sure of a welcome. Lulu still liked the high life and she expected to be treated like royalty. Show up empty-handed and she'd soon let you know about it.

Even if his mum didn't rate Marcus highly, women in general seemed to like him. He was tall, athletically built, muscled up from hardship on the streets. His hair was thick, black and straight, and he had dense black brows that gave him a dangerous look when they drew together. His eyes were so deep a brown that they appeared black, with lashes any woman would envy. His nose was almost patrician, and he had a wide mouth that rarely tilted upward in a smile.

Marcus looked hard, threatening, and – yes, all the girls said it – *very* sexy. And it didn't hurt that he was loaded. Which he wouldn't have been, if Lenny Lynch hadn't come along.

Under Lenny's guidance, Marcus's natural talent for strong-arm tactics had been honed. He had grown fit and tough and formidable, and he'd built a reputation for himself. In the streets of Soho, his was a name to be reckoned with. He had carved a place for himself and he felt secure in his ability to hang on to it. With that sense of security came confidence, and a fierce almost fanatical loyalty to the man who had saved him from a life in the gutter.

Back when he was a kid, Lenny Lynch had seemed like a god. Now that he was a man himself he saw that Lenny was just a man too, and that he had flaws. Biggest among them was that Lenny trusted people too much, whereas Marcus didn't trust them at all – he barely even trusted himself.

So he'd been doing what he did best, covering his boss's back, making sure no one was taking the piss. But he had discovered that most of them were. He had told Lenny the bad news, because it was his duty to do so. And what did Lenny say?

Drop it.

Don't go there.

So here he was, with a situation. Hang on as Lenny's number one, with all Lenny's old drinking pals laughing their bollocks off at him behind his back, or do something different?

He walked faster; it was a cold night and he stuffed his hands into his jacket pockets, feeling the reassuring rustle of his winnings in there.

Marcus was whistling 'Broken Wings' by the Stargazers. He was not exactly happy, because he had all this shit with Lenny going on, but he was cheerful enough. And why not? He had cash on the hip, he was clever and he was young

27

and strong. Anything was possible. Up ahead, parked under a street lamp that set its buffed bodywork glowing was his Jag – and now he paused and saw there were two men leaning against the front of it. He thought he recognized them from the way they moved.

Yeah, he did.

They were Lenny's boys.

He knew them. He'd even given them their orders, in the past. Dimly, in the distance, he heard the church bells ring, sounding the hour; it was eleven o'clock.

5

'You sold the watch then?' asked Kathleen hopefully, wincing as another gigantic contraction hit her. 'Ahhh, oh Jesus . . . '

'Yeah,' lied Clara, and she smiled and held her mother's hand. Kathleen's frantic grip nearly crushed her fingers.

She'd come back and fixed bread and jam for Bernie and Henry, but Kathleen was feeling too ill to eat. And so now here they were. It just kept spinning around in Clara's brain, an ever-expanding loop, a fast-spinning merry-go-round of panic.

What could she do?

Everything rested on her shoulders.

She had to think of something. Her mother was still in labour, there was no sign of the child getting itself born. Clara was climbing the walls with worry but desperate not to show her fears to her mother or to little Henry, who'd been playing Ludo with Bernie in the next room. Finally she was forced to send Bernie out again with a request that the district nurse should come urgently, the doctor, or anyone.

And once the baby was here, how would they feed yet another mouth when already they were out of their depth? She was dreading Hatton's knock on the door tomorrow. But more than that, she was dreading that this labour was going to go on and on, until her mother was too exhausted to struggle any more.

Until she was dead.

It could come to that, Clara knew. And what would become of them all then? This was what it meant, being poor. You were powerless. She hated it, bitterly. And one way or another, she was going to change it. She didn't know how, but one day, she swore, she was going to break them all out of here. The Dolans were going to be rich once more. *Fuck* this!

She took up the cool cloth and wiped her mother's brow again.

'It's going to be all right,' she said, but it was a lie, how could it be all right?

Her mother could *die*.

She thought of turning to their neighbours for help. But no. Since they'd moved into this bloody hovel, not one of them had said a kind word to the family. Clara had seen the furtive looks as she passed them. One or two of the women – one of the younger black women in particular – had glanced at her, had even smiled. But she didn't want to call on any of them for help.

What she wanted was to turn the clocks back, back to the time when Dad had been there, laughing in his madcap way, and they'd been a proper family. But that was impossible. So she fixed a smile on her face and smoothed her mother's hair back from her sweating brow.

What the hell am I going to do? she wondered in abject fear.

She'd do what she'd always done. She'd get on with it. She'd cope.

In the meantime she could only pray that Bernie was going to come back with help, very soon.

6

Lenny Lynch trudged wearily up the steps of the Blue Banana club and came out onto the rain-slicked street. Vic Damone's voice, singing 'April in Paris', drifted after him. Lenny had never seen Paris. He'd been to New York, though. They said New York was the city that never slept, but London didn't get much shut-eye either; late at night, the streets were still thronging with people, conducting trade of one sort or another or just walking. Tramps slept in doorways, cars swished by in the wet, pimps loitered, watching their scantily dressed and shivering girls; all human life was here.

He paused in the shadows of a doorway, lit a Players and took a deep lungful, then coughed mightily. Eyes watering, Lenny lifted his wrist, held the watch face up to the soaked glimmer of the street lights. It was a quarter to midnight.

It was done, then. Lenny's shoulders drooped. Marcus was taken care of and would not be seen again. Even now his dead body was being disposed of. Epping Forest or out in the Channel maybe. He didn't want to know, he'd told the boys that. A shame, but it had to be done. *He* was the one in charge, and so he would remain. A pity that Marcus had to go and forget that, the silly cunt.

He finished the cigarette and set off for his flat, two streets away. Halfway there he paused in his stride to light a second cigarette. The wind was getting up, gusting damply, blowing out the match's flame, so he stepped into a club doorway and leaned against a wall adorned with a garishly painted flame-red poster depicting two half-naked dancing girls, heads thrown back, mouths open in erotic invitation. The match flared and he took a long drag. A skinny, flashy-looking man with a black Rhett Butler moustache stepped past, bumping against him, heading for the stairs down into the club.

'Oi! Watch your fucking self, will you?' snapped Lenny. He wasn't in a good mood. He'd lost his best man tonight, and that pained him.

Lenny saw the man turn, saw the glint of a smile on his face. In a flash of recognition, Lenny realized that he looked familiar. His hand lifted and in total shock Lenny saw the gun there.

'Marcus Redmayne says hello,' hissed the man.

Lenny didn't even have time to step away, start to run, nothing. He felt the cold hard barrel of the gun drill into his temple, and then the man pulled the trigger and Lenny Lynch's brains shot out of his skull and decorated the lurid poster behind him with globs of grey and fountains of red. His lifeless corpse slumped to the ground.

A couple of people turned, looked as the man with the moustache hurried away down the wet night-time street. There'd been a noise, hard to hear over the traffic, probably a car had backfired. They saw a drunk dossing down in the shadowy doorway beneath a garish, brightly lit club sign, then someone came along and helped him to his feet, got him into the back of the car. The car roared away. Everyone shrugged their shoulders and walked on, minding their own business.

Delilah lounged against the bar after Lenny had gone home, watching the punters drink and play cards. She had thought that Lenny might be going soft in his old age, but good old Len had put her mind at rest: Marcus was going to be dealt with, thank God. Boy was getting all out of hand. Before you knew it, he'd be in here taking over, and she couldn't have that. This was *her* little piece of heaven, she'd been running this place so long now that it felt like home.

So what if Lenny had practically raised the boy? Sometimes in life you had to do things that were hard. It would hurt Lenny, dealing with Marcus, she knew it. But what the hell. Sighing, she went back to the optics and squirted herself out a measure of the dark sweet rum she favoured. Something moved behind her. Sipping the drink, she turned back to the bar to serve whoever was waiting.

The rum splattered on the floor and all down her naked torso as she choked.

Marcus Redmayne was standing there, leaning on the other side of the bar. Those black eyes of his were gazing at her unblinkingly, with steady concentration. He had a way of looking at a person that was unnerving. Like he could see straight through you and out the other side. She hated it. And hadn't Lenny said he was dealing with this fucker tonight?

'Sorry, did I startle you?' Marcus asked, his eyes not leaving hers.

Delilah's eyes were watering. She coughed again, cleared her throat, tried to think. No, it couldn't be him. It *couldn't*. Marcus should be dead meat by now, not standing here. Lenny had said he was sorting it. Eleven o'clock, he'd said.

Bullshit. Marcus was here, and he was very much alive.

Somehow she managed a ghastly forced smile of welcome.

'Or were you not expecting to see me?' asked Marcus.

'You . . . surprised me, that's all,' she croaked, coughing again.

'Yeah?' Marcus straightened and looked around. On either side of him, two big muscle-heads appeared. They looked at Delilah. She took a half-step forward, reaching under the counter to where she had the machete stashed in case the customers got lively.

'Leave that,' said Marcus sharply.

Delilah hesitated. One of the men opened the front of his coat, showed her the gun there.

Marcus was smiling at her. She sagged. *Game up*, she thought. *Game over*.

'Tonight's going to be full of surprises, Delilah,' said Marcus. 'Ring the damned bell. You're shutting early.'

The news roared through the streets like a hurricane. Lenny Lynch was no more; his number one, Marcus Redmayne, had taken over Lenny's manor. Word was that Lenny had retired to the country, snap decision, something like that. No one was really sure.

All around Soho they whispered about it. Lenny had been a fixture in the area since forever, and suddenly he was gone. So were the managers of five snooker halls and four clubs that Lenny had previously had under his control. They'd all been Lenny's people, hand-picked by him over the years, but now new faces were appearing and the old ones were history. Most notable by her absence was Delilah from the Blue Banana. A couple of days later she washed up on a pebbled stretch near the Limehouse Ship Lock. She was still wearing her boots and her birthday suit.

Suicide, they said.

Sad.

But what the fuck.

7

When the knock came at the door Clara sprang upright. *Bernie . . . ?* Yes, she could hear Bernie's voice out there. And she could hear another voice – did Bernie have someone with her? She ran to the door, unlocked it, flung it open.

'Oh my God, at last!' she burst out, hugging her sister.

One flight down, Clara could see the bulky figure of the district nurse brushing her way past the people who always seemed to be sitting, giggling, chatting and smoking foul-smelling roll-ups on the stairs. The nurse was doling out dirty looks left and right, clouting slow-movers with her bag. 'Out the way, you bastards, let me pass!' she snarled. As she came up to the top floor, she was unfastening her navy-blue cloak and gazing hard-eyed at Clara.

'Your mam up here then?' she asked.

'She is,' said Bernie.

Bernie led the woman through to the bedroom, showing her the washbasin where she could clean her hands. Clara stood aside as the grey-haired and red-faced woman eyed her groaning mother.

'She's been like this for *ages*,' said Clara.

'Right. Let's see shall we?' The nurse turned to Bernie, twitching nervously and watching with fearful eyes at the doorway, Henry round-eyed and clutching at her skirts.

'Take that bowl. Boil up some water, fetch some towels too, all right?'

Bernie ran off to do as she was told. Clara pushed the door closed behind her.

'She needs some bloody help,' said Clara heatedly to the nurse. But then she bit her tongue. At least the nurse was here.

'Well, help is what we're going to give her,' said the nurse, still smiling though her voice was edged with irritation now. 'Christ, she's not the only woman in labour in London today. I'm rushed off my bloody feet. Hold your mother's hand, girl, that's it. What's her name?'

'Kathleen,' said Clara.

Clara grimly stationed herself at her mother's side and took hold of her hand while the nurse pushed the covers back and hitched up Kathleen's nightdress. She rummaged around. Kathleen let out a moan as another violent contraction clenched her midsection. Sick with worry, Clara closed her eyes. It was as if Mum's pain was so intense she could feel it too.

She could hardly recognize her sweet-natured, contented, sunny mother in the pitiful wreck of a woman lying on the bed. The triple humiliation of the firm's collapse, their sudden homeless state and Dad's abandonment had wrecked her, Clara could see that. And now this awful pain with the baby had left her chalk-white and sweating, her once sparkling eyes now bloodshot and rimmed with red.

'Why won't it come?' asked Clara.

'Shh, girl,' snapped the nurse, trying to concentrate on what she was doing.

'It ought to have come by now, why won't it come?' persisted Clara.

'Shut up, let me see.' The nurse was silent, probing with her hand. 'Shit! It's breach,' she said.

'What?'

'The head's round the wrong way. You've sent for the midwife?'

Clara shook her head. She swallowed painfully. 'We can't afford it,' she said, and the words hurt her. They didn't have ten shillings for a midwife; they didn't have fuck-all. And oh God, tomorrow Hatton was going to be here, wanting the rent, the lecherous old bastard. She thought of the address he'd given her, burning a hole in her pocket, and shivered.

The nurse's eyes rested on Clara's face for a long while. Then she turned back to Kathleen, still squirming and groaning on the bed.

'We'll have to do the job ourselves, then, won't we,' said the nurse with a brisk professional smile at the suffering woman. 'All right, Kathleen?'

Bernie came back into the bedroom, carrying the bowl of steaming water. With shaking hands she placed it on the washstand along with fresh towels. Henry followed.

'Now off you go, you two, and shut the door,' said the nurse.

Bernie, with Henry hovering around her like a small satellite, left the room, closing the door behind her. Clara wished she could go too. She didn't want to see this. But instead she stayed there, holding her mother's hand.

The nurse was silent between her mother's legs. Kathleen groaned and twisted as the woman delved into her. *It must hurt so much*, thought Clara, tensing as Kathleen's hand gripped hers again.

'Damn,' said the nurse, emerging redder in the face than ever from her efforts. 'Come here, girl, your hands are smaller, ain't they. Get here, that's the ticket.'

Horrified at this request, Clara hung back.

'Come on!' bawled the woman, and Clara moved. The nurse directed her between Kathleen's legs. Clara, shuddering, tried not to look but there was a flash of blood, and of

37

faeces on the wet newspapers they had spread out to spare the already worn and dirty mattress when her mother's waters had broken an age ago.

Oh Jesus, help me, thought Clara.

'Do it, Clara. Please do it,' panted Kathleen, her eyes desperate as they rested on her daughter.

'Put your hand in, see if you can get a hold on the baby,' said the nurse.

Horrified, Clara did as she was told. If it helped her mother, she would do anything. Nauseated, repulsed by the stench and the awful degradation her mother was enduring, Clara closed her eyes and put her hand where the nurse directed it.

Ah, Jesus! She put her hand into the place, feeling wet slippery heat. Suddenly there was another contraction and her mother gave a long trembling moan – she was too weak to scream. Clara felt her hand being crushed as if in a vice.

'God!' she shouted in pain.

'Can you feel anything? Can you feel the leg?' asked the nurse.

Clara shook her head. She was too horrified, too terrified, to speak; all she wanted to do was run.

'Feel around,' said the nurse. 'Hurry.'

Gagging, half-crying, Clara moved her hand. It touched something. Her fingers groped. It was a leg, she thought.

'A leg,' sobbed Clara. 'I can feel a leg, I think.'

'Put both hands in and get the other one too,' said the nurse.

Ah God, this was torment, this was awful. Straining away from the smells and revolted by the glutinous feel of her mother's inner workings, Clara did as she was told. She slipped in her other hand and groped around. Kathleen screamed in pain as she did so, and Clara trembled, certain she was going to throw up at any moment.

'You feel it?' asked the nurse.

Clara nodded, biting down hard on her lip.

'Take hold of both legs. Do it quickly now,' said the nurse.

Cringing, revolted, Clara did.

'Now – Kathleen – with the next contraction you have to push, push as hard as you can.'

Kathleen gritted her teeth. 'Oh God, it's coming . . . ' she said, her face screwing up in agony.

'Push!' shouted the nurse. 'Girl, pull gently, do it now!'

One of the legs slipped free of Clara's grasp. 'Oh! I've lost it . . . ' She scrabbled around in there. *This was hell, this was a nightmare.* 'No! Here it is!'

'Pull now!'

Kathleen pushed and screamed out loud.

'Push, Kathleen, push!'

And Clara felt something give horribly then. There was a squelching sound and something seemed to come free. She pulled for all she was worth, and there at last came the blood-and-mucus-spattered little body, slippery-shiny and ghastly as an alien, then the arms and finally the head. The whole thing came sliding out onto the newspapers, and Kathleen fell back onto the sweat-stained pillows.

'Oh thank God,' she moaned.

'It's a girl!' said the nurse, snatching up a towel and rubbing the baby over. 'A girl, look.'

But then the nurse's face grew still.

She rubbed harder. Her movements frantic.

Then she stopped rubbing.

'What's the matter?' gasped out Clara.

The nurse looked at her and shook her head.

The baby had been too long trapped inside the womb. It was dead.

8

'The punters been paying one shilling for a bottle of beer – and it's watered down, trust me, I've tasted it – that's a knock-down price, but they also have to buy a liqueur, that's two and sixpence, and I've tasted that too.' Gordon clutched his writing pad and shook his shiny bald dome of a head. He pushed his glasses up his nose. 'It's watered-down fruit juice.'

Marcus nodded. They were standing in the silent, empty bar of one of the four Soho clubs that had once been Lenny's. Now Marcus had them in his power. His old school mate Gordon might be weedy, useless in a fight, bald as a coot at twenty-two, and always down with colds, but he was a wizard at maths and keeping books straight. Gordon was happily trotting around the place like a bloodhound, sniffing out boozer rackets. And there were plenty to find.

These clubs were a great wheeze for club owners. Didn't matter whether you were in Soho or Berkeley Square, the scams were the same. The licensing laws were crazy, so to get around them the proprietors had the customers sign order forms, which were sent to all-night wine retailers; in effect, this meant that the customers ordered the booze, not the club. Everyone was a winner: no laws were broken, the punters could enjoy all-night semi-legal drinking and the clubs were free to make a hefty profit.

'No reason to change an arrangement everyone seems happy with,' said Marcus, with a shrug.

'Poor fuckers,' sighed Gordon. 'All these damned hostesses have to do is bat their eyelashes and the punters stop worrying whether they're being ripped off.'

'Sounds OK to me,' said Marcus. He suspected that Gordon would kill to get one of the hostesses up close and personal, but poor bloody Gordon never had a clue with women. Figures were his strength – the mathematical ones rather than the feminine kind.

The system worked. The Bill had tried to spoil things for everyone by making it an offence for all-night wine retailers to solicit orders by giving blank forms to the clubs, but so far no court in the land had been able to make it stick.

'You know what? This is going to be good,' said Marcus, stalking around his new domain.

Gordon put pad and pen onto the bar and looked at him. 'No regrets over Lenny?' he asked.

Marcus stopped pacing and turned his steady black gaze onto his mate. Anyone else asked him that question, he'd rip their heads off. But this was Gordon.

'Nah,' he said at last. 'Had to be done.'

Gordon nodded. You had to hand it to Marcus. The takedown of Lenny Lynch's little empire had been a thing of beauty, a carefully coordinated pincer movement of military precision. Napoleon couldn't have done it any better. Once Marcus knew Lenny had turned on him, he'd swung into action. Hardly a drop of blood had been spilled, except for Lenny's, and the two boys he'd sent to do Marcus, and that mouthy bitch Delilah – and she just had to go, she'd have been a thorn digging into Marcus's side and he couldn't allow that. In a matter of days, every single club, pub, snooker hall, restaurant, rental property and whorehouse that had once belonged to Lenny had been seamlessly transferred into the hands of Marcus Redmayne.

'We'll get it all legal and above board, I can do that. Get the properties transferred and all that stuff. No problem. Make sure the Maltese or the Eyeties or that mad fucker Jacko Sears don't try to take it back off you,' said Gordon. 'All you got to do now is hang on to it.'

Marcus looked at Gordon with a grim smile. 'I bet there are people all around Soho shitting themselves right now, thinking I could be coming for them next.'

Gordon took up his notepad and pen and heaved a sigh. Marcus had been his friend just about always, but sometimes Gordon found Marcus's self-belief bloody terrifying.

What the hell made anyone so driven?

Gordon didn't understand it.

He never would.

9

On Tuesday morning, Clara took her mum in a cup of tea. She put the cup and saucer down on the hideous little curtained table beside the bed. Yesterday had been horrible, almost beyond bearing. She shuddered to think of it. A baby sister, and she was dead. Unnamed – unwanted, truth be told. Poor little sod.

Mercifully the nurse had taken the dead baby away with her, saying she'd dispose of it. She also wrapped up the afterbirth in some of the soiled newspapers, and helped Clara get Kathleen fresh sheets on the bed, get her washed and into a clean nightdress. Kathleen was still seeping blood, but that would stop, the nurse told Clara. Now all they had to do was put it behind them, said the nurse, and go on with their lives.

What lives? wondered Clara. If this was life, being here in this awful place, potless, hopeless, then she didn't want it. She'd rather be dead, like her baby sister. She trembled to think of Hatton coming to the door today, and her with no money to give him.

She went over to the curtains and pulled them back to admit the daylight, then she went to her mother's bedside and was pleased to see that Mum was still asleep. She needed her rest. Already Kathleen had shed many tears over losing the baby, but – and Clara hated herself for thinking this – maybe it was for the best.

For a moment she hesitated, wondering whether or not to wake her, but Mum never liked to lie in and she got irritable if allowed to do so. Gently, Clara reached out and shook Kathleen's shoulder.

'Mum? Wake up, it's time. Got your tea here.'

It was stuffy in the room, so Clara went over to the window and pushed up the mouldering sash an inch or two, to let in fresh air. It was raining out, and gusty; the sky was charcoal grey, ridged with thin bands of pinky white. The curtains billowed. She closed down the sash a little, she didn't want Mum catching cold, not now when she was so weak. Then, smiling, she turned back to the bed.

'Mum? Come on, got your tea,' she said.

Clara stopped there, looking down at her mother. The smile stalled on her lips. Now that the curtains were back, she thought that Kathleen's face looked faintly blue, not her usual healthy colour.

'Mum . . . ?' Clara's voice was little more than a croak. She could feel her heart beating sickly in her chest, could feel a new terror starting to take hold.

Slowly, she reached out trembling fingers and touched the hand that lay unmoving on the coverlet. She let out a gasp and quickly withdrew. Her mother's flesh was icy cold.

'Mum!' Now it was a cry. She shook Kathleen's shoulder again. 'Wake up! Come on!'

Her mother's chest wasn't rising and falling with the breath of life. Panicking now, Clara shook her roughly, and started yanking at the bedclothes.

'Come on, Mum, wake up, you're scaring me . . . ' Clara pulled back the blankets and the sheet and then stopped, staring.

The sheet beneath her mother was red.

'Oh God, oh God, no . . . ' Clara was muttering, her hands flying to her mouth, her eyes wide with shock.

The bleeding hadn't stopped as the nurse had promised. Her mother had bled to death. Clara fell to her knees and tears spilled over and cascaded down her face as she stared at her mother lying there, all the life gone out of her.

'No . . . ' she moaned over and over, sobbing with grief and disbelief. 'Oh God, Mum, please don't leave us. Not you too!'

10

Marcus had no idea why he kept coming back to see her like he did. Every time he'd say the same thing: That's it, she can stew in her own juice, the old cow – this is the last time. But a week, maybe two, later, he'd be back again, like a stuck record.

Once again he'd made the journey to Old Bond Street, where he'd selected a little something bright enough to tempt her magpie eye and – of course – expensive enough. It had to be expensive. He'd come away with the pale blue Tiffany box in his hand, tied with the trademark white ribbon, and made the journey across town to the place where she lived, the place *he* had bought her, working for Lenny Lynch.

Every time, it was going to be different.

Every time, in his mind's eye, it was.

In his imagination, his mother pushed away the gift and said: 'No matter about that, my darling, how are you?'

And she would kiss him, hug him, be delighted to see him, would chatter on, telling him about all the things she had done since they had last met. And he would tell her, proudly – because he *was* proud, dammit – he would tell her that he was in charge of the patch that had once been Lenny Lynch's, he was *minted*, he could buy her another house, a better one.

'So long as you're happy, son,' she would say, beaming with maternal pride. 'That's all I care about.'

Yeah. In his imagination.

Only here was the reality. Whistling 'Say You're Mine Again' – he loved Perry Como's voice, and the song was lodged in his brain – he knocked on his mother's door and she opened it to him. She seemed almost disappointed to see him standing there. Then she turned without a word and led the way into the house, took up her station in the armchair beside the roaring fire – which *he* had paid for, let's not forget that – and looked up at him in expectation.

Marcus knew the drill.

He handed her the pale blue ribbon-tied Tiffany box. There was a pearl-studded brooch inside it.

She gave the same sharp nod of satisfaction she always gave. Then, not even opening it, she set it aside on a small table and ran her dark cold eyes over him.

'You've lost weight,' she said.

'Have I?'

'You have.'

She didn't invite him to sit down, offer to make tea, enquire whether he wanted biscuits or cake, tell him that he needed feeding up. Marcus didn't expect that, and would have been startled if she had. His mother hadn't a single maternal bone in her entire scrawny little designer-clad body. She was always immaculately and expensively dressed, her hair beautifully styled, her make-up faultless. And all the jewels he bought her? He'd never yet seen her wearing any of them. Another poke in the eye. Another rejection.

Since boyhood he'd been doing this, trying to tease some semblance of warmth out of her. A gift, there always had to be a gift. And news of his achievements, bringing with them the promise of more. But what did he get in return? Fuck all.

47

'I've taken over Lenny Lynch's manor,' said Marcus, taking a seat even though she hadn't invited him to.

'Oh?'

'There are four clubs. Five snooker halls. Pubs. Restaurants. Rental properties.' He didn't mention the massage parlours and whoring establishments. His mother didn't like 'rough talk'. 'So I can get you a bigger house. A better one. In a better area, maybe.'

'I like it here.'

Marcus gave a tight smile. So typical of her, to toss it back in his face. 'You fancied Chelsea, you said so.'

'Perhaps,' said his mother. 'We'll see.'

'We're rich, Ma,' he said, and felt weariness grip him.

'Well, we'll see, won't we,' she said.

11

Hours after she found Mum dead, Clara was sitting at the table in the next room. She was still deep in shock and she didn't know what she was going to do. Bernie was sobbing beside her, her head buried in her arms. Henry was standing beside Bernie, struck dumb, his thumb in his mouth, reverting to babyhood in the face of disaster.

Clara had closed all the curtains, as was proper with a bereavement. In the room next door, their mother lay dead. It was beyond belief, heartbreaking. And if they had been in trouble before, now they were up shit creek for sure. With Katherine's small income as a dressmaker, they'd struggled; without it, they had no chance.

'We'll have to tell someone,' said Clara.

Bernie looked up from the table, her grey-blue eyes bloodshot, her pretty pointed little face swollen with the force of her tears. 'What . . . ?' she mumbled, dragging a shaking hand through her hair.

Clara gulped. 'About Mum.'

Bernie nodded. There was only quiet in the flat. Deathly quiet. Noise still drifted up from the flats below: music, chatter, noises from another world.

'What's going to happen to us?' asked Bernie. She was shaking.

Clara stared at her. She had always been 'big sis', the one

who cared for the younger girl, made sure she was smartly turned out in the mornings, properly washed, sitting her up on the draining board when she was little and scrubbing at her face to get her clean and ready for the day. Bernie was delicate, needy, easily upset. She bit her nails to the quick and she cried every time Hatton came to the door with that horrible great dog of his. Bernie depended on her.

Then Clara looked down at her brother. With Mum gone, Henry was her responsibility, but how would she clothe him, feed him? She had helped Mum out on the sewing sometimes. She could do that, carry on with that, maybe get more work in.

But it won't feed three of us, said a voice in her brain.

Well, it would have to. She could put cards in windows, tout the business about more. Mum had never really pushed much for work, not as much as Clara would have liked her to. She gazed at the old Singer sewing machine at the end of the table and thought of all the times Kathleen had sat there working, turning the fabric, chatting to her while she fashioned dresses and blouses for her limited clientele. And the family had scraped along, barely surviving.

Not that she was in any way criticizing her mother – God no. Kathleen had been a great woman, much too good and decent for that flashy waster Tom Dolan. But now it was Clara's turn to care for the family, and she'd do it, right up to her dying breath. Her eyes filled with tears that over-flowed and splashed down.

Mum was *dead*.

It struck her all over again, the awful gut-wrenching tragedy of it, and suddenly she was sobbing too.

'Oh, Clara – don't start, or you'll set me off,' moaned Bernie.

Clara swiped at her nose and eyes. Bernie was right. She had to be the strong one; she *had* to be. She turned a tear-bright gaze upon her sister. Gulped. 'Don't you worry, Bernie. We're going to manage just fine,' she promised. 'Now run and fetch the doctor, there's a good girl.' She swallowed her grief. 'There are things to be done, legal things.'

'I want Mum,' Henry wailed, his voice high with panic.

Clara pulled him in close to her and looked right in his eyes as she gripped his frail shoulders. 'Mum's with the angels, Henry,' she said gently but firmly. 'But listen to me. I'm going to look after you. All right?'

He nodded. Sweet little Henry, he was the most biddable, the most good-tempered child even when his world was being torn apart. Clara ruffled his copper-brown hair and he blinked up at her with big bloodshot grey-blue eyes – like Bernie's, like Mum's. Clara looked like her dad, she was the only one that did. And God, how she hated that at this moment. How she hated *him*.

Now she was remembering what they'd had to do when Gran died; they'd summoned the doctor so that he could write the death certificate. Maybe the doctor could advise them about a funeral – only they had no money to pay for one.

He came two hours later, a large moustached man, bustling into the flat with an air of brisk self-importance, wearing an ill-fitting tweed suit and carrying a Gladstone bag. Clara showed him into the bedroom. The doctor drew back the closed curtains, and in the brightening daylight Clara could see again that her mother looked awful – truly dead. All the life was drained from her, never to return. An empty shell lay there, not Kathleen Dolan. She was gone.

Clara watched as the doctor checked for signs of life, looked under the sheets. Then he glanced up at Clara. 'Wait for me next door, will you?' he asked a bit more gently.

Clara left the room. Bernie was sitting at the table, staring vacantly into space. Henry was there too. Clara put the kettle on for tea. They could afford that, at least. And Kathleen had baked a fruit cake last week, they had some of that still in the tin.

Mum's dead.

Before, their situation had been precarious; now it was truly dire. Clara clenched her teeth to stop herself crying again, and made the tea, then found a little milk from yesterday which was curdled, but what the fuck. She opened the tin and cut three slices of the stale cake, and placed them upon Kathleen's best plates, the ones she had managed to hang onto after Dad had lost all his money, the bone china ones with the lady in the pink crinoline painted on the sides.

Maybe those would fetch a few pennies? thought Clara.

Presently the doctor came into the room. Clara poured out the tea, pushed the little sugar-bowl toward him and the milk jug, and a plate with the cake on it.

'Thank you, girl,' he said, busy writing out the certificate.

Bernie sat looking at the cake as if it would choke her. She took a tiny sip of tea. So did Clara, as the silence in the room deepened. Finally the doctor stopped writing and put away his pen, took off his glasses. He looked at Bernie, at Henry, then at Clara.

'How old are you?' he asked Clara directly.

'Eighteen,' she lied. She had expected this. She was fifteen, but if she told him that then he would talk about taking Bernie and Henry into care, maybe even her too, and fuck that. She couldn't let that happen. She hoped the doctor was busy, too busy to go back to the surgery and check her records and find out that she was lying. God knows the bastard had been too bloody busy to come and tend to Mum when she'd needed him.

'And you've got work?' he asked.

'Yes. I have. Lots of dressmaking work.'

Another lie. Mum had always said she must never lie, but what alternative did she have? She didn't want her brother and sister consigned to council care, she'd heard such tales about it. They might lose touch forever if she allowed that. So she had to appear confident of her ability to keep the Dolans afloat. Even if she knew she couldn't.

'And you'll be looking after your sister, and your brother? You'd do that?'

'I will,' said Clara.

The doctor looked at the cake, took a bite. It was past its best and he put it back on the plate. Took another sip of the bad-tasting tea. Then he stood up, and looked down at the three of them. 'The funeral director will be here within the hour.'

Clara nodded. She wished she'd had a better education, she wished she could be good at something. The needle-work was nothing and she knew it. A hobby, at best. Not enough to pay for a damned thing, not really. Their Dad had been a rich man, and her parents had gone along as-suming that would always be the case, and that neither Clara nor Bernie would ever have to work because one day they would get married and become housewives.

But what sort of men could they meet, who could be a suitable husband for either of them, around here? Eight horrible, panic-driven months since Dad had left them, and neither Clara nor Bernie had even thought about school. Kathleen had fallen into a kind of dull depression and didn't care whether they went or not. The education authorities hadn't bothered to chase them up, either: not here in the slums. And what about Henry? He should be starting school soon, but he probably wouldn't. Of course, the plan had always been for Henry to follow Dad straight into the business . . . except now there was no business.

While Bernie showed the doctor out, Clara sat there, staring at her mother's death certificate. Her head swam with the shock of it. The sheer dreadful *finality* of it.

'Try and eat a little, Henry,' she said. 'Have some of the cake, for God's sake. It'll make you feel better. I'll go in with Mum for a while, all right?'

Clara went into the bedroom and there her mother lay, her spirit, her soul, all gone. Clara closed the door gently. She went over to the window and drew the curtains closed again, plunging the room into gloom. Then she pulled up a rickety old chair, sat down beside the bed, took her mother's lifeless hand in both of hers, and cried.

12

'Marcus? Honey?'

It was a woman's voice. Marcus's eyes flickered open. He pulled in a shuddering breath and sat up in bed to bright morning light and the sound of traffic outside. He pushed his hair back out of his eyes. Paulette was there, holding out a mug of tea. She had the radio on in the kitchen and he could hear the Hilltoppers drifting out, singing 'P.S. I Love You'.

He'd met Paulette last year in the Calypso, one of Lenny's clubs – now his – and he'd found her sexy and obliging so he'd bought her a flat, which was where he'd wound up overnight. Occasionally she slept over at his place – and she had been moving a few pieces of her clothing into his wardrobe, which didn't exactly delight him. She was his official mistress – most of the club owners had one – but Christ knew he didn't want to go too far down *that* road.

He took the steaming mug she offered. It was one of her set of two Coronation mugs with Queen Elizabeth II on it. Paulette was a fervent Royalist; the crazy cow had even camped out overnight in June with some of her mates on a rain-soaked Mall to see the new Queen pass by in the big gilded state coach.

It tickled him to think of Paulette – who'd been giving herself airs since she started being seen around town with him – squatting on the Mall in the rain. Now, she wouldn't do that. Now, she'd want to watch from a five-star hotel, doused in the fancy French perfume he'd paid for, wearing designer dresses with big net underskirts and tight bodices, maybe a mink over the top.

Marcus looked at her in the cold light of day. Her honey-blonde curls were glossy in the first rays of the morning's sun; her hair, he thought, was her prettiest feature. Her face was too long for perfect beauty. There was a knowing look in her grape-green eyes and her skin wasn't the best, but she was pretty enough, and – up to now – not too demanding, although she could talk the hind leg off a bleeding donkey. She had a good body and she'd been doing a lot of model-ling when he'd met her; she still did a fair bit of modelling on the side.

Undemanding, he thought. Yeah. After that dismal visit to his mother's yesterday, an undemanding woman was exactly what he needed. His mother had no heart, no soul. Well, maybe he didn't either.

She was returning his stare. 'You shout out sometimes, you know. In your sleep.'

'Do I? What do I say?' He had dreams, he knew that. About Lenny, *dead* Lenny, standing at the end of his bed in the moonlight, with half his head shot away, asking why had he done it.

'Nothing, really. You shout, that's all. And you move your legs, like you're running. You went to see your mum yester-day, didn't you.'

'So?'

She shrugged. 'Just saying. You always come back from her with a fucking face on you.'

Marcus sipped the tea. It was hot and strong, delicious. Paulette started jabbering on same as always in her high-pitched voice, so he tuned out. Minutes later, he tuned back in. ' . . . So I said it wasn't enough, not nearly enough, and he renegotiated and then I agreed. Earl's Court Motor Show! Don't you think that's great?'

'What?' he asked.

She tutted. 'Listen, will you. I'm going to be Miss Healey at the Motor Show.'

'What does Miss Healey do?'

'I lie on the bonnet of their new model car,' said Paulette. 'In an evening gown. It's all very tasteful.'

'What, every day?'

'While the show's on, yes. October twenty-first to the end of the month. Of course I have breaks.'

'Well good.'

'Is it true you've taken over from Lenny Lynch?' she said, eyeing him curiously.

'Yeah, it's true.' Marcus was used to Paulette's sudden changes of topic. She hardly ever came up for air between one subject and the next.

'I heard that blowsy tart Delilah went missing from the Blue Banana.'

Marcus's black eyes stared into Paulette's. 'I heard that too.'

'Turned up drowned, they say. Down Limehouse.'

Marcus put the empty mug aside. 'Time I was up,' he said, and Paulette took that as a signal that she was to drop the subject.

But Paulette was secretly delighted with this new turn of events. Lenny Lynch had been the uncrowned king of Soho. And now Marcus – *her* boyfriend, and God how she was going to crow about this to all her mates – was taking Lenny's place!

Marcus Redmayne was on the up.

And by God, she was going with him!

13

Clara hated everything about being poor, but what she hated most was the constant, grinding humiliation of it. It was Tuesday. At three o'clock, Hatton would knock on the door and that would be it; they'd be out of here.

The funeral directors came, and the faces of the two men were a picture of distaste as they took in the squalor of their surroundings. *They know this is going to be a council burial,* thought Clara. *No money in it for them. Not even a bloody tip for taking away the corpse.*

She couldn't fail to notice their sneering glances and the lofty way they talked down to her and to Bernie, who was clutching at Henry as if he might vanish, just like Mum would soon, when they took her body away.

Clara made the men a cup of tea, offered them the last of the stale cake – which they refused – and tried to maintain a dignified front as they sat at the table and prepared the forms that would consign Mum to a pauper's grave.

With tea and paperwork out of the way, the two men fetched a makeshift coffin from the hearse and tramped up all the stairs with it. For once, the people clustered on every flight fell silent. Bernie started to cry as the men came into the flat carrying it.

'Shh, Bern,' said Clara, patting her sister's shivering shoulder. Mum's old gold wedding band, thin as wire with years of wear, glinted on Clara's right hand. She'd taken it off her mother's body; it was a keepsake she'd treasure. She didn't want some morgue attendant wrenching it off her and selling it.

'I can't believe it,' said Bernie. 'I can't. This is *wrong*.'

'Mum wouldn't want you getting upset,' said Clara, watching Bernie with concern. Her sister had always been the caring one, the soft one; she looked like Mum and she was more like Mum in nature than Clara could ever be; sweeter, less pragmatic. Clara was the tougher of the two – more like Dad, she supposed, although she wasn't proud of that – but right now she was glad of it. She had to be tough, to cope with all this. Life had kicked the Dolans hard, and it seemed it wasn't finished with them yet.

She poured more tea for Bernie and when the undertakers came out of the bedroom carrying their sad burden, she showed them out of the flat. Down on the other flights, there were people still sitting, silent now as the men passed by with the coffin. Watching. Suddenly, Clara cracked.

'Seen enough, have you?' she yelled. Faces turned up and stared at her. She went back into the flat and locked the door and stood shaking against it.

Oh Jesus, what would they do now? How were they going to manage . . . ?

Bernie was still weeping at the table, Henry clinging on to her and grizzling. Clara went to them, her heart full of sorrow. She patted her sister's shoulder and hugged Henry.

'It's going to be all right,' she said firmly, but she could see that Bernie didn't believe it and she didn't believe it herself, not any more.

Best to keep busy, she told herself. What else could she do? She got clean linen from the cupboard, and went to strip the bed.

★

59

An hour later, she was down in the yard at the back of the building, stuffing some of the sodden newspapers into the bin. Headlines flickered past her eyes but she couldn't take them in. Some rich American called John Kennedy had married Jacqueline Bouvier. The whites had hung on to Rhodesia. A record number of houses were being built. None of it meant a damned thing. She put all the old soiled sheets into the dustbin too. The metal stink of the blood whooshed up as she did so, filling her with nausea. Bile surged into her throat. *Poor Mum.* Even if it was a wicked waste, she didn't have the heart to wash the sheets. Her stomach turned over at the very thought.

She trudged wearily back up the stairs. The young black woman who seemed to live on the second floor, the one who had smiled at her a couple of times, looked at her as she passed, seemed almost about to speak; but Clara carried on up to the top floor and knocked three times at the door. Bernie let her in. She seemed agitated – even more than usual.

'Clar?' There was alarm in Bernie's voice.

'What's up?' asked Clara, locking the door behind her.

'I dunno. I was in the bedroom, and I looked out the window, and I saw the doctor down in the road. He had two policemen with him. Come and see.'

Bernie led the way into the shadowy bedroom with its bare bed, empty of life now, all sign of Kathleen gone. 'You can only see them from in here,' she said, and nudged open the curtain to show Clara.

Sure enough, there they were, in a huddle on the pavement two doors down on this side of the road. Had they been standing a few yards further back, Bernie wouldn't have been able to see them. They were talking, and the doctor was indicating their building, and the policemen were nodding, looking up at the top-floor windows.

'What do you think they're doing?' asked Bernie anxiously.

Clara's guts heaved with dread at what she was seeing. She could think of only one explanation. The doctor must have gone back to the surgery and checked his records. Having found out that she was lying about her age, he'd returned with two helpers to do the unthinkable: take Henry and Bernie away and place them into care. If she let that happen, she would never see her brother or sister again.

'Oh God,' was all that Clara could say.

'What is it, Clara? You've gone white!'

Clara took a calming breath. Her heart was racing and she felt like she was going to pass out. She heaved in another breath. Then another.

She watched the small group move to the front of the building, picking their way through the heaps of rubbish, then they disappeared inside. Soon they would be hammering at the flat door, and if Clara didn't let them in, the coppers would break the door down.

She drew in another breath. Finally she was able to get the words out: 'Bernie – we have to go.'

They only had time to grab their coats and Clara's bag before she pushed them all out of the flat door and down the stairs. Maybe they could get out onto a fire escape? Maybe someone would help them? But who?

Leaning over the banister, Clara saw the coppers and the doctor coming up.

Fuck.

They had to find a hiding place and quickly; with the doctor and the police already on the stairs and climbing, if she didn't get Henry and Bernie off the main stairway in the next few seconds they'd meet head-on.

She herded them quickly down a couple of flights,

thinking she would go into one of the neighbours' flats and with any luck they wouldn't give them away. Why would they? All the people around here hated the police.

But for once all the doors were shut. Clara guessed that someone else had spotted the police outside and word had spread. There was no one on the stairs; no one to help. She was starting to panic, she daren't knock at a door – chances were no one would open up, and she'd only end up alerting the police to their presence.

Then she spotted the young black woman who'd smiled at her, peeping out of a half-closed door on the landing below. Seeing the stark fear on Clara's face, the woman lifted a finger to her lips and hurried out. She ushered Clara and the kids into the reeking communal toilet.

Inside, there was scarcely room to breathe – not that they wanted to. It stank to high heaven. Clara shot the bolt and they clustered together, clinging to each other like ship-wrecked sailors.

'Got to be quiet now, Henry,' hissed Clara, pulling him in close against her and putting an arm around Bernie. Clara could hear her own heart, thundering in her chest.

Outside, the tread of the coppers and the doctor kept coming closer, closer . . .

Oh God, let them keep going, please let them keep going . . .

The footsteps went on by. Moments passed and all Clara could hear was her own terrified heartbeat and the *drip, drip, drip* of the cistern overflow. Then there was a knock on the door and it was all she could do not to scream out loud.

Clara gulped, unable to get words out. 'Who is it?' she whispered.

'Me! It's me,' said a female voice.

Clara unbolted the door. It was the young woman. She made *come on, come on* motions with her hand, and Clara

pushed Bernie and Henry out and hurried down the stairs.
Then she paused.

'Thanks,' she said.

'Go. Shoo! Hurry up.'

And Clara was off, away, down the stairs and out the
door with Henry and Bernie.

14

There was a geezer hanging around Soho like a bad smell, who always seemed to make it a point to be a pain in Marcus's neck. Jacko Sears was his name; he was a newcomer to the Soho scene and was trying to muscle in on Marcus's business. Things had got to the point where something would have to be done about the tosser soon, else he might get even bigger ideas.

'I'll ask around, see what's known,' said Pete. Though his real name was Pete Driscoll, he was known around town as Pistol Pete, thanks in part to his gunslinger looks – the skinny build and Rhett Butler moustache – but also because he was handy with a gun. Marcus had known him since their schooldays, when they'd run wild together, and he was the first person he turned to in a fix. It was Pete who'd taken care of the Lenny Lynch situation for him.

Before too long, Pete came back.

'So what's the news?' asked Marcus.

Pete shrugged. 'He's from Manchester, seems him and his brothers have a bit of a reputation up there. Jacko's the youngest of the gang. The two older Sears boys, Fulton and Ivan, are still up north, but Jacko's decided to make a name for himself down here. Pulled a gun on Con Beeston over in Greek Street and told him he was taking his club over. And he did.'

Marcus digested this. His own rapid takeover of Lenny's empire was not at all unusual by Soho standards. Anyone could take a club by force then walk into a Post Office and get a club licence for two shillings and sixpence. And the temptation was strong, especially when there were so many clubs in Soho and such rich pickings to be had.

Marcus never ceased to be astonished at the sheer number and variety of clubs available to the public on these streets. Theatricals had the Kismet in Charing Cross Road, journalists frequented the Candy Box, lesbians had the Festival in Dean Street and the homos had the Duce or the Alphabet. Underworld faces drank in the Mazurka, run by an ex-Windmill girl, and there were clubs like the Premier where the Old Bill went in and took their money like a weekly wage for palling up to the villains, arranging the suppression of evidence and payments for services received. For himself, Marcus liked to run a fairly straight gambling and drinks club, but he wasn't against keeping a few tame coppers on the payroll. You never knew when it might come in handy.

'Word is, he wants to take your clubs off you,' said Pete.

'He'll find that harder going than mugging poor old Con,' said Marcus.

'He's out to cause you trouble.'

'Well, fuck him,' said Marcus succinctly, and that was the end of *that* conversation.

When he got home, had a shower, a shit and a shave, he went to his wardrobe and there was even more stuff of Paulette's in there. Fuck, she was getting keen. And he wasn't. Oh, she was a party girl, OK to pass the time with, to look good around town with him, to take to bed and smash the life out of now and then, but this wasn't part of the deal and it was starting to get annoying.

'All this stuff in here,' he said to her.

'Yeah? What about it?'

'Thin it out, will you? This ain't a fucking five-star hotel. I need some space too.'

'Christ, you're always moaning,' she complained.

Yes, Paulette was good-looking, and obliging, but she was turning out to be bloody expensive too. Every week he gave her seventy pounds, which she seemed to have no trouble at all in spending. Last Christmas she'd asked for a fucking *horse*, would you believe it? So he'd bought her one, a fine dapple-grey Arab mare for three hundred pounds, which *he* now paid to have stabled at Ennismore Mews. Turns out she was a lousy rider, always falling off the damned thing and onto her arse along Rotten Row.

A club owner had to have a showy mistress, that went without saying; so he tolerated her. And she came in handy, fending off the women who were forever chucking themselves at him. Not that he minded the odd fling, but it got annoying when they were too persistent or possessive. He'd yet to find any woman he'd trust enough to develop deep feelings for. He'd never been in love; only in lust.

Marcus toured his clubs, making sure everything was ticking over nicely, and then he made his usual duty call, first to the jeweller's in Old Bond Street, then to his mother's gaff. She was exactly the same. It put him in mind of an old saying, *pickled in aspic*, which he guessed meant set a certain way, never changing. That was his mother. She accepted his gift like always, plonked it on the table beside her chair. Didn't open it.

'You OK?' asked Marcus.

'Fine,' she said.

Silence fell. Marcus wondered where all the gifts went. Did she keep them in a box somewhere? It would have to be a bloody big box by now. Or did she sell the sodding things on?

That wouldn't surprise him.

Nothing his mother did would surprise him. The woman had a heart of stone.

Maybe he'd inherited something from her, after all.

'Took over another club this week,' said Marcus.

'Really?'

Yes, bloody really.

He stayed another fifteen minutes, and then left. Once out the gate, and certain she'd shut the door on him, he kicked the brick pillar and swore.

15

Frank Hatton could hear knocking. And he could hear something else, too: a kid crying, very loudly; a heartfelt wail that drilled straight through his sore brain. He'd sunk too many pints down the Bear the night before. As per bloody usual. Alerted by the din, Attila the Alsatian started barking out in the backyard, where he had a kennel and was secured on a chain.

Wearing only his long johns, Frank pulled himself out of bed with a groan.

'Attila, you fucking bird brain, *shut up!*' he yelled, putting on his trousers and then stumbling along the hall to the front door. Attila fell silent. Frank tugged his braces up over his shoulders, ran a hand through his dishevelled thinning grey hair. The knocking – the pounding – went on. 'Don't beat the bloody door down! What do you—'

He flung open the door. The volume of the crying soared to fever pitch. Clara Dolan was standing there, and behind her there was a younger girl with reddish-brown hair. Clinging to the younger girl's skirts was a boy of seven or eight years old.

'What the fu—' said Hatton.

Clara was staring at his face. She gulped, and got the words out.

'You said if I needed anything, I could call here,' she said flatly. 'You gave me your address. Well I do. I – *we* – need a place to stay.'

There are moments in life when everything turns, and Frank Hatton could see that this was such a one. You get up in the morning, the day's the same as every other, then bang! What you've always desired comes and lands straight in your lap. He could hardly believe his eyes or his luck, but this was happening. Little Clara Dolan with her glossy mane of black hair, her huge violet-blue eyes and her determined chin, Clara Dolan who had been haunting his drunken dreams for a long time, was here, asking for his help.

'Jesus . . . ' said Hatton.

'Well?' snapped Clara.

Hatton pushed the door open further. 'Come in,' he said.

Frank Hatton led the way into a disorderly kitchen, thick with dirt. Clara looked around in disgust. The Dolans might be poor, but they were never dirty. This place hadn't seen a duster or a broom in months. There were soiled boots on the table on a sheet of newspaper beside bike parts and a container of oil; there was a stained washing-up bowl on top of the stove. The linoleum was sticky with food spills and grubby with ingrained mud and paw prints. You could see at a glance that no woman lived here.

Sick misgiving clenched at her stomach as she looked at Hatton. Oh Christ, and he was no oil painting either, was he? Anything that had once been muscle had long since turned to fat, his skin was yellow, his eyes bloodshot, and he hadn't even bothered to wash or shave. What a state!

There was silence in the room. Henry had stopped his sobbing and Attila had given up barking. Clara slumped down at the table, and Bernie sat too, shivering and hugging herself. Hatton stood propped against the sink, looking at the younger kids. His eyes fell on Henry.

'Go out and play in the yard,' he said to the boy. 'Don't you touch that bloody dog though, he'll eat ya.'

Henry wandered off outside. Clara looked at Hatton.

'So what's going on?' he asked.

Clara told him.

'Shit,' said Frank when she'd finished.

'So can we stay? For now?' asked Clara.

On the way over, she had formulated a plan. The flat was history, and so was the Singer sewing machine that could have earned them a small crust. So she had made up her mind that something else would have to do. At least this way, the family could stay together. Bernie and Henry had been through far too much to endure any more upheaval.

Hatton was silent for a while, thinking it over.

'Yeah,' he said at last. 'Why not?'

He showed Clara and Bernie upstairs to a bedroom. It was dusty, the windows grimed from years of dirt. But there was a big metal-framed double bed for them to sleep on, big enough for all three of them, just about.

While Bernie sat down on the bed, Clara went over to the grimy window and looked bleakly out onto the street. There were people down there, going about their everyday business, nothing exciting happening, but for the once-wealthy Dolans, everything had imploded; everything had changed.

Clara's mind wouldn't stop replaying it all: first Dad's business going, then Dad deserting them when it had all got too much for him to cope with, leaving his pregnant wife and young children to scratch a living in the slums. And how were *they* supposed to cope? A visceral anger gripped Clara so hard that she shivered. They'd not only lost the roof over their head, they'd lost Mum – a loss that was too terrible, too fresh, to even think about. So Clara decided she was going to shut her mind to it and just get on with it. Do what must be done. You either sank in shit in this world or you came up and gasped in air. Clara Dolan had no intention of sinking.

'Clara?' It was Bernie, breaking into her reverie.

Clara turned, looked at her. Bernie looked very small, very pale, sitting there.

'Can we go back to the flat now?' she pleaded.

Clara stared at Bernie, long and hard. She could understand how her sister felt. It was awful back there at the flat, really horrible, but it was their last link with Mum and at least it was familiar. All this was new, and frightening. 'We can't,' she said at last.

Bernie's eyes were desperate with panic. 'What do you mean?'

'Just that. We can't go back there, not unless you want to be taken into care and Henry with you. Maybe even me too. We'll get separated. Don't you see that?'

'But Clar . . . Mum . . . '

'Mum's gone.'

'Won't there be a funeral?'

'No. We couldn't have afforded one anyway. God's sake, Bernie, show a bit of sense. All that's over, gone and done.'

Bernie's face was white as snow. 'So . . . where will they . . . '

'The council will bury her,' said Clara.

Bernie put her hands to her mouth as if Clara had struck her. Tears ran down her cheeks.

'But we won't know where,' she gasped.

'It doesn't matter,' said Clara flatly. 'She's gone.'

She had to turn away from the pain on Bernie's face, back toward the window. As she stood there, considering what options they had left, she could see her reflection in the mucky glass, faded like an old Venetian mirror.

Clara had no illusions about the sorts of things she could do to raise money, to keep the family together. She could get a job in a club tomorrow, stripping. She had a good face, a thick waterfall of black hair and a body that would fit the bill, she knew it. She was five feet eight inches tall, nine stone in weight, with richly curving hips, a small waist and full breasts that were neither too small nor too large. But she was revolted by the thought of doing that. Not when there was another way.

'Clar?' Bernie's voice was very low.

'Yeah, Bern?'

Clara didn't look round. She was afraid if she did that Bernie would see that she was almost at the end of her rope; she felt like her whole being was coming apart, that she was spinning, helpless, in a black turmoil of grief and despair. But she *had* to keep thinking, figuring out what their next move should be. For all their sakes.

'Was it my fault, that Dad left? Did he go because of me? Because of something I said?'

Clara turned around and stared at Bernie in surprise.

'*What?*' Then she saw the numb miserable certainty of guilt on Bernie's face. She went to her and grabbed her frail shaking shoulders and shook her lightly. Trust over-emotional Bernie to get the wrong end of the stick. 'No, Bern. Don't think that, don't ever think that. He got himself in a mess with the business, that's all and . . . well, the authorities could have got involved, so he had to go. It was nothing to do with you, nothing at all.'

Bernie nodded and seemed satisfied with that. At least, Clara hoped she was.

'Go and check on Henry, make sure he's all right,' said Clara, patting her sister's shoulder.

DANGEROUS

With Bernie gone from the room, Clara worked it all through in her mind again.

She was doing the right thing.

The only possible thing.

16

Bert Shillingworth was up in the dead of night, making one of several trips to the loo. He was seventy-six years old and he felt it. Everything ached – his back, his legs, his whole damned body. His bloody eyesight was going. Since his wife died, he hadn't slept well. It sounded stupid, but he missed her snoring! Now, apart from the cat, there was only him in the little flat above the tobacco shop he ran in Soho. He was glad of Tabs the cat, of another heartbeat under the roof when the nights were long and lonely.

Bert used the pot he kept under the bed to save him a trip all the way down the stairs to the outside lavvy in the back-yard, then he heard a motor revving out front. Middle of the fucking night, didn't the bastards ever sleep around here? All these clubs and strip joints and prossies and pimps hanging about on corners, music blaring out – and not *good* music, not like in the war, not 'Run Rabbit Run' or 'The White Cliffs of Dover'. No, this was new stuff, and he hated it. The place was getting worse, going to the fucking dogs.

With Tabs winding silkily around his legs, Bert tottered over to the window, yanking the curtain back. He looked out just as a car screeched to a halt outside the Blue Banana club, opposite Bert's shop. Someone got out of the car, moving quickly. There was a flare of fire, the sound of glass breaking, and then *whoomph!* The place was alight. The man jumped back in the car, and it sped away.

'Fuck me,' said Bert.

The fire brigade came out, and the police (some of whom had been drinking in the Blue Banana not three hours earlier) and it was agreed that this was a petrol bomb attack, probably gangland stuff, about which Old Bill didn't give a flying fuck. Once the fire was put out, they all buggered off home.

Marcus was summoned from his bed, shaking off Paulette's clinging hands and promising he'd be back soon. He made a couple of calls and then set off, arriving outside the Blue Banana to find the door blackened, the bricks scorched, several posters destroyed, the signage severely damaged and all the lights over it exploded from the heat of the fire.

'Shit,' he said.

Gordon rolled up, and Pistol Pete. People were standing out in the street, looking at the smouldering frontage.

'I saw it go up,' said one elderly gent, trotting over to where the three of them stood. 'I don't sleep too well. Got up to take a piss, looks out the window, there was a bloke getting out of a car, and then *boom!* Window could have blown in and the glass could have blinded me. We could all have been killed in our beds.'

Marcus guessed this was the most excitement the old geezer had had since the Blitz. The man's myopic eyes were dancing, he looked almost happy.

'You see who did it?' he asked. 'Get a car registration, anything . . . ?'

Bert shook his head. 'Nah. Sorry.'

'Nothing too drastic, by the look of it,' said Gordon, already adding up the cost of repairs in his mind.

'This Jacko Sears, you think?' Marcus asked Pete when the old man had wandered off out of earshot.

'Bloody sure,' said Pete. 'He was in the Bear last week, saying he was going to do this. Thought it was drunken bullshit. But it wasn't, was it.'

'You know what?' said Marcus. 'That prick's starting to get on my nerves.'

'So what was it?' asked Paulette when Marcus got home and crawled into bed. By which time dawn was breaking, the birds were singing, and he was very annoyed.

'Club business,' said Marcus.

'What sort of club business?' she asked, cuddling up.

'The sort that's none of *your* fucking business,' snapped Marcus, turning his back and pulling the covers over his head.

Jacko Sears.

Sears might have thrown a scare into poor old Con Beeston, but he was going to find Marcus Redmayne a tougher nut to crack. One way or another, that cunt was going to have to go.

17

There was somebody banging on the bedroom door as if they wanted to break it down. Clara shot up in the bed, fumbled for the bedside light, switched it on. Her heart was beating frantically.

A jumble of thoughts spun around her mind as she was jarred out of sleep and into wakefulness. Waking up was always the worst part, the part where reality flooded back in and struck her like a physical blow. Mum, lying dead and bloody. The baby, whose birth had killed her. The police coming with the doctor. Running with Bernie and Henry, and coming here to Hatton's place. She saw that Bernie was awake too, and sitting up. Bernie clutched at her sister's arm. Henry somehow kept sleeping. Thank God for that, at least.

'What is it . . . ?' gasped Bernie. 'Who . . . ?'

Clara looked over to the door. She'd told Bernie to give her a hand last night, and together they'd pulled the chest of drawers against it so that no one could come in.

Thank God we did that, she thought.

'Ah, come on, girl. Let me in,' said Hatton's voice. He sounded drunk.

It must be gone twelve. Clara felt anger overtake her. He'd come home from a shut-in at his local and now here he was, shit-faced and hammering at the door, scaring them all half to death.

She slipped out of the bed and went to the blocked doorway.

'Go to bed!' she hissed loudly.

Too late. There was a gasp from Henry. 'What is it? Where's Mum? I want Mum!'

'Shh, Henry,' said Bernie.

'Now look what you've done,' said Clara as Henry started to cry.

'Come on, girl,' he wheedled from outside the door. The handle rattled and the door opened a fraction of an inch. The chest of drawers stopped it moving further, but in alarm Clara flung her own weight against it too, in case it should tip over.

'No!' Clara shouted out. They were *all* awake now, thanks to this drunken stupid bastard. 'You listen to me, Frank Hatton,' she said, full volume. '*Go to bed*. We'll talk about this in the morning. You understand?'

He said nothing.

'Are you hearing me, Hatton? You're not coming in. Go to bed. We'll talk tomorrow.'

She stood there, panting with alarm. The door handle turned again, once. And then she heard him going off along the hall.

'What did he want?' asked Bernie, shushing Henry, trying to calm him down once more.

'Nothing, he's drunk, that's all, he doesn't know what he's doing.'

Bernie nodded. Her sister was the boss, she was always the one in charge and that reassured her a little. Clara always knew what to do.

It was past three when Henry cried himself back to sleep. At last Bernie was slumbering too. Exhausted though she was, Clara couldn't sleep.

We'll talk about it tomorrow.

Yes, they would talk it over. They would discuss the fact that she had her family to support; and the fact that Hatton wanted her so much that he'd be willing to stumble in here drunk and force himself on her. She had a plan, oh yes. A deal would have to be done, even if it made her sick to her stomach to do it. Come hell or high water, she was going to protect Bernie and Henry, and they were *never* going back to the slums. Whatever she had to do, she would do it.

18

There were plenty of chancers around Soho planning to take over a chunk of the action for themselves. *For Soho,* Marcus often thought to himself, *read War Zone.* Still, he was ready to fight his corner. He regretted what he'd had to do about Lenny, and he wasn't going to give up any of the ground that had cost him so dear.

These people were a constant nuisance to Marcus, causing him to send gangs of raiders into clubs and gambling houses and onto the racetracks to make the point that he was in charge. But the firebombing at the Blue Banana had taken the nuisance to a whole new level. In fact he was so pissed off at that cunt Jacko Sears that he decided to do Sears's new club in Greek Street.

So, yeah, as far as he was concerned, it was war. But before he could get in his retaliation, once again the war came to him. He was out in one of his own clubs, the Blue Bird, for an evening's entertainment when in came Sears with a gang of fifteen and started kicking the living shit out of Marcus and his men.

'Jesus!' shouted Gordon as the mob poured in. Women were screaming and men were hurtling around the room, upturning gaming tables, sending counters and chips and cards in all directions, and throwing punches. The band scattered in a cacophony of off-tune notes, right in the middle of 'Pretty Little Black-Eyed Susie'.

'Get out the back, Gord,' said Marcus, slipping on his spiked knuckledusters and picking up the hammer he kept under the table.

Gordon was away in an instant, along with the women. Marcus and his men got to work, and Pistol Pete was instantly getting the worst of it off Sears. Marcus piled in to help. Sears was a huge bald-headed git with a flattened nose from punching it out in the ring in his youth. Marcus knocked him down with a bone-cracking blow of the hammer straight in the centre of his pug-ugly mush.

Busted that nose a second time, thought Marcus.

'Shit!' burbled Sears, and Marcus dragged him back up and punched him in the jaw with the knuckledusters, snapping his jawbone and breaking the skin open like a watermelon. Blood flew and Sears collapsed to the floor.

Again, Marcus pulled him up. He wasn't going to piss about with Sears; he'd had enough. He was going to stamp it out, this last little flicker of the flame, and sadly for Sears that meant he was in deep trouble.

To his surprise Sears recovered himself enough to rear up bloody-faced and send a crashing blow into Marcus's middle.

Shit, that bloody hurt.

Wincing, Marcus flailed backward, falling over a table, then crawled upright again and hurled himself at Sears. All around them, men were cursing and shouting and falling about the place as blows landed. Marcus swung again and this time the hammer hit Sears square between the eyes. He toppled back, hit the ground and lay there, out for the count, blood all over his face.

Marcus summoned Pistol Pete, bruised and bloody but

still looking flashy with his moustache and his spivvy taste in clothing. Together they yanked Sears out into the road.

'Shit,' said Pete as they stood panting over Sears's prostrate form.

'What?' Marcus was leaning against the wall of the club, feeling like he was about to fall down. That was one *hard* bastard.

Pete was bending over Sears, a hand on the man's thick neck.

'Think he's croaked,' said Pete. Then he straightened and looked into his mate's eyes. 'We got to tidy this away.'

Marcus was nodding, still breathing hard. He pushed himself away from the wall. 'Let's get him in the back of the car,' he said.

As Pete went to fetch the motor, Marcus stood there looking down at his fallen adversary.

No more petrol bombs then, no more raids. Not from *this* arsehole, anyway.

Sears was done for.

Once they'd finished with Sears, Pete and Marcus drove back to the club and took a look around. There was an ambulance outside, blue lights flashing. Inside, stragglers were being picked up off the floor. The ambulance men were stooping over one bloke who'd got the worst of it; they were getting him onto a stretcher. Gordon appeared, stepping over fallen men and shattered fittings, to make his way to Marcus's side.

'Jesus!' he said. 'It's going to cost us a fucking fortune, kitting this place out again. There's blood all over the effing walls!'

Money! That was Gordon's God. There were men with their arses hanging off, limbs broken, faces slit with razors, gouged with bike chains; Jacko Sears had cashed in his chips for good and was mouldering in the ground right now – and here was Gordon, worrying about the cost of a tin of paint.

'You take the bloody cake!' said Marcus with a painful laugh. One of his front teeth felt loose, and his left eye was swelling shut and turning blue where Sears had punched him. His knuckles were bloody. His stomach felt like a pile-driver had hit it.

'I don't see what's funny,' sniffed Gordon.

Marcus patted his mate's cheek, leaving a smear of dirt and blood on Gordon's face.

'I honestly don't,' said Gordon, wiping Marcus's paw-print fastidiously away with a spotless handkerchief.

But Marcus was satisfied with this night's work. Sears was gone: that was the important thing. Gone for *good*.

19

Water was trickling over Frank Hatton's face – freezing cold water. He sprang up in bed and there she was, standing over him – Clara Dolan, fully dressed, holding an empty milk bottle above his head.

'What the *fuck*?' he demanded, spitting water out of his mouth. It was daylight. It was morning.

Clara stared down at him. 'Get washed and dressed and come downstairs – it's time we had a talk,' she said, and left the room.

He could hear the child grizzling again in the room next door, and the other one, the dainty little pixie-faced sister with the red-brown hair, was shushing him. Head thumping, he crawled from the bed in his long johns and went over to the washstand. Looked in the mirror. Saw grey stubble on his chin. His nose mottled red. He was getting bags under his eyes with all the booze. He splashed a bit more water on his face, dried it with the grubby towel. Rinsed out his foul-tasting mouth. Yanked on yesterday's shirt and his trousers and slippers, and trudged off down the stairs, pulling his braces over his shoulders.

Clara was sitting at the kitchen table, looking around at the place like it fell far short of expectations. Hatton felt anger stir. She'd come from a rat-hole slum with cock-roaches climbing up the walls, and she was looking down her nose at *his* place? It was OK. It was presentable. Not entirely clean, he knew that, he wasn't a fucking woman after all and he lived alone so there was no one to see to things like that.

'Make us some breakfast, will you?' he whined, slumping down at the table and putting his head in his hands.

'Make it yourself,' said Clara.

Hatton let his hands fall to the table. His bloodshot eyes took on a mean look. He stabbed the table with his finger. 'Now look here. You *owe* me, girl. I just took you in, nobody else was going to do that.'

Clara stared at Hatton like he was something nasty. 'You took me in for your own advantage,' she pointed out. 'You were trying to get into my room last night.'

'Was I?' Vaguely he remembered beating at a door and a sharp female voice telling him off.

'You were. And I won't have it.'

Hatton's eyes widened. 'You're a stroppy little mare, ain't you? You'll have whatever I choose to give you, that's what *you'll* have.'

He lunged up from the table and was halfway round it when Clara stood up and swiped her hand left to right. There was a ripping sound and Hatton felt a sharp stinging sensation. He looked down in surprise. The middle of his shirt was torn open and there was a thin line of blood seeping out, staining the dull grey-white to red. He looked at Clara's hand. She was holding his carving knife.

He felt the pain of it then, and hastily pushed the shirt up. His long johns were slit open. And she'd cut his skin. 'You little *cow*!' he bellowed, and started forward.

Clara held up the knife. Looking in her eyes, he could see that she would use it, too. He stopped, uncertain.

'Cow, am I? Not so much a cow as I'd let an animal like you into bed with me. And think on, Hatton. You might be able to take this knife off me, but there are other ways to skin a cat and if you cross me, I'll make you pay. You can be sure of that.'

Hatton stepped back a pace. Jesus, what had he invited in here? His midriff stung like a bastard, but he had to admire her somehow. Hardly more than a girl, but fiery and bloody pretty too. After a long, long moment when it could have gone either way, he stumbled back to his chair and collapsed into it like a sack of spanners. Clara stared at him, then she said: 'I'll put the kettle on then, shall I?'

And she went over to the sink and started making tea as if she hadn't just slashed him with his own knife. She filled the kettle, tossed the washing-up bowl to one side and slapped the kettle onto the range, wiping dust from her fingers with a grimace of distaste.

'This place is a mess,' she said. 'You live here on your own, do you? You're single?'

Hatton sat back and stared at her. 'Oh, sorry, don't it meet your standards?' he mocked. 'And yes, I am single. Never been married. What's it to you?'

She looked at him. 'It don't meet my standards at all. But it'll have to do. You've no kids then?'

'None I know of. And what do you mean, "it'll have to do"? What makes you think I'll let you stay?'

'Course you will.'

'Why's that?' he asked. You had to credit her for her audacity, if nothing else. All right she was a looker, a *stunner*, but she was crazy with it.

'Because you want me. Don't you?' said Clara as the kettle started to whistle.

Hatton said nothing. It was the truth, after all.

'But I can't stay in a house unmarried with an unmarried man. That isn't on. So as soon as I pass my sixteenth next month we're going to get wed, and you are going to keep a roof over my head and treat me respectfully as is a wife's due. And there's another thing.'

Hatton was sitting there goggle-eyed. *Marriage?* Had she really said that? Maybe he'd misheard. His head was still banging away with the booze.

'What's the other thing?' he asked, as she started spooning tea out of the caddy.

'You provide for Bernie and Henry too. You keep us all under your roof, and you provide for us.'

'But—'

'No arguments. It's me and them, or nothing at all. I'll go, we'll all go, we'll find somewhere else.'

Hatton sat back and eyed her, arms folded. Jesus, his middle was sore and throbbing. And sticky. He unfolded his arms with a wince. 'You ain't got nowhere else. Or you wouldn't have come here.'

Clara shrugged. She knew this was true; she'd thought about it, worked it all out. Marriage to Hatton was the only way to keep the family together, and safe. Working in clubs, even going on the game? Too risky. No, what the family needed was stability, security, a settled home; and this was the best, the *only* way of providing it. She brought the pot to the table and fetched cups from the draining board.

'I'd find something,' she said.

'You'd starve.'

'So stop me starving. Do the decent thing and provide a home for my family and for me. You're in steady work, aren't you? Rent-collecting?'

It wasn't exactly *steady*, working for Lenny Lynch. Sometimes the coppers got lively and the rent-collecting got all mixed up with the 'milk round', which he also did: collecting protection money from the clubs, restaurants, flats and whorehouses on Lenny's manor. He also went round the market collecting subscriptions for Lenny Lynch on behalf of what he called the 'stall trader's fund', which amounted to five shillings from each stallholder a week. One way or another, it all ended up in Lenny's pocket.

But he'd been hearing rumours, unsettling tales of Lenny vanishing from the scene and someone else taking over. He didn't believe it for a minute; Lenny had been in charge for years, and that wasn't going to change.

But good Christ, this was the strangest experience of his entire life. Within the space of a half-hour, the girl had poured cold water on his head, slit open his belly and proposed marriage. She was stirring the pot now, head bent in apparent concentration. Yes, she was a beauty. Mad, of course, but maybe he'd knock that out of her.

'We can't get my parents' permission. Mum died with the baby, and fuck knows where my dad's got to. So are you going to make an honest woman of me, or what?' she asked, pouring out his tea.

'What's in this for me?' asked Hatton.

She shrugged. 'Bernie will help keep the house tidy and cook the meals.'

Hatton frowned. 'And what are *you* going to do?' he asked.

Clara sat down opposite him and looked at him without even a hint of a smile. Inside, she felt sick. Felt the cold, gut-heavy anger against their father, who'd ruined them, cast them into this evil darkness. 'I'll manage the housekeeping and I'll be your wife. Aside from that? I'll do anything I damned well please. We'll have to see to a school for Henry, of course; that's important.'

They both jumped at the sound of a knock at the front door, Clara more than Hatton. She shot to her feet. Had the police found out where the Dolans were hiding, and come to take them?

Hatton lumbered up and went down the hall to the door,

flinging it open. A man charged in and came straight along the passageway. Not the police, but a man of middle years in a tatty suit and waistcoat, his face flushed to the colour of corned beef, his breathing harsh. Completely oblivious to Clara, he fell into one of the chairs, took out a dirty handkerchief and mopped at his brow.

'What the fuck's up with you?' asked Hatton, following the man into the kitchen.

The man's watery blue eyes took in Hatton at a glance. 'Me? What the fuck happened to *you*? Looks like you done ten rounds with Jack the Ripper.'

Hatton glanced down at his bloodstained and split-open shirt. 'This? It's nothing. Knife slipped, that's all. What's up?'

'I've been asking around and it's true, what they're saying: Lenny Lynch is gone. Marcus Redmayne has taken over.'

20

The wedding was a small affair, deliberately low-key; a man in his late fifties, a girl of sixteen. There seemed, to Clara, nothing to celebrate. She was doing what was necessary, that was all. The bridal gown was nothing fancy, just a big-skirted cream dress with a tight bodice that she'd bought in a department store; she'd put some sugar-stiffened net petticoats underneath it to make it flare out just right. She didn't bother with a bouquet.

She didn't draft Bernie in as a bridesmaid or Henry as a pageboy; they were still in mourning for their mother, as was she. In fact, Clara didn't even tell them she was getting married. Why would she? It was enough that she had to go through it – why drag them into it too?

Frank dusted down his one shiny suit, combed his hair, called on two old drinking mates to witness the wedding at the registry office . . . and so the day passed. There was a modest wedding breakfast in the Bear and Ragged Staff. Sausage and mash and a pudding, a few beers, and a small sherry for Clara. Then it was done and Frank drove them home in his old Ford Anglia as Mr and Mrs Hatton.

Bernie had tucked Henry up in bed, and when they came back a married couple Clara sat her sister down and for the first time told her the news.

'We're married, Bern,' she said. Frank had his arm around her shoulders. He smelled of old sweat.

Bernie looked at her in astonishment. 'You're *what?*'

'Married. We decided to make it legal. Frank's going to look after us.'

But Mum's only been gone a couple of months, Clara could see Bernie thinking.

'I don't understand,' said Bernie.

'There's nothing to understand,' said Clara crisply. 'We're married. That's an end to it.'

'You ought to congratulate your sister, girl,' said Frank.

Bernie looked stunned. Slowly she stood up and came to Clara. 'Congratulations, Clar,' she said stiffly, and kissed her cheek.

'How about a peck for your new brother-in-law?' said Frank, smiling.

Clara saw Bernie almost shrink back, then obediently she leaned in on tiptoe and kissed his leathery cheek.

'You can lock up,' said Frank. 'Mind Attila's got water. We're off to bed then.'

And this was it; the bit Clara had been dreading for weeks. Still, she followed Frank up the stairs and into his bedroom – not the one she'd been sharing with Bernie and Henry, which was where she really wanted to go.

More than anything, she didn't want to do this. Up until now, the whole thing had seemed merely an idea; not entirely real. But now, seeing the double bed made up with fresh sheets, seeing Frank eagerly peeling off his clothes as she stood there frozen at the bottom of the bed, she knew that it was going to happen; she was going to give up her virginity to keep her family safe.

It was hideous, a nightmare; he took everything off, but left on his long johns. She was relieved at that. The sight of Frank Hatton in the nude wouldn't be a pleasant one, she felt sure. Then he climbed into bed and patted the pillow beside his.

'Come on then, Clara Dolan. Clara *Hatton*, I should say.'

He was beaming, slightly drunk; he was *happy*, she thought.

Clara didn't know what to do. Go to the bathroom, undress in there?

'Get that dress off, Clara,' said Frank. 'I've waited for this, *dreamed* of it. Strip off for your husband, there's a good girl. Few minutes from now, you'll be a woman.'

His words saved her from fleeing the room. Suddenly anger replaced uncertainty. Her father had brought her to this pass. *Fucking men!* But she was going to win. This was a low point, admittedly, but it would pass, she would *make* it pass.

Angrily she approached her side of the bed. She glared into his eyes and doubled over, pulling down her stockings, her girdle, her net underskirts. Then she undid the front buttons of the dress, one by one, top to bottom, all the way down.

'Come on, let me see those lovely titties,' Frank wheedled, fingering his groin under the sheets.

Jesus, thought Clara, and in fury at him, at her father, at the Fates, at the whole miserable stinking world, she wrenched the dress open, yanked off the pointy-cupped bra. Frank's eyes were like saucers as they drank in the sight of her full naked breasts with their large coral-coloured nipples, her long slender torso, the thick black thatch of pubic hair at the juncture of her thighs.

'Satisfied?' she snapped, flinging the dress off, hating the damned thing. She glanced at the cheap gold ring he'd bought her on her left hand, then at the one on the right, her mother's wedding band. Then she stood there, upright as a soldier.

She knew she could do this. She could close her mind to disgust, to revulsion, to *anything*. She would do what had to be done.

Frank gulped. He patted the bed again. Clara braced herself and knelt up on it. His hand trembled slightly as it went to the pale skin of her thigh and rested there, smoothing over its velvety softness.

Then he pushed the sheets back and she saw his pale pink erection, jutting out from the fastenings at the front of the long johns.

God, this is how babies are made . . .

Her mother had explained it all, so she knew this was how Kathleen had become pregnant with the child that had killed her. She prayed that no child would result from this. *Begged* for it. She just wanted it over, as quickly as possible.

'What do you think, eh?' said Frank, moving the column of flesh with his hand, waggling it about as if he was proud of the bloody thing. At the same time, his free hand slid upward, higher up her thigh, moving in between her legs. 'Come on then, my darlin', come and sit on him, he wants yer.'

Be brave, thought Clara. *Just do it.*

'With my body, I thee worship,' chortled Frank. 'Jesus, ain't that the best bit? I'll say it bloody is.'

Do it. Go on.

Clara hoisted her leg over her husband's middle and clasped the thing between both hands. Frank lay back with a sigh as she positioned him, found the exact spot, and sank down, taking him inside her.

'Oh,' said Clara as she met resistance, felt a tiny hint of pain; but then Frank pushed up and it was done.

Her virginity was gone.

So was her youth.

So was her *life*.

21

1958

Ivan Sears knew he was no beauty: neither were his two brothers. The Three Little Pigs, Ma had called them when they were small. Well, small*ish*. Jacko, Fulton and Ivan Sears looked like triplet porkers even when they were in the pram. There was a year between each of them, but they could pass for identical, born on the same day. They were that bloody ugly, all three of them. Ivan knew it, and it didn't bother him in the least.

'Ten pounds each they weighed, it was like passing three fucking bowling balls,' Ma always said.

The Sears boys had matching weights, matching features; they were never going to be handsome, that much was obvious. Dad was huge and fat, Ma was wallowing around in the shallow end of the gene pool – so their kids were never going to challenge Einstein's theory of relativity or win Mr Universe. The best you could say of them was that they were big.

The brothers were all over six and a half feet tall, and they were broad across too, solid as barn doors. All three had a little dark hair to start with, but like Dad they lost it in their twenties and shaved their heads.

'They *are* different, though,' Ma would insist to anyone

94

who asked. 'In nature. And you can see it in their eyes, too. Jacko's the youngest, he has a wild look. Fulton is in the middle and has more heart than the other two. He can be soft, sometimes.'

'Yeah, and Ivan's a bastard,' said Dad, who'd discovered that your own son can and will give you a whipping once he's big enough.

Dad was right: Ivan *was* a bastard; he knew it and he was proud of it.

By the time Ivan was twenty, Dad had received a couple of hefty clouts off him. And then there was the incident with The Chair, which passed into family legend.

Dad had always had the best chair, the one by the fire – until Ivan came in one frosty day and decided that the chair should be his.

'You're in my seat,' he said.

Ma and Jacko and Fulton sat there, gape-mouthed, looking from one to the other and expecting a fight. Instead – none of them would ever forget it – Dad simply got up and vacated the chair. In that moment, that brief flicker of time when Dad could have stood his ground but decided against it, power in the family passed from the father to the eldest son.

And so it remained. Ivan and his brothers were built like brick outhouses and it was a given that they would go into a trade that enabled them to put the frighteners on people. Ivan strong-armed his way into a car dealership, where he could clock motors and flog cut-and-shuts to his heart's content; Fulton took over some doors in Manchester's clubland. Ivan wanted Jacko around to do the grunt work for the car biz, but Jacko had other ideas. He didn't want to be forever taking orders off Ivan and he said so. After a monumental row, Jacko fucked off down south to London, to try his luck around Soho.

Now something was bothering Ivan. Or rather, it was bothering Ma, so Ivan was getting it in the neck. It was the fact that Jacko hadn't been in touch for a very long while. Usually, the three brothers touched base now and again, kept in touch. Met up. But Jacko's silence had been so long-drawn-out that even his oldest brother was starting to wonder how long this latest sulk was going to go on for. None of the boys did friendship – neither did Ma and Pa, come to that – and Ivan didn't exactly *care* what Jacko got up to. Truth to tell, Ivan could hold a grudge for England and he still had the hump over Jacko bailing out and going south. Who the fuck was head of this family?

But family was family, after all.

There had been a call from a Soho phone box, during which Jacko had managed to get right up Ivan's nose yet again, bragging on about how much loot he was earning and that he'd soon be richer than any of them. Ivan had listened for as long as he could stand it, then he slammed the phone down and sat there fuming. Bloody Jacko, he wouldn't *dare* taunt Ivan like that if they were face to face.

After that, there was nothing. Silence. Jacko had always been the worst of the brothers for keeping contact, but this was pretty odd even by his standards. Ivan was prepared to bet that Jacko wouldn't turn up this Christmas either, and much as the little bastard annoyed him, that was a fucking nuisance because Ma had been upping the stakes recently, really bending his ear over it. Another yuletide no-show, and she was *really* going to start giving him a pain in the arse.

So one night Ivan finally caved in to all the nagging and decided to address the problem. Not personally – fuck that! If Jacko thought he would crawl down there himself, he had another think coming! Instead, he called Fulton into his office behind the car showroom when all the staff had gone home one evening and said: 'Got a little job for you, bro.'

Fulton sat down and stared at his older brother. Ivan was The Boss. He'd claimed The Chair. Ivan had the flashy gloss of wealth, his sheepskin coat slung over the back of his chair, his gold Ford Motor tiepin gleaming against the lemon-yellow silk tie he wore.

Fulton looked round at his older brother's kingdom and was impressed. Ivan had a big glossy walnut desk and was reclining in a thickly padded golden leather chair behind it. On top of a bank of filing cabinets, beneath a calendar showing a pouting girl in a swimsuit, was the latest radio, out of which Elvis Presley was softly crooning 'Don't'.

'Want you to go down the Smoke and catch up with Jacko,' said Ivan. 'The moody bastard ain't been in touch for a long while, as you know. Ma's chewing my arse over it. The cunt can't be doing *that* well or he'd be rubbing all our noses in it by now. Get down there, will you? Check he's OK.'

Fulton nodded his big ugly head. 'Will do,' he said, and he went straight home and packed a bag. He was bored with the doors up here anyway, he could do with a change. He knew Ivan was getting grief off Ma over Jacko, and the only reason he was sending him to London was to shut her up; Ivan didn't really care one way or the other where his younger brother was or what he was getting up to.

Neither did Fulton.

But it would make a bit of a break.

22

Frank Hatton was no model husband. Clara imagined that model husbands didn't hawk up yellow phlegm every morning, fart loudly in bed, or pick their nose in full view of their wives at the dinner table. But she blanked all that from her mind because he was as good as his word: he looked after them, her and Bernie and little Henry.

Frank hadn't even moaned too much when she'd insisted they move shortly after the wedding. He'd sold the house he'd lived in all his life, the house his parents had lived and died in, and found another, a more presentable little two-up-two down in a better area, miles away from the messy Houndsditch slums where the impoverished Dolans had spent such a short but traumatic time.

Hatton had seen to it that Clara had enough for the housekeeping, that they all had plenty to eat, and after the initial shock of the realities of marriage he'd made few demands on his wife – thank God! – in the bedroom. She'd worried over that at first, sacrificing her virginity to this grey, unappealing man; but it was nothing. The fact that he was old, and often drunk, was good in one respect: it was always quickly over.

He was a good-natured drunk, only wanting to whistle as she propped him up and brought him home from the pub, and then to sleep; he was rarely aggressive. And there was no sign of a child as a result of his inexpert fumblings; something else to be grateful for.

So, all was well. The Dolans – now the Hattons – had money for food, they didn't need to fear the rent-man's knock at the door, there were no bailiffs hammering to be let in to take their remaining worldly goods away. Life was . . . pretty much all right. And then *it* happened.

Clara always knew the exact amount of cash she had in her purse at any given time, and yet one day there it was: her purse, which was usually closed and on the kitchen table where she left it to pay the tradesmen who came to the door, was lying open. There were a few pennies scattered around on the floor, as if the person who'd opened it had been disturbed in the act. Clara picked the loose change up, put it back in the purse, counted. A pound note was missing.

'You been in my purse, Frank?' she asked her husband over his tea that night.

In the front room, Connie Francis was singing 'Who's Sorry Now?' on the radio. Soon, Frank said, they'd have a television. And stereo was the coming thing in radio; they'd have one of those too.

Bernie had cooked the dinner – pie and mash. Clara didn't mind helping with the preparation or the washing, but Bernie always threw her back into the bulk of the work around the house. She'd grown quiet, little Bernie, and seemed more jittery, more easily startled than ever, since they'd moved in here. Fourteen now, she was filling out, becoming pretty, but she wore dark long-sleeved clothing all the time. She seemed to have no interest in fashion as Clara did.

Clara tried to encourage her younger sister, lending her Louis heels and trying out the bright red Gala of London lipsticks she wore herself on Bernie. But Bernie always wiped it off. Clara worried about her, feared she was still mourning Mum even after all this time – and what comfort could she give her? None. Not really. Bernie didn't even seem interested, as Clara always was, in the news of the day: Donald Campbell's thrilling exploits in his hydroplane *Bluebird*, or even that Hillary had beaten Fuchs in the polar trek. None of it seemed to spark Bernie's interest at all.

Henry, on the other hand, had come out of his shell in an almost aggressive way since passing his twelfth birthday, becoming sullen and mouthy by turns. He took particular delight in taunting Frank's dog, Attila. Henry needed a dad, thought Clara, a *proper* dad, not an old man who wasn't interested in him. But there was nothing Clara could do about that, either. Their father was gone. And if Clara saw him, right now, she would spit in his face for what he'd done to them.

'What the hell would I do that for, go in a woman's purse?' Frank was offended.

'I wondered, that's all. There's a quid missing. Must've mislaid it.'

Clara tried to put it to one side, but it niggled at the edges of her mind for days. Then Bernie came down one morning. She looked troubled. She was shuddering, hugging herself, biting her lip – all normal, for Bernie. Her nerves were bad, and seemed to be getting worse.

'I found this under Henry's pillow while I was making the beds up,' she said, and held out a pound note in her trembling hand.

Henry was out in the backyard, standing just out of reach of the chained, lunging Attila. It amused Henry, how the dog tried to get at him, snarling and choking itself, while he calmly played, bouncing a ball off the wall. Clara, in a rage, went straight out to Henry and smacked him hard across the face.

'Clara—' said Bernie, distressed.

'You took this out of my purse,' said Clara, grabbing Henry's arm and shaking him. 'You *stole* off me.'

'I didn't!'

'And will you stop tormenting this poor bloody dog! Yes, you did. Admit it! Say you did!'

But Henry said nothing. Clara looked at the boy, mystified. 'Why would you do a thing like that? Steal off your own family? If you'd asked me for money, I'd have given it to you. You didn't have to *take* it.'

Henry wrestled his arm free of his older sister's clutches.

Clara turned away in disgust. Was there anything worse than a thief? Yes, there was. A thief in your own family. Dad had thieved off them, then left them to it. The thought that Henry could do that too was devastating.

'You mustn't be so hard on him,' said Bernie.

'Better than being too bloody soft,' said Clara.

Probably it was Bernie's bland acceptance of her brother's many little foibles that had brought them to this pass. She had been indulging him too much, never pulling him up when he stepped out of line. He wasn't a baby any more, to be endlessly indulged. He was in long trousers, and he ought to know better.

'Well *someone* needs to be,' snapped Bernie.

'What does that mean?' returned Clara.

'You don't have a pleasant word to say to him. Or to any of us, come to that.'

Clara eyed Bernie mulishly. Hadn't she done enough? It tormented her that she had been propelled into a sham marriage with a man she didn't love, could *never* love or even respect. Frank was nothing but a mean penny-pinching bastard with filthy habits. All of it – *everything* – was down to this boy, and her sister too. She had done what she had done to protect them, to keep them safe, keep them together. But the price had been high. Too bloody high, perhaps. She was in a cage of their making. And now – for God's sake – Henry was *stealing* off her. Hadn't she endured enough, without this?

Later, she decided that she would talk to Henry about it being bad to steal off your own, before his light fingers landed him in trouble at school. She probably *was* too hard on him. She would try not to be. Christmas was coming, a time for goodwill to all men.

Yeah, thought Clara. *But what about me?*

23

1959

'What you mean, you didn't see him?' asked Ivan Sears, slapping the newspaper down onto his desk when Fulton came back from his visit to London. 'Jesus, can you believe this shit? Buddy Holly's dead. Killed in a plane crash. Richie Valens too. And the Big Bopper. Never bloody know, do you? Not safe to go out the door.'

'You kidding?' Fulton asked.

'Nah. Here it is.' Ivan tossed the paper over the desk so Fulton could see for himself. 'So what's up about Jacko?' Ivan was getting bloody fed up with all this. No Christmas visit from Jacko, no card, and eating his turkey at the groaning family table while getting his ear bent by Ma. Where was her baby boy? What was Ivan going to do about it? Pa had a heart condition now, he wasn't going to last forever.

Ivan told Ma he *was* doing something about it. He didn't give a shit if Jacko had vanished off the face of the earth, but he was sick of Ma going on about the little tit. Now it was February, and *still* Ivan was getting bother. And here was Fulton, having missed the family Christmas himself, back with no result.

'He *left* his digs,' said Fulton. 'Ages ago. But the old tart

103

remembered he still owed her rent. She wanted me to pay it, the brassy old cunt. I told her to fuck off.'

Ivan frowned at this. Him and Fulton and Jacko had grown up together, done National Service together, done time in the slammer, taken up boxing, been bloody good at it too, a few cups, a couple of trophies; but then the call of crime, of dodgy deals, had whispered to them of bigger gains.

They'd kept in touch, more or less: the two younger brothers had even met up now and again, got a beer in Jacko's local down south. Not Ivan, though; if Jacko wanted to be friends again, he was going to have to come to Ivan – no *way* was Ivan going to make the move. But Fulton had been down there. Now for too long there had been no calls, no meetings, no fuck-all from Jacko. Dead silence. Nothing else. And Ma was *still* being a pain over it.

'You ask around?' Ivan demanded.

'Course I did. No bastard's seen him, honest.'

Actually, Fulton hadn't searched too hard. He'd never had much time for Jacko; in Fulton's opinion Jacko was too impulsive and he didn't have the brains of a louse.

Ivan sucked his yellow tombstone teeth at this. And then he said: 'Go on back down. Take another look.'

Fulton Sears went back to London and spoke to Jacko's landlady again. Ivan was the boss of the family and he supposed he'd better toe the line, make some effort. This time maybe he'd take a closer look, actually find that troublesome little fucker, or Ivan would have him forever going up and down to the Smoke like a whore's drawers.

'He ain't here! How many more times? Now clear off – unless you're going to pay the rent he owes me,' she said bitterly.

'No. I ain't,' said Fulton. 'You ask me again, you mouthy old bitch, I'll kick your arse.'

He left her there and went down to what he knew to be Jacko's local, the Bear and Ragged Staff. He ordered a pint and waited while the place filled up; soon he recognized a couple of Jacko's drinking pals he'd met once before; Stevey Tyler and Ian Bresslaw.

'Jacko? That you, you old bugger?' asked Stevey, frowning at Fulton.

'I ain't Jacko. I'm Fulton, his older brother. You remember me?'

'Oh!' Stevey's face cleared. 'Jesus! You don't half look like him, don't you. Yeah. Sure I remember you.'

'Come to find Jacko. Ain't heard from him in a long while. You seen him around?'

The lads shook their heads. 'Pint, is it? You want a whisky chaser with that? Nah, we ain't seen him since we done over a club, the Blue Bird, years back. Used to be one of Lenny Lynch's old clubs. Feller called Redmayne owns it now. We scarpered early on 'cos we was gettin' the worst of it. Thought Jacko was followin' on, but turns out he wasn't. We thought maybe he'd had enough and was back off up to Manchester. We knew he'd taken over the Dragon in Greek Street, but that's in new hands now, I heard. Here's the drinks, mate.'

Stevey pushed Fulton's pint glass toward him, and his chaser. Fulton picked up the glass, smashed it on the edge of the bar in a shower of glass fragments and foaming beer, and whacked it into Stevey's face.

Crimson blood spattered out and Stevey fell back, bellowing in shock and pain, minus most of his nose. Ian's face was blank with horror as Fulton, mountainous and mean-eyed, turned toward him. Ian held up his hands, shook his head.

'I don't want no trouble,' he yelled. Patrons were scattering and the barman was yanking down the metal shutters around the bar.

'You should have thought of that before you ran out on my brother,' Fulton snarled, spittle flying. 'You useless cunt. Who stayed with him then? Who would know what happened after you yellow scumbags legged it?'

'Jamesy. Jamesy might know,' gabbled Ian. 'He was there! But we ain't seen him much since.'

Stevey was writhing on the floor, screaming and gurgling past the blood, his hands cupping his shattered face.

'Jamesy who?' demanded Fulton over the din.

Ian told him, and gave him an address.

'You're lucky I'm in a fucking good mood today,' said Fulton, and brushed past the terrified man and went out the door.

And that was when Fulton saw her, for the very first time.

They would be beauty and the beast, like in the fairytale; that's what Fulton Sears thought, when he saw her at the door of the pub, holding up her elderly companion. Her dad, probably, the legless old bastard.

But just look at her!

Fulton couldn't *stop* looking at her. Oh, he knew he was ugly. He was a big, big man, barrel-chested and round-stomached, bald, with a nose knocked off-kilter too many times in the ring and a matching set of cauliflower ears. He was nothing to look at. But a cat could look at a queen, wasn't that true?

There was gleaming back hair falling all around her shoulders, her skin was like alabaster, and those eyes of a deep, melting violet-blue! She had a trim body, shapely,

large-breasted and big-arsed, not boyish. Mid-height, not
too short.

Beautiful.

Suddenly, passing the young woman in the doorway,
all Fulton's urgency to find his brother became a lot less
pressing. As she turned, supporting the old drunk, something fluttered to the floor.

A handkerchief.

Fulton stooped, picked it up, was about to hand it back
to her, but she was off, tottering along the pavement under
the weight of her burden, so instead he kept it. Lifted it to
his broken nose. Sniffed a delicate, flowery perfume. Then
he tucked it into his pocket.

He would go on looking when – *if* – he had a moment,
keep Ivan sweet, but he was going to take his time over this,
hang around down here, keep her in view. He didn't even
know her name, not yet: but he was going to find out – just
as he would probably find out what had happened with
Jacko.

Eventually.

But no rush, eh?

24

Seven o'clock, thought Clara as the alarm went off. She leaned over and thumped it irritably. Same old routine. Same old *shit*.

'Frank? Time to get up.'

Frank didn't reply. Out on the piss again last night, there he'd been, drunk as a lord, and she had been called upon yet again to guide him back home or he'd fall in an alleyway and die there. Sighing, she grabbed her robe and went over to the window and yanked back the curtains. Daylight. Pale sun. Some clouds. Another *fucking* day.

She stretched, yawning. 'Frank? Come on.'

Jesus, he's going to be in a right mood this morning, she thought. She turned back to the bed, went over there and shook his shoulder. 'Frank?'

For the first time she saw that he was much paler than normal. And very, very still.

'Frank? Wake up.'

No answer. She stretched out a hand and laid it against the bristly mottled chin. She snatched her hand back with a gasp. His flesh was like chilled meat.

'Frank?' she whispered.

He didn't answer.

Clara turned away from the bed and quickly left the room. She found Bernie sitting at the kitchen table drinking tea and reading the paper. Poor dead Richie Valens was singing 'Donna' on the radio. When Bernie was small, she'd always been fairly cheerful in the mornings, but somehow all her childhood ebullience had dropped away from her. She had become ever more jumpy, introverted, less inclined to smile. Clara had long since acknowledged that Bernie had been hit much harder than she had by Mum's death; in fact, Bernie hadn't really been the same since. But right now, Bernie's state of mind was the least of her problems. She sat down beside Bernie at the kitchen table, dizzy with shock.

'Morning, Clar,' said Bernie, turning the pages.

Clara looked at the paper over her sister's shoulder and saw the state of emergency was still in force in Rhodesia. She saw that the Macmillan and Khrushchev talks were still going on. She saw that Britain and the United Arab Republic were in agreement after the Suez crisis. She saw it all, but she didn't take in a single word.

'Want some tea?' asked Bernie.

Clara shook her head. Bernie looked at her older sister. 'What's up with you then?' she asked.

'Bernie,' said Clara, 'Frank's dead.'

It brought it back to her, the memory of finding Mum dead. But whereas Kathleen has endured an awful, painful death, Frank had slipped away in his sleep, the lucky sod. No pain for him.

Clara dutifully called for the doctor, and then the undertakers came and took poor Frank away. A massive heart attack, the doctor said; and Clara thought that Frank had drawn a long straw for once. No drawn-out illness.

No suffering.

He'd simply passed in his sleep.

'This must have been an awful shock for you, Mrs Hatton,' said the doctor.

'Yes. It was.'

Clara put on a black dress that afternoon, and told Bernie to do the same. She pulled all the curtains in the house closed.

'Will we have to leave again?' asked Bernie anxiously as they sat at the kitchen table having their tea.

'What?' Clara asked, surprised. 'What do you mean?'

'Well, when Mum died, we had to leave,' said Bernie.

Clara stared at her sister's wide, ever-anxious eyes. She saw that Bernie's lips had been gnawed until they were raw, and her nails were bitten right down. Clara leaned over and patted Bernie's hand. 'No, Bern. We won't have to leave.'

'You know, I don't think I'll ever forget it,' said Bernie.

'What?'

'Living there in the slums. The smell. The . . . desperation.' Bernie was frowning, creasing up her sweet little pixie face with concentration. She shuddered and looked at Clara. 'Sometimes I think that I should *do* something about it.'

'What?' Clara looked at her blankly.

'Something to help,' shrugged Bernie. 'Don't you think we should?'

Clara looked at her sister like she'd just sprouted another head. 'Bernie,' Clara pointed out, 'Frank made his living collecting rents on those places. His living now keeps us *out* of there. So no, I don't think we should.' The thought of having to see that place again, of maybe going back to those filthy streets, and to that mould-ridden place crawling with vermin, caused a horrified thrill to run through Clara's body. She hugged herself, blanked it from her mind. Poor, soft-hearted Bernie, she must be mad.

It was strange, how empty the house seemed without

Frank. Clara didn't actually *miss* him, but it was as if there was a hole in all their lives, and he had been a bit of a father-figure for Henry, who was no longer a sweet little boy: now he was a troublesome little sod at the best of times. Still, these things happened. *Death* happened. And at least it had been a merciful end.

25

Frank's funeral took place on a Friday, a week after his death, at the Houndsditch church he had attended as a boy. It seemed wrong somehow that spring was under way and Frank would miss it. But that was life; it went on, even if you'd rather it didn't.

Clara was surprised to find that Frank's funeral attracted a large turnout. Of course he'd been around the area for years, working first for Lenny Lynch and then for this other one, this Redmayne bloke.

After today, Clara thought, *I am never coming near this place, ever again.*

Clara hadn't known Lynch and she didn't know Redmayne either, but she was under no illusions about Frank's employment. She knew that Lenny Lynch had been the worst of slum landlords – as bad as that Peter Rachman everyone seemed to be talking about – leeching off the poorest, most desperate members of the community, sending men like Frank out to collect from them using intimidation.

And if Frank's methods failed, Clara knew that the next step for Lynch had been men with wooden staves to threaten non-payers or ultimately, if no money could be wrung from them, they would be thrown out onto the streets. Maybe Redmayne was better, who knew? Clara was only grateful that she and her family were no longer under the power of such people.

Near the back of the church, Marcus Redmayne nudged his mate Gordon. Gordon was on his left, Pistol Pete on his right.

'Who's that then?' he asked.

'Hm?'

'The woman at the front with that mousy-looking girl. The one with the black hair.' He watched as Clara turned. Jesus! 'And the tits,' he added.

Gordon sniffed. 'That's the widow. Clara Hatton.'

'You're fucking joking.'

'No, that's her.'

'You're shitting me. You sure?'

'Of course I'm sure.'

Marcus couldn't believe it. He stared hard at Clara, her face caught in profile, admiring her almost luminous white skin, so stunning against the contrast of that heavy fall of black hair, decorously tied back in a bun at the moment. He pictured it coming loose, tumbling down to those lushly curving hips, and felt a sharp stab of excitement in his groin.

Frank Hatton, that old soak, had trapped *this* in his bed? How, in God's name, had he managed it?

'What the hell did she marry a dried-up old stick like Frank for?' asked Marcus.

'Shut up,' hissed Gordon, as Saul's 'Dead March' started up. He glanced back. The pall-bearers were carrying in the coffin, stepping solemnly up the aisle with their burden. Everyone was standing up. 'Here comes Frank now, show some bloody respect.'

At the end of the service, Bernie went off home to get the funeral tea ready and check on Henry. At twelve years old,

Clara had deemed him too young to attend today. She was playing her role of dutiful widow to the hilt. And why not? Frank had been fairly good to her and to Bernie and Henry too. There had been no malice in him. Still, she was glad when the service was over.

Outside, she stood at the church door with the vicar, his cassock billowing in the brisk spring air, trying not to let her eyes rest upon the large untidy plot at the far side of the graveyard where the paupers who could not afford a proper burial or even a headstone were laid to rest. *Mum must be in there,* she thought. She gritted her teeth and shook hands with the assembled mourners, thanking them for coming to pay their respects to her late husband.

'Thank you,' she said to a flamboyant-looking young man whose glossy dark hair cascaded onto the shoulders of his military-style navy greatcoat. He had an apricot silk scarf tied around his neck and when he came close she was enveloped in a cloud of sandalwood and musk aftershave.

A peacock, thought Clara, looking into hazel eyes that beamed with warmth as he smiled, lighting up his smoothly tanned and extremely attractive face. She could see that he was vain of his beauty, but instantly she liked him.

'He was a good man,' he said. 'Frank worked for me once. Very reliable.'

'Yes, he was.'

'I'm Toby. Toby Cotton. My card,' he said, and pressed a small oblong of white vellum into her hand before moving along.

'Thank you for coming,' she said next to a thin man in glasses who shivered in the breeze.

'I'm sorry we're meeting under such sad circumstances,' said Gordon, his face colouring a little, and moved on. Clara's eyes were drawn back to that unkempt plot.

Mum's in there, she thought in anguish. *She must be.*

Now there was someone else standing in front of her. She blinked away a sudden sting of tears as she thought of dear sweet Mum, who had been ruined by loving their father, finished by it. That was a trap that Clara herself was never going to fall into. *Never.* She swallowed hard and fixed a polite smile on her face. At least poor Frank's grave would be properly marked: she'd be sorting out a headstone this week.

'Thank you for coming,' she said to a tall grim-faced man of athletic build with black hair. His intense deep-set black eyes rested upon her face with something close to amusement. His cheekbones were so fiercely sculpted that they could have been carved out of stone. Clara stared at him, riveted, feeling like she'd had all the air punched out of her.

Marcus looked into Clara's eyes and stopped smiling. 'Mrs Hatton? I'm Marcus Redmayne,' he said.

'Oh.' So *this* was Redmayne. She had pictured someone older; someone plainer. He was startlingly attractive; very masculine and tough. Suddenly her heart was beating fast and she could feel a blush creeping up from her neck to flood her cheeks with colour.

'Frank worked for me,' he said.

'I know,' she said, and it was an effort to keep her voice steady.

'I thought you'd be older,' he said.

Clara's face froze. A tear trickled from her eye and she quickly wiped it away. 'That's funny – I thought *you* would be, too,' she said, gathering herself. What was wrong with her?

'My condolences, Mrs Hatton. If there's anything I can do . . .'

'There isn't. But thank you for coming,' she said, and he moved on.

Almost without thinking, without hearing, she shook the hand of the next in line, then the next, and the next. It took an enormous effort not to turn her head and follow Marcus Redmayne with her eyes. But at last it was over, it was done. She paid the vicar and thanked him, said he would be welcome to come back to the house for refreshments if he wanted. He thanked her and said he would be happy to join them.

Back at the house, sandwiches were eaten and tea drunk, and Clara didn't see Redmayne among the mourners. She felt a pang of something dangerously close to disappointment. His face seemed to have imprinted itself on her brain, like a brand.

Toby Cotton was there, and he buttonholed her immediately. 'You poor darling,' he said, touching her arm. 'Do you miss him terribly?'

Clara looked into Toby's eyes and felt that she'd found a friend. 'Not terribly, no,' she said. 'In fact – hardly at all.'

Their eyes met and she saw surprise in Toby's before he let out a laugh. Clara moved on quickly, before she let herself down by laughing too, at her husband's wake. Suddenly, she felt light and airy and – yes – *free*.

She went out to the kitchen to powder her nose, looked in the mirror at her reflection and thought *It's true. I'm free at last.*

A laugh did escape her then, a laugh of unstoppable, purest joy. She lifted her arms above her head and twirled, ecstatic. Then she saw a long dark shape in the mirror and whirled around with a gasp of dismay.

Oh Christ – it was him, it was Redmayne. She hadn't even seen him come in, but now he was leaning in the doorway, arms folded, watching her.

'If it ain't the grieving widow,' he said.

Clara opened her mouth to speak and not a single sound would come out.

'I'll catch you later, Mrs Hatton,' he said, and turned and left.

'*Damn*,' said Clara with feeling.

But her ebullient mood refused to desert her. *Fuck* Marcus Redmayne with his black knowing eyes and his dangerous good looks.

Frank was gone and she was free.

After this, things could only get better.

26

Not long after the funeral, Clara got Henry a private tutor. She'd heard bad reports about him, that he played around at school, distracted the other pupils, caused havoc; the headmistress had complained bitterly, and so Clara had asked her very-careful-with-money Frank if they could get a tutor for him.

'Fuck off, what you think I am, the bleeding king or something?' had been Frank's reply.

Mean old bastard, thought Clara.

But now, with Frank dead, Clara was able to revisit the idea. She was able to do this because she now had a free hand around the house and had discovered that Frank kept large stashes of cash here and there – under floorboards, behind pictures, all over the bloody place – and this enabled her to do the decent thing by her young brother, get him a proper tutor who wouldn't, hopefully, put up with any of his bullshit.

Now, leaving Henry studying with Mr Gray and Bernie cleaning up around the house, Clara kept an appointment at the solicitor's office to hear the reading of Frank's will. Of course, all Frank's worldly goods would pass to her as his wife, but she was astounded to learn that he had over a thousand pounds in savings she'd known nothing about, and he owned the modest semi-detached house they lived in outright. Now, both the savings and the house belonged to her.

'Thank you,' said Clara, and sailed out of the solicitor's office on a cloud of guilty happiness and dazed relief.

She had sacrificed a lot for the family, but now she was reaping some reward at last. She owned the house! And she had money. Frank had always moaned that they couldn't afford this or that, but the lying old fucker! He'd had it all hidden away, out of her reach. Clara thought again of that sorry unkempt plot in the graveyard, her poor mother's final resting place, and counted herself lucky. *That* was how you could end up, if you weren't careful. Fall in love like a brainless fool and be taken for a mug, diddled out of your money and your house and even your life. She wasn't going to go down that road, not her. Property was cheap to buy right now but soon it would start to move upward again as the market turned. She had the means to advance herself and her family at last. *Now* was the time to act.

But when she got home, her happy mood was punctured. The house was curiously quiet as she went through to the kitchen. She was sure she could smell burning out here, like Bernie was cooking a joint of meat and had left it too long in the oven. But the oven was off; when Clara touched it, it was cold.

'What's going . . . ?' she started, and then she saw Bernie standing in the open back doorway that led out into the yard, her arms crossed over her middle, her shoulders hunched.

Bernie turned and looked at her with wide, blinking eyes. She said in a tight voice: 'Don't look, Clar. It's horrible.'

Clara hurried over and pushed past Bernie and froze.

Henry was standing out in the yard, holding an old fuel can. Out here, the burning smell was so intense that Clara started to choke. She put a hand over her mouth, her eyes starting to stream.

'Where's . . . ?' she started again, and then she saw it.

Her eyes fell in complete horror on the twisted and charred remains of Frank's old guard dog Attila, still attached to its chain.

Jesus!

She looked from the dog's smouldering corpse and her eyes met Henry's. Clara felt a spasm of sickness; a hot bolt of bile surging up into her throat. She put a hand to her mouth, staring at her brother as if she had never seen him before. Over at the side of the yard, the rabbit – Henry's pet rabbit – hopped agitatedly in its cage.

'Why?' Clara managed to croak. 'Henry, *why*? What did the bloody dog ever do to you?'

Henry's eyes were bright and bloodshot, an almost manic expression in them. He sent a look at Bernie, still cowering in the doorway, then he put the paraffin can down on the ground and said: 'It's like a Viking burial. The owner dies, and they kill the pets to be with them in Valhalla, you see?'

All Clara could see was that her brother had committed a vile, cruel act; he'd burned the poor damned dog alive. All right, none of them had loved it, but it hadn't deserved *that*.

Clara felt a revulsion so strong she wondered if she was going to pass out. She swallowed, choked again, and finally said in a chilling voice: 'You did this? You little bastard! Then you clean it up. Get rid of it. All right? Come on, Bern.'

Clara grabbed Bernie's arm, ignoring her flinch of pro-test – Bernie *always* flinched when anyone touched her unexpectedly – and yanked her back into the kitchen, slamming the yard door behind them.

*

Later, Clara went back out into the yard, to find Attila's dead body was gone. All that remained were the scorched blackened cobbles where he'd died and the kennel, which was burned out and would have to be disposed of too. She shivered as she caught the lingering whiff of cooked flesh, thinking of the inhuman pain it must have suffered as it died.

Oh dear God, what *was* Henry?

What had made him so cruel, so uncaring?

When they were clearing away the tea-things that evening, she sat Bernie down at the table and told her the news about the will.

'Oh,' said Bernie, chewing her nails distractedly. 'Well, that's good.'

'Yeah, it is.' Clara hesitated, then plunged in. She took Bernie's hand – en route to her mouth – in hers, and looked into those pretty grey-blue eyes. 'Bernie, we've never really talked, have we? About how sad it was, Mum dying like she did with the baby. I know how much it hurt you.'

But Bernie pulled her hand away and stood up so quickly that her chair fell over. 'Leave it, will you, Clar? I don't want to talk about it.'

Clara stared up at Bernie in surprise. 'All right,' she said. 'But, Bern . . . you know you asked would we have to move again? Well, I've decided we are going to move – somewhere better.'

Clara didn't want to stay here any more.

This place was done now.

It *reeked* of death.

27

Marcus had taken over two more clubs. One was the Dragon, the gaming den in Greek Street that Jacko Sears had snatched off Con Beeston, the other was a place in Old Compton Street over which the previous Maltese owner had been running a lucrative 'blue films' racket. This was the simplest game in the world: a tout stood outside, inviting tourists in to see blue movies, advertising the content with a couple of mucky postcards. Once he had their money, he directed the tourists upstairs to an empty room and then moved on to another doorway and repeated the process.

'That's neat,' said Gordon, who admired money-making skills in anyone.

'Not neat enough though,' said Marcus. 'Looks like Giddy the Maltese fell out with the coppers he had on his payroll. Maybe he didn't pay them enough. Anyway, he's been done by the vice squad.'

Giddy's misfortune was Marcus's good luck. He got the Old Compton Street club for sod all and set up business. So everything was going well, and he had a vast assortment of people in, drinking and playing poker or chemmy. Earls, tycoons, criminals – they all enjoyed the high life and a gamble, and it was nothing for one of the punters to bet fifteen grand on a single shoe. And of course Marcus took a 10 per cent cut on everything earned at his tables.

Paulette continued to be a niggling problem. She was costing him a fucking fortune, revelling in her status as his 'girl'. When he got home, there she was, dancing around his flat to 'Petite Fleur' by Chris Barber, shimmying provocatively and humming along, twining her arms around Marcus when he came in and said he was off to see Mum tomorrow.

'I ought to go with you,' said Paulette, kissing him, moving her hips against him.

Marcus thought of black-haired Clara Hatton at her husband's funeral, and felt himself harden.

'Oh! So *someone's* awake, I see,' grinned Paulette, her eyes dipping down the front of his body.

'Then do something about it,' he said roughly.

Paulette did.

Later, when they were in bed, Paulette said: 'So shall I?'

'Shall you what?'

'Come with you. Tomorrow. See your mum.'

'No fucking way.' Those visits were hard enough, without Paulette's high-pitched wittering in his ear at the same time.

Paulette sulked for days over that. But Marcus thought the 'visit mother' business was just a move to cosy up, get things on a more permanent footing. Not content with filling his cupboards with her crap and draping her stockings over his bathroom mirror – Jesus, what had he bought her that sodding flat for? – *now* she wanted to try arse-licking her way around Mum, thinking that was the way to maybe a wedding and perhaps his heart. Which it wasn't.

The way to his heart?

As far as he knew, he didn't have one.

So when he went to visit his mum, he went alone. And – of course – he took a gift with him.

28

Using Frank's carefully hoarded savings, Clara bought up four houses in decent areas, had them redecorated, and waited; the market was rising quickly but even so it was a year before her investment showed the profit she was looking for. At that point, she sold all four houses and got the decorators in to what had been her and Frank's home to work their magic there; then she sold that too.

Now they had the profit from five houses in the bank and Clara was ready for her next move. She'd just come back from a very enjoyable day of house viewings. The market was sailing ever upwards and the family home was sold, so she was going to have to act quickly to find them something new: something better. She felt on top of the world. So she was knocked off-kilter when she came into the kitchen and found Bernie sitting at the table looking tearful. Opposite her sat Mr Gray, Henry's tutor, a tall miserable-faced man of middle years. He was holding a handkerchief to his cheek, and blood was seeping into it, staining it red.

'What the hell . . . ? What's the matter? What's happened?' demanded Clara.

Bernie looked at Mr Gray, whose face matched his name. He looked grey, sick – and furious.

'This is so embarrassing,' said Bernie wretchedly.

Clara tried not to let her exasperation show. Bernie was too sensitive a soul, too big-hearted, feeling the suffering of everyone when she ought to focus more on her own and her immediate family's problems; but that was Bernie. You couldn't change her.

Despite Clara's comments when she'd first raised the subject, Bernie was doing charitable work now, down the Mission, and coming home with heart-wrenching tales of hardship. This annoyed Clara. She thought they'd all suffered enough hardship to last a lifetime, and she didn't want to hear about anyone else's.

'It's Henry,' said Bernie, her voice shaking.

Now Clara felt alarm clutch at her. She thought straight away of Attila, Frank's Alsatian, burned alive. She looked at Mr Gray's face. The hand holding the handkerchief was trembling. 'What about him? Is he all right? What's he done?'

'He ripped up all his exercise books,' said Bernie. 'Every one of them.'

'And when I tried to discipline him, he hit me,' said Mr Gray faintly. 'With my own cane. In thirty years of teaching, that has *never* happened to me before.'

'He's upstairs. In his room,' said Bernie.

Clara took a deep breath. 'Bern, make Mr Gray some hot sweet tea, will you? I'll talk to Henry,' she said, and went out into the freshly decorated hall, up the stairs. The door to Henry's room was closed, and she didn't knock; she just pushed it open and walked in.

And there he was – her brother – jumping up from the bed with a start as she came in. He was a handsome boy, with the same dark reddish-brown hair as Bernie, the same intense blue-grey eyes. He was growing up fast, thirteen now. There were scattered bits of paper and book covers all over the floor. Mr Gray's cane was lying on the rug.

'I suppose that old git told you what I did?' Henry said into the silence.

Clara had to swallow, to clear her throat. First that horror with the dog, and now *this*. 'Why did you do that? What is the matter with you?'

He shrugged, looked away. That obstinate, unyielding expression was on his face, the one she was coming to know so well. 'Dunno.'

'You little bastard!'

Suddenly Clara dashed forward and slapped him hard across the face. Henry floundered back onto the bed, clutching his head, the skin on his cheek reddening instantly.

Panting, Clara slapped him again, and again, and then she was aware of Bernie beside her, pulling her back, shouting something. Red rage enveloped her and for several moments she couldn't even hear what Bernie was saying.

Then she did. Her heart was racing; she was breathless.

'Clara, *stop*,' moaned Bernie.

Clara stopped. She stood there, gasping. She took a breath. Then another. Finally she said: 'No supper for you tonight. You hear me? You can stay in here and go to bed hungry!'

'I know you hate me!' shouted Henry. 'You had to marry that creepy old drunk to keep me and Bern out of the kids' home! I know that. You hate Bern too. You do, really! You just don't ever admit it.'

Clara staggered back. Maybe there was a grain of truth in what he was saying. Had she somehow created this thing that cowered before her, with her half-hidden resentment of the burden that had been placed on her? She had tried, so hard, to treat her sister and brother well, to care for them, but had they sensed the truth, had they seen the trap she was in?

She feared that Henry was wrong in the head. That was

her true feeling about her brother. It seemed that some vital part, some *caring* part, was missing from him. That he had ice in his veins. He was only a boy now, but one day soon he would be a man, and . . . oh God, what would he be capable of then?

'Tidy this up, will you, Bern?' Clara said, and she picked up the cane and went back downstairs.

Mr Gray was still at the kitchen table, drinking tea. There was a bit more colour in his face than when Clara had first seen him, and the bloodstained handkerchief was on the table top. Clara could see a nasty little cut on his cheek where Henry had caned him, but the damage didn't look *too* bad. She sat down, and laid the cane on the table.

'I don't know what to do with him,' she admitted.

The tutor replaced his cup in the saucer. 'He seems very difficult,' he said, and his voice was not quite steady. 'Very *troubled*. Mrs Hatton – I'm resigning my post.'

Clara nodded. She hadn't expected anything else.

'What should I do?' she asked, throwing out her hands in despair. 'The school won't take him back.'

'Do you want my advice?' he asked, wincing as he drank again.

Clara nodded. The whole problem of Henry exhausted her.

'Boarding school might knock him into shape,' said Mr Gray.

Clara looked at him. She could afford that, now. Just about. 'You honestly think that would help?'

'Yes. I do.'

Clara heaved a sad, weary sigh.

She didn't want to even *think* about Henry, not any more. She had a lovely house to buy for her and for good quiet little Bernie, and she would soon become absorbed by that. But it would be such a relief to have Henry off her hands at boarding school. She was concerned about the expense of it, but if it cured him of his wicked ways, why not? It looked like the only way forward – for all of them.

29

Fulton Sears had sorted himself out with some decent digs, got a job managing a raft of club doors for an owner called Cotton. He spent his days idly trying to trace Jamesy – who seemed to have vanished, just like Jacko. The address he'd been given had turned out to be a dead end: when he went there, he found the place boarded up, and none of the neighbours knew anything about where Jamesy had got to.

He went down Greek Street one night and looked at the Dragon club, which had once apparently belonged to Jacko. Now it belonged to a git called Redmayne, and Fulton saw Redmayne in there that night, sharp-looking, handsome – everything Fulton himself wasn't.

If I looked like that, I'd rule the whole fucking world, thought Fulton.

Clara Hatton would fall at his feet.

That was her name, he'd discovered. *Clara.* He liked the sound of it on his tongue. And after chatting to the landlord at the Bear and Ragged Staff – and bunging him a wedge for that bit of aggro with Stevey Tyler – he discovered it wasn't her dad she was hauling out of the pub on that first night he'd seen her. That was her *husband.*

This amazed him. It was incredible to think of an old fart like Frank Hatton with such a prize. Fulton didn't think that

129

Clara would have given Frank the time of day, but there you go. She was *married* to the man.

And now Frank had died, and Clara was a widow. Suddenly, he noticed when he watched her, there was a spring in her step, like a weight had been lifted from her shoulders, and she was buying houses, bustling around the place, sometimes even smiling.

When she'd been half-carrying old Frank out of that pub, she hadn't been smiling. Fulton dreamed of that smile being directed at *him*. God, she was so beautiful. Not that she'd ever look twice at him, of course not. And yet . . . a faint hope stirred in Fulton's heart.

She had married Frank Hatton.

So she wasn't *that* choosy.

30

Boarding school was the arse end of hell. That was Henry's firm assumption from day one. He pitched up in a taxi with Clara and a couple of bags, and there he was, gaping at this place. It was like that gaff in *The Wind in the Willows* – Toad Hall, that was it. Hadn't Mum read him stories from that, way back when he was small? He could barely remember, but he thought she had. He could also remember her perfume, the warm scented silkiness of her hair, and his heart always seemed to clench when he thought of that, it made him want to hit something.

The school was huge and sprawling and red-bricked and set in the country, and who the fuck wanted to be stuck out in the country? Nothing there but cows and greenery.

Oh, and the pricks in this place.

Out on the gravel turning circle, in they all came while he and Clara stood there. Rolls-Royces purred up the drive, and – fuck me! – someone had come in a gold-plated Daimler, what was that, Lady Docker or something? It was like a convention of the most expensive cars in the world, there were even *chauffeurs*, and they were all coming here to this school.

Clara – big sis – had brought him here, at huge expense, and Henry thought this was a measure of how much she

131

wanted rid of him. *Anything* to get him out of her sight, wasn't that the way it went?

Because he was a monster, after all.

And as he and Clara stood there, all the others piled out of their swish motors, didn't they. All the fucking little Lord Fauntleroys in their perfect school uniforms and pristine boaters – he'd yanked his off when Clare told him to wear it, no *way* was he wearing that bloody thing – with Mummy dripping in fox furs and Daddy smoking a pipe. Everyone talking in haw-haw tones like they had a mouth full of marbles.

Shit, thought Henry.

'You going to be all right then, Henry?' Clara asked him, taking his shoulders in her hands and – he could see it – almost *forcing* herself to look him in the eye.

She hated him. Wanted him gone, out of sight.

'Yeah,' he muttered.

She didn't kiss him goodbye, just got back in the taxi and buggered off. Couldn't wait to see the back of him. Yeah, he was a fucking monster. He looked around at the other boys, all of them sporting that creamy unfakeable gloss of old money, and thought *That's it. I'm dead.*

'Wash some of that city *dirt* out of his hair,' said Morton from somewhere above him.

'Christ, he's wriggling about like a bloody ferret,' said Archer, who was nearly pissing himself he was laughing so hard.

Morton's meaty hands were holding his head down. They'd ambushed him in the toilets, the pair of them, two of the older boys, bloody toffs, and now they had his head down the loo and they were flushing it repeatedly, half-drowning him. He couldn't speak, couldn't get his breath, couldn't do a fucking thing, they had him in such a grip.

The toilet was flushed again. Henry choked and sputtered on mouthfuls of water and thought of all the arses that had shit in this place and retched. Then they half-pulled him back out of the bog.

This was an initiation ceremony, they'd told him. All the freshers had to go through it. But funny – he hadn't seen any of their posh mates getting the same treatment. No well-connected daddy's offspring was going to be subjected to this, only *him*.

'Don't want to drown him, I suppose,' said Morton.

'Why not?' asked Archer, giggling.

Great soft bastards, they wouldn't have stood a chance if they hadn't bushwhacked him in a pair. One alone, he'd have fought off. Henry was tough. He was getting stronger all the time. And now he was furious. Free of their clinging hands, he lurched to his feet and landed a haymaker on Morton's flabby jaw; then he turned on Archer and pummelled his spare tyre with several quick jabs. Archer went down, whimpering and clutching his middle. Morton came in again, and Henry went to work. He had plenty to be angry about. And Morton got the full benefit.

And then one of the tutors arrived on the scene, and pulled Henry off or he'd have killed Morton stone dead.

'We don't have *this* sort of behaviour at our school,' said the tutor, cuffing him around the ears.

Archer was groaning on the floor. Morton was nursing his jaw, seemed unable to speak.

Good. Prick never had anything of sense to say anyway.

Morton and Archer got the rest of the week off from studying.

And Henry?

He got detention.

31

1961

The new house was a world away from Frank's modest little place, and far removed from the mean Houndsditch slums. It had a nice garden, two receptions, fires in every room. Clara strolled around it, and felt proud. *She* had pulled her family out of the mire, rescued them from penury by her advantageous marriage to Frank, God rest him. Her only regret was that she hadn't been able to do it sooner, and save their mother too.

Still . . . it wasn't the grand place they'd once known, back in their other life, their *real* life. Once, the Dolans had lived in palatial style, with servants and actual grounds. Then disaster had struck them, pulled them down. Clara walked around her house and thought that even now it wasn't enough. The money was running out too fast. They were solvent, yes, but they had to watch the pennies still. She had invested, purchased another couple of houses: she carefully studied the markets. But what was needed was more cash. Her dwindling resources, the cost of Henry's schooling, *everything* worried her.

Sometimes she still dreamed in the night that she was a girl again and that Dad had come back, that all was well. Then in her dreams he would vanish somewhere in that old

134

hideous Houndsditch flat and she would search and search but be unable to find him. She would wander dark cavernous hallways looking for him, and she would finally see a door ajar, the door to a bedroom, light flooding out from a fire.

She would push the door open, and find not Dad there but her mum, dear sweet Kathleen, her face bleached of colour, her eyes closed. Not asleep, but dead. Dead in a fireside chair, blood pooling on the rug at her feet, the cold blue dead child cradled on her lap.

At these times Clara started awake, drenched in sweat, trembling with fear. She had to turn on the lights, go downstairs, walk around the house as she was walking around it now, to reassure herself, to calm herself down. There were no horrors here. There were no cockroaches swarming on the walls. The paper wasn't peeling off with black, foetid-smelling damp. Her mother wasn't there, coughing with the chest condition that had plagued her ever since they moved into the Houndsditch place. Only then, once she knew it was just a bad dream, could Clara try to go back to sleep.

No. As much as she had now, *it still wasn't enough*. It wouldn't keep the family in luxury for the rest of her days. And then she was out one day, shopping in Regent Street when she saw a familiar handsome hazel-eyed face. The man had long dark hair and was wearing a dove-grey velvet coat and a hat tilted at a rakish angle. He was coming out of Selfridges as she was going in. He paused.

'Mrs Hatton?'

Clara stopped walking.

'Toby Cotton – we met at your husband's funeral a year ago.'

Clara did remember him; he was good-looking, of course she remembered. He'd been just ahead of that Marcus Redmayne person in the queue of mourners. She had barely noticed Toby, because Redmayne had been very distracting. She didn't need distractions. She felt sure he was a bad lot; he certainly looked it with his bold black eyes and his mocking smile, and she felt a hot flush of shame when she remembered him watching her in the kitchen after she'd buried Frank.

'It was *two* years ago, Mr Cotton,' she corrected him.

'As long as that? And how are you, Mrs Hatton? You look well.'

'I am well, thank you. And you?'

'Fine. Are you free? Would you join me for tea in the Palm Court . . . ?'

They took tea together, and talked. He was in nightclubs, he said; he had six Soho clubs and business was good, exceptionally good; he was into music, and booking up-and-coming bands like that new foursome called the Beatles, who were proving difficult, their manager upping their fees all the time, and for God's sake, they weren't even well known.

Clara was made further aware of how good his business was when they emerged from the store and his Rolls, complete with uniformed chauffeur, was waiting there at the pavement, ready to collect him.

'Can I drop you off somewhere, Mrs Hatton?'

'No, thank you. Look, call me Clara.'

'Clara. Fabulous. Is there any possibility that you would agree to another meeting?'

Clara gave a slight smile. 'I think I still have your card . . . '

'Take another,' he pushed a new one into her hand. 'If I might ask for your address . . . ?'

Clara gave it. She said goodbye.

'Goodbye, Mrs Hatton,' he said, 'for now.'

Clara strolled away, aware that he was still watching her. Once out of sight, she looked at the card. The address was a good one, but just to be sure she hailed a cab and sent the driver past Toby Cotton's house on the way to her own, to check it out.

Fulton Sears loitered among the crowds and watched Clara talking to the man he recognized as Toby Cotton, a night-club owner. He watched Cotton get into the Rolls, watched Clara hail a cab and ride away. He couldn't get enough of looking at her, following her around the town, and he thought that maybe this was a bit of a sickness in him, something bad maybe, but still, he loved spending his every waking moment tagging along behind Clara Hatton.

He didn't think he'd ever summon the nerve to actually speak to her. In his dreams, he walked with her, talked with her, even did things, *sexual* things, with her, but in real life? The very thought made him shake inside.

He still had Ivan bending his ear over Jacko. Less and less these days, so maybe Ma wasn't giving Ivan so much grief over it any more, not since Pa died. Fulton knew that Ivan didn't personally care whether Jacko was ever found or not. Ivan had offered – not with any great interest, it seemed to Fulton – to have some of the boys come down from Man-chester, help out maybe, but Fulton had said, Why bother? Jacko was abroad somewhere, no doubt about it. As for Fulton himself, he was happy in London, doing door work here and there, renting a little place, he was more or less his own boss and the days were free for him to follow Clara around – so that was pretty bloody perfect.

32

Down at the Houndsditch kitchen, Bernie and the other volunteers and Salvation Army people made vats of soup and begged old loaves of bread from grocery stores to serve up with it.

Bernie loved doing this: helping the poor, having people pat her on the back and tell her she was the salt of the earth. It made her feel good, and she'd *never* felt good, not since Dad left them. They had their regulars in here, and they also had the cheeky ones, the ones who queued once and then queued again for more. And lately . . . well, she had another reason to feel pleased with herself.

Lately, a photographer had been showing up at the soup kitchen, taking impromptu shots in and around the place, until one of the Sally Army captains asked him what he was up to.

'Taking a few natural shots. Black-and-white, for texture. I think people should see this, should know that people are destitute, that they have to queue up for food.'

'What's he doing?' asked Bernie. She found the man fascinating. He was so tall, with long thin limbs and an offbeat, arty way of dressing. His sand-coloured hair was scraped back in a ponytail, and he had warm blue eyes. When he caught her staring, he smiled. He had a lovely smile.

He was still there when they were closing up. She hesitated, then went over, fidgeting warily.

'Hello,' she said, as he squatted in a corner removing a roll of film from his camera. He licked it, stuck down the end paper, then put the roll in his pocket. He stood up, turned to face her.

'Hi. I'm David.'

'Bernie,' she said, and shook his hand. She nodded at the camera slung around his neck. It looked expensive. 'You ought to watch it, coming around here with that. Someone's likely to nick it off you.'

'A couple of people have tried,' he said. 'They'd have to take me with it. I can't function without this.'

'So . . . is this a hobby? Taking pictures?' she asked, chewing her lip.

'No, I rent a studio. I do this for a living. Such as it is.'

'Really? I'd love to see it,' said Bernie impulsively. She'd never met a photographer before.

'How about now?' he asked.

'Oh!' Surprised, Bernie looked around. Clara wouldn't expect her back until late, there was nothing else she had to do. Why not? 'OK. If you don't mind.'

'Why would I mind? I'd be delighted.'

33

Toby was simply adorable. There was no other word for it. Clara was so delighted to have found him. He took her to the theatre and to the opera; he loved the arts, music, and it was pretty clear that he loved her, too. He sympathized over her difficult brother (although she didn't confide even to Toby just how difficult Henry truly was), agonized with her over Bernie's social shortcomings, seemed to understand her and empathize with her in a way that no other man ever had.

Annoyingly, Clara found that, attractive as Toby was, she didn't feel a physical pull toward him in the way she had felt toward Marcus Redmayne. But she was very fond of Toby, and felt cosseted and adored in his company, and he was rich, so what more could any woman want?

You know the answer to that, a voice in her brain told her.

Oh yes. The sexual stuff. That wild fizzing in the veins that told a woman she desired a man. She'd felt it, the moment she'd clapped eyes on Redmayne. And stifled it, too, instantly. Such madness had dragged her mother down, left her penniless, pregnant, without a hope. That was *not* going to happen to her.

She toured the clubs with Toby, asking questions, meeting the acts, and slowly they became a couple, gossiping happily together over what was happening around the venues, laughing at private jokes. They became a fixture on the Soho club scene. Wherever Toby went, wending his flamboyant way around the streets, there was Clara, stately as a queen, at his side.

'Who is that?' asked Paulette, tapping Marcus's arm as they sat at his usual table in the Blue Bird one evening. 'I've seen her out with Toby Cotton a few times now.'

Marcus looked where she was indicating and saw Toby Cotton sitting down at a table with a stunning dark-haired woman. One of the hostesses went up to them and took their drinks order.

Fuck, he thought. It was her again. Clara bloody Hatton. She drove him mad with her ripe luscious body and her cold-as-ice ways. He watched her for long moments; she was wearing a plunging red silk gown and those looked like real diamonds in that necklace she wore. There was a white fox fur stole over her shoulders. She was fucking *beautiful*. And cold as Christmas.

'His girlfriend, I suppose,' he said, looking away. He picked up his whisky and drank it in one hit.

What he wanted . . . what he *wanted* was to go over there and slip his hand inside that low-necked dress and squeeze one of those fabulous tits of hers until she shrieked. He wanted to fuck her until she could barely walk. He wanted *everything* with her, to see her exhausted and wrung out in his bed. But she was like ice; untouchable. A couple of times their paths had crossed since Frank had fallen off the twig, Marcus had come on to her – and she had knocked him straight back, hard.

'But I thought he . . . ?' Paulette was still staring at Toby and Clara.

'Look, who gives a fuck?' snapped Marcus, and Paulette

fell sulkily silent. He clicked his fingers for another drink, and the hostess hurried over.

'Isn't that Marcus Redmayne over there? He's staring at you, darling,' said Toby.

'Is he?' Clara looked vaguely around. Her eyes settled on Marcus. 'I hadn't noticed,' she lied, because the minute they'd entered the building she'd been aware that this was his place, that he might be here, that she might see him.

He wanted her. She knew that. He'd made it clear. But she wasn't ever going to risk losing control, and with him she knew she would. No, she liked wonderful, laugh-a-minute Toby.

'I'm not surprised he's staring, you look gorgeous,' said Toby, leaning over and kissing her cheek. Then he sat back and smiled. 'We've been getting on so well, haven't we,' he said.

'We have,' smiled Clara. No wild excitement, no maddening crazy impulses, not with Toby. Toby was *safe*. And safety, wealth, the cocoon of luxury, all that was what he could provide, and she loved him for it.

Toby reached into his pocket and extracted a black velvet box. He held it out to Clara.

'What's this?' she asked, her smile broadening as she took it. Toby was always giving her gifts. She opened the box. There was a gold ring set with a large dark sapphire surrounded by tiny diamonds inside it. 'God, that's gorgeous,' she said, and looked up at Toby with a laugh.

'It's an engagement ring, darling. I would like you to marry me,' said Toby. 'Will you?'

Clara was shaking her head in disbelief, still smiling. She took out the ring and slipped it onto her finger. 'It's a perfect fit,' she said.

'Like us,' said Toby.

Clara's eyes met his. 'Of course I'll marry you,' she said, and Toby called for champagne to celebrate.

34

Clara was dismayed that house prices were falling again. But she was comforted by the sapphire engagement ring she now wore, comforted by the extent of Toby Cotton's wealth, if not entirely happy about the business he was in. Clubs in Soho! It wasn't what she might have wished for. But it was obviously a rich, thriving business; the new music scene was something Toby was enthusiastic about and keen to promote at three of his venues, while the other three were gaming and drinking clubs. She couldn't wait to get gorgeous, flamboyant Toby up the aisle and take a proper look at the business situation.

Toby escorted her around all the clubs, and they hugely enjoyed each other's company. He gave her extravagant gifts of silken blonde furs and dazzling white diamonds, treated her to lunch at the best places.

At the Savoy he had the waiters bring vintage Dom Perignon to celebrate their engagement, and Clara said: 'But, Toby – my sister Bernie and my brother Henry, you do understand that they come with me, don't you?'

'Of course, dear heart.' He smiled his wonderful crinkle-eyed smile and they clinked glasses and drank to a happy life together.

Being so pleased with her new engagement, Clara was puzzled by Bernie's fixation with the slums they'd crawled out of, the slums she had pulled them out of by the skin of her teeth. She had worked hard to make sure they could leave all that behind them; but now here was Bernie, coming home late again, exhausted but flushed with inexplicable good cheer, having spent yet another day in that pest-hole.

'The soup kitchen's doing well,' Bernie enthused.

'Really?' Clara didn't want to hear about it. She was reading the papers, flicking through the news. The GPO were going to build a 507-foot tower that would be the tallest building in Britain, and there was still fighting going on in the Congo and Angola.

'We can hardly keep up with demand.'

Clara was exasperated. Poor stupid soft-hearted Bernie. If you were ill, Bernie was right there at your bedside. If you were a loser? Ditto. She'd be there with the tea and sympathy, every time. Bernie was so sweet. Shame Henry didn't have half her feeling, half her heart and compassion; then he might yet be salvageable. Maybe that ridiculously expensive boarding school would do the trick. Maybe he was even happy there. He never came home in the holidays – she never invited him, either – so how would she know?

'Who is this "we"?' asked Clara. She supposed she ought to take some interest, if only to please Bernie.

'Other women with some time and money to spare, and the vicar donates all he can too. And there's a photographer who's helping us out – David Bennett. He takes pictures of the slum dwellers. Actually, he's quite poor himself. He's a wedding and portrait photographer mostly.'

'Oh.' No surprise then that he was half-starving and happiest among the poor. In her experience, photographers rarely made any real money.

'As a matter of fact, I'm going to start helping him out in his studio,' said Bernie.

'Is he going to pay you?'

'Well, no. Not at first.'

Not at all, thought Clara, closing the papers with a brisk rustle.

Bernie irritated her to death sometimes. Clara stared hard at her sister. Why didn't Bernie make more of herself? Attract someone with prospects for a change? Her long-sleeved drab clothes, bitten nails and lack of make-up all added to her plain-Jane aura, when really she was quite pretty – if only she'd show it.

'He can't afford an assistant yet, but he will, one day. I'm going to help him with paperwork, doing up the proofs, that sort of thing.'

'When you're not trailing after him around the slums.'

'Don't be horrible, Clara. We can't all be like you, engaged to a wealthy, interesting man like Toby. He's so handsome too. And so nice. You're lucky.'

Clara knew she was lucky. Toby was an absolute find: chatty and sweet, and he loved to fuss over her. He wasn't very demonstrative physically, he was not a passionate kisser or forever groping her tits, but after marriage to Frank, that didn't bother her in the least.

'David says that people should see this,' Bernie was droning on. 'People should know the conditions these poor souls live in. He's going to get his pictures into the national newspapers one day.' Bernie started to sit down at the dinner table.

'Oh. Right.' Clara was dubious about this. It seemed to her that pigs might fly first. Toby had told her that some of the newspapers were conducting campaigns against the clubs in Soho, claiming that they were hotbeds of drug-taking and prostitution and other terrible perversions. The newspapers were no friends of Toby, and so they were no friends of hers, or of Bernie's either. Clara wrinkled her nose. 'Bernie, can you wash first please? And get those clothes off. They smell.'

Bernie rolled her eyes at her sister. 'You lived there once,' she said.

'I know that. You don't have to remind me. It's a flea-infested rat-hole – and please don't ever ask me to help out in your soup kitchen, because I would brain you with the fucking ladle if you did.'

35

Fulton was almost annoyed when one of Jacko's old drinking mates showed up after having been abroad for a couple of years and said that he might know where Jamesy was. Anything that distracted Fulton from his long-running fascination with Clara Hatton irritated him, but he supposed he'd better show willing. The old mate said Jamesy was at his sister's, so Fulton went there to see what was happening with him, and if he could shed any light on Jacko's whereabouts.

Fulton thought about it on the drive over. For fun, he'd nicked a Morris off a garage forecourt and had Ian Bresslaw – who was scared shitless of him after Stevey Tyler got glassed – fit a set of fake plates to it for him.

Of course, Fulton reasoned that it was perfectly possible his brother had simply gone off somewhere, to the Costas maybe, and that was fine, who gave a shit? But that far-distant fight in the Blue Bird being the last-known sighting of Jacko gave him pause. Had something happened to Jacko that night, something *fatal* maybe? Either way, Ivan would expect him to make the effort to find out, if he could, and maybe Jamesy could supply some answers.

'Well, you can try,' said Jamesy's sister when he got to her door. She was a worn-looking middle-aged yellow-blonde with varicose veins, a fag smouldering in her hand and a

148

network of lines on her face that British Rail would be proud of.

'What does that mean?' asked Fulton.

'Come through and you'll see,' she said, and led the way down a gloomy hall to a sitting room. It was very hot in there, and smelled stale and shitty.

Jamesy was there, and straight away Fulton could see he'd had a wasted journey. Jamesy was sitting in an armchair, his head bent over, his eyes vacant, a string of drool sliming its way down his chin.

Fulton had seen all sorts but he was shocked. He had seen Jamesy once on a visit down here – and this wasn't anything like the Jamesy he remembered. Those days, Jamesy had been upright, short, bald and bow-legged as Popeye, with a big grin and a quicksilver way about him. Now, all his previous vigour was gone. He looked like he'd left planet Earth and forgotten to die first.

Fulton looked at the sister. She took a long pull at her fag and stared straight back at him.

'See?' she asked.

Fulton saw all right. On top of Jamesy's bald head there was a half-moon scar about four inches long, coloured angry red.

'The doctors said there was nothing more they could do. Someone fractured his skull in a fight, knocked bits of bone into his brain and left him like this. I thought of a home, but I didn't want to do that.' She sniffed and blinked back a tear. 'Not at them prices, anyway. He was a lovely boy, but look at him now.'

Fulton sat down in a chair opposite Jamesy and stared at him. Jamesy didn't look up.

'Does he speak?' asked Fulton.

'Nah. Well, sometimes. Rarely. Don't even seem to know I'm here most of the time. He takes food and I see to him,

149

bath him, get him to the bog or he'd mess himself right there in that chair.'

Fuck it.

Fulton stood up. 'Sorry to take up your time,' he said. 'I didn't realize.'

'That's all right.' She walked him out of Jamesy's presence, and down the hall to the front door. 'What was it you wanted to ask him, anyway?'

'The fight when he got injured – just wanted to know if he'd seen anything of my brother, Jacko Sears, since then.'

The sister dropped her fag-end on the dirt-speckled lino at her feet and stubbed it out with a slippered foot. 'Well, no. He was laid up in hospital for weeks after the brain op.'

'Right. OK.' She opened the door and Fulton stepped out into the black drizzling day.

'But I was there with him that night at the Blue Bird when the fight happened, if it helps,' she said.

36

Clara was coming out of one of Toby's music clubs a week before the wedding. She'd lost her comb somewhere and was rummaging in her bag, hoping to find it, not looking where she was going. She bumped straight into a tall man with hair as black as her own and deep, dark eyes. It was like walking into a wall. She stumbled, and he stopped her with a hand on her arm.

'Clara Hatton, isn't it?' he asked.

Fuck. It was him again. Marcus Redmayne. She hadn't seen him to talk to much since Frank's funeral. She had seen him around town, of course, in the clubs, and she knew that if she ever gave him the slightest encouragement, engaged or not, he would pounce on her like a starving lion on a gazelle, but she wasn't about to do that. Just a couple of moments in his company on the day she'd buried Frank, and she had soon been hungering for more. That wasn't like her. She hated feeling that her emotions were beyond her control. She had her future carefully mapped out – and *he* wasn't part of it.

The truth was, whenever she clapped eyes on Marcus Redmayne she felt something shift inside her; a sort of softening, weakening sensation. She didn't like that. She had a purpose in life and that purpose was to become rich. So rich that no one could ever take it away from her. She didn't want to muddle any of that up with sex. Feelings of the romantic variety for a man – any man – did not fit with her plans at all.

'Yes. Hello,' she said coldly. 'Have we met?'

That half-smile, teasing. She could see he was remembering her triumphant little dance in the kitchen after Frank's funeral. 'Yes. We have. I'm Marcus Redmayne. We met on the day of your late husband's funeral. And we've met a couple of times since.'

'Oh yes,' she said. *Bastard*, smirking at her like that.

'I asked if there was anything I could do to help you.' He paused, his eyes on her face and then dropping to her left hand where the large sapphire glinted darkly. His eyes returned to her face. 'But you seem to be managing pretty well on your own. About to get married again.'

Something about the way he spoke made Clara bristle with anger. He was implying she was a gold-digger. Well, she was. If not for her, her family would still be in the gutter, and there was no way she was having that. So she wasn't about to apologize for using her looks to attain a certain standard of living. There were worse ways to pay the bills, that was for sure.

But you sent Henry away, whispered a voice in her head. Yes, she had. Boarding school might yet knock all the kinks out of him. She hoped so. His form tutors had sent her so-so reports of him. She hoped she had done the right thing. She hoped that he might come out of that place *normal*, that they'd turn him back into her sweet little brother Henry.

'I am getting married. Next Saturday,' she confirmed.

'To Toby Cotton, I hear,' he said.

'That's correct.'

'He's a pretty rich man,' said Marcus, pulling her to one side of the door so that they shouldn't get in the way of other pedestrians. She wished he wouldn't keep touching her. She stepped back, kept a distance between them.

'So I've heard,' she shrugged.

'Oh, you've heard right. He is.' He indicated the pillar-box-red club door. There were posters up on either side of it, trumpeting new bands performing there. 'This is one of – what, five . . . ?'

'Six.'

'I thought you'd nail the exact number,' he said.

'I don't like your tone,' she said.

'Oh?' Now he was smiling. 'Well, I like yours. You're some act, Mrs Hatton. Bold as brass, aren't you, with your peachy arse and your chainsaw brain. That's a dangerous combination. Look, I've got an idea.'

Clara stared at him with hostile eyes. *What* had he just said? 'Oh? What's that?'

'I've got money too. More than Toby – whose fortunes may be about to turn.' His eyes were moving up and down her body, taking in the Russian blue fox coat she wore – a gift from Toby – which didn't hide the luscious curves of her breasts and hips, the tiny indentation of her waist. 'How about it, Mrs Hatton?'

He was playing with her, making it obvious that he had seen straight through to her very soul. That was rubbish, what he said about Toby's fortunes, too; she'd seen the books, the whole thing looked sound. And what was Marcus offering? It certainly wasn't anything respectable.

He knew she was a woman on the make, and was treating her accordingly. She felt hot furious colour rush into her cheeks. She hated him. She felt found out, invaded, offended. What the hell did *he* know about what it was like for a woman trying to get ahead in this dog-eat-dog man's world? Yes, things were changing, but not that much, and far too slowly. You could get the Pill now, to stop you getting pregnant, and some girls even talked about sexual equality – but that, as far as Clara could see, was the same tired old joke it ever was. Only money made a woman a man's equal – and having learned that lesson she was now clawing her way ever-upward, back to where she belonged, at the top of the pile.

'You bastard,' she snapped.

'Oh, that's better. Although the language don't quite match the furs and the finery. That's the *genuine* Clara Hatton, right there.'

'Get out of my way.'

He stepped aside. 'Of course.'

Clara sent him one last seething glance and stormed off along the pavement, losing herself among the crowds.

'The offer still stands, Mrs Hatton!' he shouted after her.

She didn't answer.

Marcus watched her go. There was something about her, something strong and downright ruthless, that he could only admire. Then he turned, still half-smiling to himself, thinking that one way or another he *had* to get her into his bed.

He went to Paulette's flat and there she was, pacing the carpet in her skin-tight jodhpurs. Times had certainly changed, where she was concerned. As his own standing had grown, so had Paulette's upkeep. She was so glossy now, perfectly turned out, her fingernails painted, her skin massaged to a rosy glow, her hair coiffed and gleaming.

Yeah, and I paid for it all, thought Marcus. Which was fair enough; if you had an expensive mistress it made you look good around town, gave you a certain air.

Paulette was just back from her late-morning ride on the Arab mare that had also cost him an arm and a leg, and she was cursing her agent and whining that he was letting her down.

'Then ditch him. Get another one,' said Marcus. Christ, how she went on.

Paulette blew out her lips and flounced over to the bed and sat there, looking at him.

'Actually, I'm getting tired of the modelling,' she said with a sigh.

'Do something else then.'

Paulette's eyes sparkled suddenly. 'We could get married. Make it legit.'

Here we bloody go, thought Marcus. She'd skirted around the marriage thing before, but this was the first direct approach.

'We're not getting married,' said Marcus. 'Get a new agent. Get some better jobs. And *don't* mention that again.'

He walked over to the bed and stood looking down at her, tried to fathom out what the attraction had been in the first place. But all he kept thinking about was Clara Hatton and those violet-blue eyes of hers. He undid his tie, started unbuttoning his shirt.

'Get those bloody jodhpurs off,' he snapped, because he was aroused again.

Paulette stopped pouting and gave him a smile.

37

'What do you know about infinity?' asked David.

Bernie stared up at him. She could see infinity in his sweet blue eyes, she thought. Since that first visit, she'd come to the studio often. David was gorgeous. Or he would be, if he'd put that fag out for five minutes; it was making him squint. That was the scent she was coming to associate with him; tobacco mingled with Old Spice. She watched him in admiration and listened dreamily to the Marcels crooning 'Blue Moon' on the desk radio.

David was dressed today in chestnut-coloured cord trousers, a baggy white shirt and a sheeny brown waistcoat. His long face was soulful, his sandy-brown hair pulled back in its usual ponytail. He chain-smoked and chewed his nails to the quick, but that was OK; he was an artist, highly strung, he could turn a brat of a child into a cherub through the power of the lens, could turn a plain bride into an angel. Bernie understood taut nerves; she suffered from them herself, after all.

She had already learned so much from him. She admired the fact that he hadn't followed that flashy newcomer Bailey and gone into high-end fashion shoots for *Vogue*, even though that was where the money was. Bailey, Donovan and Duffy – the Black Trinity, as Norman Parkinson called them – they were famous. But David was worth much more in her opinion. He was a social photographer, he had high principles, and if it didn't pay much, well, so what.

She was sitting at the desk in the tiny reception area of his rented studio, surrounded by brown woodchip walls on which were hung large gold-framed misty close-ups of brides, beautifully contrived portraits of couples, a lovely oval canvas of two children, darkly lit in a Rembrandt style, and posed beside a cream-coloured Victorian nursing chair.

Bernie was cutting corners off 5 x 3½-inch proofs, matching the negative number to each one, then writing that on the back, beside the studio stamp.

'Infinity? I know it's on the camera lenses, but apart from that? I don't know much about it,' Bernie said, watching as he turned the costly Leica camera over in his agile long-fingered hands.

He'd taken out a huge loan to buy it, he told her when she'd asked, and a Hasselblad too. The Leica was 35mm and lighter, more easily portable for portrait shoots, but the Hasselblad had a bigger negative, and a fabulously 'soft' lens; it was perfect for weddings.

'I don't know why I have to cut the corners off these wedding proofs, either,' said Bernie.

'Isn't it obvious? You cut one corner off every proof because otherwise customers will hold on to them and put them in frames or folders and not order proper prints. With one corner missing, they can't do that, can they? A proof is just that: a sample to order from, that's all. So the customer has to take a note of the neg number on the back, and order more prints from the studio, instead of pinching the proofs and using those – thereby taking the food out of my mouth.'

Bernie frowned at the prints. There was so much she didn't know. She didn't begin to understand the process of photography – and David wouldn't let her into his darkroom down in the basement, couldn't risk any light penetrating that red-tinted black hole of his. Which was awkward, because he kept the filing cabinet in there with all his paper-work and negatives stored inside it, and she had to wait for him to come out before she could go in.

'What if you put the studio stamp on the front, across the print?' she asked.

The door onto the street opened, dinging the little bell overhead.

David straightened. 'Tried that. Big trouble. Customers complaining the stamp was across the faces, or they couldn't see the pattern on the dress. Tried a gold blocking machine, too, but that wasn't popular either.'

He turned, putting on a big smile for the customer who'd entered. Then Bernie saw the smile instantly drop away from his face.

Standing just inside the door was a striking sight. It was a hugely tall black man – easily as tall as David himself, but solid with it, not skinny – and he was wearing big looping chains of gold around his neck and wrists, a black Stetson hat on his head and a long black-and-white pony-skin coat that nearly touched the floor.

'Yasta,' said David, and all at once his manner was ob-sequious. When his smile reappeared, it looked sickly.

He's afraid of him, she realized.

The man came over to the desk, looked down with molten brown eyes at Bernie. 'And who is this?' he asked, in a voice so deep it seemed to come from his boots.

'This is Bernie. Bernie Dolan,' said David. 'Bernie, this is Mr Frate.'

Yasta Frate reached out a hand, took one of Bernie's in a bearlike grasp, and raised it to his lips.

'Charmed,' he said, and Bernie had to fight the urge to snatch her hand back. Then he turned his attention to David. 'Want to talk,' he said. 'Might have something for you.'

'Right! Let's take a walk,' said David, and led the way to the door. He glanced back at Bernie.

'Can you call the customer when those proofs are ready?' he said. 'See you,' he called over his shoulder, and was gone.

38

When Jamesy's sister, Susan, dropped that bombshell about her having been there on the night of the fight, Fulton, who was standing on her doorstep and on the verge of leaving the place without ever knowing, said: 'Why didn't you fucking well say so?'

Her lips puckered up in a scowl. 'I'm saying so now, ain't I? Of course, if you don't want to hear about it . . . ' She was starting to shut the door in his face.

Fulton put one shovel-like hand up, stopping the door closing. 'Let's not be hasty.'

'No. Let's not, eh? So what's it worth, this information you're so keen to get?' asked Susan, her eyes narrowing with avarice.

Fulton exerted sudden force on the door and Susan staggered back, tripped over her own carpet slippers and nearly fell on her arse in the hall.

Fulton pushed his way inside, closing the front door behind him. He grabbed Susan by her frizzy blonde hair and walloped her against the wall. Then he leaned in close and stared into her startled eyes.

'Hey! What the f—' she started to holler, then saw the look in his eyes and went quiet.

'You see what happened to Jacko that night? *Did* you?'

'Look, don't take offence over the money thing. A girl's got to live, you know,' she babbled.

'Tell me what you saw.' He slammed her head against the wall again.

'All right!' she panted out. 'No need for that. I saw him getting a pasting, OK? But I was running outside, everyone was running, it was a madhouse in there. It was only when I got out in the street that I realized Jamesy wasn't behind me, and I didn't dare go back in. They did for Jamesy, that lot. Curse their black souls.'

'What else?'

'Nothing. I was waiting for Jamesy to come out, and he didn't. It was hours . . . then when it had all quietened down, I went back in, and found him on the floor. The state of him! I called the ambulance from the club.'

'You didn't see Jacko?'

'No, I didn't. I was so upset about Jamesy, I can't be sure, but I don't *think* Jacko was still in the club when I went back in there.'

'Who'd you see fighting with Jacko?' asked Fulton.

'The thin one with the 'tache who's always there. The one they all call Pistol Pete, 'cos he's a hit with the girls.'

Fulton went to a phone box and checked in with Ivan.

'What you been doin' down there? Taking a fucking holiday?'

Fulton bristled at that, but after all Ivan was The Boss. He had taken The Chair, had kicked Dad into second place.

'I've got a job down here, I'll hang around a bit.'

'What sort of job?'

'Door work.'

'Fuckin' hell.' Ivan sounded disgusted. He ran a big dealership that was expanding all the time. Had cash to burn.

Door work? Granted, you could make a fair whack on the side dealing, but there were better jobs.

'I like it,' said Fulton obstinately. He did too. It was bloody heaven, because he saw her, Clara, nearly every day lately, saw her passing through the clubs. Sometimes he even talked to her. She seemed to be good friends with that limp-wristed fucker Cotton.

'You still looking?' asked Ivan.

'Sure I am.' Fulton told him about Jamesy, and the sister.

'Well, keep it in mind,' said Ivan, not too bothered because Ma had gone off the boil now, she was getting old and it had got to the point where she sometimes thought *he* was Jacko, so what the fuck.

Then the pips went and Fulton put the phone down and headed back to his flat, made himself some tea and went over to where he had set up a corner table, a sort of shrine to *her*. He had the handkerchief there, and now he had her comb too, with a few strands of her hair still attached to it. He picked up both items and sniffed: smelled her perfume, so faint, so tantalizing.

One day she'll be mine, thought Fulton.

He didn't believe these 'engagement' rumours.

She wouldn't marry Toby Cotton, for God's sake.

She *couldn't*.

39

This wedding, Clara's second, was totally different from the first. It was grand, no expense spared.

'I love fine things, my darling, and you are *extremely* fine. Nothing's too good for the wife of Toby Cotton,' said her fiancé, kissing her cheek warmly. And he set out to prove it too.

Clara's wedding gown was designer, a shimmering cascade of chiffon over the finest ivory silk. Her shoes were handmade white satin, her bouquet a waterfall of white lilies. Toby took a keen interest in what she was going to wear on the day.

'But it's unlucky, isn't it? For the groom to see the wedding dress?'

'Bullshit,' said Toby, and so they had a lot of fun together, touring the boutiques and department stores. But none of the dresses met with his approval, so he took her to an *atelier* near Bond Street where they found the right, the *perfect* designer, who made her wedding dress.

'You look so beautiful,' said Bernie, twitching around, arranging the veil as she and Clara stood with a silent, moody Henry on the church steps. Much as Clara disliked the idea, Henry was her only male relative and so was to give her away.

'How's it going at school?' she'd asked him brightly when

he arrived, trying to connect with the Henry she'd once known, the sweet little boy, and not with this bulky, hard-eyed, fifteen-year-old stranger.

'Shitty as ever,' said Henry, and that was the end of that.

Clara thought that Bernie looked beautiful too, her bronze-tinted hair and pale pink complexion offset by a deep moss-green satin dress with three-quarter-length sleeves and a bouquet of antique pink roses, but Clara's day had been somewhat blighted by her sister's insistence on inviting along 'the slum photographer' as she always now thought of David Bennett.

She hoped that Bernie wasn't getting too close to that man. He had a poor look about him; even now, all dressed up for the occasion, you could see his collars and cuffs were ragged, his clothes were badly fitted and shiny with wear. Granted, he was OK to look at in a pale, over-tall, thin Byronic way – a look that was guaranteed, she thought, to tug at Bernie's soft heart-strings – but she didn't want any-thing serious developing there.

The atmosphere between Henry and his elder sister was frosty, although Clara was pleased to see that boarding school had at least given him some polish. He was taller than her now, and looked quite thickset and handsome in his dark morning dress.

Girls must swoon over him, Clara thought, and then she thought of the manic darkness in Henry's soul and she shivered for those girls and wished they'd stay away.

The groom almost eclipsed the bride on the day of the wed-ding. Toby wore a bespoke buttercream-coloured three-piece suit to match Clara's gown, and an ivory straw Panama hat. And while her side of the church was nearly empty but for her brother and sister and David Bennett, his was packed with scores of Bohemian types in trailing scarves and exuberant hats.

They warmly exchanged their vows. Then, at last, she was Mrs Cotton and the huge house, the lavish clothing and the life of safe comfort she'd craved were all hers.

After the reception – held in a massive marquee in the grounds of Toby's house, with guest appearances from some of Toby's newly discovered bands – she retired to the master bedroom with Bernie and slipped into her going-away clothes for the honeymoon trip to Venice.

'Oh, this is so lovely,' sighed Bernie, zipping up her sister's pale taupe gown and then slipping the fawn cashmere coat, trimmed at the cuffs and the collar with ginger fox fur, onto her shoulders. They were travelling first all the way. *Better* than first, Toby had told her: by a private jet he'd hired for the occasion.

'Help me with these . . . ' said Clara, and Bernie reached behind her sister's neck to fasten the clasp of a double string of real luminescent pearls. Finally Clara picked up her gloves and bag, slipped her feet into her elegant flesh-coloured courts. There in the mirror, the sisters stared into each other's eyes and smiled.

'Do I look all right?' asked Clara.

'Wonderful.' Bernie chewed her lip, as if hesitating over saying something more.

'What?' asked Clara. 'Spit it out, Bern.'

'Do you love him, Clara?' she asked at last.

Clara's eyes locked with Bernie's for a long moment. Then she smiled and shrugged. 'Yes, of course.' She *did* love Toby, in her way. He was a dear, dear friend to her, which was quite enough – *more* than enough.

There was a knock on the door and Bernie went to open it. Henry stepped inside and leaned back against the closed door.

165

'You look very beautiful, Clara,' he said.

'Thank you, Henry,' she said politely, feeling that slight stiffening of distaste that she always felt in her brother's company. Henry's voice was deep now, his attitude both condescending and guarded.

'Pity it's all going to be wasted on that prancing fairy,' he said.

Both Clara and Bernie gasped in shock at that.

Henry smiled.

Clara went over to where he slouched arrogantly against the door, hands in pockets, one ankle crossed casually over the other. That stance reminded her of Marcus Redmayne, and today of all days she didn't want to be reminded of *him*. 'Take that back,' she said.

'Why should I? It's what he is. But he's rich, and that's all that matters.'

'*Take it back*,' hissed Clara.

Bernie rushed over. 'Clara . . . ' she said, putting a restraining hand on her arm.

'I'm not taking it back,' said Henry.

Clara lashed out, striking Henry across the cheek. His skin reddened instantly and he put a hand up to his face.

'How dare you stand here in his house and say a thing like that?' Clara shouted.

'You're such an act, Clara dear,' said Henry, smiling, dropping his hand away from his face as if her blow had been no more than a moth-wing brushing against his skin. Which probably it had. Henry was growing up very fast, and very tough, scowling at everything – angry, it seemed, at the entire world. His words reminded her of Redmayne too, stopping her outside Toby's club: *You're some act.*

'What do you mean?' she snapped.

'Clara . . . ' said Bernie again, hopelessly.

'I don't know how you do it, I honestly don't,' said

Henry. 'Crawling into bed with that old drunk Hatton, and now with *this* poncy bastard. I suppose you do know what he is, and the things he's into? Maybe you don't. And you hit me again, sister dear? I'll hit you straight back.'

'I've done everything for this family,' said Clara icily. '*Everything*. Just to keep us together and keep us fed and housed.'

'Keep us together? You couldn't *wait* to get rid of me,' he said.

Again she saw it, she saw it all, flashing through her brain. Her mother lying dead, Bernie's tears, their desperate flight from the slums, and then Henry, this twisted little *bastard*, stealing from her purse and then – horrifyingly – murdering Frank's dog.

'Get out,' she said, her heart breaking. He was her brother and once she had loved him. But no more. He had become a monster, a thing beneath contempt.

'Pleasure,' he said, turning and opening the door.

'*Get out and don't come back!*' yelled Clara as he closed it behind him.

40

Later, Clara could admit that she had known there was something amiss right from the start. She spent her wedding night alone in the master bedroom, while hearing the noises of laughter and singing still going on downstairs late into the night. She didn't mind. Not then. Exhausted after the hectic day, she slept deeply and awoke next morning, refreshed, ready for the upcoming trip to Venice.

Their hotel, an exclusive haven on the island of Giudecca in the Venetian lagoon, offered a water taxi service over to St Mark's Square, and the day after their wedding Toby took advantage of that service before she was even awake.

So she was left alone. But it *was* a honeymoon, after all. And a marriage had to be consummated to be legal; Clara understood that. She had acknowledged that fact when she married poor old Frank, and she had done her duty, gritting her teeth, determined to get it over with. She acknowledged it now, with Toby Cotton; get the deed done, and all would sail smoothly on. Frank had never bothered her much; she was grateful for that. And she was convinced that Toby, who had never gone in for overly physical displays of affection during their engagement, would not be too different.

Get it over with, she told herself firmly. So that second night she had the candles lit in their luxurious suite with its fabulous views of the Campanile across the lagoon. She put on a virginal white negligee, wore her long black hair brushed out loose and glossy. She arranged herself against the pillows, and waited. Laughter drifted up from downstairs, the sound of footsteps, doors slamming.

She waited.

And then she waited some more.

Finally, after midnight, she fell asleep. And when she awoke next morning, it was to see Toby, still dressed in yesterday's clothes, rummaging in the wardrobe.

'Sorry, darling. The poker game went on longer than expected,' he said, seeing her questioning look.

'Oh,' she said.

'Sorry.' He found his robe and went into the bathroom, closing the door behind him.

No further mention was made of it all that day, but at least Toby took her with him on his travels this time, to see the island of Murano and the glass blowers there.

'All the furnaces were transferred from Venice to the island in 1295 to prevent fire in the city,' said Toby, avidly consulting his guidebook.

'Really,' said Clara, too worried about this strange situation with her new groom to even think about the Venetian glass industry.

Then they moved on to the Piazza San Marco to see the Basilica. Toby bubbled over with excitement and enthusiasm. Clara was starting to feel so wound up that she nearly cried with relief when they returned to the hotel to rest, clean up, and have dinner. Once again, she prepared herself to cement her marriage to Toby.

Again, he didn't come to bed. All she heard was men's laughter downstairs, until she drifted off to sleep, tired of waiting. She snapped awake next morning and there he was again, looking through the contents of the wardrobe, fishing out his robe.

'Were you playing poker again last night?' she asked. She remembered that she'd heard them down below, Toby's happy braying laughter mingling with that of the other men staying in the hotel.

'Yes, I was. Sorry.'

Now Clara began to puzzle over this. He'd never married and he was in his thirties. Was he perhaps nervous of women? But with his looks she didn't think it was likely. She thought that she should probably reassure him, say something. This was his *honeymoon*, for pity's sake. Newlyweds were supposed to be close, unable to keep their hands off each other. Here they were in the city of romance – and he'd barely been near her.

They were supposed to be in love.

As she thought of that, a pang of something like sadness gripped her. She remembered Bernie's anxious, hopeful face, those pretty blue-grey eyes meeting hers in the mirror.

Do you love him?

Much as she cared for Toby, the truth was, she didn't feel any true intensity of passion for him. All there had ever been for her was the driving need to pull her family out of the shit. She was ready to seal their deal now. But Toby wasn't interested. He took himself off on a gondola down the Grand Canal, leaving her alone once again.

If he continued to be uninterested, that might jeopardize her position as his wife. One of these days he could say – and now the sadness turned to unease – that he found her unappealing, that his selection of her as a bride had been a mistake and he wanted the marriage annulled.

Clara couldn't, under any circumstances, allow that to happen.

She sat in the cool grandeur of the lobby during the day, watching the comings and goings of the guests and staff there; and then she saw Toby come back in from his day's sightseeing, saw one of the handsome waiters hurry up to him, saw them exchange low words and smiles. Their heads were close together, it looked almost intimate . . . and then Toby spotted Clara sitting there, and he jerked back, away from the young Italian.

'Clara! Darling!' His smile was vivid as he dashed over to her, kissed her cheek, sat down beside her. 'Say you'll come out with me tomorrow, Clara. We're going to the Bridge of Sighs.'

We? thought Clara. Well, at least he was including her this time.

That night, he was absent from the marital bed again. And next day they went to the bridge over the Rio di Palazzo that connected the prison to the interrogation rooms in the Doge's Palace.

'It's called the Bridge of Sighs because prisoners saw their last glimpse of the city as they passed over here, and sighed with regret,' said Toby.

Clara felt like sighing herself. She felt like kicking him. She'd read the guidebook he was so engrossed in – she'd had fuck-all else to do yesterday – and she'd seen the part about the bridge, and about the local legend that said lovers would be granted eternal bliss if they kissed under the Bridge of Sighs as the bells of St Mark's Campanile tolled. She felt like kicking the idiot who wrote that, too.

Finally, irritated beyond belief by this farcical situation, she pulled him to one side and said: 'Toby.'

He mopped his brow and looked at her. 'Yes, my sweet?'

'Will you come to bed tonight?' she asked.

There was a look of absolute horror and embarrassment on his face when she said that. She almost wished she'd shut up, kept quiet. But this *had* to be resolved. She wasn't one to shirk her responsibilities, and first among them was getting this marriage set in stone.

She touched his arm tentatively. He almost seemed about to shrink back, but maybe she imagined it. 'I would like you to come to bed with me,' she said.

He hesitated. Then he gave a faint smile and patted her hand, and they moved on.

By now, she didn't honestly expect him to arrive in the bedroom that night. But in preparation she abandoned the virginal white negligee and sat up among the pillows naked, bare-breasted, her hair flowing down to barely cover her nipples. She hoped that the sight would stimulate some smattering of desire in her reluctant husband, although she was beginning to doubt that it would.

But there he was! Toby came into their bedroom at ten o'clock, closed the door and stood there staring at her. Slowly, he walked over to the bed.

'Oh my angel. Look at you! You're bloody beautiful,' he said. 'I've always thought that, right from the first day I met you, at poor old Frank's funeral.'

'Thank you.' Clara determinedly pulled back the sheets further, in what she hoped was an inviting and provocative manner.

Just get it over with, she thought.

After this, she didn't think Toby was going to trouble her much at all. Get this done with, and she could relax, enjoy her comfortable life with no fear of any more unpleasant surprises.

Toby didn't start to get undressed. He just stood there, her handsome, flamboyant husband, staring down at her, all her curves lit by the glowing bedside light. He stood there for so long that she even thought he might lose his nerve and bolt out the door. Sensing his indecision, she pushed the sheets right down to the bottom of the bed, revealing her full nakedness.

Toby merely stared. Then he said: 'No. No, darling.

Don't do that.' He went to push the sheets back over her, to cover her up. Then he hesitated and said: 'Um – turn over, will you?'

Clara turned over. Whatever worked for him, she was prepared to do. Unable to see his face now, she could hear that his breathing was deepening, hardening, becoming almost like a gasp.

'Get up on your knees,' he said.

Clara did so, leaning her elbows and her face into the pillow.

Perhaps he was shy, and couldn't look her in the face while he did it? Yes, that could be it. She was confused by this. Toby was so gorgeous, why would he doubt his own abilities as a lover?

Now his breathing was very loud and she could hear him fumbling with his clothing. *This was it.* She felt the bed sway as he got up onto it. She felt him touch her waist and tried not to flinch. She felt his manhood, hard but silky, against her buttocks and felt exposed, ridiculous; she longed for it to be over. And soon it would be. Thank God.

And then – there was pain. Unexpected, *excruciating* pain.

Clara screamed aloud as he pushed his cock hard into her arse. The pain increased as she clenched against it, tried to stop this intrusion and couldn't. It was horrifying; hadn't he had a woman before? Didn't he know this was wrong?

'Toby – no . . . ' she shouted, trying to strain away from him.

'Shut up,' he said sharply, pounding into her, hurting her.

She gripped the pillow, tears of anguish squeezing out of her tightly closed eyes, and still he kept on hammering at her. It felt endless, she couldn't endure it for another single moment . . . and then he shuddered, clutched hard at her waist, and stopped.

Slowly, his breathing steadied. Quickly now, satisfied, he withdrew. Clara collapsed onto her side, in pain. She opened her eyes and saw him there, her lovely Toby, tucking his penis back into his trousers, refastening his fly buttons. Without a word or even a glance at her, he turned and left the room. Clara curled up, dragging the sheets up to cover herself, shivering and shaking with shock.

41

'Pistol' Pete Driscoll was a good-looking man and girls flocked around him. As sidekick to Marcus Redmayne, he held a lot of kudos around Soho and worked it to its fullest extent. Thin but with a good head of dark hair and that dashing Rhett Butler moustache, he favoured cowboy boots and spivvy bootlace ties; he could pull in the women with ease.

Not that he wanted to.

He kept a girl, one *special* girl, in a flat off Greek Street. Sonya was Swedish or Russian or Norwegian or *some* damned thing – he had never taken the trouble to enquire. Pete only cared that she was blonde and sweet with a knockout body. She spoke halting English, and understood little of what he said to her, and that was fine. Catch *him* keeping a mouthy cunt like that Paulette who Marcus had on a leash, he didn't think so.

As a matter of fact, him and the boys were laying bets on how much longer Marcus was going to put up with the cow. Paulette had become a firm fixture, trailing after Marcus like a lost puppy, clearly sensing his cooling interest and scared to let him out of her sight in case some other woman nabbed him.

Pete thought that Paulette could be out the door by the end of the year. He knew that Marcus was more than a little interested in that black-haired bint who'd just got herself hitched to Toby Cotton, but then she definitely wasn't mistress material. It was the ring on the finger or nothing for that one – and Marcus would never go down that route.

Pete was coming out of Sonya's place after a night of sexual acrobatics and sound sleep, passing the paper shop where all the headlines were shouting about that poof ballet dancer Nureyev defecting in Paris. Pete was feeling pretty bloody cheerful. He planned to have breakfast in his usual café – Sonya was no Fanny Craddock and never fed him, but who gave a shit? – and then he'd hook up with Marcus, see what the day required.

He was minding his own business, whistling along on his way to eggs and bacon, when he was thumped on the back of the head and everything went black.

Pete came round by slow degrees, thinking *What the hell . . . ?* The back of his head hurt. He was in bed maybe. He tried to sit up. Found he couldn't, because he was already sitting up, and in fact he couldn't move his hands because they were behind him, and they were bound. Tried to move his feet – ditto. Opened his eyes. Looked around.

He was in some sort of empty warehouse. It was a big, echoing space, concrete on the floor, rusted pillars, a little dust-covered workbench over to the left. No bastard ever came here, he could see that. His eyes ached. His mouth felt like it had been sandblasted, it was that dry.

Standing in front of him was the biggest, ugliest bastard he'd ever clapped eyes on and for a second he thought, *That's it, I've lost it, now I'm seeing ghosts*. It was Jacko Sears – wasn't it? Only Jacko Sears was dead, and . . . no. There was something different about the eyes on this huge butterball. Something softer, maybe. Or maybe not. Jesus, his head really hurt.

'You don't know me,' said the man-mountain. 'But you knew my brother.'

'Who . . . ' rasped Pete. He coughed, cleared his throat, tried again. 'Who the hell are you?'

'I'm Fulton Sears. You knew my little bro, Jacko.'

Pete was shaking his head while thinking *Oh shit*. 'I knew *of* him, sure. He used to hang around here.'

'Now that's funny.' Fulton Sears started pacing around, arms folded over his barrel chest, looking at Pete. 'Because I got it on good information that you were among the last people to see him before he vanished.'

'Vanished?' Pete gave a dry laugh. 'Vanished like in a magic trick you mean?'

'No, I mean vanished in like . . . oh, let's say . . . like someone done away with him. A friend of mine was in the Blue Bird when there was a fight. She saw *you* fighting with my little bro Jacko, and after that night, you know what? It's strange, but he ain't been seen again.'

'That's just a coincidence,' said Pete. 'Yeah, it's true we had a fight. Round here, there are always fights going on, we don't take that too seriously. Last I saw of your brother, he was heading out the door. Gave me a kicking, and took off.'

'Now *that's* funny too,' said Fulton, pausing in front of Pete and looking at him with eyes that were . . . no. They weren't soft at all, those eyes. Right now, they were beady, and they were mean. 'Because you know what? My information says that Jacko never came out of the Blue Bird at all. He didn't walk out. That's for certain.'

Shit, shit, shit, thought Pete.

'So now, my friend, I might have to hurt you but it's just to get to the truth, you do understand that, don't you?' asked Fulton.

'Now whoa, hold on there,' said Pete, his heart in his mouth.

'You got something to say?' asked Fulton.

Pete stared into those muddy brown eyes for a long time. Then he slowly shook his head.

'Shame,' said Fulton, sounding genuinely sad about this. Then he walked over to the bench, and picked up the cleaver.

42

David's tiny rented studio had become the centre of Bernie's world. She loved answering the phone, ordering prints, doing up wedding albums, and most of all she loved him. While he worked in the studio, she manned the phone in reception; they were a team. Before too long they would take lunch together, either going out to a Wimpy Bar or going up to David's poky bedsit over the studio where they ate cheese on toast and listened to the radio on his little red transistor, with 'Run to Him' by Bobby Vee, 'Walk Right Back' by the Everly Brothers and 'Stand By Me' by Ben E. King in the charts. She'd sing along to them, and David would smile.

Bernie was in heaven. This, then, was what love felt like. She had only to see him at a distance for her stomach to turn over. When he kissed her – and he kissed her more and more now – she was besotted but felt no real desire. She trailed after him around the slums, carrying his bags at weddings, put up with the stroppy guests and the mothers-of-the-bride, who were nearly always on the verge of hysteria on their little girl's 'big day' – and she helped him in the studio, setting up lights and adjusting umbrellas.

But David seemed reluctant to move things forward. They were in love! What was holding him back? She wanted to do it, to know what it was like. They were up in the bedsit

'He didn't say anything to you? I mean, he didn't . . . ?'

'No! Nothing like that. He makes me feel uncomfortable, that's all. Why does he keep coming round?'

'Oh, just business. You know.'

Bernie didn't know.

And about Yasta Frate?

She didn't *want* to know, either.

43

Clara realized, bitterly, that Toby had used her, just as she had used him. Now she understood why he favoured the company of men over his bride. Now she understood all those secret shared smiles and pats and pawings he'd got up to with his new male friends and with the handsome Italian waiters at the hotel.

Next morning – the morning after their marriage had been 'consummated' – Clara crawled, wincing, horribly sore, from the marriage bed, alone once again. She looked at the sheets and found a small amount of blood on them. He'd *ripped* her, she discovered when she gingerly examined herself with trembling fingers in the bathroom.

Shuddering, disgusted, she ran a bath and lay in it, dreading that he might come in; but he didn't. Her aching body relaxed in the warm soothing water while her mind spun in turmoil.

She forced herself to face facts. Her husband was what they called a bender. He enjoyed men, not women, and that was why he'd entered her from behind, that was why he'd been reluctant to get into bed with her. And the discomfort she was now suffering was her own fault, not his. If she hadn't insisted, she felt sure that Toby would not have come near her for the whole week – or for the whole of their lifetime together.

He'd used her while no doubt dreaming of one of those dusky-skinned Italian boys who served the hotel guests with drinks and food and probably much more besides. She felt insulted, hurt. But there was no denying the truth . . . *she'd made use of him and he'd made use of her.*

Well, didn't this just serve her right? She'd blundered along, looking for new ways to improve her family's lot, until she'd hit on this marriage to Toby, a wealthy club-owner who could afford the best but who she had somehow always sensed had little real interest in women. If she stopped and thought about it – and now she did, rather too late – she had known, in her heart, what he was. But she had ignored her gut feelings. True to form, she had been like a steam train, running along a line, unstoppable. And now she was lying here in tears, her body stinging and aching, blood on the sheets and an undreamed-of future stretching out in front of her.

He had used her.

Toby's marriage to her was nothing but a blind to stop any speculation about his night-time habits. If people thought he was homosexual they might also think he was something less of a man, something soft and not fit to run a tough business. She could see that Toby had made a decision; he would acquire a good-looking wife and the talk would stop.

That good-looking wife was her.

And now she stood up from the bath, water streaming off her skin, off her lovely, desirable, unloved and unwanted female body, and thought about it properly. She still had a husband. He was handsome and he was kind. She still had the lifestyle she had wished to create. The one thing she *wouldn't* have – if she was sensible – was the pain of the invasion she had endured last night. *She* had instigated that. In future, she would be careful not to do that again.

She smeared Vaseline on the place where he'd torn her, and felt a little easier. Gingerly she dressed and went downstairs to breakfast, finding him at their usual table. He looked up at her, her gorgeous husband, and stood up, his face pink, his eyes evasive.

'Good morning, Toby.' She smiled coolly.

'Morning, my darling,' he said, and resumed drinking his coffee.

The waiter brought her coffee and toast, smiled at her, and at Toby. She sat down tentatively, aware of that sore place, wincing. He'd hurt her badly. Was it her imagination that she caught a glint of something, something more than she had previously been aware of, passing between her husband and the handsome young man who was serving them?

No, it wasn't her imagination. And she was going to have to get used to it, just soak it up. Because one thing was certain; there'd be a lifetime of that to come. And if she was clever, she could turn it to her advantage.

'I can't wait to get home,' she said.

He looked at her. 'Perhaps Venice was a bad choice.'

'It's all right.' She shrugged and buttered her toast, thinking that she would always hate this place now, beautiful and romantic though it was. She had discovered awkward truths and suffered pain here. But she would survive. She always did. 'I really do want to help you in the business, Toby. When we get back home.'

'Are you sure?'

'Of course. Business interests me.' Making money, expanding his wealth, yes, that did interest her. Very much. So long as her family thrived and her home was secure, those were her only concerns. 'I'm happy to help in any way I can.'

Toby's eyes narrowed. 'You know, things have been a little below expectations for a while. Perhaps a fresh eye . . . ?'

'I'm here to help.'

Toby still looked a bit shamefaced, but at the normality of her tone, he seemed to relax. He knew what he'd done last night had been wrong, that he should have talked to her, told her the truth instead; but it seemed he was forgiven and he was happy to forget it – now that they understood one another.

'You know, Clara,' said Toby. 'When you are . . . like me, sometimes it's difficult. People disapprove. They get the wrong idea. They think that having certain tastes means that a person might be . . . weak.'

It was almost a confession. Clara leaned forward, interested. 'And how do you get around that?' she asked.

'By being vicious,' Toby smiled. 'By setting booby-traps.'

'What kind of booby-traps?'

'Oh, loose stairs, tripwires, and some other things, very tricky and quite bloodthirsty things.'

'Sounds bad,' said Clara, intrigued.

'Yeah. But necessary. I'll show you. And of course I hire vicious men, to handle the rough stuff.'

'Who are these vicious people you've hired then?' asked Clara.

'I've got an ex-boxer called Fulton Sears running the doors on all the clubs to keep out the riff-raff. He looks *ferocious*, I'm telling you. Quite scary.'

'I think I've seen him.' Once seen, never forgotten: Fulton Sears. 'But you're not scared of him?'

'No . . . Well, perhaps a bit. I'm paying his wages, so I'm safe enough. Sometimes I think that having Sears about the place is like having a tiger by the tail. But I needed someone tough to do the job, and Sears is as tough as they come.'

The waiter returned to their table with the food.

'That boy's very good-looking,' said Clara pointedly to her husband when he'd served them and departed.

'What? Oh! God, yes,' said Toby, eyeing the waiter's rear as he sashayed away.

Then Toby's eyes met Clara's. She felt they'd passed a difficult point, but she could see him almost visibly relaxing. Toby leaned in.

'Straight, though, darling,' he whispered. 'One for you, not for me. I could fix it, you know. If you wanted me to.'

'We'll see,' said Clara, and they exchanged a smile.

44

Marcus Redmayne was still expanding his empire throughout Soho but Jacko Sears, even all these years after his death
during the club fight at the Blue Bird, was continuing to be
a sharp pain in his arse.

No doubting it, Sears had been a tough bastard. And
now there was *another* Sears boy on the scene, Fulton Sears,
who was apparently searching for his missing brother – and
not having a lot of luck with it, either.

Jacko was long gone. And Marcus's plan was to get rid of
this brother too, if he proved too much bother. He'd heard
that Fulton had been put in charge of all the doors on Toby
Cotton's clubs. Meanwhile, he was wondering where Pete
had got to. Days, he'd been missing. Sonya had been in,
crying, saying Pistol Pete hadn't been round hers lately, had
he ditched her?

But it wasn't unheard of for Pete to go off on one,
Marcus had reassured her. Sometimes he hit the bottle a bit
too hard, there was nothing to get steamed up about. He'd
be back.

Sonya was not happy as she made her way home after going
to see Marcus about Pete being missing. *Bloody men*, she
thought as she walked back to her little flat. Well, it was

Pete's flat really, he paid the rent, but he kept her there, paid the bills, and she loved it.

Fucking men.

They never listened to you, never took you seriously. She was so worried that Pete had gone off somewhere, couldn't sleep for worrying, and what did Marcus say? It's nothing. Don't worry. He'll be back.

Easy for him to say, but what about her? The sun was dazzling today, she pulled her sunglasses lower, shielding her blue eyes from the glare. Seething with frustration at her lowly place in the scheme of things, she kicked a can along the gutter. She was going to run out of cash soon, and what could she do then? She didn't want to go back on the open market, back on the game.

She liked being kept by one man, even if he wasn't a head man, not like Marcus. His girl, Paulette, looked down her nose at Sonya, she knew it, put on such airs and graces, pretended she was *better* than her. What a laugh! Sonya was a one-man woman. She didn't like orgies, and it had been Paulette – before her involvement with Marcus, of course – who had taken her along to one at a smart address in Mayfair.

The shock that night had given her! Ministers and members of the aristocracy with their trousers around their ankles, copulating with tarts. Champagne and caviar on tap, servants wandering around naked except for their socks, and all the women completely undressed except for suspenders and stockings.

No, she hated all that. She couldn't go back to it. She *couldn't.*

As she passed the paper shop, 'The Writing on the Wall' was blaring out from the vendor's radio, sung by Adam Wade. Well maybe *this* was the writing on the wall for her.

Maybe Pete was tired of her, and this was his way of telling her so.

'Mornin', gorgeous,' said a man, jumping down out of a lorry's cab, grinning at her.

Sonya gave him a freezing look, drew her chocolate-brown mink coat even more securely around her and walked on by, approaching her flat, her home, sanctuary.

She loved Pete. She loved his dashing good looks and the fact that he kept her safe from all the vultures who roamed these Soho streets. With Pete at her side, no one bothered her. She liked that. Without him, what was she? Just another girl in a flat over a shop, touting for business.

Ah, she hated the business.

If I have to go back to that, I'll kill myself, she thought. *I really will.*

She came up to the flat door beside the sweet shop.

'Sweets downstairs and sweets upstairs,' Pete always said, making her laugh.

Oh God, Pete, where are you . . . ?

There was a brown cardboard box on the step, about eighteen inches high, eighteen inches wide. She looked around, surely the postman hadn't brought it . . . ? Fishing out her key, she looked at the box. Couldn't see an address on it. And the top of the box was open. She bent and pushed open one flap. Then the other.

Then she looked inside.

And then she started to scream.

Marcus had expected trouble from Fulton Sears and sure enough here it was. Fulton was badmouthing Marcus around the streets, trying to take over some of his best-paying protection work and he couldn't have that. So Marcus took a few of the boys with him to Cotton's Star-light Club when he knew Sears was going to be in there, and kicked the crap out of the place. Taken by surprise, Sears found himself on the receiving end of a working-over from Marcus, who came in late and pulled him up from the floor, which was littered with bits of tables and chairs.

The smoky air was frantic with the shouts and cries of patrons and hostesses. Marcus leaned in to Fulton Sears's great ugly face and said: 'We've done the Paradise too. And the Heart of Oak. And listen: if you persist in being a troublesome cunt, I'll gut every one of Cotton's clubs and then, Sears, believe me – I will gut *you*.'

45

Clara and Toby arrived home from Venice to a blissful English summer. Clara surveyed her new kingdom and was well pleased. Toby's house was very grand, a spacious Kensington town house with an elegantly drooping wisteria blooming on its back wall and old cabbage roses growing in the grounds, all tended by gardeners. Living here, Toby might almost be a merchant banker or a wealthy entrepreneur, but he was a Soho nightclub owner. It wasn't perfect, but it was good enough.

'Clara!' Bernie was there to welcome her home, hugging her delightedly as she and Toby came in the door. 'This place is *wonderful*. Did you have a lovely time?'

'Yeah, terrific,' lied Clara, smiling and embracing her sister.

Toby only stopped to freshen up, then he was out again, checking up on business. Clara and Bernie sat in the drawing room overlooking the gardens while tea was brought in by a maid. Clara sat down gingerly. She was still sore. But she ignored the discomfort and looked around her. Her home. She had achieved this by *her* efforts. So she had suffered for it. But so what?

'When I think of where we came from . . . ' said Bernie, when the girl left the room. 'When I think of the fleas and the cockroaches, and the mould on the walls . . . '

'Don't,' said Clara with a shudder. She looked at this beautiful place, *her* lovely home, and let out a sigh of contentment. 'How are you, Bernie? Still caring for the great unwashed?'

'Don't talk about them like that!' Bernie was half-smiling. 'Yes, I still go down Houndsditch with David, and the soup kitchen's doing very well.'

'Oh, so it's still "with David",' mocked Clara.

Bernie went red in the face. 'Of course! He's such a nice man. So kind.'

'So long as that's *all* he is.'

'Meaning?'

'Meaning the bloody obvious. The wife of a photographer can only look forward to a starvation diet and an impoverished old age.'

'You're such a cynic.'

'Yeah? Well, it pays to be,' Clara said, sharply enough to wipe Bernie's smile away. 'Seriously – don't even think of getting involved with him, Bern. It won't do.'

'Perhaps it would do for me,' said Bernie obstinately, gnawing her lips to ribbons. It *would* do for her. She didn't like the sex part much, but she liked *him*. She *loved* him.

Clara rolled her eyes and quickly dropped the subject. 'So how's Henry? Have you heard from him?'

'Ah.' Bernie looked awkward, evasive.

'Bernie?'

'He phoned and said he'd had a gutful of boarding school.'

'What?'

'He left, Clara. Just cleared out. No explanation, nothing.'

'Well . . . where is he? Is he here?' Truth be told – and she wasn't proud of it – Clara didn't honestly care *where* Henry was, so long as he was nowhere near her.

Bernie shook her head. 'He did phone though. He said he's staying in town.'

Clara was frowning. Would that boy never settle, never do as he was supposed to? Never be the brother he *should* be?

'So, is he working in London then? Looking for a job?'

'He didn't say.'

An hour after Bernie departed to do good deeds, Toby came back in. His face was white as milk.

'What's wrong?' she asked.

'Three of the clubs have been wrecked. Sears said it was Redmayne and his thugs.'

'Wait a minute. I thought you hired Sears to *stop* things like that happening.' *Marcus Redmayne. Again.* Sometimes, she felt like he was haunting her.

'So did I. The Paradise and the Heart of Oak were hit, and I'm just off to the Starlight to see what the damage is there.'

Clara stood up. 'I'll get my jacket,' she said.

46

It was even worse than they'd thought: the Starlight was a wreck. Toby walked around, broken glass crunching beneath his feet.

'Bloody vandals,' said the manager, his eyes shifting away from Clara's when she introduced herself as Mrs Cotton and asked him what the hell had happened. Toby went on up to the office while Clara surveyed the smashed tables, broken bottles, shattered chairs. All the mirrors behind the bar had been destroyed, only jagged shards remaining in the frames.

That's an awful lot of bad luck, she thought.

A couple of the waiters in white aprons were languidly sweeping up the debris, chatting, cigarettes hanging from the corners of their mouths. They looked at her without interest.

'When did this happen?' she asked the manager.

'Few days ago,' he said, and shrugged as if this was the natural order of things.

'Hey! You!' said Clara sharply. One of the young waiters paused and stared at her. 'Yeah, you. Put your back into it, will you? Every day from here on in, if this club's closed up with damages it's a day of your wages lost.'

The manager's attention sharpened at that. 'Here, we can't have that. You got to pay the staff—'

195

'When they're leaning on their bloody brooms like that? I don't think so,' said Clara. 'And that goes for you too. Get this show on the sodding road by the weekend's trade, or you're out the door.'

Soho was a whole new experience for Clara, but business was business and she had a feeling for it, a sure touch. From the Starlight she went with Toby on a tour of the other damaged clubs, rallying the troops, getting things moving.

'Let's hope to Christ Sears has tightened up on the doors,' said Toby as they sat in the office over the Heart of Oak a week later.

Clara blew out her lips in exasperation. Talking to Fulton Sears was like addressing a slab of rock. The lights were on but the dogs weren't barking, that was the impression she got of Fulton Sears. He was a gormless idiot. He'd been bruised and battered but unapologetic when they'd queried him about the damage to the clubs. She wondered if he had the intelligence to run doors. She wondered if Toby had made a big mistake in hiring him. And that manager at the Starlight! His casual attitude had enraged her and she wasn't about to overlook it.

'That Starlight manager's a lazy bastard,' she said. 'And the staff are taking it easy, knowing he doesn't give a stuff.'

'What do you advise?'

'Sack him. And those two no-hopers he's got there – Flash and Lightning, the so-called waiters. Get someone in who'll have the job done fast. This rate, you'll be losing money until Doomsday.'

'I'll see to it,' said Toby, eyeing his wife with a new respect. He'd been reluctant to wed, but it had become a necessity. He'd been stung a couple of times by chancers thinking to 'out' him or milk him of money to keep the secret of his shameful homosexuality. Marriage had been his solution, but initially it was a resented one, a *hated* one. Now, he could see that there might be advantages to it: he and Clara could work together, and it could prove beneficial to both of them.

'Why don't you have a good look around the other clubs?' said Toby. 'See what you think.'

'OK,' said Clara.

Clara hated to see inefficiency. It galled her. And if it was allowed to go on in Toby's clubs it would cost her, and Bernie too. She couldn't forget that. So she carried on touring the clubs, reporting back, working hard.

She was both fascinated and appalled by the things she heard on the streets of Soho: slavers and chinks and Eyeties and all kinds of sex for sale. It was all new to her. But it was exciting too, exhilarating. She relished the chance to make her mark.

She called in at the Juniper, where the clientele was mostly of the 'queer' variety and all the hosts were pretty young boys with lavishly made-up eyes. This, she guessed, was where Toby would spend his evenings, given the choice. But could he? Probably not. He had a reputation on the streets to protect, and she was part of that. His wife.

She felt sorry for Toby, protective of him. He was a bender and couldn't help it; but the situation was fraught with risk. He could easily get caught in one of these 'badger traps' so common in Soho, where people – even pillars of the community – were lured into compromising positions with young men and then blackmailed for the rest of their days or reported to the police and prosecuted for acts of gross indecency between male persons.

All the beautiful boys in the Juniper eyed her with scorn and she felt that they probably knew, all too well, that her marriage was a lie, that her husband preferred the company of men. She was what they called a 'queen's moll' or a 'fag hag'. But she had to maintain the deception, live it every day; just like Toby.

In the Heart of Oak, she couldn't fail to notice the poor quality of the 'hostesses'. The Juniper's array of young male beauty, probably having been personally chosen by her husband, was of a much higher quality. These girls looked like exactly what they were: part-time low-end brasses.

She continued her tour of inspection, determined that none of the clubs should escape her attention. She had promised Toby that she would do the rounds, and suggest things – if he didn't mind? He didn't. All in all, Toby seemed very happy to have her on board as part of the firm's management, was clearly content with their sexless 'marriage' – and he was obviously relieved that she didn't bear a grudge over Venice.

A few more clubs, and she had seen and assessed them all. She reported back to Toby one evening in the office over the Carmelo Club. He was behind his desk, puffing on a thin cheroot, flicking through *Today* magazine. He looked every inch a ruler of the streets in a bespoke toffee-beige suit and dark-blue watered silk waistcoat.

There was a malacca cane leaning against the desk that Toby sometimes carried with him. It looked like an affectation, but Clara knew it concealed a long, vicious steel blade. Toby had meant it when he told her about the booby traps. When they left this room tonight, she knew he would not only lock the office door but also set up tripwire so that anyone trying to get in there would go arse over tit straight down to the bottom of the stairs.

'Paul Raymond's in the shit again,' said Toby.

'For what?' asked Clara, sitting down.

'He's been up in Marlborough Street Magistrate's Court,

charged with keeping a disorderly house. He's appealing against the verdict.'

Clara shrugged. She'd fast become anaesthetized against the shock of Soho life. All the journalists called it 'the Square Mile of Vice', and they were right. The sheer diversity of the people on these streets – Italians, French, Cockney barrow-boys, Chinese, Caribbean islanders – was staggering. Tarts chatted on street corners, espresso machines hissed in over-heated cafés, bookies loitered to take illegal off-course bets, teenagers clustered in coffee bars, tapping their feet to rock'n'roll, touts enticed suckers into clip joints. And clubs like Toby's, like Marcus Redmayne's, like Paul Raymond's, walked an uneasy line between lawlessness and keeping the authorities sweet.

'Well, what do you think, now that you've seen the lot of them?' asked Toby.

Clara got out her notebook. She thumbed through the pages. 'You're right, the takings in some of the clubs don't seem that good. And I can see why. The girls are rough. When a man comes into a club where he's going to be fleeced for a lot of money, does he really want to see a col-lection of unwashed whorebags lounging about the place? I don't think so.'

'Tell you what,' said Toby, 'why don't you start taking the girls in hand? Would that suit you?'

'Perfectly,' said Clara.

Then Toby frowned. 'Actually,' he said, stubbing out his cheroot in a green marble ashtray, 'I've been meaning to talk to you about something, Clara. Marcus Redmayne has made me an offer on the clubs.'

'Well . . . ' she paused, absorbing this bombshell. 'Is it a good offer? Would you accept?'

'No! Fuck him. Sears says Redmayne was behind the clubs being vandalized. He saw him in the Oak while it was going on. I asked Redmayne about it. He denies it, of course, but Sears was certain. There's a grudge thing going on between those two, so I don't know *who* to believe. What I think is that Redmayne is trying to intimidate me and he's put in a very low offer. I don't want to accept, and I've told him so.'

Clara let out a breath. She felt relieved. She was starting to enjoy the club work, she didn't want to lose it quite yet. Bloody Marcus Redmayne! She didn't like the idea of him damaging their livelihoods, their clubs – and she thought he would make a dangerous enemy. Would he accept a refusal? She had a feeling he wouldn't.

'So that's that, then,' she said, but she felt uneasy.

Toby's mouth jerked upward in a smile. 'Yeah. Let's hope so.'

They went home together – the separate-bedroom situation had been sorted out to their satisfaction right from the outset – and they were sitting chatting into the night, sharing a brandy, when Bernie arrived home.

'Oh – I didn't think you'd still be up,' she said, blushing when she peeked into the drawing room and found them there.

Clara was aware of some other presence out in the hall, someone standing behind her sister. She stood up; so did Toby.

'Come in, Bernie, don't stand there like a lemon,' said Clara.

Bernie came reluctantly into the room; and behind her came David Bennett, the photographer. Clara bit her lip and out of politeness stepped forward to be introduced to the man who seemed to be always tagging along behind her sister like a bad odour.

'Mrs Cotton? Nice to meet you,' he said.

Clara shook his hand. He was too tall, too pale, too thin. He looked like he needed mothering, and she thought that probably appealed to Bernie.

'This is my husband, Toby,' she said, and the two men shook hands.

Clara could see that Toby wasn't immune to David's charms either.

'Sit down,' he said. 'Will you have a drink?'

And so the evening passed pleasantly, with Toby and Bernie happily chatting away to David while Clara watched, smiled, listened – and thought that she was going to have to find a way to nip this relationship of Bernie's in the bud.

She watched the interplay between Toby and David with interest and wondered if David might be bisexual. If Toby liked the man, even if he bedded him, it was no skin off her nose. Perhaps, if things went that way, it would turn out for the best, spare Bernie from marrying some nobody without a pot to piss in. She didn't like the adoring way Bernie looked at him. She didn't like it at all.

David Bennett, one way or another, was going to have to go.

47

Fuck all that for a game, thought Henry as he came up from the subway station at Leicester Square. He felt elated. He'd walked out of the Claremont School for Boys and hadn't looked back. He was free as a bird. He'd just turned sixteen, he had a change of underwear and a few pounds in his bag, and here he was in the big city.

His plan was to get to Soho, there were hundreds of clubs there, get a job as a bouncer on a door. He'd sleep rough for a few nights if he had to, until he got his first pay packet. That was OK. Anything was better than being back at Claremont with the Hoorays.

He couldn't forget that it was big sis Clara who had condemned him to that. Sent him away. *Disposed* of him like he was rubbish, like she couldn't bear to have him anywhere near her.

And why not?

He was, after all, a monster. The thing with the damned dog. And the thieving, let's not forget that, and turning on that poor tutor, acidic old bastard. All his fault, all down to *him*, of course. So Clara had kicked him out the door, sent him off to posh land where he'd had to toughen up quick, or die. Well, maybe she'd done him a favour. Because now he could fend for himself, big time. Now he was tough, and strong, and no one crossed him if they knew what was good for them.

Henry went knocking on doors that evening, approaching doormen and saying, 'Your guvnor in? He got any jobs going?' Girls wandered up to him, but he ignored their 'Fiver for a shag' offers and walked on. That night, he slept on a bench in Soho Square, keeping his penknife in his hand in case anyone should disturb him during the night.

No one did.

He was one more vagrant, one more loser dossing down rough on the streets.

The following day, he got some food in a café and then that evening tried again. Door to door to door. He felt dizzy in the end, he'd tried so hard, but no luck.

He began to feel that maybe he'd be better off back at the rotten Claremont, where at least he'd be fed and sheltered. Next day followed the same pattern, and every doorman turned him down, said, 'Shove off, mate, we ain't got no vacancies,' and more girls wandered up, propositioned him.

He'd end up dossing on the bench again, he could see it coming. The clubs were starting to close up for the night. It was dark, drizzling rain and he was shivering. Then another girl came up to him, a tall blonde, and said five quid for a shag, how about it, lovey?

'All right,' he said. Anything was better than being stuck out here.

So she took him back to her flat.

Fifteen minutes after coming for the first time, Henry was ready for a reload and Sal – that was the girl's name, and she had the body of an angel, with fabulous tits and an arse you could balance a pint on – climbed aboard again, pumping at him until Henry exploded once more with the force of his desire.

'Blimey!' Sal fell back laughing onto the bed. She was panting and sweaty. 'That your first time then?'

Henry went red in the face. 'No,' he said.

'It was. Go on. Admit it to your Aunty Sal. I won't tell.'

'It's not my fucking first time, OK?' said Henry angrily. It was. But no way was he going to tell anyone that. He was good at keeping secrets. He'd had to be.

'Don't worry, this bed's like the confessional,' said Sal cheerfully, reaching over for two cigarettes from the pack, lighting them, then drawing a deep drag on hers while inserting the other between Henry's lips. He'd been smoking on and off since he was eleven, so this was nothing too shocking. 'Anything said in here, *stays* here. All right?'

Henry looked at her and decided that she was all right. Her flat was a tip, and it was in Houndsditch, which held bad, *bad* memories for him, but Sal herself was OK. Good enough, anyway. Now all he had to do was persuade her – somehow – to let him linger here until tomorrow, just spend the night.

Not that he could *afford* a night.

If one shag took half an hour at a fiver, then he'd have to stump up forty quid by breakfast, and he barely had a tenner left. So it was time to turn on the famous Henry Dolan charm. He could do that – charm the birds out of the trees, when he wanted to. And he wanted to, *needed* to, right now.

'You're something special, you know that?' he said to her, smoothing back a wisp of blonde hair from her face. 'You're beautiful.'

Sal wasn't, and she knew it. She had big poppy eyes and he knew now that she was *not* a natural blonde. She looked down his body. A very *fit* body, it was, strong and muscular and with fine smooth skin. The hair on his head was copper-brown, but around his penis the hair was a brilliant fire-engine red. She liked that. She smoothed her hands over his chest.

'It's nice to be appreciated,' she said.

'I can't believe anyone wouldn't appreciate you.'

Sal's mouth twisted. 'You'd be surprised.'

'What's this?' Henry took her jaw in his hand, brought her face down to his and kissed her mouth. 'Boyfriend trouble?'

'Take a tip from your old Aunt Sal,' she said, pulling away, lying on her back, blowing out a plume of smoke from each nostril. 'Never fuck your landlord.'

'What, is he giving you grief then?'

Sal rubbed her forehead and frowned. 'Well, he *has* been. You don't ever want to get too involved with a bloke like Yasta Frate. Wish I'd thought of that before I let him . . . well, anyway, old stuff. History.'

Sal sat up suddenly. Her back was long and strong. Henry ran a hand down over it, trailing a shiver of sensation from the nape of her neck to the base of her spine. She peeped at him over her shoulder.

'You want to stay tonight?' she asked. 'No charge, OK?'

Henry nodded, sat up, put his mouth where his hand had just been.

Gotcha! he thought.

48

'Christ,' said Marcus.

Gordon and a couple of Marcus's other boys were with him in the office over the Calypso; he was sitting behind the desk and they were standing. All of them were looking at what was on the desk.

The sodden eighteen-by-eighteen-inch cardboard box was on the floor now. Its gruesome contents had been removed and set out on Marcus's desk, with a newspaper to soak up the blood.

Not that Pistol Pete's head was bleeding much any more; someone had cut it from his shoulders quite cleanly and now there it sat, his face staring almost serenely ahead, blind to everything, his eyes filming over, his skin tinted a waxen grey. On either side of Pete's head were his hands, neatly sliced off at the wrists.

Gordon looked sheet-white and sick. He pulled a chair toward him, and slumped into it. 'Where did you say they found it?' he asked, gagging.

'On Sonya's doorstep. She phoned me straight away. Fucking hysterical, she was,' said Marcus.

Christ, he thought. *Pete.*

He'd known Pistol Pete like, always. And now . . . where the hell was the rest of him? Nothing but his head and hands here, cut from his body with something, looked like a machete maybe, or maybe not. So *neat*. There'd been no note, no phone call, no warning of anything more to come. Someone had just taken Pete, his right-hand man, off the street and chopped his head and hands off, and presented it at his girlfriend's door like a sick perverted *gift*.

Only a few days back, he'd been talking to Pete, laughing and joking with him.

Now, he was dead.

'I want to find out who did this,' said Marcus.

They all nodded.

'I want *their* heads, too,' he said. 'And their *dicks*,' he added, as an afterthought.

49

'All right. Here's what we're going to do,' said Clara. It was late afternoon and she'd gathered together all the girls who worked in the Heart of Oak, which was mostly a drinking and gaming club. 'Or rather, here's what *you* are going to do.' She gazed around at the girls and felt something close to despair. Dirty clothes. Scuffed shoes. Matted, unbrushed hair. The stench of days-old sweat overlaid by cheap perfume and a whiff of stale cigarettes. Toby hadn't been interested in the way the girls appeared to the punters because the girls didn't appeal to him. 'You look a state, the lot of you.'

'Cheeky mare,' said one of them, a tall woman with a face hard as a hatchet, her dark bulbous eyes mocking and her too-blonde hair bleached to fuck.

'I heard that,' said Clara.

'You were meant to,' said the blonde.

'Whatever you think of it, it's the truth. Now Mr Cotton tells me that you have no clothing allowance.'

This seemed to amuse the girls greatly.

'*Clothing* allowance! We ain't in the clothes long enough to bother,' said the blonde, laughing and looking around at her pals for support. They smiled. A couple of them tittered.

'Really? Well, we're not actually running a whorehouse here, so that could be where you're going wrong,' said Clara.

'Ain't had no complaints,' said a dumpy little brunette, round as a barrel, folding her arms.

'Yeah, but then you haven't seen the books, have you?' retorted Clara. 'Fact is, takings are poor. You, as hostesses, are supposed to encourage the punters to spend like there's no tomorrow. And you're not.'

'So what about this clothing allowance then?'

'From now on, you get one. Not a big one – don't get excited. This is not a fucking benevolent fund. It'll be just enough to see you nicely turned out. I want to see evening gowns, girls, not tatty old blouses and skirts with the hems coming unravelled.' Clara looked at the blonde. This was precisely what she was wearing. The blonde's face was thunderous.

'So you'll get your allowance,' Clara went on. 'And there's more. Let's get on to the subject of personal care, shall we?'

The dumpy brunette heaved a sigh.

'You all stink like polecats,' said Clara.

'Hey!' said the blonde.

Clara held up a hand. 'You bloody do. That's rule number two. Number one, you dress nice. Number two, you make sure you wash every day. Number three, you wear make-up, but not so much slap that you look like an eighteenth-century tart. And you clean your teeth, make sure your breath smells nice, suck on Parma violets . . . '

'I know what I'd rather suck on,' said hatchet-face, to a chorus of giggles.

'That's number four,' Clara went on. 'Number five, you sort your hair out.' Clara looked pointedly at the blonde. 'Six? You smile. No matter what a customer says or does, you smile.'

'That's easy for you to say,' said the brunette.

'What, do they give you lip?'

The blonde laughed out loud. 'You ain't got a clue, have you?'

'If they get like that, you report to the manager and he'll get one of the door staff to see them off. You don't start fighting it out hand to hand with the clients like an alley cat. You behave like a lady, you got that?'

'Holy shit,' sighed the blonde.

'What's your name?'

The blonde looked around at her mates.

'You – the blonde with the mouth,' said Clara. 'You got a name?'

'Sal,' said the blonde.

'Well, Sal,' said Clara, 'let me put it like this. Them's the rules. You don't like them, you can piss off. Simple as that.'

Sal's eyes narrowed. 'How big's this allowance then?'

'Enough to get you a couple of dresses and a few bits and pieces besides.'

'That queer Cotton OK'd this, did he?'

Clara stiffened. She walked over to the blonde and stood nose to nose with her. Her voice when she spoke was cold as ice. 'You know what? You're *this close* to going out that bloody door with a thick ear.'

'Christ, I'm scared to death.' Once again Sal glanced around at her cohorts. 'Look at me, I'm tremblin'.'

'You don't ever call my husband – *your employer* – that, you got it? I hear one more thing like that coming out of your mouth and I won't be answerable for my actions.'

Sal blew out her cheeks. 'Right. I'm *really* afraid.'

Clara hit her. Her open palm connected forcibly with Sal's cheek. There was a resounding *thwack*, followed by a collective gasp of surprise from all her mates as Sal's head whipped to one side with the force of the blow. Sal's jaw dropped, then set in a furious line. She stepped toward Clara.

Her little fat friend grabbed her arm.

'*Don't*, Sal. You bloody asked for that, you got to admit it. You want to lose this job? Don't be stupid.'

'Yeah, Sal. Listen to her. You don't want to lose this job, do you? And that's what will happen if you don't shut your mouth,' snapped Clara.

Sal stood there, panting with rage. Everyone else held their breath. The dumpy little brunette kept hold of Sal's arm. Then the tension went out of Sal and she shrugged.

'All right,' she said to Clara. 'Keep your bloody hair on. I didn't *mean* anything by it. Just joshin', that's all.'

'I mean it. I don't want to hear anything like that, ever again,' said Clara, hard-faced.

'All right, all right.'

Clara drew back. Standing in among the girls, she was even more strongly aware of their odour. She wrinkled her nose. The dumpy little brunette released her hold on Sal. The moment of danger had passed.

'Let's get some class back into this place, shall we?' Clara said, looking around at their faces. 'God's sake, what's the matter with the lot of you? We'll all profit from this. We'll trial the new working rules for a month. I'll bring in the cash tomorrow, and you'll all get yourself kitted out. In long black evening gowns.'

'*Black?*' said Sal.

Clara nodded. 'Black. Suits everybody, flatters everybody, and if you're all in the same colour it's like a uniform, isn't it. Like the Ford Motor Company – black is the required colour.'

50

Sal introduced Henry to Fulton Sears and told him he wanted work.

'You fit?' asked Sears.

'Try me,' said Henry.

So Sears sent him out around the manor collecting protection money; Fulton had a good few restaurants and other businesses staked out; he'd avoided those already under the control of the Triads and the Maltese, and he'd tried a few that the Redmayne crew covered, only to be shoved back, hard. He wondered how Redmayne felt about that little gift he'd left on his right-hand man's girlfriend's doorstep. From what the man had said before he'd died, it was Redmayne who'd done for little bro Jacko. And Fulton was going to sort that out, very soon.

Very soon.

And he was going to enjoy doing it, too.

'Persistence is the thing if they're kicking up at paying,' Sears told Henry, and by God was Henry persistent.

At Sears's instruction, Henry targeted a drinking venue in Wardour Street, first phoning the owner and offering insurance.

'I'm insured,' said the owner, and slapped the phone down.

Henry phoned back. 'This insurance is different,' he said.

'Fifty pounds a week. All the club owners around here have got it. We chase up late payers for you, deal with any trouble.'

'Fuck off,' said the club owner.

Next, Henry approached the man directly, with Joey, another of Sears's boys, as the bloke was leaving a boxing match at Earl's Court. They dragged him into an alley, knocked him to the ground and scarred his face with a bike chain.

Soon as he was out of hospital, Henry was on the phone to him.

'You were lucky. Next time you might not get off so lightly. Have you thought about covering yourself? With our insurance?'

Finally, the owner caved in. Henry collected the money and Sears was pleased. Sears had little else to please him right now. Granted, he was on to Redmayne over Jacko's death and there was a score to settle there. But Clara – *his* Clara – had married the bender. Fulton comforted himself with the little shrine he'd set up back in his flat. A shrine to *her*. Her comb. Her handkerchief. *Her* things. One day soon, she was going to see the light; she *had* to. It couldn't be too long before she came to her senses and realized that he, Sears, was her man.

51

The clubs began to prosper, takings were boosted; there were some good bands playing in the three music venues and the others were paying too.

'Stuff the Beatles,' said Toby one night to Clara. 'A hundred quid? That Epstein bloke's having a laugh. I only pay Screaming Lord Sutch sixty.'

But then Toby saw the band had got a good write-up in the *New Musical Express*. He phoned them back, and now the price was a hundred and fifty.

'For a *night*?' Toby demanded. 'Or a fucking fortnight?'

Reluctantly, Toby let the Beatles pass him by, just like the Decca record label did. There were other bands, *great* bands, so what the hell.

Toby introduced Clara to his lover, Jasper – a stunning blond youth with fabulous heavy-lidded blue eyes that glared into hers with jealous fury. Clara saw the way Toby looked at Jasper and she thought that Jasper was off his head; Toby was besotted with him, and *she* was no competition at all.

Clara found she had a new nickname – Black Clara – around Soho, for her black hair and the fact that she had made all the girls in the various Cotton clubs dress themselves in funereal black gowns.

It seemed to be paying off though, and Clara was pleased. She liked to look around the clubs at night, see all was well, while Toby busied himself with Jasper. Sal and her mates at the Heart of Oak were behaving themselves, they'd tidied themselves up and were now smiling like Cheshire cats even if they had a period or a toothache. And the other girls at the other Cotton clubs had followed suit. The tills were ringing. Toby and Clara were happy.

One evening she finished looking through the books at the booming takings, closed them and placed them in the safe with a sigh of satisfaction. Then Sal came up and tapped on her door.

'What is it?' she asked, surprised. Sal's face, never the prettiest, was set in truculent lines.

'I s'pose I'd better tell you before some mouthy git does it for me,' she said. 'Some of the girls are jealous, see. I reckon they're getting set to blow the whistle on me, so here I am doin' it before they can, the bitches. I don't include Jan in that, she's a good 'un. But the others think *they* should be doing it, making a bit extra. But I'm *still*, see. I can hold a pose for ages. That makes me perfect for the job, not like them, twitchin' about the place.'

Clara thought that Sal was going to tell her that she was on the game after the club closed in the small hours. Clara knew a lot of the girls were, and what could she say about it? She had made them look decent while they were inside the club, had even persuaded Toby to up their wages a penny or two. But what they did outside club hours? That was their business.

'It's not as if it interferes with anything I do here,' said Sal. 'It ain't the same thing, at all.'

'What isn't?'

'The posing. There's no harm in it, and I get a bit of wedge for my trouble.'

'Pose for who? A painter?'

'Nah, a photographer.'

'Well? What do you want me to say about it?' Clara was tired and she was wondering what the hell Sal was bothering her with this for.

Sal was rummaging in her little black velvet evening bag, pulling out some photographs. She laid them out on the desk. Clara took a look and her jaw dropped open. There was Sal in various stages of undress. Say what you like about Sal's face, her body was that of an angel; white, silken, curving. Then there were other shots too; Sal, legs akimbo, an extremely well-hung West Indian man fucking her while taking care not to get in the way of the camera.

'Good God,' said Clara.

'They're suggestive, you see. That's all.'

'*Suggestive?*' Clara was frowning at the man in the photos. 'Don't I know this bloke? Haven't I seen him around the clubs?'

'Oh! Probably,' said Sal. 'That's Yasta, Yasta Frate. Owns a couple of cellar jazz clubs.'

'And likes having his picture taken,' said Clara dryly. 'Sal – your tits are on show. And the rest, too. And *this*,' she brandished the pic of Sal with the man, 'is porn.' She looked at a couple more; they were even worse. They were horrible. A young white boy flashed briefly in front of her eyes in a tangle with Sal and the man and she quickly put the prints aside and handed them back. 'It's nothing to do with me, what you do in your own time, Sal.'

Sal was stuffing the photographs back into her bag. Her face was flushed. 'You mean none of the girls have said anything to you?'

'I expect they were winding you up,' said Clara. Sal was mouthy, but she didn't have much of a brain. Clara, however, had developed a liking for rough, cheeky old Sal. And she appreciated the fact that she was always brutally honest. 'I hope they pay you well for those.' The sight of the boy in those pictures with Sal and the man had caused a cold shiver of revulsion to go right up Clara's spine. 'They'd have to pay me gold nuggets, and even then I'd pass.'

'Those cows downstairs! I'll give 'em a kickin' they won't forget.'

'Don't mark their faces!' called Clara after her, as Sal stamped off down the stairs. Then she heard the woman coming back up again. Shit, what now? Clara moved around her desk, put her bag down on it, and started to pull on her coat, give the hint that she was off, going home. Give Sal half a chance, and they'd be standing here all night chewing over the rights and wrongs of smutty photographs, and Clara felt too tired for that.

'We'll talk about it tomorrow,' she said, not turning round. 'All right?'

'Why not now?' said a male voice close behind her.

Clara spun round. It was Marcus Redmayne.

52

'D'you mind not creeping up on me like that?' she snapped, stepping quickly back, away from him.

'I wasn't creeping anywhere. Didn't you hear me come up the stairs?'

'What are you doing, in my club?' Those stupid gutless wonders on the door! Why hadn't they stopped him? And wasn't that thick oik Fulton Sears downstairs too? Hadn't she seen him there earlier? What the hell were they paying him for?

'*Your* club?' He folded his arms and smiled. 'I thought Toby owned it. Jesus, you're a sharp operator, Mrs Cotton. Previously Mrs Hatton. Previously Miss Dolan. You believe in climbing up the ladder, don't you? And I don't think you'll stop until you get right to the top. What, has that twat signed it over to you already?'

'I *meant*,' said Clara through gritted teeth, 'that Toby is my husband and so, broadly speaking, what's his is mine.'

'Oh, right. I've never caught you very long between husbands, have I. Onward and upward, that's the plan, right? Well, I've told Toby and now I'm telling you. I want these clubs.'

'And as Toby already told you – they're not for sale. Anyway, the price you offered was pitiful.'

'Don't be hasty. You might want to think it over. Maybe discuss it with me.'

'I don't want to discuss anything with you.'

'God, you're a hard cow, Black Clara. Have you found out the truth about him yet? Happy being a fag hag, are you?'

Clara's face tensed with fury. 'Get out of my club. Or do you want me to have you thrown out?'

He stepped toward her. Clara quickly moved back, and bumped up against the desk.

'Try it,' he invited.

'All right, I will,' she said, stepping around him to get to the half-open door.

Marcus grabbed her arm, pulled her up short. His black eyes were staring into hers, then wandering down, over her body.

'What a fucking fabulous creature you are,' he said. 'All that nerve, all that power and guile and determination, and you're bloody beautiful too. But what a flaming waste. First you marry that poor old crock Hatton. And now you're wasting yourself on a shirt-lifter.'

Clara could hardly get her breath. 'I don't know what you mean. Toby and I are perfectly happy.'

'Yeah, and I'm the Pope.'

'Let go of me,' ordered Clara.

'It's a sin against nature, wasting yourself like this. So why not dump Toby – I'm sure he won't even notice, he's too busy with his boyfriends – and try me instead?'

'And what would you give me? Exactly?' she challenged.

'Why don't you try me and see. You want wealth? I've told you. I've got it. I'm richer than Toby by a country mile. And I think – physically – we could suit each other very well.'

'I'm a married woman, Mr Redmayne. And I am going to stay married. To Toby.'

'And what about your family? D'you know your brother Henry's running wild?'

Clara stiffened. Bernie had told her Henry was in town, but that was all she knew, all she'd wanted to know. 'What do you mean?'

'He's mixing with some bad faces, that's all. Sears, that goon you got in charge of the doors, has a lot of deals going on, and I've heard your brother's involved in a big way. It strikes me you ought to be thinking less about building up your cash reserves and more about what your family are getting up to,' said Marcus.

'Your concern is noted. If it *is* concern,' said Clara. 'More likely it's self-interest. Toby has told me about the friction between you and Sears. And it was *you*, wasn't it, who trashed our clubs.'

Marcus's smile broadened. 'Only to give Sears a bloody nose. See what I mean, right there? You're sharp as a tack. You ought to have been born a man, with a brain like that.'

'You ought to be grateful I wasn't, or I'd have knocked you flat on your arse by now.'

'Oh, Clara.' Now he really was smiling, leaning in closer; resting his hands on either side of her, trapping her between the desk and his body. 'I like it when you flirt with me.'

'I'm not flirting,' said Clara, wishing he'd leave her alone. There was something about him that disturbed her, terribly.

'No?' Now his voice was low and husky. He was so close that she could feel his breath, warm on her face. He smelled clean, soapy; and his lips were inches away from hers. His head moved, lower, lower . . . he was going to kiss her! 'You're such a tease,' said Marcus. 'All this "untouchable" business is just a front. I bet you're wet as April. And nobody to satisfy you either. It's tragic.'

'Don't you *dare*,' she muttered, straining away from him.

'Shut up, Clara,' he said. 'This was always going to happen, and you know it.'

His lips were on hers, warm, moving, stirring up things in her that she thought she would never feel. She'd never *wanted* to feel them, either. In panic she bit down, hard, and he jerked his head back, blood trickling from his lip. Marcus raised a hand to it, and his fingers came away stained with red. He looked from his fingers to her face.

'You know what?' he said. 'You're starting to fucking well annoy me.' And he wiped his blood off on the front of her coat.

Clara gasped. 'That's pure cashmere, that cost me over forty pounds, what are you *doing*?' she demanded.

'Clara, you know the cost of everything and the value of nothing,' he said, taking out a handkerchief and dabbing at his lip. His eyes met hers. 'Cards on the table then. I want these clubs. And I want you.'

'Well, you can't have them,' she snapped. '*Or* me.'

'We'll see.'

'No we bloody won't.'

'Yes. We will,' he said, and with a last parting smile he went to the door and was gone.

53

Clara took a cab back home. She looked forward to these late nights when she and Toby could talk business, discuss how things were going, chat about what was in the news, the Berlin Wall going up and the ban on nuclear testing, all that stuff. But what she really wanted tonight was to talk to him about Marcus, how he was pestering her. Not pausing to take off her coat, she walked from the hall straight into the study, and he was there, reading the paper.

'Hello, my darling,' he said with a smile, putting the paper aside.

'Hello, Toby.' Clara sat down. 'Good news on the Oak's takings. Up by a third.'

'That's good,' he said. He frowned. 'Clara, there's blood on the front of your coat.'

Clara looked down. 'Oh . . . it's nothing. One of the girls cut herself on a glass, that's all. Toby . . . ' said Clara.

'Clara . . . ' said Toby at the same time.

'Go on,' said Clara.

'No, you first,' said Toby.

'No, you. Go on. What were you going to say?'

'Just . . . ' He stared at her face . . . 'You've been a great asset to me. And . . . ' his eyes dropped and a faint colour came into his cheeks . . . 'and I'm sorry. It's . . . Jesus, Clara. You've been so good, so understanding, such a diamond, and it's played on my mind something horrible. That fucking farce of a honeymoon. You didn't know, and I should have told you beforehand. Instead of . . . '

Clara remembered – and she could see that he was remembering – the night when he had forced himself to enter her, how he'd hurt her, then left her in distress.

'It's forgotten,' she said, although it wasn't. Of course not. He'd given her the shock of her life that night. But she had forgiven Toby. And she had grown so very fond of him.

Toby stared at her. 'You've been a terrific wife to me, Clara,' he said.

Clara had to smile. 'And you've been a great husband.' Her smile widened. 'No trouble at all.'

'I should think not! Oh, Clara I'm sorry I can't be different.'

'I wouldn't want you different in any way.'

And that was true. She had never felt the least physical attraction for her husband. But they were workmates, friends, part of a successful team. And she worried about him. 'You ought to be careful, Toby,' she warned. 'People don't understand. It's frowned upon.'

Toby was nodding. He knew. Every week there were reports of homosexuals being charged as perverts and forced to undergo aversion therapy. Clara couldn't bear the thought of him ever having to suffer through anything like that.

'You saved me, you know,' he said. 'Early on in the marriage, things were . . . shall we say, tricky?'

'Tricky in what way?'

Toby sat back with a sigh. 'There was talk of Redmayne snatching the clubs by force. He's done it before and he'll do it again, you can be sure of that. See an opportunity to shove his way in, and take it. Look at what happened to Lenny Lynch. And others, too. But fortunately he didn't, and now I'm wondering if I have you to thank for that.'

Clara was frowning. Marcus *fucking* Redmayne. Hadn't he said something to her at the time? Something about Toby's fortunes being about to change? Yes, he had. She was certain of it. But Toby's fortunes, since she'd been on board as his wife, had only risen. Not diminished.

Now Clara knew that she could never tell Toby about what had passed between her and Redmayne tonight. That the blood on her coat was *his*, that he'd kissed her and nearly snatched her breath away, and that far from being deterred by Toby's refusal to sell, he had set out his intention to have both her and all Toby's clubs for himself.

'Did I ever tell you about my parents?' he asked.

'What? No. You never did.'

'My mum died young, when I was eight. Dad raised me. He wasn't exactly an understanding sort of man.' Toby pulled a face. 'In fact, he was a thug. A big bullish type who didn't think any son of his could ever turn out to be . . . well, queer.'

Clara's eyes were resting on his face. 'That must have been horrible for you.'

'It was, pretty much. When he realized – I never told him, but he caught me once, with someone – well, when he realized, he tried to beat it out of me. He whipped me. He said he'd get this *evil* out, one way or another. I was a disappointment to him, and he thought I should be ashamed. When he died, I was so pleased!' Toby let out a laugh. 'I hated his guts. The clubs were his, you see, and I never thought I'd get into the club business, but I inherited them and so I made a go of it. A pretty good go, actually. Had to learn a few dirty tricks to survive – I've shown you a few – but I did it.'

'You did,' Clara agreed.

Toby looked at her, head cocked to one side. 'Are you happy, Clara?' he asked.

'What sort of question is that?'

'I want you to be happy.' Now Toby looked faintly embarrassed. 'I am, you know. Jasper and I . . . well, it's only been a year, but it's serious, it's love, he's my best beloved. Does that sound stupid?'

Clara felt her throat catch with emotion at the tenderness in Toby's voice. *Best beloved*, she thought. It sounded sweet, indulgent.

'It doesn't sound stupid at all. And I'm glad you're happy. I'm happy, too. Don't worry about that.'

'You could take lovers, you know. Discreetly. I've no objection. Of course we have to do our best to maintain the illusion of a married couple . . . '

Clara thought of Marcus Redmayne. No, she had no intention of complicating her life with that. 'I don't think so.'

'Then let me buy you something nice. Some more furs, perhaps? A winter break? Some jewels?'

'Some jewels would be good.'

'Jewels it is then. I'll have Asprey send over a tray of goodies.' He laughed. 'We have fun, don't we, Clara?'

'Yes. We do,' she agreed. It was a marriage. It wasn't hearts and flowers, a bed of roses. But it worked. All that thrilling, heart-stopping nonsense with Redmayne was nothing more than daydreams. And they were dangerous ones, at that.

54

Marcus had never forgotten that night at the Blue Bird when Jacko Sears died on him, and now his brother Fulton was still causing ructions. Pete had been there with Marcus that night, he'd helped him put Jacko Sears to rest out Epping way. Was it such a big stretch to think that Jacko's brother had heard something, taken revenge, targeted Pete?

Maybe Fulton would be coming for Marcus next. He was going to have to be *very* careful, but he'd lived under threat for most of his adult life; he was used to it.

He carried on bedding Paulette, moved her into a better, bigger flat in the hope that this would stop her leaving all her shit at his. And when he fucked her? He dreamed, always, of Clara Hatton who was now Clara Cotton. Clara with her solemn blue-eyed gaze and her tumble of black curls. Somehow – he didn't know how – she was stuck in his brain. Just the thought of her was enough to set his blood on fire. And she'd rebuffed him, then gone and married that nancy-boy Cotton. Even knowing what Cotton was, it still drove him crazy-mad with jealousy, thinking of her with someone else, not him.

And meanwhile?

He had Paulette – who had now added a yappy little apricot poodle to her repertoire of things designed to irritate the crap out of him. The thing chewed his belts and shoes, and Paulette cooed over it like an idiot when it pooped on the floor. Fucking thing. He thought of ditching her, taking up with Pete's old party girl Sonya instead.

Oh yeah, bright idea. Then every time you fuck her, you'll see Pete's decapitated head and dead hands on your desk.

He still couldn't get over Pete. They'd taken the remains, him and Gordon, and buried them way out in the sticks. He'd even said a silent prayer over the grave site; he didn't know what for, but it made him feel better somehow. And he'd given Sonya a job in one of the clubs, because Pete would have liked that.

In an attempt to lighten his mood, Marcus bought another car, a phallus-shaped red E-type Jag, and drove it first to Old Bond Street and then over to his mother's.

'What do you think?' he asked Mum as she stood at the door to let him in.

'It's a car,' shrugged his mother.

The women in his life? They gave him no joy at all.

55

'What do you think of these, sweetheart?' said Toby, coming up behind Clara, who was looking in the drawing-room mirror at the two glimmering strands of pearls around her neck. He held up a pair of fire opal screw-on earrings. Each opal was ringed with a circle of tiny bright diamonds.

Asprey had sent over a tray of jewels this morning. The jeweller was standing patiently in front of the closed hall door; there was a security guard on the other side of it. Clara paused, looked at Toby and the opals, and smiled.

'Aren't they beautiful?' he said. 'These would match your eyes. Deep shimmering blue. So pretty.'

'Don't they say opals are unlucky?'

'Do they? Superstitious crap.' He lowered his voice to a whisper. 'I wonder if Jasper would like them? I could wear one on each bollock, what do you think?'

Clara gave a snort of laughter, then glanced at the jeweller, standing there pretending not to listen. Toby caught the direction of her gaze and sighed.

'I love these pearls,' said Clara.

'They are extremely fine, madam,' agreed the jeweller.

'Would you like them, darling one?' asked Toby.

'Oh, darling, could I?' They were playing now, their eyes filled with mirth as they looked at each other in the mirror.

'Of *course* you could, sweetness.' Toby nodded to the jeweller. 'And the matching bracelet, perhaps . . . ?'

'You're so good to me,' said Clara, giving him a kiss on the cheek.

'Darling, nothing is too good for you,' said Toby, hugging her.

So the transaction was completed and Clara felt herself to be very lucky. She had an indulgent husband, a fabulous home, and now she had a double strand of real pearls in a necklace and a double-stranded bracelet too, both necklace and bracelet finished with matching sapphire-encrusted fasteners – and Toby had bought his fire opal earrings.

Annoyingly, the bloodstain on the cashmere coat wouldn't come out, though; and soon, Bernie dropped a bombshell that wiped the smile right off her sister's face.

'David and I have decided to get married,' said Bernie a couple of weeks later over dinner.

Clara nearly choked on her salmon. 'You *what?*' she asked, incredulous.

'David and I have decided that the time is right for us to be married.'

Toby and Clara exchanged a long look. Then Clara said: 'But . . . he doesn't have a bean, Bernie. How will he keep you?'

'We'll manage,' said Bernie.

'*Manage?*' Clara let out a hollow laugh. 'I don't think that's good enough. Manage how? I mean, where will you live?'

'David has a room over his studio.'

'Which he rents. He doesn't own that room. He doesn't even own the studio.'

Toby cleared his throat, dabbed lightly at his mouth with a napkin. 'Clara, if they are happy . . . ' he started.

'How can they be? Oh, they might be happy *now*, but it can't last. Bernie, don't you remember what it was like, living hand-to-mouth? You can't want to go back to that!'

'Perhaps I could find a job for David?' suggested Toby.

Clara scowled at him. *I'd be happier if you'd fucked him*, she thought. But that hadn't happened. David was straight as a die, and now Bernie was going to waste her life on the tosser.

But Bernie herself quashed Toby's offer. 'David's a photographer. A *brilliant* technician. That's all he wants to do. He couldn't work in a *club*.'

'Yes, but with a wife to support, he'd have to think again,' said Clara.

'I wouldn't want him to "think again",' said Bernie. 'That's what he does, that's how he chooses to make a living, I wouldn't want to dissuade him from carrying on with that.'

Clara was shaking her head. 'You're not thinking straight.'

'I love him, Clara,' said Bernie firmly.

'Love? What good is that going to do you, when you're dirt poor and pregnant? Don't be mad, Bern. It's out of the question.'

Bernie scraped back her chair and stood up. Her face was livid and she was trembling hard.

'Look, we can't *all* forget our feelings and just marry money,' she snapped.

Clara stood up too.

'Oh, now look . . . ' said Toby, ever the peacemaker.

'I won't allow it,' said Clara.

'You can't stop it,' said Bernie, and marched out of the room, slamming the door hard behind her.

56

Clara was sitting up in the office at the Heart of Oak one evening, thumbing though the day's papers, glancing at yet more Ban the Bomb demonstrations as American and Russian attitudes hardened.

It was over a month since she had last visited the Oak, a month since she had seen Marcus Redmayne. Since then, she'd heard no more from him and had even begun to relax, to think that he was all talk, like most men. And she had other things on her mind. More and more Toby was leaving the bulk of the running of the clubs to her while he swanned about the town with Jasper. She didn't mind; she liked the work, the feeling that for all she took out of the business, she was putting something tangible back.

Bernie worried her, though. She seemed set on this idea of marriage to that no-hoper Bennett, and what good could ever come of it? But Bernie was determined. She was talking about a formal engagement now; and they'd argued again last night.

'Could he afford to buy you a ring?' Clara had scoffed – Clara, whose fingers, thanks to her careful choice of second husband, were bristling with cabochon-cut emeralds, starry diamonds and stunning sapphires, and, of course, with her most treasured item, her mother's old thin wedding band.

'He'll give me his mother's ring. It has sentimental value.' Bernie had looked scathingly at Clara's hands. 'It actually *means* something to him, besides what it's worth.'

Then they'd been off again, shrieking at each other.

God, she didn't know what to do about Bernie. And now, dumpy little brunette Jan had come up the stairs to tell her that Sal hadn't been in.

'For how long?' asked Clara.

'We ain't seen her since a few days after you last came in here.'

'Well . . . she's probably just moved on.' Staff turnover was high in all the clubs. Girls found other jobs they liked better, or drifted back full-time onto the streets. Very rarely did they bother to give any sort of notice.

Jan was shaking her head. 'Nah, Sal wouldn't do that. She liked it here, with all her mates.'

'You been round to her place?'

'Yeah, I been round. Didn't get no answer, though. I thought maybe she's moved out of the area, who knows?' Jan looked worried. 'But I don't think she'd do that. Not without telling me. We been friends for years.'

'Where's she live?'

'Houndsditch.'

God! That place. 'Don't worry, she'll turn up,' she said.

'She won't. I know she won't! Look, would you come round her gaff with me? See she's all right?'

'God, Jan, I'm up to my arse in—'

'Please! For God's sake, anythin' could have happened to her.'

'Isn't she a bit of a drinker? Don't she like the gin?'

'Yeah, she does,' admitted Jan. Sal had been known to go off on a bender and roll in a week later – Clara had chewed her arse about it on more than one occasion. But it was getting on for a month now . . .

'That could be it. She might be off on one.'

'No! It's too long,' said Jan fretfully, echoing Clara's own thoughts.

Shit, thought Clara. Jan was looking to her to do something, take some action. But Houndsditch . . .

She remembered it. She'd never forget it. The stink of the slums. The damp and the despair. She shuddered to even think of it. She didn't want to go back there.

'*Please*, Clara. Come round there with me will you? I'm getting scared now.'

Clara took a breath. *Fuck it*. 'Look, we'll go tomorrow morning, all right? You and me. Come in here at eleven, I'll meet you and we'll go.'

'Thanks, Clara,' said Jan, looking relieved.

Shit, shit, shit, thought Clara. *Houndsditch.*

57

Next day they set off in a taxi into Clara's deepest, darkest nightmares. The driver, a big bluff Londoner, stopped at a certain point and wouldn't go any further.

'This is as far as I go,' he told them.

'Oh, come on . . . ' said Clara. It was pouring down outside.

'No, lady. Now get out, OK?'

Sheltering under an umbrella, Clara and Jan hustled on foot along the streets and Clara thought that it was like being fifteen again: the dank air, the rubbish mouldering on the pavements, the unwashed bodies hurrying past, trailing their feral scent of poverty.

'Is it much further?' asked Clara, teeth chattering, desperate to be gone.

'Not far.'

'Do you live round here too?' asked Clara.

'Here we are, up in these flats. I live over in the next street. Sal and me, we see each other a lot. It's not like her to just not turn up.'

Now Jan was hurrying up stairs to the top floor, going along a rubbish-strewn landing. Lines had been set up and strands of washing flapped tiredly in the faint breeze. They could hear televisions blaring inside the flats; all the paint on the doors was peeling and there was the strong scent of cats in the air up here.

Shivering with disgust at actually *being* here again, streets away from where her poor mother had died and where they had lived such desperate and miserable lives, Clara followed, cursing Sal and Jan equally. The sooner they roused Sal from what was probably nothing but a drunken stupor, the sooner they could get out of this filthy hole and back to civilization.

'Here we are . . . ' Jan stopped outside a door and knocked on it.

Clara felt sick. She couldn't believe she'd been dragged here, it felt like a ghastly dream.

'Oh . . . ' said Jan.

'What?' asked Clara, through chattering teeth. She looked round, focused on the door. It was ajar. When Jan knocked, it had swung inward.

Jan was staring too. 'When I tried last time, it was shut,' she said.

'Well, let's get in, at least it'll be drier inside . . . ' Clara moved past Jan and the door swung open further. She stepped into a small, semi-dark room. Something jingled under her feet. She looked down. Small change on the floor, and a red purse, open, as if it had been dropped there. Then . . .

The smell hit her like a blow, straight between the eyes.

'Oh – Jesus!' shouted Jan.

Clara reeled back a pace, barrelling into Jan and nearly knocking her flying. 'What the fu—' said Clara, her hand clamped over her nose. Oh Jesus, that *smell*.

Then Clara became aware of the noise. At first she thought it was the rain hammering on the roof – it was heavier now, and there was dripping, somewhere in this hellhole there was a leak. She heaved sideways, wondering if she was going to be sick, and her foot knocked against tin.

A bucket. The roof was leaking water, and Sal had placed a bucket there, to catch it. She reeled over against a small table, and there was Sal's little black evening bag. Numbly Clara picked it up. And . . . oh Jesus, *what was that?*

Things were pitching on her clothes, buzzing against her face. Big black things were crawling over the expensive cream wool of her coat, landing on her neck. With a shuddery cry of disgust she brushed them away.

Meat flies.

There was something rotten in here, something festering and dead. Her eyes flickered around the place, the dirt in here, the stench, the . . . oh God, there was a bed in the corner, there was something on the bed, and she didn't want to look but her eyes were drawn to it, to the image that would haunt her for weeks, months, *years* to come.

There was Sal.

Her face was blue, her bulging brown eyes opaque and staring, her mouth open in a silent scream, and there were – oh God! – maggots writhing and scrambling over the exposed mass of her spilled innards.

'Jesus!' said Jan.

Clara elbowed her aside and went out, away from this nightmare, out onto the walkway. Suddenly bile rose in her throat and she was sick, retching violently. Brushing a trembling hand at her mouth, she stumbled back to the steps and halfway down them Jan bustled past her, almost knocking her over in her haste to get away from the horror up the stairs. They were running as if there was a mad man coming behind them.

Gasping, they reached the bottom of the steps. Clara couldn't hold herself up any more. She collapsed onto the bottom stair, seeing Sal in her mind's eye, eviscerated, dead. Big mouthy Sal. Gone.

'I'll get . . . I'll get help . . . ' Jan was saying.

Shaking, shivering, Clara nodded. Somewhere, she'd dropped her umbrella. The rain was pouring now, drenching her. Jan stumbled away into the gloom, leaving Clara on the step. People were hurrying past, no one taking the slightest notice of the crouching woman there. She had to move, had to get up, had to leave. If only she could gather her strength. But she felt drained, weak as water. Someone bumped against her knee, stumbled; a man.

'Sorry,' he muttered, and then instead of moving on, without any warning, he grabbed her hand, pulled off her sapphire ring, and the diamond, and the emerald, wrenching at her fingers, hurting her.

Clara let out a scream. The man shoved her so that she fell back against the steps, and then he ran away. She looked at her hands. The only ring he hadn't taken was – thank God! – the only one she really cared about. Her mother's gold band, that was still there. Now there was someone else, coming closer. Clara shrank back, one hand in front of her face, waiting for another attack.

'Clara?' he said.

Clara dropped her hand slowly and stared up at the man's face. There was a lean, hungry look to him. A camera hung on a strap around his neck. It was David, Bernie's soon-to-be fiancé.

'Oh . . . it's you,' she said faintly.

'What on earth are you doing here?' he asked, staring at her like she'd landed from another world.

Well, she had. She'd left this place far behind her – and good riddance to it. And now she'd come back to find poor Sal, done to death. Clara opened her mouth to speak, but nothing came out.

'Come on,' he said. 'Let's get you somewhere warm and dry.'

He put a hand under her elbow and helped her to her feet.

58

It struck Clara then that David was probably a very nice man. Poor, yes; but caring, pleasant, even handsome in his gangly long-limbed way. He took her to his grubby little studio and she felt a bit faint and had to sit down at his desk while he fetched some water.

When she'd recovered, he put the CLOSED sign on the door and led the way upstairs to his surprisingly clean but untidy flat. He made her tea, sat her down, gave her a towel to dry her sodden hair. Clara became aware that she still had Sal's black evening bag on her lap, that she'd carried it with her out of the flat. She saw a portrait of Bernie, smiling shyly at the camera, up on the mantelpiece.

'What the hell were you doing there, of all places?' he asked, when they were sitting down and he'd switched on a two-bar electric fire. It felt chilly in here; Clara thought that he could probably not afford to run the damned thing, and probably never did, but was doing it because she looked so cold and shaky.

A nice man.

Clara sipped her tea, clasping the mug between her hands, feeling the warmth seep into her frozen body. She glanced at her left hand, bereft of rings.

'Someone stole my jewellery, just before you came by,' she told him.

'Well what were you doing, wearing stuff like that around that area? It's asking for trouble.'

'One of the *poor* you have such sympathy with,' said Clara.

He shrugged. 'They're desperate. You must have looked like easy pickings.'

Clara didn't answer that. It had been a terrible day. Finding Sal like that, and then being robbed. She was still shuddering, still seeing that awful scene in her head. She wondered if she would ever forget it. Someone had *murdered* Sal. Her brain could hardly absorb it; it was too horrible. She had been lying there dead, undiscovered for weeks. Jan had called by, but no one else had knocked at her door. No one else had cared. Suddenly all Clara wanted was to get home, to see Toby, tell him all about this. She was lucky; she had a husband, a home, a sister, people who cared about her. She could have ended up like poor Sal.

But . . . hadn't the rent man called in all that time? And hadn't Jan said the door was closed last time she'd called, and this time it was open?

'I know you don't like me,' said David.

Clara snapped her wandering attention back to what he was saying.

'And I can understand why,' he went on. 'But I love Bernie, and I want to make her happy.'

'But you can't, can you?' said Clara. 'How are you going to earn a living, with a family to support?'

'We'll manage,' he said.

Clara put her empty mug aside. She eyed him cynically. What a pair of dreamers they were, him and Bern. Fortunately she had a clearer view of the situation. She nodded to the photo on the mantle. 'That's a lovely photo of her,' she said.

'She's very photogenic. Good bones.'

'Does she come up here often to visit you?'

'She does. I suppose you don't like the idea, but it's serious, Clara. We're not just messing around. She sits in that same chair you're sitting in, every time she comes.'

'Could I have another cup of tea?'

He smiled and went to fetch it. When she'd finished it, she said: 'I think I'd like to go home now,' and stood up.

'You're sure? You can stay here for a bit, if you're still shaky. What were you doing over there, anyway? You never said.'

'Visiting a friend,' said Clara. 'That's all.'

He eyed her with disbelief. 'Can't imagine you having any friends down there. Still. Not my business.'

'No. It's not.'

'I'll get my coat,' said David, and left the room.

When he came back, they went down the stairs and out into the street. The rain had nearly stopped and everything looked brighter, raindrops catching on trees and shrubbery and glittering with rainbow shades. People were coming out into the streets again. Life was going on.

But not for Sal.

A feeling of deep unease gnawed at Clara. She had seen death close-up today, and it was shattering. And on top of that, she had just done a very wicked thing. Necessary – but wicked.

59

At four in the afternoon the cops called in at the Heart of Oak, wanting to speak to all the staff. Jan wasn't in. Neither was Toby. Clara had got home yesterday to find he wasn't there. He was obviously off around town with Jasper.

Now, for the first time, Clara wished for a *proper* husband, someone who would always be there for her, instead of gallivanting around the gambling dens and nightclubs with his handsome young lover.

All last night Sal's tortured face had haunted her dreams, pulled her sweating and half screaming from sleep time after time. To find herself alone. No Toby. No Bernie, either, sleeping in the next room. When Clara checked, she found her bed hadn't been slept in. She must have stayed over at David's.

There was nobody to confide in.

Well, she was used to that. Carrying all the responsibility. Making all the decisions. But it seemed to be getting harder all the time, and this fresh disaster had made her feel fragile, cast adrift.

Where the hell was Toby when you needed him?

And where was Jan?

She found *that* out quickly, when a police inspector came up to her office to take her statement and told her: 'Miss Cutler is taking the day off, trying to get over the shock.'

Thinking about that hideous scene again, Clara suppressed

a shudder. Poor bloody Jan; if she felt anything like *she* did, she needed a day off. The difference was, she was getting it. Clara couldn't enjoy such luxury. She had to soldier on.

'It was a particularly vicious crime,' said the inspector. He was tall, cadaverous, and his pale eyes looked like they had seen far too much. 'Miss Cutler was very shaken at finding her friend like that, and she was upset you left the scene.'

'I'm sorry. I think I just panicked. Do you have any idea who . . . ?' asked Clara, dry-mouthed.

'Not yet. We're making inquiries. So Miss Dryden worked here. Would you say she seemed happy?'

'Sal was never happy. She loved to have a moan, it kept her going.'

'Any problems she discussed with you or her workmates? Boyfriends? Anything?'

Clara thought of Sal's photos but shook her head. 'Sal had a bit of an attitude, she was mouthy but we all knew that. You took no notice.'

'Had she upset one of the customers? Anything like that?'

'Not that I know of.'

The inspector stood up. 'I'll have a talk to the staff.'

An hour later, he was back in Clara's office. 'A couple of your staff have told me that Miss Dryden did some model-ling on the side. Under-the-counter stuff, I believe.' He sniffed. 'Do you know anything about that?'

Clara shrugged. 'She did mention it, in passing.'

'But you didn't think to mention it to me,' he said.

'No. Well, it was nothing. It slipped my mind.'

He was staring at her face. Then he stood up. 'Well if anything *does* cross your mind, call me,' he said, and dropped a card onto the desk.

When Clara got home later that day, she went straight to Toby. She found him in front of the mirror in his bedroom, holding two silk ties in front of his pale blue Turnbull and Asser shirt, whistling along to Roy Orbison singing 'Ebony Eyes' on the radiogram. He smiled when he saw her. 'Darling, what do you think? Blue or dove grey?'

'The grey,' said Clara, and went and sat on the bed. 'Toby, something's happened. Something awful.'

Toby put the ties aside and came and sat beside Clara. 'What is it?' he asked.

Clara took a gulping breath and spilled everything out to Toby, barely keeping the tears at bay.

'Oh, Clara, how fucking awful! Come here, my darling,' said Toby, hugging her. 'You poor little mare.'

'The police came into the Oak today, questioned me and all the staff. They'll probably want to talk to you at some point.'

'Me? How would I know anything about it?'

'You don't, obviously. I'm only warning you, in case they do.'

'Why don't you stay home today, have a rest? It must have been horrible for you.'

It had been. But Clara's brain was spinning, she couldn't rest. Her mind kept re-running the events of yesterday and today like some obscene art-house movie stuck on a never-ending loop. Sal's gaping mouth, her belly slashed open, the coins on the floor, the photos in Sal's bag . . . yes, the photos. Thinking of them reminded her of what she'd done, and gave her a feeling that was dangerously close to shame.

No, she'd done what was necessary.

She had to keep telling herself that.

And she did – right up until Bernie came home a few nights later, sat down at the kitchen table, and cried her heart out.

60

'What's the matter?' asked Clara, and she was thinking *Oh shit.*

Bernie couldn't speak; she was crying too hard.

Clara put an arm around her sister's shaking shoulders and thought *I did this. I am a bad person. A wicked woman.*

'Can't you tell me what's happened?' she asked after a while, when Bernie's sobs had abated enough for her to be able to form a sentence.

'It's David,' said Bernie, gasping, looking in her bag for a tissue, blowing her nose loudly.

'What about him?'

'I found some photographs in his flat.'

'Well, he *is* a photographer.'

Bernie was shaking her head. 'No! These were . . . horrible. Real hard-porn things. Kids and stuff. Disgusting.'

'Then he couldn't have taken them,' said Clara. She hated this, seeing the pain in Bernie's eyes. 'He does weddings, portraits, innocent stuff like that.'

'I thought that, at first. God, I was so shocked when I found them. He was in the kitchenette making tea, and I sat down, and there was something rustling, something papery, and I felt down the side of the cushions and dug out these shots of a girl and a man . . . Well, I won't tell you what they were doing. And I turned them over, and there was David's studio stamp, right on the back of them. They're *his* photos.'

'Did you confront him about it?' asked Clara. Her heart was beating fast; she felt nauseous. It had worked, better than she had hoped it would. But now she wished she hadn't done it. Wished she could have spared Bernie this pain.

But it's for her own good. He's a loser, he's poor, he's a nothing.

'I did. Of course he denied it. Said they were nothing to do with him. But I know they are. They were stamped with his own studio mark, how could they not be?'

That started up a fresh wave of sobs. Clara patted Bernie's shoulder, soothed her, and felt sick to her stomach now, really churned-up. She thought of Marcus Redmayne's harsh words to her: *gold-digger*. Well, that was her, wasn't it? She was a gold-digger, she'd married twice for money and now she was making damned sure that her sister was going to do the same, live a comfortable life, not one of hardship and desperation, trying to keep the wolf from the door.

But . . . she felt disgusted with herself.

Still, she could make this better. She would start introducing Bernie to some more *suitable* men, now that arty David with his slum-loving ways had been kicked into touch. Clara gritted her teeth and thought *It will be OK. Bernie will get through this, and she'll be happier for it.*

'He takes these disgusting shots and I was going to *marry* him, not even knowing.'

Clara grasped Bernie's shoulders hard. 'At least you found out,' she said firmly. 'It's better that you know. Isn't it? Before it's too late?'

Bernie nodded, her face a picture of misery. 'Yes. I suppose it is.'

But Bernie didn't look convinced.

She looked destroyed.

61

'Someone was asking for you earlier,' said Fulton Sears, who was standing at the Starlight's front door when Clara went there a week later.

She paused. 'Oh? Who?'

'Bloke called Bennett. In a bit of a state. Said he was going to call back tonight, see if you were in. You want to see him, do you?'

No. She really didn't. Clara stared up at Sears's face. God, he was ugly. And right now, after all that had happened, he was hanging on to this job by the skin of his teeth. 'Yeah, let him in when he comes,' she said, and walked on, into the club, aware of the goon staring after her. *Great lummox*, she thought.

It was only ten but it was already busy, the atmosphere thick with cigarette and cigar smoke, the lighting low and intimate. All the hostesses were circulating, chatting up the punters, drinking overpriced booze with them at the long red-lit bar and at the tables. Clara was pleased to see the regulation uniform on each and every one of the girls, the plain black satin evening dress, the neatly groomed hair, an aura of cleanliness and friendliness about them.

Up on the tiny half-moon stage, a brunette in emerald green was crooning 'Where the Boys Are' under the spotlight. Clara moved over to the bar and ordered a G & T. She

perched up on a bar stool and sat listening to the girl singing about a man who was there, with the boys, waiting for
her.

God, was that all everyone thought about? Love?

Toby was in love with Jasper, he was always talking about
him, obsessing over him. Toby *had* his love. Whereas she . . .

An image of Marcus Redmayne, dark-haired and dangerous, drifted into her brain and she kicked it straight back
out.

Love didn't last. Look at her dad, running out on Mum
when she most needed him. And in her own life, oh yes,
there had been husbands. For security, for making sure
the family got by. But love? She had only ever tolerated
Frank Hatton. In her way, of course, she loved Toby. They'd
become friends, companions; they understood each other,
valued each other's input. But love, the true love they sang
about in songs, the heart-wrenching, gut-clenching love that
drove people to madness or despair . . . she didn't know
about that. And she didn't want to, either.

The girl finished her song and the punters clapped
loudly. Then Clara saw David, face set in grim lines, weaving his way through the packed tables toward the bar. He
looked a bit unsteady, like he'd been on the drink. She
braced herself.

'So you're in then,' he said when he reached her.

'Yep, I'm in,' said Clara.

The girl on the stage was bowing, then turning to the
piano-player and nodding. He played the opening bars of
'When the Boy in Your Arms' and she was off again. Really,
she was very good. They'd have to see to a little pay-rise for
her, or someone would poach her to sing in their clubs,
instead.

'I tried to catch you at home, but you're never bloody
there. Always out around the clubs. Counting the takings, I

suppose,' he said bitterly. The barman came up. 'Whisky,' said David.

Clara nodded and the barman went to the optics.

'So what can I do for you?' she asked David.

He stared at her face. He hitched himself up onto the stool a little; yes, he'd been drinking already. He was unsteady, swaying. Finally he let out a caustic laugh.

'What a piece of work you are,' he said, as the barman came back with his whisky. David lifted the glass to his lips, threw back his head and drained it in one hit. Then he slammed it back down onto the bar.

'Go easy,' warned Clara.

'Get me another,' said David to the barman.

'No. Don't,' said Clara, and the barman moved away. She looked at David. 'Say what you've got to say, then.'

'You absolute bloody bitch. It was you, wasn't it?'

'What?'

'You planted those fucking pictures in the chair. I *told* you she sat there every time she came, and she found them just as you intended she would.'

'I don't know what you mean.'

'And the fucking studio stamp. You didn't miss a trick did you? Coming over all faint so I'd leave you alone long enough for you to stamp those pictures. Well, you got your wish. She never wants to see me again.'

Clara looked at him straight-faced, but her heart was thumping. 'Sal showed me the prints. Weeks ago. They were disgusting.'

He stared at her. 'How did you know? Come on. Tell me. How did you know?'

'What?' Clara looked back at him blankly.

'Fuck's sake!' He leaned both elbows on the bar, dragged his hands through his hair, then turned to face her. 'How could you know I'd taken those bloody things? Or . . . ' Now he was staring at her face. 'Oh Christ. You didn't, did you? You were just going to fit me up with them, put Bernie off me. You didn't know that I'd actually taken them!'

62

'What did you just say?' Clara was staring at him in shock. David Bennett, friend of all mankind, had taken that stuff which it had nearly choked her to look at? The children, the cringing women, Sal's unhappy face while her body was being abused by that huge bull-like man . . .

'Christ,' he muttered, realizing he'd said far too much. 'Oh, Christ . . . '

'No. I didn't know,' said Clara, her lip curling in distaste. 'But now I do? I'm *glad* I did what I did. If only to keep Bernie away from you. What were you thinking, getting involved in filth like that?'

Now he was laughing without mirth, staring at her, his eyes full of hatred. 'Well, sadly we can't all be so fucking choosy as you, can we? I'll tell you why I did that shoot, *those* shoots – there were quite a few of them and they turned my stomach, but I did them because do you know how much a Leica camera costs? Or a Hasselblad? Or the lenses or a decent tripod or proper studio lights? Even a bloody cable release? No? Well, it all costs a fortune. I told Bernie I took out a loan to buy the cameras – all right, I *lied* to her, but I couldn't get a loan, the interest would have crippled me, it was too much. So when someone asked me to take a few porno pictures, I said yes.'

'I see,' said Clara.

Now he was shaking his head, smiling sourly. 'You never thought I was good enough for her.'

'You got that spot-on. I didn't. I thought she'd have a miserable life with you.'

'We're in love.'

'Oh, please. That wouldn't feed my sister, or a family.'

He was staring at her, mouth half-open, looking at her as if she was something from an alien species. 'I *helped* you,' he said. 'I fucking-well helped you, you cow! I don't know what the hell you were doing there—'

'I told you. Visiting a friend.'

'That's bullshit, isn't it? But still. Maybe I'll find out.'

'Keep your nose out of my business.'

'I'll be glad to. I don't think I'd have the stomach for looking into anything much to do with you, Clara. Christ, what a cold-blooded cunt you are. You're *nothing* like your sister.'

'Don't bring Bernie into this. And I think you lost the moral high ground when you decided to take photos of people fiddling around with women who looked like they were being raped at gunpoint, and with innocent kids. Bernie's better off without you.'

'Oh, you think so? What would you know? You only marry for money, don't you. You don't know the meaning of the word "love". All you do is count the cash – am I right or am I right?'

'You're right,' said Clara flatly. 'I've never had any interest in marrying for anything else. I don't want to live that way – the way that you would have inflicted on my sister, given half the chance. I'm pleased to say that she's escaped all that, and soon she'll find someone with a bit of substance to them and a bit more of a conscience too.'

'Someone with big fat wads of money, you mean.'

'Yes, that. Why not? And then she'll forget all this stupid business and she'll be happy.'

'Like you are? Are you happy, Clara? Or Black Clara, as they call you? Oh, you're black all right. Black-hearted. Black to the core. *Rotten* to it.'

Clara froze as he hurled the words at her like stones. Was she happy? She was . . . content, she supposed. She'd done well, she'd single-handedly pulled the family out of the poverty their father had left them in. She'd made a success of her life, despite all the struggles, all the sacrifice. But . . . happy?

The brunette was doing a snappier number now: 'Up a Lazy River', made famous by Bobby Darin.

'What do you know about Sal Dryden?' asked Clara, changing the subject.

His eyes widened. 'Who?'

'Oh, come off it! Sal. The tall white blonde in the pictures, the one that bastard was fucking. What was his name? Sal told me.'

'Frate,' said David. 'It was Yasta Frate.'

'Oh! Selective memory. You know him, but not her?'

'All right. I know the girl you mean. And I heard she'd been found dead, it was in the papers and on the news. What has that got to do with me?'

'I don't know. But the funny thing? You were right there, outside her flat.'

'That's who you were visiting then? Sal? Christ, did you find the body? Was it you?' David was nodding now. 'It was you. That's why you looked so shaken up, wasn't it? You were sitting on the bottom step looking like you were about to hurl up your breakfast. And that's why.'

Clara ignored him. 'So who did you sell that filth to, to raise the money so you could play with your expensive cameras?'

David shrugged and leaned his elbows on the bar. 'A couple of club owners. A few doormen.'

'My guess is you didn't take those into Boots to get them printed off,' said Clara sourly.

'No. I printed them myself. I've got a darkroom – they're black and white, not colour, it's easy enough.'

'And these random people, they can order more prints from you? You've got the negatives?'

His head swivelled round and his angry eyes met hers. 'What is this, twenty fucking questions? Sure, I kept the negatives. And people can re-order if they want.'

'Bet you do a brisk trade,' sniffed Clara.

His gaze froze. 'We all do things for money, Clara. You can't talk.'

'Oh, fuck off, David,' she snapped in irritation. 'Whatever I do, it has absolutely nothing to do with you. Keep your nose out in future or I'll have someone cut the thing off, do you get me?'

He leaned in closer and the scent of liquor hit her in a wave. 'You cold bitch. Married to an old man and then a bender! Does the money keep you warm at night, Clara? Does it?'

'I said fuck off,' said Clara sharply, drawing back. 'You'd be well advised to do that before I have one of the boys on the door toss your drunken arse into the street.'

He stood up. 'Don't trouble yourself. I'm going.'

He walked away, weaving unsteadily through the tables, then up the stairs to the club's entrance.

Sticks and stones, thought Clara, as the brunette on the stage let out a last exuberant trill of sound. The audience clapped enthusiastically. Clara clapped, too. But inside, she felt unnerved, and his words echoed in her head.

Does the money keep you warm at night?

She knew the answer to that. It didn't. But what else was

there? The brunette left the stage to a round of applause. Clara ordered another G & T, and drank it down. She shuddered at the memory of those photos. So Saint David was no saint after all.

63

It was a shame about Sal, a real crying shame, but what the hell. Shit happened – Henry thought he was living proof of that, after all that had come crashing down on his head since he was a small boy in short trousers – but what could you do?

In her line of work, it was inevitable that sooner or later Sal would come to grief, and now she had. Not so shocking, really. Certainly not surprising. And him? He was all right. Life went on. De Gaulle was in town for talks with Macmillan, and the Immigration Bill was causing fights in Westminster, and here on the streets there were fights too and births, and deaths. After what happened to Sal . . . well, *happened* . . . and he was sorry as hell about it but there you go, that was life, he'd had to go get himself some other digs.

And not a moment too soon, as it turned out. Since then he'd learned that the Bill had pulled in a photographer called Bennett for questioning two or three times, and there was a black club owner called Frate who had been implicated in the porno stuff involving Sal – but everyone knew that Yasta Frate had the cops in his pocket, so nobody could make even a teaspoon of shit stick to that slippery bastard.

Henry was grateful to Sal for all she'd done for him – for letting him stay with her in her ratty, disgusting, leak-ridden flat. It wasn't much, but it was better than the streets. And he was grateful to her for slipping him in the back door to see Fulton Sears, who was overseer of the doors on all the Cotton clubs and who also was getting a pretty impressive protection racket going among the businesses around Soho.

Of course there was the connection, the *family* connection. But was he even a part of that any more? Clara – big sis – had married Toby Cotton, signed up for a life of ease and privilege. But Henry was a *long* way down the pecking order from big sis, their paths need never so much as cross if he put his mind to it, and he would. He didn't relish door work anyway, it was boring. No, he liked doing the milk round, collecting the cash payments from the traders. He was bulky now, muscular, he frightened the fuck out of the poor bastards.

Pay up and there'll be no trouble, he told them.

He admired the way the Triads over in Chinatown went about their business; it was stylish, he thought; they worked the streets – Lisle, Newport, the south side of Shaftesbury Avenue, Wardour, Gerrard and Macclesfield – demanding protection money, and getting it too. They called it 'tea money', a tribute; violence was only applied when a certain series of steps had been observed. If a restaurant owner didn't pay on the first approach, a negotiator was sent in to take tea with the proprietor in a private room at a hotel. If he *still* refused to play ball, a knife wrapped in a Chinese newspaper would be presented as a final warning. After that, if the man continued to object, a 'chopping' would take place. He would be cut with a fourteen-inch beef knife.

And after that?

He would be killed.

Yeah, thought Henry. That was *style*.

64

After David's departure, Clara did what she always did in the clubs: checked and rechecked that everything was running as it should. And it was; the manager of the Starlight was doing a good job. She caught up with the singer Babs Morley in her dressing room, praised her performance and gave her a pay rise.

She knew that David would calm down, and eventually he would move on. He'd been drunk, making empty threats and swearing at her to ease his bruised feelings. Always playing the do-gooder, the friend of humanity, he'd been scorched with embarrassment to be found doing something most decent people would find disgusting. He'd had to lash out at something, and she was the obvious target. So be it. All the rest was empty posturing, nothing more.

It was after two in the morning when she finally left the club and headed home.

On the way there, a fire engine, lights flashing, sirens wailing, shot past her taxi.

'Phew, someone's got trouble,' said the driver.

'Yeah,' said Clara, uninterested, tired. Exhausted, actually. And . . . David had rattled her.

The truth hurts . . .

Yeah, it did. It hurt a lot.

257

She was a cold, heartless woman, marrying for money, caring nothing for love.

Love . . .

Marcus Redmayne . . .

Jesus! How could she even think about *love* for a man who'd hounded her, trashed three of her and Toby's clubs, caused her nothing but trouble?

Another engine roared past, and another, all heading in the same direction. As the taxi moved on, Clara became aware of a glow lighting the sky up ahead. The fire was close and it was big. There was still traffic about – in London, there was *always* traffic about – and as another huge red Dennis came past, lights blazing, sirens letting out a deafening din, the taxi driver and the other drivers coming up behind him were nudging their cars into the pavement, giving the engine space to get by.

The closer they got to Clara's road, to her home, the more her guts clenched in anxiety. The fire was *very* close. And . . . fuck, she could see flames now, huge gouts of flame shooting up into the night sky, and . . . there were the engines, parked all ways across the road, across *her* road, barring any further progress, and the firemen were unravelling the hoses, sending mighty arcing jets of water up into the flames and . . .

'You live right here,' said the driver. 'Don't you?'

Clara couldn't speak. Her house – her beautiful, fabulous house, the one she and Toby had bought treasures for, had decorated together, had debated over colour schemes for and had such fun with – was on fire.

She couldn't think straight. Somehow she remembered to peel off some notes and thrust them at the driver, then she was out of the black cab and running.

Out in the street, all was chaos. Immediately the smoke choked her. The wind was strong and blowing thick black curls of smoke and burning cinders and ash downward so that everything at street level was grey and hazy. Clara coughed and held a hand in front of her mouth. Her eyes stung and started streaming. She could barely breathe. There were people coming out from their houses on the other side of the road to gawp at the spectacle. There were parked police cars, blue lights flashing, and there was shouting and manic activity at the front of the house.

There were only two thoughts in her head as she dashed toward the burning building.

Toby.

Bernie.

She was running for the front door, which was blackened, all the paint peeling away, and there was such thick awful oily smoke, enveloping everything, choking her. Mindless with terror, she was stumbling toward the door, she had to get to Toby, to Bernie, she had to get in there.

Someone grabbed her around the waist. 'Whoa! Steady on, miss, you can't go in there.'

One of the firemen. She twisted in his grip like a cat, determined to be released, to complete her purpose.

Now another man grabbed her too, and between them they held her steady.

'Miss! You can't go in there, you can't,' said the second officer.

And then Clara saw that there was a bundle laid out near the front of the house, a bundle of what looked like blackened rags.

'Is that . . . ?' she choked, and then she couldn't speak any more, the smoke was too dense, too awful, it tore the breath from her lungs. With a gargantuan effort she pulled free and was off, stumbling toward the pile of rags. Ambulances were arriving now, medics piling out. Clara ran, fell, righted herself, ran on. Because that wasn't rags, it was a *person*, she could see that now.

Bernie? Oh Christ! Not Bernie . . .

Here in the front garden of her lovely house she could feel the furious roaring heat of the fire; it seemed to blast at her skin, to snatch her breath. She fell to her knees beside the person laid out on the lawn. There was a fireman bending over the body, and he looked up in surprise when Clara arrived on the scene.

'No – miss – go on, get back, get away . . . ' he said, and he was choking too, coughing, trying to get the words out.

'*Bernie?*' Clara managed to say. She reached down, pushed back a section of blanket, and let out a gasp of horror.

It wasn't Bernie.

It was Toby.

And he'd been burned.

65

Toby's eyes were the same. That was all she could think as she stared down at him. His face was smeared with soot, his skin was scarlet and peeling away from his face in strips, his thick, gorgeous hair had been reduced to frazzled fluff, scorched to blackened tufts, his handsome looks were gone, never to return. He was nearly unrecognizable. But his eyes were the same, even if his brows and lashes were burned off. His left hand rested on the blanket they'd put over him, and it was like a mummy's claw, dried and seared and ruined.

Oh God, he'd been afire, he'd stumbled out of the house in flames, hadn't he. She could see it, could picture it in her mind. His hand was black and red and . . . she went to touch it, and she couldn't. She was afraid to. It would feel . . . horrible. And she might hurt him even more than he was hurt already. But his eyes were still exactly the same, still recognizably Toby's. Hazel-coloured and beautiful. They stared up at her and the expression in them was dazed, agonized and terrified.

He was alive.

Somehow Clara forced a smile onto her lips, willed her voice to be steady, to be strong. Inside she was screaming *Please, not Toby, please no!*

'It's all right, darling,' she said. 'You're going to be fine, it's all right.' Then she said: 'What happened? Can you tell me what happened?'

He wheezed; couldn't speak.

'Where's Bernie, Toby?'

Toby wheezed in another gasping breath. His eyes held hers. But he said nothing. Could he speak? Had the heat seared his lungs, damaged them? She thought it had.

'We couldn't find anyone else in the house, miss,' said the fireman, crouching beside her. 'Look, the ambulance crew are coming now . . . '

Toby's eyes were still on her face. Somehow Clara didn't cry. He wouldn't want her to cry. She had to be calm and resilient, to reassure him that this was only a temporary thing, that he would recover, that all would be well.

It wouldn't. She knew it wouldn't. She could see it.

'Now, Toby, don't worry,' she said with terrible forced brightness. 'The doctors will help. They're going to take you to the hospital and make you well again.'

'Clara . . . '

He could speak! But his voice was cracked, and the effort of speaking was exhausting what little strength he had left.

'I'm here, darling. I'm right here.' Her tears were spilling over. She couldn't stop them now.

'Clara . . . ' he gasped, and then his eyes turned up in his head.

'Toby!' Clara leaned in closer. '*No! Oh, please . . . Toby . . .* '

The medics came then, shoving her to one side. Choking, sobbing, she reeled back and the fireman pushed her away, further, out of the gate, to where it was safer. Her eyes were fastened on the pitiful bundle that was Toby, fastened on the people now clustering around him, talking, putting an oxygen mask over his ruined face, pumping at his burned torso.

She couldn't look away.

All around her there was turmoil, the house still burning, firemen running, directing hoses, cursing the wind and saying loudly that they had to keep this from spreading to the other houses, they had to contain it. The flames leapt like demons. The fire was like a living thing, straight from hell, and it had grabbed Toby and burned his body to a crisp.

All the time Clara stared at that little group surrounding Toby, how they worked at him, how they struggled. And finally . . . at last, after minutes that felt like hours, how they gave up, stood up, shook their heads. She watched one of them pull the blanket over Toby's face.

No. Oh God, please don't take Toby too. Not him!

'Clara?'

She turned, dazed, tear-stained, soot-streaked, toward the voice. Bernie was standing there, staring at her, then her gaze was going past her sister to the burning house beyond. Clara almost fell forward and grabbed her sister in a desperate hug. 'I thought you were in there,' she moaned.

'Where's Toby?' asked Bernie, pushing Clara away. Clara thought that Bernie's voice sounded strange; her face looked somehow wiped of emotion.

Clara couldn't say it. She indicated with a trembling hand the spot where the ambulance people were now loading Toby's blanket-shrouded remains onto a stretcher.

Bernie's eyes widened. 'Oh my God. Clara! He isn't. Please say he isn't.'

Clara couldn't speak; she could only nod.

'Oh Jesus . . . ' Bernie started to cry. 'Oh no.'

Clara felt the strength leave her. She slumped down onto the garden wall, and sat there, head in hands. She thought of Toby, laughing with her, trying on jewels, mincing around, sending himself up, making her laugh. Making her *love* him. He'd been no husband, it was true, but they'd weathered that storm without too big a fuss and come through it until finally they were the best of friends.

And now he was dead, gone from her forever.

Oh Christ, she thought. *Toby*.

66

There were things to be done. There were always things to be done, lots of things, and although life had lost all meaning for Clara she struggled to attend to business, as always. Crippled with grief though she was inside, on the outside she continued to cope, to be the same old upright stern Clara.

Having to maintain the pretence of control was a help to her in the grim days after the fire. The insurance men came and grubbed around in the shell of the gutted house, her once-beautiful house full of all the wonderful things she and Toby had acquired over their pitifully short time together. The chimney was still standing, but everything else was a scorched, dripping skeleton of something that had once had life. Now the house itself had perished, along with Toby. And Clara felt that something within her had died, too.

But she pressed on. Bernie seemed to have shrunk away from her even more since the fire, which puzzled and wounded her.

'We'll stay at the flat over the Oak,' said Clara to her sister. 'There's room enough for two. Until we sort out what we're going to do next.'

But Bernie shook her head. 'No, I . . . a friend of mine, Sasha, has offered, I'm staying with her.'

'Oh. All right. If you want.'

'Yes. I do.'

So Clara stayed alone at the poky little flat over the Heart of Oak nightclub, had all her mail redirected there. Toby's club. *Hers*, now he was gone.

After Frank's death, she could remember the feeling of release, of sudden freedom. Guiltily, she had also felt that at last she owned something worth having; all that Frank had owned before his death was now hers. Now she owned the clubs that had once been Toby's, but that thought filled her with nothing but sorrow. She felt numb and alone.

The insurance men poked around some more, and left. She had to sort out the death certificate, do all the paperwork at the registrar's. Then she visited the local undertaker's, and arranged a splendid funeral for her late husband. Bernie kept her distance. Seemed almost like a stranger.

Alone, Clara sat in the flat over the Oak, trying not to weep over Toby – and failing. At least he'd lived as he wished to live, happy with his boys and – she hoped and firmly believed – happy with her, too. She clung to that, a tiny life-raft in an ocean of despair. And then, all too soon, the day of his funeral arrived.

It was a wet December day, cold and damp. All the girls and boys from the clubs, all Toby's friends and business acquaintances turned out, the church was packed to the rafters. Clara gritted her teeth and endured throughout the service, the hymns – all the while staring at the coffin there on the dais. It was deep red mahogany, its brass handles and name plate buffed to a brilliant golden shine, and the whole of it was draped in mounds of sumptuous white lilies. It was just as Toby would have wished, just as Toby would have done for her.

He would have loved this, she thought.

Throughout the service, as she stood shoulder to shoulder with Bernie – thank God, at last they had shaken off that loser David Bennett – she couldn't take it in. This was *Toby* they were burying. Toby's ruined body lay inside that exquisite casket. Her flamboyant, gorgeous Toby. And . . . she glanced around and caught the eye of a beautiful young blond man, tears cascading down his face.

Oh Jesus.

It was Jasper. This was bad for her, horrible, but it must be equally bad for him. When her eyes met his, he looked away.

Soon, it was over.

There was the sad little scene beside the open grave, a blessing, and then it was done. Toby was truly gone. Clara found herself wishing that she could go home to their lovely house with its glamour and its grounds, but that was impossible; the place was a wreck, beyond saving; it would have to be demolished. Their neighbours had been lucky; the Cotton house had been an end property and the adjoining house had suffered a little damage, but nothing major.

She arranged a buffet in the Heart of Oak, and everyone came. Well, nearly everyone. Clara's eyes searched the crowd for Jasper, who must be suffering over this, but he wasn't there.

'My commiserations, Mrs Cotton,' said Marcus Red-mayne, coming to stand in front of her.

'Thank you. Help yourself to something to eat and drink.' Quickly, she moved away. Marcus Redmayne always made her feel shaky, and she was shaky enough today, without having to act cool in front of him.

'Toby was a great bloke,' said the new manager of the Starlight, shaking her hand. 'A real character. I'm so sorry.'

'He was,' she agreed.

'One of the best,' said someone else.

'Yes. He was,' she said, and seeing Bernie loitering near

the buffet table – which was nearly empty of food now, and thank God for that because that meant this day would soon be over – Clara went to speak to her.

'Are you all right, Bern?' she asked. 'You had something to eat?'

Bernie shook her head. 'No, I couldn't face it,' she said, then her eyes rested on Clara's face. 'Clara?'

'Yes, lovey?'

'I've heard people saying that Toby was . . . well, "queer". Did you know about that?'

Clara let out a breath. 'Yes. Of course I knew.'

'But you were *married*,' said Bernie.

'We were friends,' said Clara.

'It can't have been much of a marriage.'

'It was a very good one, actually.'

Bernie's expression grew cold. 'I don't think you know what's good and what's bad when it comes to marriage,' she said. 'All you ever seem to want from any of your husbands is money.'

'Bernie!'

'Don't "Bernie" me in that hurt tone of voice,' she snapped. 'David told me that you set him up. He told me you put those photos down the side of the chair in his flat. And you nicked a rubber stamp from his studio to convince me he'd taken the shots. He says he didn't.'

'That's a lie,' said Clara. 'He admitted to me that he *did* take them. Bernie, it's just lucky we found this out before it was too late.'

'All I know is I'm miserable without him. And I keep telling myself, you wouldn't stoop to such a thing, to set him up – but you would.'

'He was no good for you, Bernie. Whatever *I* may have done, the fact remains he's as guilty as fuck. And it's always better to be a rich man's darling than a poor man's slave.'

'There we are. Back to money again.'

'Oh, come on, Bernie . . . '

'No! I don't want to talk to you, Clara. I don't want to hear any more.' And Bernie hurried away, up the stairs, out of the club.

I've lost her, thought Clara. Her guts were churning in anguish. She'd lost Toby; she couldn't bear to lose Bernie too.

She was relieved when the day was over, when at last she was able to crawl off to the flat upstairs and lick her wounds and cry her bitter tears in peace. The postman had delivered the mail earlier, and she read both letters while sitting slumped on the sofa, feeling exhausted, wrung out, full of misery.

The first was a bill. There were always bills. Clara slit open the second and gasped in a breath. It was from the insurance brokers and they were talking about 'accelerants' having been used during the house fire.

Clara dropped the letter into her lap and stared ahead, unseeing.

They were saying the fire had been started deliberately, and so they were not going to pay out. They were saying that Toby could have started the fire himself, to reap the insurance money. But Clara knew that was rubbish. She *knew* Toby. He'd loved that house as much as she did. And Toby had no need of a big cash payout, the clubs were all doing well, he had no money problems that she knew about.

But *accelerants* . . .

If Toby hadn't started the fire himself – and she didn't for a second believe that he had – then someone else had started it. And by doing that, they had murdered him, in cold blood.

67

She was single again. Fulton Sears watched her come and go in the clubs and in his heart he rejoiced. She was single, she was free. He went on with his life, sorting out aggro on the doors, dealing puff and a little coke, running the boys out on the street making collections from the business interests all around Soho, but in fact, all the while, his mind was elsewhere.

He couldn't wait to get home to his flat and the shrine he'd set up in his front room. There was her handkerchief, the one she'd dropped while ferrying her first husband home from the pub. It still smelled faintly of her perfume. And there was her comb, still with strands of her black-as-midnight hair attached to it.

Now he had her watch, too – a beautiful Cartier thing she'd put down in the women's toilets and forgotten to pick up. The cleaner had handed it to him, and he'd kept it.

'Clara, Clara,' he whispered as he stood there and lit the candles on either side of the small table in the far corner of the room. He listened to Elvis Presley singing 'Surrender' on the Dansette and thought, *Yes, oh yes*.

Soon, Clara Cotton was going to surrender, she was going to be his. He'd waited patiently, let her get all this *wildness* out of her system. Soon, he would propose and he knew she would accept. Of course she would.

She *had* to.

68

1962

Christmas had passed for Clara in a dismal and solitary blur. She was still staying at the flat over the Heart of Oak and it was pretty much business as usual, only with added tinsel and Bing Crosby singing 'White Christmas' over and over again until she felt she would shriek, and loads more drunken punters.

She toured all the clubs during the week: the Starlight, the Paradise, the Carmelo, the Juniper and the CityBeat – which was a favourite drinking-hole for the mods, who rolled up, stoked up on amphetamines, on their Lambrettas and Vespas to party all night. Clara had heard of bad clashes between the mods and their fierce rivals the rockers – leather boys in jeans with greased-back hair – but there was no trouble in the CityBeat. Whatever Clara's personal view of Fulton Sears, she had to admit that mostly he did manage to keep things peaceful. For herself, she was grateful for the necessity to be seen, to be functioning, because otherwise she felt she would have crumbled to dust, sat in the flat alone and cried, done nothing at all.

She had Toby's contacts book, which he'd left in his desk at the Oak, and that helped her. She phoned round all their suppliers, placing new orders, establishing new lines of communication with the band managers, and everywhere she phoned people said how sorry they were, what a tragedy, if there was anything they could do she must let them know; everyone loved Toby.

Not quite everyone, she thought. She wanted to contact Jasper, see if he could shed any light on what had happened. But there was no entry for him under his Christian name in Toby's contacts book, and she had no idea of his surname.

Along with the house, all her clothes, all those sumptuous furs and beautiful designer outfits she had so treasured, all her jewels, all her expensive lingerie – everything was gone. She went up West and bought herself some essentials, but she took no pleasure in it. Once, she would have had Toby to advise on outfits, he had a fine eye and would say, 'No, darling, that's too outrageous' or 'Darling, that is so you.'

Now she shopped alone. Bernie hadn't been in touch since the day of Toby's funeral. The police called and questioned her about the fire, but what did she know? Precisely nothing. They also asked if she had anything else to say about the death of Sal Dryden, but she hadn't. She knew nothing about it.

The inspector gave her the same sceptical look he always did, and left. Then Jan came up to the office and told her Marcus Redmayne was downstairs waiting to see her.

'You been speaking to the Bill?' Clara asked her, more to distract herself than anything. Deeply though she grieved for Toby, when she'd heard Marcus's name, her stomach had actually flipped.

Jan shook her head firmly. 'I wouldn't speak to the Bill. Nobody on these streets would, that's a thing you never do, turn grass.' Jan looked disgusted at the very idea. 'They still don't know who done Sal then? Or Mr Cotton?'

'No. They don't.' Clara thought of the coins on the floor

in Sal's pitiful little flat. 'Probably a punter in Sal's case, don't you think? I suppose she was on the game a bit, on the quiet, was she?'

Jan's fleshy cheeks went pink. 'No, course not.'

Clara was staring at Jan's face. 'You're a rotten liar, Jan.'

'No, I . . . '

'Oh, come on. We both know the score. A lot of the girls turn tricks on the side, don't they.'

Jan said nothing. You had to admire her loyalty, and Clara did. 'Who's her landlord then? Do you know?'

'Same as mine. That bastard Frate. You seen him around town?'

Clara had seen more of Yasta Frate than she wanted to. 'Did he . . . what about rent collections? Did he go and get it himself?'

'Yeah,' said Jan with a frown. 'He likes to play the bully, does Frate. Likes to frighten people. He still collects mine now, gives me the creeps, think he's goin' to put a ruddy hoodoo on me or something.'

Clara stared ahead, thinking. 'He must have called, then, while she was lying there all that time. To get the rent. Had she fallen out with someone, Jan? Do you know?'

Jan shrugged. 'The filth asked me the same thing. And no, I don't. She seemed a bit more flush with cash lately, I do know that. She bragged to me about it. And . . . ' Jan's voice wobbled . . . 'The poor cow's *dead*, ain't she, regardless who did it.'

There was a knock on the office door. Both women jumped.

'Come in,' called Clara.

The door opened. It wasn't Marcus and irritatingly Clara felt disappointed. Towering, square-shaped Fulton Sears stood there instead.

'Sorry,' he said. 'Wanted a quick word.'

'I'll see you in a bit,' said Jan to Clara, and she edged past him out the door.

69

'What is it?' asked Clara. 'Only I'm really busy, so make it quick.' Clara looked pointedly at her bare wrist and frowned. Toby had bought her a Cartier Tank watch, engraved *With Love*. She'd adored that watch, treasured it, and she thought she'd put it down in the ladies' loos, but she'd gone back an hour later and it wasn't there. It had been like losing Toby all over again, losing that. She'd wept actual tears over it.

'I just wanted to say . . . ' Sears muttered.

'Yes?'

He gulped and managed to get the words out at last.

'I . . . I want you to marry me,' he said.

Clara stared, transfixed. *What?*

'I'll look after you. I'll make you happy. I'll . . . '

'Wait a minute.' Clara let out a gasping laugh of incredulity. 'What on earth are you saying?'

Fulton Sears cleared his throat. Stared at her. *His* Clara. She was so beautiful it hurt him to look at her sometimes. But that would pass, and they would be happy together, contented. They would have a fabulous life, own all these clubs, and he would run them for her, they would be a terrific team. He knew it.

'I want you to marry me,' he said again. He was clutching

his fists together, wringing his hands. This wasn't going the way he'd expected.

In his *mind*, her response would be to fall into his arms, be grateful, be nice.

But she was . . . oh fucking hell, she was *laughing* at him.

He thought of all the keepsakes back at the flat. Her handkerchief, her comb, and the new addition, her watch. Engraved *With Love* by that fairy Cotton. But he, Fulton, was a real man, he was what she needed, all he had to do was make her see that.

'Are you off your head?' Clara demanded. 'What are you *saying*?'

Fulton couldn't bring himself to repeat the words. She was looking at him like he was mad. He stood there, choking on emotion, unable to proceed, unable to take the words back.

'Look . . . ' Clara was clutching at her head. '*Look*, I'm terribly flattered. Really. But . . . I had no idea. And of course I can't marry you. In fact . . . I'm sorry, but in view of this I think it's best you go, don't you? Look for work elsewhere. I'll give you a good reference, of course. That goes without saying.'

What?

She was sacking him.

He wouldn't see her any more.

This was a disaster.

This was . . .

Someone was knocking on the door.

Go away, thought Sears. *My life is ending here, just fuck off!*

It opened and Jan put her head round it. She looked at him, at Clara.

'Marcus Redmayne's still waiting,' she said, and then she pushed the door wider, and Marcus stepped in.

And Fulton saw it then. He saw the whole picture, straight away. He pushed past Marcus, and nearly fell out of the room.

70

Clara braced herself to confront Marcus again. He always put her on edge. His masculine arrogance annoyed her. She was so miserable over Toby. And she was still reeling from that ridiculous thing that nutter Sears had said. Marry me! What the fuck was he on?

But then, maybe it was just as well he'd finally come out and said something stupid; she'd been unhappy having him around, staring at her, giving her that wounded puppy-dog look, for a long time, and *that* was the final straw, the perfect excuse to fire his arse.

As Marcus came into the office, she watched him warily. Uninvited, he sat down across the desk from her and said: 'Mrs Cotton.'

'Mr Redmayne,' she returned coolly.

'How are you?'

'Do you care?'

He smiled at that. 'How are things?'

'What things?'

'Oh, business, that sort of thing.'

'All fine,' she said.

'You must miss Toby's input.'

'Yeah.'

'Coping OK?'

'Yeah.'

'No trouble then?'

'Trouble?'

'Nobody trying to muscle in . . . ?'

'Nobody.'

He pursed his lips. 'Well, that won't last. Things can only get worse now.'

'*Worse?*' She stared at him like he'd gone mad. 'Would you mind explaining to me how the hell things could get any worse? Someone *gutted* one of my staff and the Bill have been sniffing around here ever since. Someone has *killed* my husband and the insurance people have said that he must have started the fire himself, which is a damned lie. I told them Toby was financially sound, he didn't need a cash payout from the house fire, but then they said he must have wanted to expand, buy more clubs or a yacht in the Med or some bloody thing, who knew? And so they won't pay out.'

'You don't think Toby could have started the fire himself?'

'I just told you. There was no reason.'

'Maybe he had a reason you didn't know about.'

Clara shook her head. 'No. I don't think so. And anyway, *if* Toby burned the house down – and he loved that bloody house as much as I did, so why would he do that? – then he'd have been a bit too clever to burn himself to death in the process, don't you think?'

Marcus leaned back in the chair, clasped his hands behind his head and stared at her face. 'You've thought a lot about all this.'

'Of course I have.' Her voice wobbled as she thought of Toby lying there, burned and dying. If someone had done that deliberately, she wanted them to suffer – just as he had. 'I've thought of nothing else.'

'Then let me give you something else to think about.

Things *could* get worse, Mrs Cotton. Far worse than you know.'

'Is that a threat?'

'It's a warning.'

'What, you think now Toby's gone the time is right for you to walk right through here, take over my clubs, offer me a pittance for them? Is that it?'

He shook his head slowly. 'I'm not talking about me. There are others. You're a sitting duck. So why not make it easy on yourself?'

'In what way?'

'Admit that running these clubs is a man's game. Accept that and hand the reins over to someone who can handle the situation.'

'Oh – like you, you mean?'

'I've said it before and I'll say it again, Clara – it's too dangerous. I can see that you want to carry on with it because it's making you money, but I'm telling you now, that won't be the case for much longer. You've already lost your house, why wait until you lose more?'

Clara sat back and studied him. 'It could have been you who set fire to our house, couldn't it? Or any other hustler with gang money behind them, come to that.'

'Clara.' Marcus dropped his hands onto the desk. He leaned forward and stared into her face. 'Take some advice, for Christ's sake. Give it up.'

'And do what?'

'I've told you what. You want money, I've got money. Let me take the strain, you just spend the loot.'

Clara heard Bernie's voice then, echoing in her brain: *That's all you care about, money!*

Marcus Redmayne thought that about her, too. And it wasn't true. She'd done what she had to do to crawl out of the filthy trap of extreme poverty Dad had left them in.

She'd married an old man to put a decent roof over her family's head, even if the idea did make her skin creep. Then
Toby, dear Toby, who had made her wealthy again, who'd
become her best friend. Her only friend. She hadn't cared
that he preferred bedding boys. After marriage to Frank, the
comfortable settlement that she had reached with her second
husband had in the end proved a joy for them both.

Now she looked up at Marcus with his intense brooding
black eyes and knew that any liaison with him would be very
different. Marcus wasn't old. He wasn't homosexual. And he
was nobody's idea of a gentleman. She'd heard about him
around town with a woman, a party girl, heard the rumours
that he kept her in a flat somewhere, nice and convenient.
And he'd want the same with her. Tuck her away, use her for
his pleasures, spoil her with mink and diamonds.

Then she thought of all the work she had done on Toby's
clubs, how she had turned them around, made them pay:
she had done that, no man had taken control. *She* had. And
. . . she had relished it. Enjoyed the work, found it fascinating and satisfying.

Because you've got nothing else in your life, said that voice
in her head again.

Well, that was true. Bernie wasn't talking to her, and
she didn't even know where her brother Henry was. All
she knew of Henry was what David had told her while he
was drunk, that Henry was into gangland life, working for
Sears out on the streets – and was that even true? Meanwhile, she was kipping upstairs in the Oak, because she was
temporarily homeless. And now Marcus Redmayne was sitting there like God Almighty, saying she could lose more
unless she played ball with him.

'Well,' said Clara at last. 'Thanks for the kind offer. But I
like running the clubs. And I have muscle if I need it.' Well,
she did. Sears might be gone, but there were others.

He was shaking his head. 'There's no loyalty, particularly not now Toby's gone. It's survival of the fittest and toughest around here, Clara. I mean it.'

Clara shrugged. 'Frankly, I don't give a shit what you think.'

Marcus straightened and stood up. 'That's your final word?'

'It is.'

'In that case I'll say goodnight –' He went to the door, opened it, then he turned back. '– and good luck,' he added, and went out and down the stairs.

71

Fulton Sears was trembling as he stood in front of the little altar to Clara Cotton. His boxer dog Charlie came nuzzling at his hand and he kicked him away. Charlie let out a whine and scooted off.

'Fucking *cunt*,' said Fulton under his breath. 'Fucking, fucking, fucking *cunt*,' he said, and he swiped an arm across the altar, then swiped again, back and forth, sending the watch flying, and the handkerchief, and the comb with her hair still attached.

'*Bitch!*' he yelled.

Charlie whimpered from across the room.

She'd laughed at him. And why wouldn't she? He'd turned dumbstruck as a lovelorn teenager when it came to actually talking to her, actually coming out and *saying* it.

Marry me.

Sacred words, beautiful words, and she'd laughed in his face as he'd spoken them, thrown it all back at him.

That *cow.*

And Redmayne. Marcus *fucking* Redmayne, strolling in there like cock-of-the-walk, so bloody good-looking, dark and tall and like fucking Heathcliff or something out of a bloody book, and oh there it was, the thing that had been under Fulton's nose all along, the thing he should have seen, if only he'd had the sense to look.

The way she'd reacted to Redmayne. All the little signs that were there, clear as day. Her lips parting; her pupils dilating. The downward flutter of her lashes. The inrush of her breath.

It was that bastard Redmayne she wanted. Not him. *Never* him.

He went through to the bathroom and stood there looking at his great ugly moon face in the mirror. Well, why would she want *that*? Tears were coursing down his ruddy heavy-drinker's mug now; he looked ridiculous, an overgrown baby crying for what it couldn't have.

I'll give you a good reference, that goes without saying, she'd said.

A reference!

He wandered back into the living room and Charlie cowered in his basket, accurately judging his master's mood. Fulton didn't kick the dog again. Instead he went to the scattered altar and snatched up the Cartier Tank from the floor. With a snarl he smashed the watch against the wall. Then when it failed to break he flew through to the kitchen, took a meat mallet from the drawer and pounded the damned thing on the worktop. It smashed now. But he kept on hitting it, over and over again, sobbing all the while, until it was nothing, it was gone, it was beyond hope.

And soon, *she* would be the same.

Her and Marcus *fucking* Redmayne.

72

It happened on a Saturday night, not long after Marcus came into the Oak trying to scare the arse off her. She was at the Carmelo, in the office upstairs, when there was a commotion down in the body of the club and Mitch came running in looking shit-scared.

'It's fucking Sears!' he shouted, then ran out again, leaving the door swinging behind him. From the club below she could hear glasses smashing, tables being overturned, screams and shouts.

Cautiously she went out and down a couple of the stairs and peered over. There were fist fights going on, men hurling punches, women running, shrieking in fear. Clara's heart seemed to stop in her chest. At the middle of the scene was a big bald man swinging left and right with brass knuckledusters, his hands red with blood right up to his wrists.

Shit.

It was Fulton Sears. He'd made that laughable proposal, and then vanished. She'd posted a glowing reference to his home address, and then heard no more.

But now he was back. And he was wrecking her club.

Limp with fear, Clara crept back up the stairs, trying to be invisible – but to her horror he looked up and saw her there. He was *grinning*, wallowing in this bloodbath like a hippo in the mud. Clara went back into the office and slammed the door closed. Instinctively she fumbled for a bolt or latch, but there was no lock on the inside of the door – why would there be?

So instead she jammed one of the chairs up under the handle and stood there, watching it, panting with fright. Then she snatched up the phone and dialled 999, all the while her eyes fastened to the handle, waiting for it to turn, for that monster to try to get in at her.

She could hear Toby's voice saying *Whatever happens in the clubs, we don't ever call the police. We never involve the Bill, not even the ones on the payroll. We sort things out ourselves.*

Clara paused for a long moment. Then she slammed the phone back onto its cradle. Looked around for a weapon, anything, to defend herself. Sears had gone crazy, there was no telling what he might do.

There was nothing.

Sweating, trembling, all she could do was stand there, listening to the chaos downstairs and waiting for the handle to turn. How long would a chair hold him? Not long. She stood there, staring, unable to look away.

Oh God, please help me, she thought, her heart hammering in her chest.

The noise downstairs seemed to be fading. She could hear only men's voices now, shouting, no more screams. Groaning, did she hear groaning? She thought she did. And . . . oh sweet Jesus, she could hear someone coming up the stairs. She could hear *him,* moving stealthily, creeping up the stairs. Her eyes were riveted to the handle. To the door. To the chair. She couldn't move, she couldn't even breathe.

The handle was turning.

Slowly, excruciatingly slowly, it was starting to turn.

With a desperate cry Clara flung herself forward, put her full weight against the flimsy barrier of the chair. Her chest was tight with fear. She was right up against the door, she could almost *feel* him there, right there, on the other side of it.

The handle continued to turn. She could feel his weight go against it, felt it shuddering through the wood. The chair bucked beneath her. He was going to get in here. He was going to get her.

She waited, sweat trickling down her temples, sliding down her back. She could smell her own fear. If he got in here . . .

There was no *if* about it.

He was going to.

A faint, deep-throated chuckle. She had laughed at him and now he was laughing at her. He knew she was in here and he was mocking her. She waited, watched the handle; he would come in soon, he would burst in here and kill her or hurt her, do something horrible, something awful to her. She could picture him on the other side of that door, barrel-chested, bloodstained, sadistic and out for revenge.

Oh God, please help me, she thought in desperation.

There came a ferocious kick at the door.

Clara flinched.

Then another.

Jesus, God, help, please help . . .

Then another kick. Door and chair flew inward, and Fulton Sears burst through into the room.

Sears didn't speak. He just stood there, breathing heavily. Christ, he was ugly. And she could smell the pungency of his sweat, stale and reeking – disgusting.

Clara froze. That was what Toby had always told her to do, and now she heard his voice in her head, clear as a bell.

If they're unarmed, let them come to you. They'll grab you from the front. Let them.

But she hadn't realized the amount of willpower it would take to do that. She stood still, rock-still, and this leering, stinking monster came at her like a bear, *rushed* at her – and grabbed the front of her clothes, sank his fists around the costly cloth, yanked her in toward him, yanked her right off her feet.

Clara saw blackheads all over his nose, his wet repulsive mouth, smelled his foul breath, she was enveloped in his stench. They were eye to eye for seconds. And then slowly an expression of puzzlement came over Sears's face. His dark bloodshot eyes, which had been glaring into hers, dropped to look at his fists.

There was blood streaming from his hands, dripping down over Clara's jacket.

'Uh?' It was a grunt almost, a sound of bewilderment, that came from his mouth.

On Sears's right hand, his thumb detached itself and tumbled to the carpet as the razor in her lapel bit cleanly through it and cut it off. *Booby traps*, she thought. *Thanks, Toby*.

Sears unclenched his hands automatically and stared at the deep, heavily bleeding cuts. A finger peeled off one hand and dropped to the floor. Then Clara shoved her knee hard into his groin and he doubled forward with a shout.

Clara ran. She stumbled past Sears and flew out the office door, falling over the chair, righting herself, throwing herself full-pelt down the stairs. She raced across the main body of the club, where people were still fighting, still throwing punches and chairs and bottles, and then someone grabbed her arm and she was dragged to a halt.

'Bastard! Let go, let go!' she shrieked, crazy with fear, and then she looked, and saw that it was Henry, her brother.

Their eyes locked. Clara was panting as if she'd run a mile. So was Henry. His fists were red, bruised, bloody. His face was flushed with exertion. Would he let her go? She didn't think so. He would hold her here until Sears recovered himself and came down and finished her off.

'Henry—' she started.

He let go of her arm.

Clara stared at his face for a second longer, then she turned and ran, out of the club, out into the night and away.

73

It turned out that Sears and his bully-boys had a busy Saturday night all round. As well as the Carmelo, they'd hit the Oak, the Paradise, and the CityBeat, taking in a gang of rockers to flatten the mods drinking in there with bike chains and knives. Half of the clubs had been decimated in one massive hit.

When she got back to the Heart of Oak early on Sunday morning, it was to find it in a similar state of devastation. Exhausted, wrung out with anxicty, she locked the doors (luckily the locks were still intact, they were about the only thing that was), then she crawled upstairs to the flat beside the office, which was untouched. She shoved one couch in front of the door and sprawled out on the other, and was asleep in minutes. If Sears's lot came and burned the whole damned thing to the ground, she'd die in it. And she was getting to the point where she was past caring one way or the other.

Her gloom increased on Monday, when only one of the staff turned up for work – porky little Jan, who seemed to have adopted Clara as her best mate.

'Where is everyone?' Clara asked her. She was downstairs in the decimated body of the club, trying to sweep some of the mess up with a broom. It was like fighting the tide, it seemed to achieve nothing.

'They won't come back,' said Jan. 'Bloody great warning off Sears? They won't come back after that.'

Clara looked at Jan in exasperation. She was telling her she had no staff. No muscle. No nothing. That she was truly alone, trying to clear up all this crap, without assistance.

'Then why are *you* here?' she asked.

'Came in to see how you're coping.'

'Oh, bloody fucking marvellous. Three of my clubs down the Swannee, and no staff to get them back up.'

'Nobody's going to work these clubs, not after Sears made his feelings plain. Everyone's shit-scared that he's going to come back in and beat them senseless. Toby's dead and everyone knows you can't handle the situation. You'd best just pack up, get out.'

Clara stared at her. She thought of confronting Sears last night in her office, and shuddered at the memory. But she had done him damage. She was glad of that. She thought of Henry down in the club, catching her arm. For a moment, she had thought he was going to betray her totally; but he hadn't.

'You don't understand,' she told Jan. 'I've lost my house. I've lost the income from three clubs. I can't *afford* to get out.'

Jan gave a snort. 'You can't afford not to. He'll see you off any way he can, you know. He'll walk right over you. Well, he has already, hasn't he.' Jan gave a nod of affirmation. 'Listen to me, Clara. Just *listen*. The sensible thing to do now? Go. While you still got legs.'

'What does that mean?' asked Clara.

Jan leaned in and said with ghoulish relish: 'He chopped the foot off a bloke over in Greek Street when he refused to pay out. Right off, *crunch*! Just like that. Left the poor bloke with a stump. He's on disability now, he's fucked.'

Oh shit, thought Clara.

74

A few days later, a bleak cold windy day well suited to her mood, she did a tour of the three clubs that had been hit. There was no one there in any of them – only wreckage, only carnage. Bloodstains and smashed mirrors, wrecked chairs and upturned tables, all the optics drained and smashed, all the stock pinched, slivers of glass all over the place.

This was a fucking disaster.

She went on to the clubs that were still in operation. Or they *should* have been. Only there was no staff in any of them. No barmen, no bouncers, no hostesses, no singers or dancers, no bands. Not a bloody soul. Clearly everyone had heard about what happened to the other Cotton clubs and they were taking no chances.

She finished up outside the Juniper. She unlocked the shutters and pulled them up; unlocked the main doors. Then she walked in. The place was empty, echoing, devoid of life.

She stood there in the deserted club and thought of the horror she'd seen happening in the Carmelo, with the thwarted Sears standing gigantic and bald and powerful with his hands red with blood. Seeing Henry there, standing shoulder to shoulder with that horrible bastard, had chilled her right through to her soul. No one had died that night, but that had been more luck than anything.

293

If Toby's and even Sal's deaths were a warning to her to clear out, she was still too stubborn to take the hint. Then she thought of Jan, telling her about the man who'd been maimed for life. It had been so vicious an act that she felt sick just thinking about it. But along with the revulsion she could also feel fury like a fire deep in her belly, like those leaping flames that had enveloped her beautiful house and her dear, sweet husband.

All her life, men had caused her grief. Her father, abandoning her. Henry, cheating, stealing from her, appalling her with his mindless acts of cruelty, standing among Sears's thugs trashing the Carmelo. Her own brother. Fucking *men*, thinking they could just plough through her like she was nothing. Then Sears with that fucking proposal. Marry me, or else. That cold, horrible chuckle on the other side of the door as Sears realized she was hiding from him, both of them knowing how easily, so easily, he could break down her flimsy defence and come in. But she'd marked him. Like a cornered cat, she'd lashed out and hit her mark, thanks to Toby and his tip on razored lapels. Anyone grabbed you by your coat, they cut themselves to ribbons. And it had worked.

Booby traps, he'd told her. And thank God he had.

As she stood there amid the wreckage, she heard a noise behind her. She whirled round, her heart in her mouth, expecting to see *him* there, massive and menacing, come to get her. There was no one there. Only the main door, banging shut in the wind and then opening again with a low creak.

Now she was jumping at shadows. Sears had terrified her, she was expecting him everywhere.

Had she really come through so much, suffered and tried and endured, just to have it all snatched away from her? She had scaled the heights but was now in danger of slipping right back down the ladder of bad luck and ending up in a situation that filled her with horror – poor again, destitute. All of it gone. And she had worked so hard to get here, *so bloody hard.*

The thought of ever again landing up in an overcrowded slum filled her with sick dread. That *couldn't* be allowed to happen. She flatly *refused* to contemplate such a future. She drew herself up, took a deep breath. No. She wouldn't let it happen. Clara Dolan only ever played by her own rules, never by anyone else's. Clara Dolan never stopped thinking, not for an instant, and she never let her heart rule her head. She told herself that, very firmly. It was the truth. She was cool and calculating, and she was going to stay that way.

The door banged open again, and she jumped.

Oh fuck this.

Sears thought he could just bulldoze over her, did he?

Well, she'd see about that. Clara left the empty club, closed it up again.

She had two things to do. And then they'd bloody well *see*, the whole sodding lot of them.

75

'I want to report something,' said Clara to the inspector, the same one who had come in asking about Sal's murder, the fire, Toby's death.

She'd gone to the police station and asked for him by name. Then she'd sat and waited with a drunk on one side and a prostitute bellowing about her innocence on the other, until he'd appeared and ushered her into a gloomy back office.

'Report what?' he'd asked, when they were both seated. He had a young fresh-faced PC with him, who produced a notebook and pencil and looked at her expectantly.

'Fulton Sears ran the doors on my clubs. Since my husband Toby Cotton died, he's taken it into his head that he's going to marry me and take over. I wouldn't play ball, so he wrecked three of them and I want you to charge him.'

The PC was writing in his notebook. The inspector looked at her sceptically.

'You actually saw him . . . ?' he asked.

'I did. And I'd swear to it in court.'

'You people don't usually refer things like this to us,' he said.

'Look, I'm a private citizen being menaced by a thug, and I want protection.'

'You have any evidence that Sears was involved in this?'

'I told you. I saw him in the Carmelo club the night it happened. And he saw me.'

'And what was he doing?'

'Hitting my staff and my punters. With knuckledusters.'

'You'd testify to this?'

'I would.'

Now both men were staring at her. This was something unique – a Soho club owner talking to the police about *anything* was a shocker. But to say they'd give evidence? It was unheard of. Of course they'd heard nothing about this before Clara's visit. The local plod had, as usual, turned a blind eye. And there were enough boys in blue on Soho's streets on the take to make sure that happened; a sad fact of life.

'Also, I think he could have been involved in the death of Sal Dryden.' If Clara was going to hang Sears out to dry, she wanted to make a thorough job of it.

'Why would you think that?'

'He was terrorizing her,' lied Clara.

'What does that signify? Nothing, in my book.'

'And what about the fire at my house? What about the death of my husband? Sears was trying to get to *me* – isn't it possible he wanted to get Toby out of the way?'

'All right. We'll look into it,' said the inspector, and dismissed her.

'What you been up to?' asked Jan when Clara got outside in the cold February fresh air again.

Clara clutched a hand to her heart. Jan had peeled away from the wall outside the cop shop, she hadn't expected to see her there. 'What the hell you doing?' she demanded.

'Following you.'

'Well don't, for God's sake. You nearly gave me a bloody seizure.' If Jan could follow her, so could anyone. That wasn't a nice thought. And she had just done what no one else in the whole of Soho would dare to; she had dropped the snubbed, rejected Fulton Sears in the shit. Gone to the law. Turned grass.

'What you been doin' then, talkin' to the Bill?'

'Go home, Jan. It's none of your business.' Clara started walking away, very fast.

Jan half-ran to keep up with her. 'You been tellin' them about what happened in the clubs? I don't believe it.'

Clara stopped walking and gave Jan a hard shove in the shoulder. 'Look,' she said hotly. 'Mind your own, Jan. This has nothing to do with you.'

'Well, pardon me,' sniffed Jan, looking hurt.

'I don't want to have to tell you again. Fuck off,' said Clara, and walked on. This time, Jan didn't follow. And Clara was glad. Jan was safest being a long way away from her. She was poison now, she'd gone beyond the pale, and soon everyone would know it.

One job down; one to go.

She went to the Blue Bird that night, paid on the door to get in just like every other normal punter, then asked the muscle in there to take her to their boss.

'Who wants him?' asked one of them, eyeing her suspiciously.

'Tell him it's Clara Cotton.'

The muscle disappeared upstairs, then reappeared within a few minutes.

'Come on up,' he said, and she followed him up a set of steep stairs and along a short gloomily lit corridor. He knocked on a black-painted door to the right, then opened it.

'Clara Cotton, boss,' he said, and ushered her inside, closing the door behind her.

'Well, this is nice,' said Clara, looking around the cramped office. Actually it wasn't nice at all. It was a box, full of filing cabinets, a desk, three wheelback chairs and Marcus Redmayne, who was leaning back in a ruby-red leather captain's chair behind the desk and staring at her like she'd appeared out of a puff of smoke.

Finally he said: 'What do you want, Clara?'

'That's an easy one,' she said, taking a chair and settling herself on it. 'I want you to marry me.'

76

The silence in the office was total for a long time. Finally Marcus said: 'Why would you want me to do that?'

Clara shrugged. 'You said it yourself, didn't you. You have money. I want money.'

'Right. I heard your clubs got a going-over.'

'They did. And frankly it looks like I'm going to have to cut my losses there and admit you're right. Running clubs is a man's game. And you know about the insurance, don't you. They claim the fire was started deliberately. It probably was. But *not* by Toby. They mentioned accelerants. Which all leaves me a bit short, as you can imagine. And so I thought, why not? You mentioned it first, and I suppose now would be a good time to take you up on the offer. You want the clubs. You said so.'

'And you've come here because you're strapped for cash.'

'That's right.'

'That's the only reason.'

'Of course.'

Marcus narrowed his eyes and stared at her face. 'Why don't I believe you?' he pondered aloud.

'I don't know. Why don't you?'

'I bet you're a great poker player.'

'I never gamble.'

'No, I think chess would be more your game. You only go for certainties.'

'That's right.'

He was shaking his head now. 'No, there's got to be something else, some angle you're not telling me about.'

'No, there's nothing.'

'Clara, Clara,' he sighed. 'If only I could believe that. I've watched you work people over before, remember. Poor old Frank, and then Toby. You're cold, you're devious. Do you ever stop thinking, plotting your next move? I doubt it.'

'So you don't want to marry me then? You don't want to have those clubs that were Toby's?' asked Clara.

Marcus sucked in a breath. 'You know what? Actually, I think I still do. Even if half of them *are* in a damaged condition. Of course I could just buy them off you now, couldn't I? With all this aggro and the state they're in, it would be a knock-down price. Or I could take them off you. For nothing.'

'Marcus. I need security. Your "muscle", if you like. Of course I expect to live to a certain standard,' said Clara. 'When we're married.'

He shrugged. His mother was the same. Give her gifts, give her the world, and she was happy. Nothing less would do. Fucking *women*. And marriage? When the hell had he ever mentioned *that*?

'I've never mentioned marriage to you. Not once,' he pointed out.

'No, you haven't. But that's the only way you get the whole package, Marcus. The clubs. And me. The *only* way.'

He was silent, staring at her face. She meant it. 'What the hell happened to you?' he asked at last.

'I don't know what you mean,' she said, but she did.

'I mean, what made you like this?'

Too much pain, thought Clara. *Too much shit.*

301

'I am what I am,' she said. 'So . . . ?'

Marriage! Fuck's sake! Marcus stared at her. Yes, he wanted her. Wanted the clubs, too. But *marriage* . . . 'I suppose the Registry Office would be acceptable? After all, you've already been married twice.'

'And widowed both times,' Clara reminded him. 'Not divorced.'

'What, you want a church wedding then?' Marcus couldn't believe he was having this conversation. Yes, he'd wanted her for a long time. Now she was here, offering it on a plate . . . but marriage. Christ! He'd been dodging *that* for years.

'No. I don't.' After all, this wasn't going to be a love match, was it. She wanted his money, he wanted her business and her body. The way he made her feel . . . well, she could deal with that. She *would* deal with it. 'I want an equal partnership,' she pointed out. 'I want that understood right from the start. Equal shares. I want just as much say as you in the way they're run, both your clubs and mine.'

He was watching her. 'Long engagement?' he asked.

'No. Short as possible.'

'Engagement ring, though.'

'Of course.'

'Preferences?'

'Diamonds.'

'Very marketable. And easy to remount.' He looked at her hands: no rings there at all now, except for a thin, worn gold band on her right hand. 'What's that then?' he asked, curious.

'Oh, this?' Clara looked down. 'My mother's wedding ring.'

'Yeah?' Marcus thought of his own mother. 'What's she like?'

'She's dead.'

Marcus nodded slowly. 'We'd better go shopping, then. Tomorrow.'

'Yes. First thing.'

'Where are you staying?'

'The Ritz.' The little flat over the decimated Heart of Oak was far too risky now.

Marcus sighed. 'Should have guessed.'

77

'People are saying that Fulton Sears has been pulled in for questioning by the police,' said Marcus when he picked her up in reception next morning.

'Really?' asked Clara, all innocence. 'What about?'

'Trashing your clubs, I heard. And that hostess who died? Sal something? Her murder. And maybe Toby's murder too.'

'Sal Dryden. Someone must have tipped them off then,' said Clara. 'I suppose.'

'Yeah.' Marcus followed her out, then hailed a passing taxi with its yellow light aglow. 'I wonder who.'

Diamonds truly were a girl's best friend. The inside of Asprey was as welcoming and as sumptuous as a fabulous box of chocolates, Clara thought, and she remembered all the times she had come in here with Toby, both of them happy as children playing in a sandpit as they selected this jewel or that.

It came over her, time and again when she least expected it. The memory of Toby, lying there burned, made ugly, ruined. Someone had done that to him. She shivered and had to swallow hard and blink back tears.

'You all right?' Marcus asked.

Clara snapped back to the present. She was trying on a diamond solitaire ring, mounted on a platinum band, and both the jeweller and Marcus were staring at her as she stood there, saying nothing. She fastened a smile on her face.

'It's lovely,' she said bracingly. 'Took my breath away for a minute there! Yes, this one. It's perfect.'

They had lunch at Claridges, then Marcus asked what she would like to do next.

'Look at the Crown Jewels,' said Clara.

'Haven't you had enough diamonds for one day?'

'I never have enough diamonds,' said Clara. 'Haven't you heard?'

'I'll book the Registry Office for next week. Friday. All right?'

'Fine,' said Clara. That would give her time to make her peace with Bernie so that she could have her as bridesmaid. She thought of Henry, but she kept seeing that scene at the Carmelo, Henry flailing about among the blood and the smashed wine bottles like he was enjoying himself – while he wrecked his sister's club. Like he was finally having his revenge on her.

No, she wouldn't be inviting Henry to her wedding.

When they got back to the hotel late in the afternoon, Clara was surprised to find she'd had an enjoyable day.

'I'll see you tomorrow,' said Marcus as he got back into the black cab and was driven away. Clara stood there on the pavement and stared after it. Her brand-new fiancé hadn't even tried to kiss her goodbye. And why would he? This was a business deal. That was all. Then someone tapped her on the shoulder. She whirled around, her heart leaping into her mouth. It was Jan.

'Christ, you again! What do you want?'

'Was that Marcus Redmayne?' asked Jan.

'Yes. Not that it's any of your bloody business.'

'Keep your wig on. I wondered where you'd got to, and I thought, where would I find Clara? Knew it had to be a posh hotel and I'd heard you mention this one.'

'Well done, Sherlock. What did you want to find me for?'

'Just to tell you what I heard on the street.'

'Which is?'

'That Sears is being detained.'

'I know that. Marcus told me.'

'Yeah? Well you better hope they *keep* detaining the bastard, because penny to a pinch of shit he's going to hear about your visit to the cop shop from one of his tame plods – and he ain't going to be too happy with you when he gets out.'

78

Next day Clara went to the address off Regent Street where Bernie was staying with her friend. It was a tall, airy house divided into flats; Sasha had the top one. Clara trudged up four flights of stairs to find herself in a small and stiflingly hot attic room that must once have been servants' quarters. There was a sweetish scent in the air; pot, she thought.

'Oh, hi,' said a languid brown-haired girl, opening the door to Clara. 'Come in.'

Clara entered. The room she stepped into was shabby, dust-motes floating in the diffused light that fell from an uncleaned window. Sofas were draped with red and orange rugs that had seen better days. Indian dream-catchers dangled from the ceiling and extinguished joss-sticks lay on the mantelpiece above the boarded-up fireplace. Two closed doors led off to what must be bedrooms. She wondered if there was the luxury of a bathroom in the flat or if they had to share with the other tenants on the floors below. The thought brought back memories – not good ones.

A door opened and Bernie stepped out, wearing a knee-length white skirt – no miniskirts for Bernie – with burgundy go-go boots and a matching long-sleeved blouse. Her copper-brown hair was loose on her shoulders; she looked lovely. But her eyes when they rested on her sister were cold, and her face looked lifeless. Her lower lip looked sore from bite marks.

'Hi, Bern,' said Clara.

Bernie said nothing. Sasha looked between the two of them, then said awkwardly: 'Let me give you folks a moment . . . ' and sidled off into the room that Bernie had just vacated, closing the door behind her.

'Can I sit down?' asked Clara.

'If you want,' said Bernie, making no move to do so herself. She moved about the place restlessly, pacing, picking up ornaments, putting them down again, shooting glances at her sister all the while.

Clara went over to the rug-draped sofa and sat down. She looked up at Bernie.

'So, what did you want?' asked Bernie, folding her arms.

'I'm getting married. Next Friday.'

'What? Who to, for God's sake?'

'Marcus Redmayne.'

'Doesn't he own nightclubs?'

'That's right.'

'I didn't know you'd been dating anyone. I didn't know you were engaged.'

'Oh! Yes, the ring. We got engaged – officially – yesterday,' said Clara, holding out her left hand. On it sparkled a vast white diamond.

Bernie stared at it. She didn't move any closer. 'You got engaged yesterday and you're getting married next Friday. That has to be the shortest engagement on record.'

'We saw no reason to delay.'

'What, you're madly in love are you?' Bernie laughed. It wasn't a pleasant sound.

'Of course we are,' said Clara.

'*You?* God, you're really having a laugh. You don't even understand the word love.'

Clara took a breath. Whatever she felt for Marcus Red-mayne, and she wasn't sure yet, next Friday come hell or high water she was going to marry him. And he was going to marry her . . . yes. To get her clubs. And her body. Because of course he didn't love her. The very idea was laughable.

'I wanted you to be my bridesmaid. If you would.' This was a gesture of kinship, an olive branch; she didn't need a bridesmaid, not for the Registry Office, but she wanted Bernie there with her, with all the bad blood between them forgotten.

'Right.' Bernie nodded. 'Let's see what we have here. You deliberately wrecked my relationship with a perfectly nice man who loved me, purely because he had no money. You've made me miserable, made me lose the man I loved. And now you pitch up here and ask me to be your brides-maid? Christ, you've got a nerve.'

'I did what I thought was best for you, Bernie. I always have. You know that. And he was a pervert or at least he *pandered* to perverts.'

'I loved David. I was happy with him. Then you had to destroy it, ruin it, because it didn't suit you. Clara, you really are a prize bitch.'

Clara stared at her sister. Bernie was pale, she looked washed-out, jittery, exhausted. As though misery had eaten into her soul.

I did that, thought Clara, and the knowledge hurt her. She'd done what she thought was best. She always did. But now she wondered if she had made the wrong call.

No, she thought. Bernie, her much-loved sister, con-demned to a poor life? No, she'd done the right thing. And sometime – not any time soon, she could see that, but some-time in the future – Bernie would meet a man who could offer her more than back streets and poverty and a seedy, disgusting living and then she would realize that Clara had been right.

'Look,' said Clara firmly. 'It's over, you and David. You'll find someone else.'

Bernie let out a harsh laugh. 'We don't all have your facility for making loveless marriages, Clara. I suppose that's what this one is, too? Like you and Frank? Like you and Toby?'

Now Clara was angry. 'Can you honestly say they were bad matches? Can you? My marriage to Frank rescued us from the gutter. My marriage to Toby saw us nicely set up.'

'And then it all came crashing down, didn't it.' Bernie was nodding, biting her lip, walking around the room while sending scathing looks at her older sister. 'So now, with Toby barely cold in the ground, you move on to your next victim. I bet he's rich.'

'He is,' said Clara.

She understood Bernie's anger, and it was best to let her get it out of her system. She deserved to be shouted at, railed against; but soon she hoped that Bernie would accept that she had been right, and let it drop. She wanted them to go back to being the sisters they used to be, close, loving each other – as they always had before that bastard Bennett had pitched up on the scene.

'Of course he's rich!' snapped Bernie. 'You wouldn't give him a second glance otherwise, would you? D'you still get them, Clara? The nightmares? The ones you used to get, about trying to find Mum in that big empty house? The one where you found her and the dead baby?'

Clara felt her jaw set with tension. Yes, she did. Hideous dreams, wandering and finally finding that horror, her dead mother, the dead baby, sitting by an empty grate, with the blood on the floor beside the chair.

Clara shook her head, brushed the thought of those night-time terrors aside. 'I would like you to be my brides-maid, Bernie. I really would.'

'Yeah?' Bernie stopped her pacing in front of where Clara sat and bent over, leaning in close. Her whole face was set with tightly contained rage. 'Well, you know what, big sis? You can just go and *fuck* yourself.'

'Bernie—'

'No, I'm not listening to you any more. You did the same thing to Henry, didn't you? You made an enemy of him, and now you've made an enemy of me. You're so fucking black-and-white in everything. There are shades of grey, you know. People fall in love without worrying about wage packets. People make mistakes—'

'What did I ever do to Henry? Except give him the best education I could afford.'

Bernie drew back. She went to the mantelpiece and leaned against it, her eyes glued to Clara. 'We've been in touch, Henry and me.'

'Have you?'

'Yeah. Actually, we're quite close now.'

Clara thought about Henry. The pilfering. The casual killing. The truculent, almost menacing air about him. And seeing him trashing her club alongside Sears. She stood up. 'Well, I wish you good luck with that,' she said.

'What an unforgiving bitch you can be, Clara.'

Clara looked at her sister. 'Bern. He's no good. Never was, never will be. You know my clubs were trashed? He was there, helping that thug Sears. I *saw* him.'

Bernie looked taken aback. 'Well, he couldn't have known the clubs were yours.'

'Oh, come off it! He was vandalizing my business, my livelihood, and he was enjoying it. So I'd say you ought to be careful, mixing with Henry. He's not right in the head.'

79

It seemed ridiculous, really, to spend a lot on a wedding outfit, so Clara found a white mini dress in Selfridges and thought that would do. There would be no bridesmaid Bernie; no Henry, for certain, although Clara supposed that Bernie would have told him that she was getting married. There would be two witnesses – Marcus's friend Gordon, and Clara, who had no real friends to speak of, had to fall back on dumpy little Jan.

'Really? You want me to be a witness at your wedding?' Jan had beamed all over her face when Clara asked her. And Clara felt mean then. She had asked Jan out of necessity, but Jan's delight at the invitation made her realize that she saw this as something special.

'What shall I wear?' Jan wondered instantly.

'A dress? A hat? Anything you like,' said Clara.

'What are you going to wear?'

'This,' said Clara, and there in her room at the Ritz she showed Jan her purchase.

'Oh! Well, that's nice.'

Clara looked at her. 'You think so.'

'Well, if it's only a simple do . . . '

Clara pursed her lips. She could tell Jan was under-whelmed with the dress. But actually she liked it. It was Empire-line, low-cut at the neck and with big bell chiffon sleeves and a deep ruby-red sash ribbon under the bust that tied at the back. The red suited her, suited her dark hair. Teamed with white sandals and a quickly purchased bouquet made up of dyed red feathers, it looked perfectly presentable.

She felt hurt by Bernie's rejection and uneasy at the renewed closeness between Bernie and Henry, like there were things going on that were under her radar, kept secret, tucked away. And Bernie leaping to Henry's defence as she did made her feel that somehow Bernie was condoning what Henry had done that night at Sears's side – and that wounded her.

The wedding party – her and Jan, Marcus and his goofy mate Gordon – pitched up at Chelsea Registry Office at eleven on the following Friday, sandwiched between a ten-thirty raucous wedding party with a bride in an elaborate gown, and an eleven-thirty West Indian gathering with big hats and huge happy smiles.

This is a bit different, she thought, as she and Marcus stood soberly before the Registrar with their two witnesses and said the words that would join them together as man and wife. They both knew the score. Well, Marcus knew part of it, at least. And the rest would become clear to him as time went on.

'You may kiss the bride,' said the Registrar at last, and it was over. Marcus leaned in and Clara waited. Then he kissed her on the cheek.

'Woohoo!' shouted Jan, throwing confetti when they were outside on the steps. She stuffed a handful of it down Clara's dress.

'Don't bloody do that,' snapped Clara, but Jan only smiled.

They hadn't even hired a photographer. All four of them piled into Gordon's car and went off to a restaurant for the 'wedding breakfast', which was a stilted affair because Gordon wasn't much for social talk and Jan couldn't open her mouth without effing and blinding like a trooper on a route march. The more she swore, the more Gordon seemed to sink into himself, shutting up like a clam.

Feeling tired by late afternoon, Clara went back with Marcus to the flat over his biggest club, the Calypso.

'There's going to be a party downstairs tonight,' he told her when finally they were alone.

Clara looked at him in surprise. 'What? You didn't tell me.'

'I'm telling you now. I told Jan before she left, Gordon's going to pick her up and bring her back at eight.'

Clara didn't want a party. They hadn't even booked a honeymoon. Remembering the disastrous Venice trip with Toby, she wasn't too sorry about that either. Clara sat down on the couch in the comfortable living room, feeling somehow deflated. She looked down at the diamond ring on her left hand, which now had a matching platinum band beside it.

Married again.

Suddenly she felt more than tired. She felt exhausted, drained of life.

'Drink?' Marcus offered, going over to the drinks cabinet.

'Thanks. Gin and tonic.'

He fixed a whisky and soda for himself and brought the drinks back over, placing them on the side table.

'Well, here we are then,' he said, fixing her with that dark unnerving gaze of his. 'So when were you going to tell me that it was you who shopped Sears to the Bill?'

Clara took up her glass and gulped down her drink. She'd expected him to find out quickly, but not *this* quickly.

'Later,' she said.

'Yeah, when I was committed. Gordon told me just before the ceremony started.'

'So why didn't you pull out?'

'As I told you – I want your clubs.' He took up his glass and drained it. 'You're a devious cow. I ought to kick you straight up the cunt for pulling a stunt like that.'

Clara shrugged. 'You married me to stop anyone else getting my clubs. I think that's pretty devious, too.'

'Sears is going to want your backside on a toasting fork for this,' he pointed out.

'But I have your muscle now. Your protection. Don't I?'

Marcus was shaking his head in wonder. 'Jesus! You've got some front.'

'You're using me for your own ends. What's the difference?'

Marcus looked at his empty glass. 'Want another?'

'Yes, please.'

He went over to the drinks cabinet and poured her a second gin and tonic.

'Not joining me?' she asked, when he didn't refresh his own.

'No,' he said. 'Things to do. I'll see you later.'

And he left her there, his new bride, on her own in the silence of the flat.

80

'Twistin' the Night Away' was pounding out of the speakers. Everyone who was anyone seemed to be in tonight. The place was heaving with celebs. Diana Dors was in a corner with her husband, and Ronnie Knight was on the floor, twisting with a blonde.

'I just spoke to Albert Finney!' said Jan excitedly when she came upstairs to the flat to see if Clara was ready. 'I was standing *this close* to him, can you believe it? Christ, I wish poor old Sal had lived to see this. She'd have loved it.'

It was an unpleasant reminder in the midst of what should have been a happy day. But Clara seemed to have lost her facility for happiness, so what did it matter? Another business deal had been done. She had slipped down the ladder a little, come perilously close to falling further, but here she was, back on top again.

Married to a rich man.

Richer than Toby, with more clout than Toby.

But Marcus was cold toward her. At least she and Toby had become friends. Somehow, she couldn't see that happening with Marcus. She felt too much for him; he felt too little for her. That much was obvious. It hurt her, but she'd make the best of it, like she always did.

'The police still haven't got to the bottom of it, you

know,' said Jan. 'Poor bloody Sal. Someone carved her up proper.'

'Jan,' said Clara sharply. 'Could we not talk about that, today of all days?'

'Sorry. So what are you going to wear tonight then?'

'I'm not changing.'

'Oh! OK. You're not going away then? You know, on a honeymoon like normal people do?'

'Shut up, Jan.'

After Marcus had left her alone, she had fallen asleep on the couch. When she woke, it was already dark; she'd been more tired than she realized. And he hadn't come back. She turned on a couple of low lights, went to the bathroom, freshened up. And still he hadn't come back. She could hear the party – well, her wedding reception – was in full swing, and she thought that traditionally the bride and groom ought to enter together, to cheers and catcalls . . . but he hadn't come back.

I stitched him up.

Yes. That much was true. What she had done was the equivalent of throwing a stone at someone and then ducking behind the nearest large object. Marcus was that object. And he was mad as hell about it. This was her punishment, being left alone.

'Come on. Let's go down,' she said, taking Jan's arm.

People were bopping around on the dance floor to 'Duke of Earl' by Gene Chandler now. Everyone seemed to be having a good time. Even while people were congratulating her, saying what a dog Marcus was and how the hell did she catch him? Clara found herself anxiously looking around for him, wondering where he'd got to.

Finally she spotted him over by the bar, talking to a big bruiser of a man. As she looked at him, his eyes roamed around the room and settled on her. He said something to the man, who turned his head and gave her a long look. Then Marcus moved through the crowds to where she was standing.

'Good sleep?' he asked.

'What?' Clara was wrong-footed. 'How did you know I was asleep?'

'I came back up. Saw you were dead to the world and left you there.'

'Oh.' She didn't like the idea of him watching her sleeping.

'Tiring, getting married,' he said.

'Yes.'

'Well, you'd know.'

'Third time lucky,' quipped Clara.

'Or unlucky, possibly.'

'You could always divorce me.'

'Yeah, I could. Right this minute?' There was a flare of anger in his gaze. 'I could do that. Easily.'

'Time to cut the cake,' said someone, and they were ushered over to the table where all the finger-food in the buffet was being devoured. They'd managed to get a cake at the last minute, a single-tier sponge, nothing fancy, and someone had stuck a little plaster bride and groom on top of it. A knife was fetched from behind the bar, and Marcus and Clara cut the wedding cake. Flashes fired as the guests took photos.

'Dance! Dance! Come on! Dance!' Jan shouted, and the rest of the crowd joined in, clapping and cheering as slices of cake were handed round.

'Oh fuck,' said Clara.

'Well it *is* traditional. The first dance as a married couple,' he sighed.

Egged on by the crowd, the DJ put on 'Love Letters' by Ketty Lester.

'Jesus,' said Clara as a space magically cleared all around them.

Marcus pulled her in close against the front of his body, linking his arms around her waist.

'Do we have to?' groaned Clara.

'Yeah, we do,' he said. 'Look happy. Pretend you're cuddling a wad of tenners or something.'

She wasn't sure how she felt. But that remark did hit her, right where it hurt. He would like to divorce her and he thought she was a money-grabbing tart. She didn't like him touching her, she never had; it unnerved her, made her feel somehow sad. But she put her arms around his neck and tried to look the adoring bride.

'You're stiff as a plank of wood,' whispered Marcus in her ear as the watching crowd stamped and applauded.

'You're a bastard,' said Clara sweetly. Her eye was arrested by a woman in the crowd, blonde and very pretty, who was staring at Clara as if she'd like to cut her heart out. 'Who's that?' she asked.

'Hm?' He raised his head, looked around.

'The blonde giving me evils.'

'Oh, that's Paulette.'

'Girlfriend?'

'Mistress.'

'And where's your family? Aren't they here to celebrate?' she asked sourly.

'I've only got my mother left,' he said.

'And she's not here?'

'She doesn't get around much any more.'

'What about your father?'

'Dead.'

'Do you have to hold me so bloody tight?'

'Just making it look real. Like we're in love.'

'You're cutting off my air.'

'I'd like to.'

'Stop it,' said Clara as the pressure of his hands increased on her back.

'Uh-oh,' said Marcus.

'What?'

The music halted with a screech, as if someone had torn the record from the deck. Clara looked. There was a confrontation going on at the far side of the room with the DJ and someone else. Punches were being thrown and the heavies were rushing over. And the interloper looked familiar. It was him who had taken the record off, and now he hurled it to the floor, where it smashed.

It was Henry, her brother.

81

'Don't hurt him,' said Clara as she and Marcus rushed over. Then she stood there and thought *What am I saying?* Henry deserved a thick lip at the very least, crashing in here.

'Don't . . . ?' Marcus hesitated, looked at her face. 'Wait up. Do you *know* this joker?'

'Course she bloody knows me,' shouted Henry, who was turning slowly purple as he was being clasped in a headlock by one of the bouncers. 'I'm her effing *brother*, you tosser.'

Marcus let out a breath. 'Let him up,' he told the bouncer.

The heavy reluctantly let Henry go. Henry staggered sideways, then started to grin at Clara's white, set face.

'Come to wish my big sis a happy wedding day,' he said. '*Another* one, for fuck's sake. You're making a bit of a habit of this, ain't you, Clar?'

'What, like you smashing my clubs up?' she retorted.

Marcus turned to the DJ, who was mopping at a cut over his right eye and trying to retrieve smashed bits of vinyl from the floor as the crowd surged avidly round, entertained by all this.

'Stick on something a bit lively,' he told the DJ. Then he looked at the bouncer. 'Bring him up.'

Marcus grabbed Clara's hand and led her to the stairs. The bouncer and Henry followed. The DJ put 'The Young

Ones' on the turntable, and gradually the crowd dispersed and people moved out onto the dance floor once again.

Up in the flat, the bouncer shoved Henry down onto the same couch Clara had earlier fallen asleep on. Marcus closed the door, but the bass beat kept thumping up through the floor.

'What the fuck you doing here?' asked Marcus, staring down at Henry in disgust. 'I know you. You work for Sears. Seen your ugly mug before.' Marcus glanced at Clara then turned back to Henry. 'So you're not a strong believer in family loyalty then,' he said to him.

'What, me be loyal to *that*?' asked Henry with a mocking grin at his sister. 'You want to watch it, mate, she'll fleece you then move on to the next poor bastard she thinks can keep her in better style. And all her bridegrooms have a habit of winding up dead, in case you haven't noticed.'

'But you came here to congratulate her on her wedding, you said,' said Marcus.

'Thought it might be fun to crash in.'

'Bernie refused to come,' said Clara with a sigh.

'Wanted her for your bridesmaid, didn't you. After you fitted up her boyfriend? Some bloody hope.'

'So why the hell *are* you here, Henry?' she asked irritably. 'To make a bloody scene, I suppose. As usual.'

'Nah, thought I'd deliver a message. Think you know who it's from.'

Clara's heart clenched. 'You mean that bastard Sears? The one I saw you with, wrecking my bloody club?'

'That's the one.' Henry grinned. 'Well, surprise surprise, sister dear. Despite all you said and all you did down the cop shop, guess what? The Bill aren't going to press charges. They've dropped the case. Of course they bloody have, most

322

of them are in Sears's pay, for God's sake, didn't you know that, you dumb bitch?'

'So you're saying . . . ' said Clara.

'I'm saying Sears is out,' smiled Henry.

Fuck, thought Clara.

'So now you and lover-boy here are really in the shit,' said Henry, smiling at both of them as they stood there before him. 'Your days are numbered. That's why I'm here, to tell you that. He's *very* upset with you. Turning grass, Clara! Becoming a copper's nark! So now he's gunning for the pair of you, new husband and new wife. I'd bloody well watch out if I were you. Sears is out on the streets again. And he's out for blood.'

82

The first thing Fulton Sears wanted when he got out of the cop shop was to send his boys to get Dutch Dave. They were pleased to do that, because it was better than hanging around Sears when he was in a temper like this, his bloody hands still bound up, red seeping through the bandages.

One of the doctors on their payroll had done the job, sewed up three stumps where once there had been fingers and a thumb. Sears was in pain, both his hands and his bollocks stinging and throbbing like a bastard. He was sniffing a lot of puff and coke to make himself feel better, and he was spaced-out but not mellow: he was sweet-tempered as a bear with a thorn stuck up its arse. He was *losing* it.

They found Dutch Dave in the pub, lounging at the bar with his tied-back mop of long grey-blond hair and his pale-eyed stare. He was a scrawny six foot four with skin like old tanned leather, and abundant tattoos. He looked like the sort of bastard you wouldn't want to mess with. During the war, Dave had been a crack shot, a sniper in one of the regiments, picking off Nazis with a rifle and notching up each kill on the barrel. He wasn't known for his patience or his tolerance. He was known for his aim.

'Dave?' One of Sears's boys sidled up to him. The Shadows were playing on the juke. Dutch Dave was drinking

Southern Comfort. He sent a pale, cold glance toward the one who had disturbed his drinking.

'Do I know you?' he asked.

The boy was one of Sears's best, tough as old boots, but he gulped. 'No, I'm a friend of Fulton Sears,' he said.

'Then you call me Mr Jones,' said Dave.

'Sure. Mr Jones. We got a job for you,' he said.

Dutch Dave drained his whisky and gestured to the barmaid to pour him another. She did so, then stepped away to serve another customer.

'I don't come cheap,' he said.

'Mr Sears knows that. He's happy to negotiate a price that suits you, Mr Jones.'

'So what's the job?' he asked.

'Little clean-up thing,' said Sears's boy.

'Clean up who?'

'A grass.'

'Yeah? Who?'

'She's called Clara Redmayne.'

83

When the bouncer had dragged Henry back out of the flat and away down the stairs, Marcus closed the door and looked at Clara.

'You know what you've started?' he asked.

'I had to do something.'

'No, you didn't. You should have come to me, talked it through. Now Sears is spitting blood and we're in the middle of a fucking war because I'm married to the woman who shopped him to the police. In case you don't realize, this is all bad news.'

Clara said nothing. She sat down on the couch, feeling wrung out. Sears was out for her blood. The cops – most of them, it seemed – were on his side, and who could tell who was good cop these days and who was bad? Her family had turned against her; Bernie had washed her hands of her, and Henry was now standing with her enemies, despite all she had done for them over the years.

And her husband – she had to remind herself, firmly, that Marcus was her husband, although this whole wedding day had passed in a blur that felt surreal – was looking at her like she'd gone crazy. Actually, he was looking at her like he wanted to wring her neck.

Marcus came over and stood in front of her.

'Jesus, you really are the fucking bloody limit,' he said, and grabbed her arm and pulled her to her feet.

'Get off me,' complained Clara as he pulled her closer.

'You *what*?' He was staring at her face from inches away, holding her tight to his body like he had on the dance floor. Now he started to shake his head, very slowly. 'Oh no. I don't think so. We're both fucked, thanks to you. Christ knows what Sears is going to come up with as a suitable punishment for what you've done, and the whole of Soho will be on his side now, not mine – and certainly not yours.'

'Look, I didn't—'

'You didn't think. Or maybe you did.' He was staring into her eyes from inches away. She could feel his breath on her face, could feel the angry tension in his body. 'Yeah, you did. I'm starting to know you, Clara, and it's scaring the shit out of me. You calculated who had the most clout and then you decided you would back me against him. Right?'

It *was* right. It was so right that Clara could only nod.

'You cold-blooded cow.'

'Marcus,' said Clara, bunching her hands against his chest. 'I'm sorry . . .'

She *was* sorry. She had hoped the cops would hold Sears and charge him. But his influence clearly went far inside the Bill as well as out on the streets. They'd just let him go, he was on the loose and it was her fault.

'No you're not.' He stared into her eyes for long moments. Then he said: 'Well, fuck it. If this is a sham marriage, so bloody be it. But I'm going to get *something* out of the damned thing, that's for sure.'

'What are you doing?' asked Clara when he bent and picked her up in his arms.

'What does it look like?'

'You've got guests downstairs.'

'Fuck 'em,' and he went over to a side door and elbowed

it open. He walked in, tossed her down onto a double bed, and then went back and closed the door behind him. 'Right, get undressed.'

Clara shook her head. 'Not until you calm down.'

'*Calm down?* I'm not going to calm down. I'm mad as hell.' He was throwing off his jacket, flicking off his tie, unbuttoning his shirt, kicking off shoes and socks, glaring at her all the while.

Clara sat there shaking her head.

'All right then.' Bare-chested, Marcus came over to the bed and yanked her to her feet. Then he ripped the wedding dress open, right down the front.

'What the *hell* . . . ' complained Clara.

'Shut the fuck up,' said Marcus, pushing the remains of the dress down her arms. It fell in a heap onto the floor, leaving her in white bra and pants. He reached round and undid the clasp of the bra. Clara slapped his face.

'Oh, so *that's* how you want it?' he muttered.

'Don't you bloody *dare!*' she protested as he pulled the bra off and shoved her back onto the bed.

'I said shut up.' He wrenched off her pants.

'You bastard! You like it rough, do you? Is this how *she* likes it too, that blonde bitch downstairs?' panted Clara, naked now and struggling to get off the bed. Angry as he was, she didn't feel afraid. She felt furious that he was treating her this way – but she also felt turned on and triumphant. She'd made him lose his cool. She was driving him crazy. She liked that.

Marcus threw off his trousers and pants and then shockingly they were both naked. Clara recoiled when his body touched hers, but he pulled her to him, held her very close to him, running his hands down over the small dip of her waist and over the full curves of her hips and buttocks.

'I'm going to fuck your brains out,' Marcus warned her.

'That's what I've wanted to do, ever since I first saw you in the front pew at Frank Hatton's funeral.'

'So do it!' Clara tried to appear nonchalant, but she was gasping for breath and the blood was singing in her ears, her pulse hammering like mad. When she looked at him naked, a sound almost like a whine escaped her. Marcus Redmayne in the nude was the most beautiful thing she had ever seen.

Oh Jesus, she thought.

He was narrow-hipped and broad shouldered, his skin swarthy and so much coarser than hers. There was black hair on his chest and it feathered down the front of his hard-muscled body. His nipples were dark as chocolate drops. Crazily, she found herself wanting to kiss them.

'You've got some bloody nerve, I'll say that for you,' he snapped out, and then he was on top of her, pushing her thighs open.

Clara writhed, trying to knee him in the balls.

Marcus twisted away then grabbed her wrists in one hand above her head, keeping her there, immobile. Pinned, helpless, Clara let out a cry of surprise as he eased his cock inside her. He pushed forward, frantically.

'You're such a bastard,' she said, half-laughing, half-gasping because this was something new, this was something *strange.* Now wasn't the time to think of poor old Frank's rare night-time attempts at copulation, or of the sexual desert that had been her marriage to Toby, but think of it she did. And this was completely different.

'Oh God,' she moaned as he thrust furiously into her.

'Finally! Something that shuts you up.'

Clara felt herself opening, softening, and then he released her wrists, cupped her breasts in his hands, roamed further, touched her, caressed her. She felt a sensation building, an entirely new sensation, and suddenly she was arching her back, and screaming, unable to stop herself, as the exquisite feelings pulsed through her.

'Jesus,' she cried out, and then he shuddered too, and she watched his face, saw him bite his lip, saw that quiver of extreme pleasure shake him, take him over.

Finally they lay still, like exhausted adversaries. All too soon Marcus detached himself, sat up on the edge of the bed, glancing back at her.

Don't go, she thought. But she was too proud to say it.

'Well, that's the marriage consummated,' he said, his eyes moving down over her body.

'Yeah,' said Clara, sitting up on the opposite edge of the bed. She felt strange, not herself – weak, somehow, her breasts tingling, her eyes filling with emotional tears. She reached down, picked up her ruined wedding dress. 'What am I supposed to wear now?' she asked.

'There's some stuff in the wardrobe,' he said, getting up, putting on his trousers.

The blonde's stuff?

She didn't ask. She didn't want to know the answer.

'I'll see you later,' said Marcus, pulling on his shirt. He picked up his socks and shoes and his jacket, and left the room, slamming the door shut behind him.

He hadn't uttered one single word of affection, not a word of warmth. No 'sweetheart', no 'darling'. No 'best beloved'. Her third wedding was following the pattern of the first two; it was going to be a loveless wasteland.

Best beloved.

That was what Toby had called Jasper. Clara sat there on the bed and all at once she had it: she reached for her bag, rummaged in there past the pan-sticks and the comb and her violet eye shadow, pulled out Toby's contacts book and slid her finger down the alphabetical leaves at the side.

She flipped it open at B. And there it was: an address and phone number.

BB. *Best Beloved.*

She'd found Jasper.

84

The party was still going on. She could hear and feel the heavy thudding of the bass through the floor as she got up from the bed and went over to the wardrobe.

Fuck Marcus Redmayne. If he thought she was going to cower up here like little wifey, firmly put in her place, after *that*, then he didn't know her at all. She rummaged among the garments there, wrinkling her nose at the blonde's flashy taste in outfits. Finally she pulled out a geometric-patterned black-and-white shift dress and yanked it on. It was too tight on the chest, too loose on the hips, and too short, but she didn't care. Angrily she tugged on her white sandals and went off downstairs again.

'You all right?' It was Jan, rushing up and looking at her like she might be in need of gas and air.

'I'm fine,' said Clara. 'Shouldn't I be?'

Clara's eyes were scanning the dancing crowds for Marcus. And there he was. With the blonde, who looked angry. They spotted her at just about the same time as she spotted them, and she saw the blonde's eyes go to the dress she was wearing, saw her mouth tighten, saw her say something. Although something churned in Clara then – something she refused to acknowledge as jealousy – she waved airily to her husband and his companion, and set off for the bar with Jan trailing after her.

'He looked mad as hell when you went upstairs,' said Jan, having to shout in her ear to make herself heard over Ray Charles's dark-brown voice singing 'I Can't Stop Loving You'. It was a real smooch number. But Marcus and the blonde weren't smooching, they were arguing.

Well, good, thought Clara.

'Gin and tonic,' she said to the barman. He poured the drink for her, and she downed it in one. 'Another,' she said.

'Easy,' said Jan.

'What'll you have, Jan?' asked Clara.

'Same, please. I thought he was going to beat the crap out of you, to be honest. The way he looked.'

'Well, as you can see, I am unbeaten,' said Clara, downing her second drink. What was it they said? *Bloody but unbowed.* Yeah, that was her. That was her entire life, right there.

Actually, she felt quite strange. Quite *different*. Sort of energized, almost glowing. She was aware that Marcus was watching her. And the blonde was, too. And more than anything, she was suppressing a strong desire to go over there and kick the blonde straight up the arse. Cheeky mare, staring at her like that.

'Who the hell is she then, this "Paulette"?' Clara asked Jan. 'Do you know her?'

'Sure I do. Surprised you don't. Marcus Redmayne's been keeping her for years. In some style, I heard. Got her a flat, a horse, even a fucking French poodle.'

Clara's heart sank. She wished it wouldn't do that.

'Yeah. And I guess she's pissed as hell that he's gone and married you,' Jan went on. 'Word is, she's been trying out the M word on him for as long as anyone can remember. Hey, did you know the old Bill came and saw me again the other day, about Sal?'

Clara's attention snapped back to Jan. 'What did they say?'

'Nothing much. Just checked my statement again.'

'Fuck! Is that all they've got?'

Jan let out a sigh. 'They said investigations were ongoing.'

'That means they haven't got a clue.'

'She didn't deserve that,' said Jan gloomily.

'No. She didn't.' Clara had liked Sal. She was common as muck, but gritty. Had she lived, Clara thought they would have become friends. She had admired Sal's in-your-face toughness, her refusal to kowtow. Now, all possibilities were gone. Sal was dead.

'Hey! You,' said a female voice over the tail end of Ray.

Clara and Jan turned as one and stared at the blonde who was standing in front of them. It was Marcus's blonde, the one whose dress Clara was now wearing. The blonde was looking it up and down. Then her eyes fastened on Clara's face.

'That's my dress,' she said.

Clara nodded. 'I know. Marcus said to help myself from the wardrobe upstairs, so I did. He ripped my own dress off me, so rather than come down here stark naked I had to put this dish-rag on.'

Clara heard Jan take in a whooping breath and start choking on her gin as she said that. The blonde's eyes grew wide. '*What* did you just say?' she demanded.

'Think you heard.'

The blonde was shaking her head. 'You don't even love him, do you?'

Clara gave a smile. 'He wanted my clubs and I wanted his clout and his money. So everyone's happy.'

'You're a cold-hearted cow.'

'It has been said.'

'I'm going to smack that stupid grin right off your fucking face,' said the blonde, and surged forward.

'No you're not,' said Marcus, appearing at her elbow and yanking her back, away from Clara. He glared at his new bride. 'Stop winding her up, will you?'

'*Me?*' Clara's mouth opened in innocent surprise.

'Marcus, fuck off. Let me *at* her,' raged the blonde, struggling to get free of his grip.

'You ought to keep that in a cage,' said Clara, watching the blonde in fascination. 'I've seen chimps with more self-control. What was her name again? In case our paths should cross.'

'I already told you. This is Paulette,' said Marcus, as Paulette started to scream swear words at his wife. She writhed and struggled, and dropped her clutch bag, which opened on impact, spilling out a Tampax, a small bottle of French perfume, a broken-toothed comb stuffed with dark-rooted blonde hairs, and a shower of coins.

'You've got to admire that vocabulary,' said Clara as small change rolled in all directions and settled on the floor. Just like it had when young Henry stole the pound note from her purse. Just like it had when they'd found poor Sal's butchered body in that disgusting hole she lived in. Something nudged at her brain then, but it was there and then it was gone.

'Bitch! Cow! You want to watch your *step*!' Paulette threw over her shoulder as Marcus snatched up the bulk of the items and marched her away, toward the club exit.

Jan was nearly choking, she was laughing so hard. 'I thought she was going to rip your head right off your shoulders,' she giggled, gathering up the coins from the floor.

Clara took the coins off Jan and put them in the staff tip box. She wasn't smiling. She'd already dismissed Paulette from her mind. She was thinking about Henry, and about David and Jasper; and she was also thinking that if the Bill didn't shift themselves and get some answers then she would get to the bottom of what had happened to poor Sal, and to Toby, her best friend in all the world, if it killed her.

85

Someone was knocking at the door but Jasper Flynn couldn't wake up; couldn't face the day. The sunlight was coming through the curtains and he knew he'd have to get up sooner or later, but right now? He didn't want to. With shaking hands he reached out to the bedside table and with sore, aching eyes he peered at its surface.

There was a little coke left, misting the wood grain like talcum powder. He was going to have to stir himself at some point today, if only to get to his dealer. He snatched up the fiver, rolled it unsteadily into a cylinder and inhaled the last of the dope. Then he lay back, dropped the fiver, and then . . . ah, *bliss*.

Bastard banging at the door, but did he care? He felt better – lighter than air. Gone was the rage and the depression and the pain that had sapped him, robbed him of all strength and purpose, ever since Toby's hideous death. He couldn't think about that, he *refused* to think about it.

These good feelings wouldn't last long, he knew that, but for now . . . ah, fuck the world. He felt *fine*.

Someone was rattling the letter box now.

'Jasper! You in there? Open this bloody door.'

It was a woman's voice.

Maybe he would get up. Maybe he would answer it. He felt a little stronger now. Slowly Jasper pulled on his grey silk robe, the one Toby had given him for his last birthday, the last present he would ever receive from his lover . . . *Ah, God, don't go there, don't think about it*, he told himself.

The coke thrumming through his brains, he fastened his robe and stumbled out into the hallway. 'All right, I'm coming,' he mumbled, and shot the bolt back and opened the door.

She was standing there.

'Oh for fuck's . . . ' moaned Jasper, thinking that this was too much, this was insult on top of injury. Toby's *wife*, for Christ's sake. That fucking *bitch* was standing there. All right, he'd known Toby would have to appear straight to get on in his business, but when Toby had said he was going to marry some bit of skirt, Jasper had hit the roof. He'd been mad with jealousy. *Demented* with it. And now she was here.

'What the fuck do *you* want?' he demanded.

Clara pushed past Jasper and stepped into the hall. She noticed that his eyes were swivelling like he was drunk or something, his pupils were massive. He was swaying on his feet. His blond hair was dishevelled.

'Sorry, did I wake you up?' said Clara. She glanced through the open bedroom door, saw the disordered bed, the rolled-up fiver, the dust on the bedside table. Jasper was a cokehead.

'You did, as it happens,' said Jasper, pointedly closing the bedroom door with a slam.

'It's two in the afternoon.'

'So?'

'Can we sit down? Talk?' said Clara.

'I've got nothing to say to you. And how did you get this address?'

'Out of Toby's contacts book, of course. *Best Beloved. BB.* That's you. That's what he called you, wasn't it? Come on, for God's sake, talk to me. We both loved Toby.'

Jasper's face twisted in a sneer. 'You didn't love him. He wouldn't have married you at all if he hadn't been forced to.'

'I loved him as a friend. He was my *best friend*. I know that's very different to what you had with him, and I'm sorry. Losing him that way . . . it must have been horrible for you.'

Jasper's face lost some of its truculence. He leaned back against the wall and folded his arms over his skinny chest and stared at her. 'So what do you want to talk about?' he asked.

'Do you know anything about it? The fire? What happened that night?'

'How would I?'

'You weren't there? Only I know that you two sometimes met when I was busy round the clubs. Were you there that night?'

Jasper gulped. Clara could see this was painful for him. 'I was there at eight. We had dinner. I went home at about ten. He was alive then.' A glint of tears shone in Jasper's eyes. 'He was alive, and he was well, when I left him. We were talking about meeting up the next day. He kissed me good-night in the hall and your sister came in and he pulled away, which made me mad. We argued. I'm ashamed to say it, but we did. About that and about you, of course. I hated that he'd gone down that route, trying to lie to the world. I gave him a very hard time about it. It all seems stupid now.'

Clara kept quiet; let him speak. So they'd argued. Had Jasper become so upset that he'd lost all reason and killed the object of his adoration?

'But then,' Jasper gasped, stifling a sob. 'The fire. I didn't know anything about it, not a thing, until I showed up at the house the following day and found it burned to the ground.

Some people who lived in the road told me what had happened. That he'd . . . oh Jesus, that he'd *died*.'

'So you left at ten?' Clara was eyeing him closely.

Jasper's mouth dropped open. 'What, you think *I* would do a thing like that? We argued a lot. But we loved one another. I only wish to God he'd never set eyes on *you*, never seen you as a solution to his problems. I hated that he went home to you, that you were his wife, and I was only a bit on the side, a *nothing*. It's true we had a fiery relationship. Oh shit.' Jasper realized what he'd just said and clamped a trembling hand over his mouth. Tears spilled out of his eyes and ran down his cheeks. Then he tried to gather himself. He dropped his hand and stared at her. 'I would *never* hurt him. I don't know how you could even think that.'

'I don't think anything, Jasper, I'm trying to make sense of it, that's all,' said Clara, wondering if he was telling the truth. If he was into drugs in a big way, who knew what lies he was spouting? Who knew what might go on in that fried brain of his? 'The insurance people wouldn't pay out, you know. They said the fire had been started deliberately. They talked about accelerants.'

'Was it you then?' snapped Jasper.

'*What?*'

'You had the most to gain by his death, didn't you. The insurance and everything. And it wasn't a proper marriage at all. Maybe you wanted to get him out of the way so that you could get your grasping hands on everything he had.'

'No,' said Clara firmly. 'Not true. I wouldn't hurt Toby, any more than you would. You're talking rubbish. If I'd wanted to do a thing like that – and I never would – I would have been a damned sight more subtle. No accelerants, for a start. Because someone used them, the insurance company are saying I can go and fuck myself, they're not paying a penny. They're sure it was started deliberately.'

'Maybe Toby started it?' said Jasper, rubbing a hand over his brow. It was obvious the hit from the coke was wearing off now, and all this talk of Toby's death was exhausting him.

'But why? Toby loved that place as much as I did.'

'Then someone else. But who?'

'I don't know.'

'Well, will someone find out? Please?' Jasper gave a hitching gasp and wiped at his tear-streaked face. 'Whoever did this, I want them to suffer. I want them *dead*.'

86

'Where the hell have you been?' asked Marcus when she got back to the Calypso.

Clara looked at her husband with surprise. After the wedding reception had ended last night, she'd slept alone; he hadn't come near her again. Then she'd got up, washed and dressed, had a bit of breakfast and gone off to see Jasper in a taxi.

Now she was back, and none the wiser for her visit, and Marcus was sitting in the main body of the club with all his boys, including weedy little speccy-four-eyes Gordon, gathered around him, and she walked in and got both barrels, straight between the eyes.

'Visiting a friend,' she said, and walked on past him because that was all he was going to get. He didn't *own* her, for Christ's sake.

'Don't do that. Don't wander off alone,' said Marcus.

'What, you think Sears is going to jump out of a bush and grab me?' asked Clara with a laugh.

She didn't *feel* like laughing, but she had to maintain a front. It had taken a lot of bottle to walk out of the door this morning, knowing that Sears had it in for her. And she wondered about Sears and the house fire that killed Toby, too. Had he been behind that? It was possible. He'd had some sort of weird fixation on her, and she'd been married to Toby. Maybe Sears had killed him, wanting him out of the way to clear a path to her. The idea made her shake with rage.

'Let's take this upstairs,' said Marcus, standing up and coming over to her.

'Yes, why don't we?' said Clara, and preceded him up the stairs and into the flat over the club.

Marcus closed the door and leaned against it and looked at her.

'Are you totally bloody crazy?' he asked.

'Me?' Clara threw her bag onto a chair then turned and faced him. 'Excuse me, *I'm* not the one who invited my bloody *mistress* to my own wedding.'

'I didn't invite Paulette. She turned up. What was I supposed to do, kick her out?'

'Yes.'

'What, are you jealous then?' He was watching her closely.

'Oh, don't flatter yourself. But I do expect to be treated with a little respect, and I don't think that was very respectful.'

'Oh, I am sorry, your majesty,' he said.

'Don't mock me.'

'Clara.' Marcus pushed away from the door and came and stood right in front of her.

'What?' She eyed him warily.

'I don't think you understand the situation here. I'm not old Frank the rent man and I'm not a poofter like Toby.'

Clara's stare hardened. 'Don't call him that. Don't you *dare.*'

Their eyes locked. 'Good Christ,' said Marcus. 'You actually felt something for that poor bastard, didn't you? Perhaps you have got a heart and not a block of ice after all.'

Clara gulped. Every time Toby's name was mentioned,

she felt close to tears. It crucified her that his life had ended so horribly. But she wasn't going to start trying to explain her feelings to a hard nut like Marcus.

'Just don't call him that. *Never* call him that. OK?' she snapped.

'Clara?'

'What?'

'You can't order me about and expect to get away with it.'

'I wasn't aware that I was ordering you about.'

'You were, you stroppy mare. So come on. What's the big mystery? Where did you get to?'

'I went to see Jasper. Toby's boyfriend.'

'Why?'

'Because he might have known something about the fire. He was there the night it happened.'

'What did he tell you?' Marcus looked interested now.

'He left at ten. According to him, Toby was fine then. By two o'clock, when I got home, the place had burned down and Toby was as good as dead.'

'Maybe he's lying,' said Marcus.

'Maybe. They were arguing, he said. About me, about Toby's marriage to me.'

'Or maybe it's down to someone else.'

'Don't say me, for God's sake. That's what Jasper said.'

'What about Toby himself? Christ, Clara, he had enough secrets, God knows. Was Jasper his only boyfriend, do you think? Maybe there was something else going on.'

'I can't see why Toby would start the fire to get an insurance payout,' said Clara, holding her head in both hands. 'I've thought about it over and over again, and I just can't see it. He had no money problems. I knew the business inside-out, it was thriving. And he adored that house. Besides, he was clever. You know he was. He'd have had the sense to do the thing a lot more carefully than that, if he was going to.'

'Sears then. What about him? He was trying to frighten Toby into handing over the clubs, and it got out of hand. Or maybe he didn't realize Toby was at home that night. And speaking of Sears . . . '

'Yeah? What about him?'

'Seriously. No more wandering off alone. I've been hearing rumours around the streets.'

'About what?'

'They're saying he's put a contract out on you.'

'He *what*?'

Marcus nodded. 'There's a price on your head. So no more fucking around. Word is, you're to be delivered up to Sears, Clara. Dead or alive – but preferably dead.'

Clara sat down hard on a chair as he spoke the words. 'What did you say?'

'He wants you dead. Big surprise.'

'What should I do then?' she asked blankly.

'Stay close. In fact,' Marcus gave a winning smile, 'I think it's time we did a little socializing – as a married couple.'

87

Marcus's mother was a tiny withered thing who lived in a stately mews house in Chelsea. She was dressed for her son's visit with his new bride in a dark navy velvet gown that had probably cost a working man's weekly wage. The gown had a neckline edged with creamy guipure lace. She had cold black pebbles where her eyes should be, and a perfectly coiffed head of startlingly white hair. She opened the door to them, supporting herself on an ivory walking stick.

'She's older than you'd expect,' Marcus had warned Clara on the way over in the E-type. 'She had me when she was forty-nine.'

'Black hair!' said Marcus's mother, leading the way into an overheated sitting room where she sat down by the fire. She laid the walking stick at her feet and stared at Clara. 'Well, well. She's got black hair, like yours. Like mine, too. I had black hair once. I was a beauty, you know.' The gimlet eyes held Clara's. 'An absolute catch. But there's something Celtic there, maybe Irish, with her pale skin and blue eyes. It's a pretty effect, anyway. Whereas in us it's dark eyes and dark skin to go with the hair. I think *that's* something Latin.'

'Hello, Mrs Redmayne,' said Clara, wondering how this doll-like creature could have produced a fabulously robust bruiser like Marcus. She was glad now that Marcus had told her about the late age at which his mother had him – this woman looked old enough to be his grandmother. And she had a chilly judgemental glint in her eye that made Clara decide instantly that she didn't like her at all.

'Mother,' said Marcus, going to her chair and kissing her cheek, while his mother's eyes remained glued to Clara.

'She's got a confident look about her,' said the old lady, and it didn't sound like a compliment. Clara thought that this old cow would have preferred someone like Bernie – compliant, meek, easily intimidated – someone she could dominate.

'Well . . . ?' the old lady said, and held out her hand.

For an instant Clara thought the woman was holding out a hand to her; but then Marcus produced a blue Tiffany box tied with white ribbon from his jacket pocket and laid it in his mother's palm. She didn't open it. She merely nodded, lips clamped tightly together in grim satisfaction, and put it aside on the small table beside her chair.

'Sit down,' said the old lady.

Clara sat. *This is going to be a* long *afternoon*, she thought.

'So – what do you think of her?' asked Marcus on the journey back to the Calypso.

'She's a monster,' said Clara.

Marcus smiled. 'Yeah. Thought you might have that in common.'

'*I'm* not a monster.'

'Don't suppose she thinks she is, either.'

Clara stared at his face, intent on the traffic. 'What, you think I'm like her? You think I'm like *that*? You think that every time you see me – I'm guessing it is every time, isn't it? Yes, I thought so – you have to present me with a gift? That's not true, Marcus. Not at all.'

He glanced at her. 'No?'

'No.' Clara thought of trying on the jewels with Toby, the great laughs they'd had. Toby had gifted her with rubies, emeralds, diamonds – and most of them had been lost in the fire. Worse – far, far worse – he had been lost too.

Some things you just couldn't replace.

She was starting to know that now. She had no family to speak of any more. She'd lost Frank, who had at least been kind to her, and Toby, who she'd loved dearly. Now, what did she have? A husband who married her as a business deal, to get her clubs and have her in his bed.

She'd listened to him talking to his mother today and thought, *Yes, that's what drives him.* He had told the old witch that he'd taken over Clara's clubs. Not strictly true – they were equal partners – but Clara hadn't argued the point. And she had seen something like hope in his eyes as he'd said it. But his mother had seemed unimpressed.

I bet he's been trying to impress her forever, thought Clara. *Trying, and failing. And bringing gifts to her feet, like a dog that longs for a pat of approval from its master.*

'We were bombed out during the war. I must have been, oh, fourteen, fifteen,' said Marcus as he drove through the traffic. 'And the thing I remember? She didn't look for me to see I was all right. When it was over, I found her grubbing about on her hands and knees, searching for her jewellery box among all the bricks and shit and stuff that had blown in on our fucking heads. That was all that mattered to her.'

Marcus drove into the alley beside the club's side entrance, and Clara got out as soon as he killed the engine. She heard a 'pop' like a kid's toy gun going off, and something punched into the open car door, sending a quiver of vibration up her arm.

'What the f—' she said in surprise, and then Marcus

came barrelling around the front of the car and knocked her flat to the ground.

Another 'pop' and a second hole appeared in the gleaming red finish of the car door. Another one zinged off the top of the bonnet.

'Keep down,' said Marcus by her ear.

What else could she do? Flattened under Marcus's weight, she could only lie there and wait for one of those bullets to find its mark. *Someone was trying to shoot her.* She couldn't believe it, but it was true.

Someone was trying to *kill* her.

'Crawl around the front, we'll get to the other side and then we've got some better cover,' said Marcus.

Clara was almost too scared to move, but Marcus shoved her forward and she moved around the motor's long bonnet. Another shot dinged into the car, and she had a horrific flash of it thudding not into metal but into her body, smashing its way into her flesh, her bone, her veins, stopping her heart.

'Oh Christ,' she gasped as they got round the other side, in between the club door and the car. The shots were all hitting the far side, whoever was shooting at them must be up in the office building on the other side of the alley, maybe even up on the roof of that building. One of the bullets hit the front tyre, and the E-type sagged wearily.

When the club door opened, Clara nearly bolted for it in panic.

'Wait,' said Marcus, taking hold of her arm.

Another shot fired. Another. Then another.

'He'll have to reload now. Let's go,' he snapped, and shoved her ahead of him toward the club door.

It was the longest few steps Clara had ever taken. At any moment she expected to feel the numbing impact of a shot in her back, but none came. She was in the door, Marcus running behind her, and then it was slamming shut and the sniper had had time to reload, because two shots crashed into the closed door as they backed away from it.

'Jesus!' she cried out in terror, clinging on to Marcus.

'It's OK, it's over,' he said, and his face looked bleached, almost grey; she'd never seen him looking so grim.

Over? Of course it wasn't.

Clara wiped a hand over her eyes.

Someone had just tried to put a bullet in her. She didn't know who'd fired the gun, but she certainly knew who'd ordered it.

88

'You want to go *where*?' asked Marcus the day after the shooting. He'd been out for most of the day, not even telling her where or what he'd been up to.

'David Bennett's studio, I want to talk to him.' Clara's voice was edged with irritation. She'd been about to go out to hail a taxi, but her legs had turned to jelly at the thought of stepping out of the door. Now she was getting the third degree.

'Someone tried to kill you yesterday,' Marcus reminded her.

'I know that!' she snapped. She was trying not to think about it. Trying to carry on as normal. Only nothing felt normal any more. She was relieved that Marcus hadn't come near her last night; on top of all that had happened, it would have been one shock to the system too many. Irritatingly, though, while there was relief, there was also this niggling feeling of *so where the hell was he? With sodding Paulette?*

'And you were going to walk out the door alone?'

'I'll go mad, cooped up in here.' Actually, she didn't think she *could* have gone out alone. She felt limp with fear at the thought, and she hated that.

'Better cooped up than dead,' said Marcus.

'So come with me. Bring the pit bulls too.' Clara indicated

the two burly men who were propping up the bar while their boss and his wife were having this conversation. 'Let's go mob-handed, why not?'

'Is this important?' asked Marcus.

Clara thought of Sal, eviscerated. Poor bloody Sal, selling her body for profit and winding up dead for her trouble. All for the entertainment of men who would snigger and wank over the images of her in those stark black-and-white shots.

For a moment Clara felt too choked to speak. Instead, she pulled a couple of the remaining photos out of her bag and showed them to him. 'That girl there – she used to work for me. She's dead now, murdered. So yeah, it is important.'

Marcus stared at the prints. Then he handed them back to her. 'OK. Let's go.'

'Oh Christ, not you,' said David when Clara stepped into his studio's tiny reception area.

He was sitting at the desk, matching up negs to proof prints. There was a stack of wedding albums on one side of the desk, a pile of 8 x 6 pictures on the other. He looked impatient, annoyed.

Probably misses Bernie's input on the grunt work, thought Clara. *Well, good.*

Marcus followed her in. The pit bulls stationed themselves outside the studio door.

'Yeah, me again. Wanted to ask you something,' said Clara.

'What, for Chrissakes? Can't it wait? I'm up to my arse here . . . ' The phone started ringing and he snatched it up. 'David Bennett Studios, can I help you?' he asked in a completely different voice. He was silent, listening. Then he said. 'You see, I did explain this to the bride. To your daughter, yes. It's what's known as anomalous reflectance. That is, the bridesmaid's dress was lilac, but it's come out pale blue. It's caused by the chemicals in the printing reacting to certain dyes in the dress.'

David rolled his eyes and rubbed at his brow as the person at the other end of the phone spoke again.

'We tried that, adjusting the colour balance, but the *other* bridesmaid's dress is pink, and adding extra cyan made that too dark and also gave a pink cast to the bride's white dress, so it was no good. It *does* happen, I assure—'

Marcus snatched the phone out of David's hand and threw it back onto the cradle.

'What did you do that for? That was the bride's mother, now she's going to think I put the phone down on her. Can't this wait?'

'No, it can't,' said Clara. 'Those pictures of Sal . . . '

'Not this again. The police have asked me about this. Now you. I don't know a fucking thing. I took some photos, I was paid for them. That's all.'

Marcus stood there, looking down at David. 'And who is this anyway?' David demanded. 'What's with the goons out-side? What—'

Marcus leaned over and grabbed the front of David's collarless granddad shirt. He pulled David over the desk. Some of the albums thunked onto the floor. Marcus stared into David's startled eyes from inches away.

'I'm Marcus Redmayne,' he said. 'That's who the fuck I am. Those are my goons outside the door. This is Clara Redmayne, my old lady. So you keep a civil tongue in your head when you speak to her. Got it?'

'All right, keep your hair on!' David blustered, struggling against Marcus's grip.

Marcus shoved David back down into his chair. He sat there, winded, eyes wide, looking from Marcus to Clara and back again. Marcus stepped back, waved a hand to Clara, indicating that the floor was hers.

Clara didn't know whether to be impressed or annoyed.

'Those pictures,' she said, looking down at David like he was shit on her shoe. 'I want to know details of who you sold them to. Did someone actually commission the damned things to start with?'

'I've said all this. The police gave me a caution over it. People have asked me before about taking stuff like that. I turned them down. But when I needed the cash to get started with this business . . . '

'Yeah, and then you forgot your high-minded scruples, I know. When did you take them?'

'Last summer. Around June.'

Just a few months before Sal was killed, thought Clara.

'You got off lightly, didn't you,' she said. 'People can get banged up for producing pornography, David. And when it involves kids, the cons inside can get rough.'

Clara heard Marcus sigh heavily behind her. She ignored him.

'All right, all bloody right!' David burst out. 'Jesus, like any of it matters any more anyway! A cellar club owner paid me to take them and he said I could sell them on afterwards, reprint them anytime I wanted because it made him look good.'

'How the hell could it make him look good?' asked Clara.

'Made him look fearsome, see? Ferocious. The bastard's built like a bull.'

'I don't get it,' she said.

'Yasta Frate set me up in business here. He's the one who paid for the sessions. Drafted in the girls and the boys too.'

'The *children*, you mean.'

'Them, yeah.'

354

'Yasta Frate,' said Clara. 'Haven't I heard that name before? Who is he?'

'He's the guy in the photos. The West Indian.'

Something went *click* in Clara's brain as she remembered what Jan had told her about Yasta Frate. He was Jan's landlord. And he had been Sal's, too.

89

When they stepped out of the studio, it was to find one of Marcus's heavies yanking a piece of paper off a telephone pole.

'What's that?' asked Marcus.

The heavy said nothing, just handed it to him. Marcus unscrewed the paper and Clara peeped over his shoulder and went white. *Clara Redmayne's a copper's nark*, it shouted. Marcus put it in his pocket.

'For fuck's sake,' said Clara.

'Oh, come on. You can't say you're surprised. *I'm* not,' he snapped, and they went over to the car.

Clara felt exposed now, out on the street. She couldn't forget the noise those bullets had made, *thunking* into Marcus's car. The damage they'd caused to the metal. They could easily have hit her. And now things tied onto lamp posts; she was looking at everyone who walked past thinking *Who put that up there?* And then a woman passed by, gave her a sneering look, spat at her feet and walked straight on.

'Jesus!' Clara sprang back and collided with Marcus. Then she turned and started after the woman.

'Hold on, Tiger,' he said, grabbing her arm and hustling her into the back of the motor while his two pit bulls got in the front.

'Have you heard of this bloke? This Yasta Frate?' Clara

asked Marcus as one of the heavies drove out into the traffic.

'What?' He gave her a pained look.

'Yasta Frate. The man in the photos. Do you know him?'

Marcus stared at her. 'Clara. You're in trouble here. People are spitting at you in the street. People are sticking your name up on lamp posts. Yesterday, someone took pot-shots at you. And you're asking me who Yasta Frate is? For fuck's sake, who cares? The girl's dead, let her rest.'

'You do know him, don't you?' said Clara.

'Let it go.'

'No!'

'All right. I do. He's small-time. Runs a couple of cellar clubs around the area. Lives in one of them, I heard.'

'And he pays nonces like David Bennett to take photos of him shafting women and kids.'

'You're thinking he had something to do with her death?' Marcus frowned. 'Why would he kill her?'

'Have you heard of snuff movies?'

'You think there are other photos going around? Ones that show him *killing* this girl? That he'd get some sort of sick kick out of it? That he'd let incriminating stuff do the rounds? You're mad.'

'Well, they wouldn't be "going around". Maybe he keeps a private collection of stuff like that.'

Marcus was staring at her.

'What?' she asked.

'Christ, what a mind you've got. What sort of dark fucking horrible things go on in there?'

There had been horrible things. Things that haunted her still, although he would never know about that. That recurring dream of her dead mother, the cold blue lifeless child cradled in her arms. The night-time horrors, the fear of going back there, to that awful place, the terror of never truly escaping the slums.

'These things do happen,' she shrugged, staring right back at him. She couldn't read him, not at all, and she could read most people. She stared into those almost-black eyes, as deep as pools of oil and just as expressionless.

She shivered. Did he care that she was under threat? If anything happened to her, she was his wife and all that she had would pass directly to him. She remembered what he'd said on their wedding day, that he wished he could divorce her straight away. Would he truly be sorry if she died?

She didn't think he would.

Not for a minute.

And she *could* die, easily.

Ever since that sniper thing, she had felt that she was being watched. That someone was keeping their eye on her, biding their time. And if the worst happened? Marcus would just carry on, take over her clubs. He had Paulette for recreational purposes. And probably – oh, and this made Clara's guts heave – maybe he was keeping Paulette still, in her flat, in luxury; a convenient piece of arse on the side.

90

Jan was there at the Oak with a couple of the other girls, all getting set for the evening's trade. She beamed like a beacon when she saw Clara walk into the bar with Marcus.

'Hiya, Clar,' she said, bouncing up, pleased as a puppy when its master comes home.

'Don't call me Clar,' said Clara, and got out the photos.

'What's this? Oh these aren't . . . ' Jan's smile vanished as she looked at them. 'God, poor old Sal. What a way to go, eh?'

'You know the man in these shots, don't you?'

Jan looked from the naked couple in one shot and then up at Clara. 'Course I know him. That's Yasta Frate. Sal used to be on the game in Notting Hill, Frate came over on the boat and moved in with her and ponced off her, took most of her earnings, the poor cow. Then she got out from there, got that other place – the one where we found her – and started working at the Oak. But he took over the flats and wound up as her landlord. He was mine, too. Still is.'

'So they fell out, her and Frate?' said Clara.

'He couldn't have been too pleased, she was his meal ticket way back and he's the sort to bear a grudge. She took up with another bloke last year, a younger man. You know him. He was here at your wedding reception.'

Clara looked startled. '*I* do? What d'you mean?'

'Course you do. He was causing trouble, you remember? Smashed up the DJ's deck and some of his records.'

'But . . . that was my brother. Henry. You're talking about Henry.'

'That's right,' said Jan. 'That's the one.'

Oh shit, thought Clara.

91

It was the middle of the day but Yasta Frate was asleep on the couch in the room behind the Gallipoli, safe and secure as a bug in a rug. These cellars, they'd come all through the war untouched. Like the Windmill, they were below ground and solid as could be. He always felt *safe* here.

Safe to shoot up.

Safe to do *whatever*.

While the brothers partied in the basement club, he was back here counting the takings, doing whatever the fuck he liked. So, when there was a hammering and a banging on the door upstairs and it woke him up, he didn't worry. He had boys up there, take care of anything.

Annoying, though. Waking him up like that. He stretched and yawned and pulled his pony-skin coat closer over him. Big trouble with cellars, they were several degrees cooler than street level. Nice for keeping your wine in; not so good for anything else. He'd had a heavy night last night, and his head . . . well, it wasn't the best, not today. All that banging about the place, he could do without it. Seriously.

Then the door crashed open and he shot off the couch like a bullet.

'Hey! What the fuck?' he roared, and two huge men came at him, grabbed him and pinned him down on his knees on the floor, pulling his arms up behind his back until he was on the point of screaming in agony. He looked up. There was a black-haired white woman standing there, and a tall black-haired man.

'You're Yasta Frate,' said the woman.

'What *is* this, man?' hollered Yasta.

'You were Sal Dryden's landlord. And more besides.' Clara fished in her bag. She held the photo out to Yasta Frate, so that he could see it. 'Much more, by the look of it.'

'So?' asked Frate, then he shrieked as more pressure was applied to his arms. 'Man, wassup? Don't break my limbs, for Chrissakes!'

'Tell me about you and Sal,' said Clara.

Frate was looking at Marcus. 'I know you. I know the *pair* of you, I seen you around here.'

Marcus stepped in and punched Frate hard on the jaw. He let out a yell and shook his head wildly. 'Fuck! What you do that for?'

'Answer the question,' said Marcus.

'All right, OK! She was my whore once. Then she decided she wasn't.'

'Upset you?' asked Clara.

Frate hesitated. Marcus stepped forward.

'Hold it! Yeah, it upset me, but what can you do? Anyway, I was *glad* to see the back of her. You want the truth? She cheek me, that girl. She cheek me bad.'

'And now she's dead.' Clara stared hard into Yasta's liquid brown eyes. Thought of all that he'd done to Sal, and felt nothing but disgust. 'And you were her landlord.'

'*So?*'

'You do that?' asked Clara. 'You kill her?'

'No! God's my witness, I didn't.'

'Making some of these sick prints? What, you do films too? *Snuff* ones?'

Frate said nothing. Marcus stepped forward.

'Whoa! Wait! All right.' He was panting, his jaw starting to swell. 'We did the photo stuff, but I didn't kill her!'

Clara stood there, staring down at him. If he was telling the truth . . . oh God, if he was, where did that take her?

To somewhere I don't want to go, she thought. To Henry, who cold-heartedly killed Frank's dog to make Frank's death like a Viking funeral. Henry who'd been with Sal last year. Henry who pinched money from her purse and left coins on the floor – and there'd been coins on the floor that day at Sal's place when she found the body.

She put the photos back in her bag. Turned to Marcus. 'Let's go,' she said.

The heavies released Yasta Frate and he pitched forward onto the floor. His jaw was on fire and his arms felt like they'd been wrenched right out of their sockets.

'*Bitch! Whore!*' he shouted after the woman.

But Clara was already gone.

92

'It's time we had a honeymoon,' said Marcus later when they were up in the office.

Clara looked at him. A moment ago he'd been going through the books with Gordon, the pair of them acting like Scrooge on Christmas Eve, gleefully crowing about this new and lucrative source of revenue – *her* clubs. Only they weren't just hers any more. Now they were his, too.

'What?' Clara stared at him moodily. She had that scene stuck in her head, the two of them exulting in their good fortune, Marcus counting out notes and Gordon adding up lines of figures.

He's done well out of this marriage, she thought, and it hurt.

All her life she'd married for security, for money – and now Marcus had done the same to her, hadn't he. And the truth? It cut her like a knife.

How must Frank have felt?

And Toby?

'A break, that's all. Not a long honeymoon. The business will look after itself for a few days.'

'What are you up to?' asked Clara.

His eyebrows raised. 'Me? I'm not the one chasing around after someone that'll never be found. And I'm not the one who's being shot at in the street, or spat at, or having notices posted—'

'All right, for God's sake! So where are we going?' she demanded. Fuck's sake. He hadn't even been near her since their disastrous wedding day, when he had practically *raped* her in a fury over what she'd done, and now he was spouting on about honeymoons like it was all a big romance and not a business move.

'I've got a place down near Winchester. We can go this evening, be there by dark.'

'That's a bit sudden.'

'Nah, gives you an hour or so to get packed after we've had some dinner here. Strictly casual.'

'On a *honeymoon*?'

'It's nothing fancy,' he said, and then he smiled at her the way a shark must smile before it chomps a seal into dead meat.

Well, he hadn't been exaggerating. It really was nothing fancy. In fact . . .

'It's a shit-hole!' exclaimed Clara when they pulled up in the Hillman Super Minx Marcus had borrowed from Gordon. The E-type was in the garage, getting the panels replaced. Evening was coming in, the light fading fast. Soon it would be true spring, the clocks would go forward, it would get lighter.

After about an hour on the road, they'd come up a dirt track, the suspension groaning and creaking under the strain of it, and now they'd stopped outside this place. It was an old farmhouse, probably Victorian, thought Clara, and there was a cracked cement yard to the side of it where she guessed the cows had once come in for milking. Half the chimney was missing and the roof, outlined against the cloud-streaked purple sky as the sun sank into the west, was

365

bowing in the middle, which Clara knew from her days of speculation in the property market was a very bad sign.

'What the hell is this place?' she asked, getting out of the car and slamming the door. She walked around to Marcus's side as he hauled their bags out of the boot. He tossed Clara's to her and she let out an 'oof' of surprise as it smacked her in the midriff.

'Bought it to do it up a couple of years ago,' he said, as she went to the rusted metal gate and pushed it open. It jammed. She shoved it. It was still jammed.

'I'm not staying here,' she said as he kicked the gate open. It hung there, sagging tiredly from its ancient, rusted hinges. Clara surged through and Marcus grabbed her arm.

'What?' she snapped. How did he have the fucking nerve to bring her to a tip like this?

'Don't stray off the path,' he said. 'Molehills.'

Clara couldn't see any molehills. She could barely see the path, it was darkening so fast now. All she could make out was a ton of unkempt shrubbery and huge thickets of brambles; a couple of rogue daffodils gleamed yellow here and there, but really? The front garden was a wilderness. 'Oh, perfect. I'm going to freeze my arse off and on top of that I'm likely to break my bloody neck the minute I go outside.'

'Stay on the path and you won't. Dunno what you're moaning on about. It has all mod cons. Well, a bed, anyway.'

'How much land does it have?' Clara was shivering now, thinking of the slums. She couldn't believe he'd had the nerve to bring her to a disgusting old dump like this.

'Couple of acres.'

Marcus unlocked the front door and nudged her into a cavernous dust-covered entrance hall with a big central staircase. Glancing left and right, she could see through one open door a dark kitchen with a range that must have come out of the ark, it looked so old. A farmer's wife would have black-leaded it once, and kept orphan lambs alive in the bottom oven. *Fuck's sake!* She looked to her right and there was another open door, leading into a sitting room with an old dusty threadbare couch and an empty brick fireplace.

'This is a wreck,' she said, flicking at a light switch. Nothing happened. No lights. No heat. No nothing.

He closed the front door, locked it and threw the rusty bolt across.

'Home sweet home,' he said, turning on a torch to light the way. 'Come on, let's get to bed.'

He grabbed her by the arm again to guide her toward the stairs. Clara walked into the newel post. 'Careful,' he said.

'Fuck you!' said Clara, but he only laughed.

93

The first thing Marcus did when they got upstairs was put down his overnight bag; then he pulled up a floorboard beside the bed and took out a shotgun and a box of ammunition. The second thing he did was to pull the curtains and light a couple of candles. Yes, there was a bed. And it was freshly made up, by the look of it.

'What the hell?' asked Clara, dropping her own bag onto the floor in shock when she saw the gun.

'Security,' he said, and sat down on the bed. He loaded the gun and laid it on the floor. The spare ammo he placed beside it.

'Is there anywhere I can clean my teeth? Have a wash? Anything?'

He shook his head, his eyes watching her as she stood there in the candlelight. 'There's no running water. Not yet. There's a well out in the yard and a pump, but that's out of bounds overnight, all right? Stay in this room, and if you've got to use the toilet . . . '

'Yeah? What then?'

'There's a bucket on the landing. Think you kicked it on the way in.'

'For God's sake!'

'Come here.'

Clara frowned at him. 'What for?'

'What do you *think* for?'

Clara stared at him. He was a very handsome man, she thought, her husband. And very conniving, very calculating. He'd set this up, made the bed, sorted out candles, stored the gun away at the ready. He must have done all this earlier today, while she'd wondered where he was and – of course – no one had told her.

Was that the plan then, get her out of the way down here? Shoot her with that damned gun, bury her dead body out in the wilds somewhere, everything sorted in one fell swoop? She knew he could do it. Troublesome copper's-nark wife disposed of, so no shit sticking to *him*. He could just say she'd run off somewhere, God knew where, it was sad but there it was, a fact of life, she'd gone – and then he'd take over her clubs without her bothersome input and go back to his tart Paulette a richer man than he'd started out.

'What?' he asked, returning her stare.

What the hell. If he was going to kill her, she saw no way of stopping him. She stepped around the bed, stood in front of him.

'Well, here I am,' she said lightly, but her heart was pounding with fright and anxiety.

'Yeah,' he said, pulling her down onto his knee. 'Here you are.' He pushed her hair aside, kissed her collarbone. 'You're shaking. Cold?'

Terrified, she thought. And now she was remembering their wedding night, the amazing sensations he'd aroused in her, things she had never experienced before. She nodded.

'Then let's get you into bed,' he said, and pulled the zip down on her mini dress and slipped his hand inside.

Clara flinched as his skin touched hers. Then he was pushing the fabric down off her shoulders. Every inch of her flesh felt sensitized, every brush of his fingers over it causing a quiver deep in her gut.

'Why not an earl, a viscount, something like that?' said Marcus.

'What?' she queried vacantly. What was he talking about? His hands were everywhere, touching, caressing.

Don't stop, she thought.

'You, Clara. Why settle for Frank or Toby or anyone like that? Why settle for me? Why not set your sights higher, if money's all you want and clout is all you need? God knows you're beautiful enough to get any man.'

Clara shook her head. She was finding it hard to think. 'Not many earls in Houndsditch,' she said.

'Or in Soho,' said Marcus.

'No. Oh *God*,' she moaned as he unclasped her bra and pulled it off. Her nipples were hard as rocks, and when he touched them, slowly running his palms over them, she felt like she might just disintegrate, just *die* with bliss.

Now he was turning with her still in his arms, pushing her back down onto the bed, yanking the dress off her, pulling her tights and her pants out of the way. Then he sat back and looked at her for long moments.

Do it, thought Clara frantically. *Please, just do it.*

Marcus pulled off his shirt, took off his shoes and socks, kicked off his jeans and pants.

'Jesus,' she groaned.

'Tell me what you want,' said Marcus, coming to her, brushing the full length of his hard lithe body against hers.

Clara gasped, licked her lips. She felt choked, emotional, almost beyond words.

'You,' she managed to say. So what if he killed her later? Now, right now, she was in heaven; she was exactly where she had wanted to be, ever since their wedding day. 'I want you.'

'Good. Like this?' he said, and bent his head and touched her nipples with his mouth, sucking them in, rendering them so sensitive that she cried out again. 'Or like this?' he asked, moving between her legs, opening her wide, touching her with his cock, arousing her so much that she could only pant for breath.

'Yes,' she groaned. 'Like that.'

Marcus pushed into her. Clara clung to him as he kissed her lips, as his tongue entered her mouth. This was different, so very different, from that first time when he'd been so furious, so aggressive. This time he was slower, taking his time, making her wait until it was her that surged forward, clasping him, welcoming him in, and then and only then did he push forward too, hard yet silken, filling her to the hilt.

I don't care if I die, not after this, she thought.

Their bodies locked together. This was what her mother must have felt for her father, this all-consuming rush of uncontrollable lust, *this* was what had killed Kathleen. *Love* had killed her.

I don't care, thought Clara. *Just let me die right now, I don't care.*

And when it came, her orgasm was so intense that she screamed, every gorgeous pulsing wave of it hitting her, tossing her into warmth, exhaustion. They were still twined together when she fell asleep, right there in her husband's arms.

94

She was wandering through a big empty house, a flickering candle on a saucer in her hand.

No, she thought. *Oh no.*

She couldn't bear it, not again, but her feet kept moving, she had to keep walking through these cavernous halls and there, oh fuck *there* was the half-open door, and inside there was the light of a fire.

She wanted to turn, run the other way, only her legs wouldn't move in any direction but forward, toward the door. The candle in her hand, the wood of the door, peeling pale-blue paint, it was all real, oh and cockroaches scuttling around her feet this time, crunching beneath them as she stepped on some of them, it was real, this was *real*.

Clara wanted to scream, wanted to run away, but her hand reached out and pushed the door wide and she knew exactly what she would see here, she knew it, she had lived it a thousand times.

And there she was, her mother Kathleen – sitting in the chair beside the lit fire, the flames falling upon her blue-grey face with its closed eyes, the firelight lapping at the form of the slumbering blanket-wrapped child asleep in her arms.

Only the baby's not asleep, is she? She's dead, like Mum.

There was blood on the floor. Clara wanted to scream,

but she couldn't, she was dumb, unable to break free. And then her eyes moved and she saw the other chair, and her veins turned to ice.

Toby was there.

Toby was sitting there, his eyes closed – but not the Toby she had known, not Toby the flamboyant, the beautiful. This was a smouldering wreckage of twisted blackened sinew and bone that somehow had Toby's face.

Toby's eyes were closed.

'Toby . . . ' she wanted to say, to run to him, to help him.

His eyes opened.

They were black, inhuman. Not Toby's eyes at all. Slowly, his head turned and those awful eyes fastened upon her. The scarred mouth twisted into a grin.

Clara, said his dry, cracked voice in her head, and Clara fell back, screaming.

She awoke with a start, to darkness and stillness. She was drenched in sweat and her heart was racing. She lay there thinking that Toby was coming for her, that soon her mother was going to rise from the dead too, and she would hear the creaking shuffling sounds of two dead people coming to get her, and the baby would wake and it would gurgle and if it did that then she knew she would go completely, utterly mad.

She lay there, panting, disorientated.

There was no traffic noise. It was weird, no traffic noise. In London, it was the background track to her entire life. Then her scattered senses sharpened. She could hear an owl, hooting. This was different to when she normally awoke from the nightmare. Very different indeed. Someone had their arms around her. Someone was breathing in her ear.

Slowly, she came back to herself, back to reality. She was

here in this disgusting hovel with Marcus. They had made love. She could still feel the dampness of his seed on her inner thighs.

Oh God, the way he made her feel . . .

She was slightly sore, he had *made* her sore, and she didn't care.

After that she had fallen asleep, and now – thank God! – something had woken her up, she didn't know what. Maybe that bloody owl. The candles had burned down to nothing. Now the only light in the room was the faint alien wash of the moon, glimmering through the tatty old curtains.

Something had disturbed her, snapped her awake. But what?

There was another sound now, an unearthly sound. Her heart picked up speed. What the hell was *that*? She edged out from beneath Marcus's arm, started to sit up. His hand caught hold of her wrist.

'Where you going?' he asked.

'I thought you were asleep,' she hissed.

'Fox barking. Woke me up.'

'Is that what it is? Sounds like someone being strangled.'

'Come back here,' he said, yawning.

Clara lay down again. She could see his eyes gleaming darkly as he wrapped her in his arms again. She was very glad of Marcus's strong arms around her, driving the bad dreams away.

Then there was another noise. Louder. A shriek, loud enough to make her skin crawl.

'Shit! What was *that*, then?' she demanded, as yet another sound ripped through the still night air. It was horrible, like a long-drawn-out scream. 'You can't tell me that was a bloody fox.'

Marcus let out a long sigh. He sat up, swung his legs to the floor, pulled on his trousers and picked up the loaded gun and the torch. She saw his outline moving across the room toward the door. 'Stay right here. Don't move from this room. All right?'

Clara said nothing.

'Did you hear me?' he said.

'I heard you.'

'Good.' He opened the door, stepped through it, closed it behind him.

And nobody gives me orders, thought Clara, rummaging around and finding her dress, pulling it on, zipping it up. She scuffed her feet into her shoes and, shivering, she followed him out. On the landing she could see the bucket lit by a faint shaft of light. She stepped around it and carefully groped her way down the stairs. Ahead of her, she saw the front door opening, saw the torch's glimmer as Marcus stepped into the stark white moonlit world outside. She followed.

95

Clara could see the torch wavering ahead as he walked down the path, and she trailed in his footsteps, thinking of the molehills he'd warned her of earlier and how easy it would be to turn her ankle in the half-dark, break her fucking neck.

'Holy *shit,* oh fuck, oh God . . . ' someone was swearing steadily and viciously up ahead. She followed the beam of Marcus's torch. It was a man's voice, and now that man gave a cry like a wounded animal, a noise that made the hair on the nape of her neck stand up.

Marcus had moved off the path, into the thick shrubbery to their right, and cautiously Clara followed. Then she saw Marcus stop, saw the torch's beam stop too, and light up a wizened and tortured man's face. His grey-blond hair was caught in a long ponytail, and his swarthy features were contorted into a grimace of pain. There were garish tattoos on both his muscled forearms, and even on the ground and writhing in pain, he looked big; threatening somehow.

'What the hell—' said Clara out loud, and hurried up.

Marcus half-turned and swore. 'Didn't I tell you to stay in the fucking room?'

'What's going on? Is he hurt?'

In the torchlight Clara could see there was a rifle on the

376

ground, just out of the man's reach. Marcus kicked it further away. His own gun was still in his hand.

'What's he doing here?' asked Clara. 'He's got a gun with him!'

'Yeah, good question, pal. What the fuck *are* you doing here? Or should I take a guess?' Marcus kicked the man in the ribs and he writhed and yelled.

'Christ, get it off me, will you? For fuck's sake get it *off.*' The man started sobbing with pain.

And now in the torchlight Clara could see what he was talking about. Clamped onto the man's right leg below the knee was a huge dark metallic thing shaped like a whale's jaws. He'd clearly stepped into it, springing the trap, catching his leg in its grip. There was blood seeping out; it gleamed dark and wet in the torchlight.

'Oh Jesus, that's a mantrap,' she said in horror. She'd heard tales of the things, they'd been used years ago to keep poachers off estate lands, but she'd never seen one before. She'd heard they could snap a man like a twig. And from the peculiar angle of the man's leg as he lay there, she could see that it had done just that. The leg was broken; it would never be the same again.

'Yep, it is,' said Marcus. 'Works too, don't it.'

'Get me out of here, you cocksucking son of a whore!' snarled the man.

'Who sent you?' asked Marcus.

'Fuck you!'

'I *said* who sent you?' Marcus repeated, and emphasized the question with a kick to the man's ribs.

'Fuck! Oh shit, oh Christ . . . '

'Tell me,' said Marcus. 'Or that leg's gonna be the least of your problems.'

'Fuck off!' snarled the man, his face convulsed with pain.

Marcus kicked him again. Twice.

'Jesus!' the man yelled, agonized, trying to roll away, then shrieking as his leg moved against the trap.

'Save yourself the trouble,' said Marcus. 'Tell me a name.'

'No . . . ' He was gasping, sweating, half-crying with the pain now.

Marcus drew back his foot to land another kick.

'No! Wait!' the man shouted. 'All right! I'll tell you.'

'Go on,' said Marcus, and his voice was so cold it made Clara shudder.

'Sears! Fulton Sears.' The man sent a pain-filled nod in Clara's direction. 'I had a hit to do on *her*. Clara Redmayne. He wanted it done, he wanted her out of it.'

Clara felt all the blood in her body rush straight to her feet.

Marcus turned to her. 'Go back to the path. Go back *exactly* the way you came. Carefully. Don't step to the left or right, got me?'

Oh Christ, the place is littered with those things, she realized suddenly.

Marcus had come down here today and he'd set these traps because he knew whoever had tried to shoot her, whoever Sears had paid to do it, would follow them down and try to finish the job. Her husband had staked her out in the wilds here like a piece of bait – and it had worked. They'd caught their gunman. But what the hell were they going to do with him?

'What . . . ' Clara asked, her mind floundering, her stomach churning with revulsion, her eyes on the man's ruined, crippled leg. 'We have to get him out of that.'

Marcus looked at her. 'Go back to the path,' he said. 'Go on. Do it.'

Clara turned and stepped carefully, oh so carefully, back toward the path, fearing that at any moment she would hear a movement, feel a gigantic snap of ferocious metal teeth and then she too would be in a death grip, unable to escape.

Molehills! She remembered him grabbing her so roughly yesterday, pulling her back onto the path when they'd arrived here. He'd set this whole thing up, and he hadn't told her a thing about it.

The blood humming in her ears, crashing crazily in her veins, she found the path and exhaled sharply, shaking, as she stood on it once more, in safety. Breathing hard, she looked back at the semi-darkness where she had left Marcus and the crippled gunman. She could see the torch flickering, and hear the man's desperate cries as the metal clawed ever deeper into his flesh.

She trembled and stood there, hugging herself for warmth.

And then came the shot, deafening in the still night air.

Clara flinched and let out a cry.

Then there was only silence.

96

Ma Sears was gasping her life away in a dingy little side ward in a Manchester hospital. Dad had already passed on, about two years earlier. Now there was just Ma. Ivan sat there at her bedside and wished she'd hurry the fuck up. They'd called him in overnight, said if you want to see your mother still alive, you'd better come now.

So he'd driven over, ready to play the good son, thinking there would be things to do when it was all over, *lots* of things, take ten skips and a fumigator to clear all the shit from the house before he could put the fucking thing up for sale, the crap she'd gathered around her over the years. Jumble sales, charity stuff, Ma loved all that and came home with ridiculous things, saying they'd come in handy. A camera tripod, for God's sake. A gas mask from the war. Oh, and wouldn't that little toy guitar look sweet on the mantelpiece . . . endless sacks of the stuff, brought home and left in bags here there and everywhere.

So hurry up and die, for Christ's sake, and I can get on, thought Ivan, watching his mother's face now, hoping for a sign of life.

And then she opened her eyes, tiny dark orbs in the folds of pale wrinkled skin all around them. He nearly jumped, he was that shocked. They had said she was on her way out, and now her eyes were open and they were staring at him.

'Jacko?' she croaked.

Ivan cleared his throat and took her icy-cold hand. It was heated to tropical in here, and she felt stone cold. 'No, Ma. It's me, Ivan.'

'Where's Jacko, my baby? I want him. And Fulton, where's Fulton?'

Ivan sighed inwardly. Jacko was fuck knew where and he didn't care anyway, why would he? The only reason he'd sent Fulton down to London to look for the little tosser was because Ma had been carping on, and then after Pa died Ma had entered her *confused* period and hadn't bothered him any more about it, which was all good news as far as Ivan was concerned.

Recently, she'd been mistaking him for Jacko a lot. Sometimes for Fulton too. But she hadn't actually asked for either of them in a long, long time, and that surprised him.

'They're away, Ma,' said Ivan. 'Business. Down south.'

'I want them here,' said Ma, and a tear trickled from her eye and dampened the hospital pillow. 'I want them *here*,' she wailed, and Ivan saw the nurses watching from their station.

Well, fuck. Ivan supposed that when you were on your deathbed you could ask for anything you wanted. He hadn't touched base with Fulton in a long while, and the car business was quiet right now.

Besides, with a bit of luck, by the time he'd been down to London and back, Ma would be dead and gone. Plus he could do with a break from Milly. His missus had been bending his ear for weeks, wanting to know how much longer the old cow was planning to hold on; she was counting the days till they could sell that bloody bungalow and make a fortune. Few night away, take in the sights, smash the life out of a barmaid or two . . . Ivan was warming to the idea. And then he'd get home – alone, of course – and the whole shebang would be over anyway.

'I'll get them for you, Ma,' said Ivan. 'I'll fetch them. Both of them.'

That seemed to settle her.

Wonder if she'll last the night? thought Ivan. He stood up. Her eyes were closed again.

Good, he thought. *Just make sure it's fucking permanent soon, OK?*

After driving down, Ivan parked up his flashy new motor outside Fulton's flat, pulled his sheepskin collar up against the wind and rain, and rang the bell.

No answer.

It was three in the morning and Ivan knew that Fulton knocked off at two, so he should be home by now. From the hospital, Ivan had gone back to his house, skirted around Milly, who was giving it all *that,* as usual – *Is she dead yet? What are we going to do about the bungalow? Who's going to clear out all that crap the old girl keeps?* – told her he was off to London because Ma had asked for Fulton and Jacko, and Fulton wasn't answering his phone – which was true. He packed a bag, kissed her cheek, goosed her arse, and left. Now he was standing out here in the dark and the rain and the cold, and Fulton wasn't answering the bloody door.

He rang again, and pounded a fist on the door.

Finally, just as he was about to give up, go away, a light came on in the hall. And then the bolts were thrown back and the door opened.

'What the f—' asked Fulton, standing there in pyjama bottoms.

Ivan looked at his little brother and wondered what sort of shitstorm had kicked off to leave him looking like this. He had bloody bandages on both hands. He was limping. His eyes were bleary and bloodshot, almost like he'd been crying. A large boxer dog nudged its way to the door, stumpy tail wagging, and Fulton booted it up the arse. It vanished back inside the flat.

'What d'you mean, what the fuck?' said Ivan. 'What the fuck happened to you, bro? You look like someone's taken a dump straight on your head.'

And then Ivan went inside. There was dust and mess and dog shit and women's things scattered over the floor. He put his overnight bag down on the couch and looked around him, spotting a woman's hankie, a comb, a watch that had been smashed to smithereens.

'Ma's about to croak,' he told his brother. 'She wants you and Jacko up there. You *seen* Jacko?'

Fulton shook his head. He looked like he'd done ten rounds with Henry Cooper; he looked *finished*, Ivan thought.

'Christ alive! How many years has it been? Thought you were going to track him down.'

Fulton looked at Ivan, the boss of the family. He knew he'd let him down. Somehow that bitch Clara had eaten into his soul, sucked him dry like a bloody vampire, screwed with his head. Cut off his fingers and his thumb. Kicked his balls so hard they swelled up like watermelons and he wasn't sure they'd ever be right. She'd rejected him, laughed in his face.

Now, he hated her. Now, Dutch Dave was sorting that out for him.

'You'd better tell me what the hell's been going on,' said Ivan, and sat down.

97

Clara didn't even want to think about what happened after that. She'd gone back to the house, crawled back into bed, cold right through to the bone and shivering with horror. It was a long time before Marcus came back to bed, and when he did he smelled of damp earth and the faint tang of fresh sweat. Clara cringed away from him but he pulled her in tight against him, held her close so they lay like spoons in a drawer.

'Christ, I'm fucking frozen,' he complained, cuddling in against her. He *was* cold. His feet were like ice, his hands when they slid around her and cupped her naked breasts were chilling, but she didn't complain. What she wanted to say was *What did you do with him?* But she was afraid of the answer. She *knew* the answer. She lay there in a state of bewilderment, because he had removed a threat to her but he had also used her to lure that threat, and it could all have gone very badly wrong.

Why would he want to save me? she wondered. The clubs were as much his as hers now, and they would be totally his if she died. No her-indoors to cramp his style, he'd have what he'd always wanted. He'd be King of Clubs, King of Soho, no questions asked. And he wouldn't be saddled with a copper's nark for a wife, either.

If he let her die.

But . . . he'd knocked her to the ground when the sniper had struck outside the Oak. Marcus had *saved* her. And now, by getting rid of the gunman tonight – probably the same man – he had saved her again.

She could feel Marcus's skin warming, little by little, as he absorbed her body heat. Maybe *this* was all he'd done it for. To have her in bed. After all, he'd never made a secret of the fact that he wanted her. She'd heard rumours about him, that he'd had a bad time with a cold mother and it had affected his feelings toward women in general. Having met his mother, she could now believe it. Her fear was that, despite his good looks, despite the charm he could turn on like a light when he chose to, despite all that, deep down he *hated* women. Soon, his breath against the back of her neck deepened and slowed.

He was asleep.

But she couldn't sleep. She couldn't work out what was going on here. Not at all.

In the morning, Marcus packed up the car and they set off back to London. She didn't ask him what had happened after she left him outside last night, and Marcus was silent, not volunteering any information. He dropped her at the Oak with her bag, and drove off, saying he'd catch her later.

'Oh! You're back already. I thought you said you were going on your honeymoon?' said Jan, bouncing up to her as she sat in the bar with the bag at her feet, feeling too wrung-out, too emotionally exhausted after the night she'd just had, to even shift herself to crawl up the stairs for a bath.

'Marcus had business to get back to,' she said.

He killed that gunman last night. Deliberately lured him in, trapped him and shot him. Then he buried him somewhere out in the wilds. I know he did that. He's smart, he wouldn't leave a trace.

She shivered at the thought. Her husband. She was now married to a man who disposed of his enemies without a single qualm.

But that gunman was my *enemy.*

'You two not getting along then?' asked Jan, hoisting her bulky little frame up onto a bar stool beside Clara, then eyeing her with a frown of sympathy.

'We're getting along fine,' said Clara through gritted teeth.

'Only he *is* bloody gorgeous.'

'So what?' snapped Clara.

'I wouldn't kick him out of bed, that's for damned sure.'

'You wouldn't kick *anyone* out of bed, Jan.'

'That's uncalled for.' Jan sniffed and looked genuinely affronted. 'I'm not like Sal, you know. Poor cow, God rest her, she had more dick than I've had hot dinners. You know what? I always knew she'd come to grief. The risks she took, the things she did. And all to scrape a bit of bloody cash together. Cash was all she cared about, our Sal. She even had a bloody bank book, can you believe that? She was always on about how much money she had in it. Well, it ain't doing her much good now, is it.'

Clara looked at Jan's troubled face. Maybe she *had* been a bit harsh. 'Sorry,' she said.

'I miss her a lot,' said Jan, and Clara could see the raw pain on her face. 'This sounds bloody desperate, I know, but she was my only friend.'

Clara felt bad now, being rotten to Jan. The woman had feelings, after all. And it struck Clara that with her only friend dead and gone, that explained why Jan was always hanging around her. Jan wanted, *needed*, a friend, and she had clearly decided that Clara fit the bill.

Clara jumped down off the bar stool and snatched up her

bag. 'I need a bath,' she said, and left Jan sitting there while she went off upstairs to clean up.

By the afternoon, Marcus was back. Somewhere along the way he'd changed his clothes, and when he came up to the flat over the Oak and kissed her cheek he smelled fresh and was clean-shaven and wearing his usual woody after-shave. Yesterday, when his jaw had brushed against her skin, it had been like sandpaper. It had also been hugely erotic, and she felt aroused just remembering it. She couldn't help but think of their bodies twined together in that candlelit bedroom, of how wonderful it had felt. But then, it hadn't meant anything to him, not really. The whole thing had been planned as a trap – that was all.

'Here,' he said, and put a small blue box in her hand.

Clara stood there looking at it. A white-ribboned blue Tiffany box, identical to the one he had presented to his mother days ago. Yesterday he'd staked her out like a sacri-ficial goat, and yes, she couldn't forget it – on their wedding day he'd let his bloody mouthy girlfriend Paulette attend their reception instead of kicking her scrawny arse out the door.

Something in Clara snapped at that thought and she threw the box straight at his head. He stepped aside and it sailed overhead and *thunked* against the wall, dislodging the biggest of a trio of flying ducks. Both duck and box fell to the shag-pile carpet.

'What the fuck?' said Marcus.

'I'm not your bloody mother!'

'What?'

'You heard! I'm not like her, always with my hand out for something or other. Is that what you think? That every-thing's about what I can get?' snarled Clara. 'What is more, I'm not some *tart* you have to pay for sex – is that what you think of me? Do you give that whore Paulette this sort of thing after you've jumped her bones?'

'What are you raving on about?' he asked, glaring at her as he came in close.

'You don't have to keep me sweet with little presents all the time. Some *honesty* would be far more appreciated.'

'You want honesty?' He grabbed her shoulders and shook her. 'Here it is then. You're more fucking trouble than you're worth so far, so don't push me, OK?'

'*I'm* trouble? You're the one who stalks about in the night killing people with a shotgun.'

Marcus stared into her face. 'I don't understand you,' he said.

'You made that clear enough.'

'Most women like gifts,' said Marcus.

She wanted to tell him that she'd *had* all that, with Toby. And where had it ended? In a funeral pyre. Toby, done for. All her furs and jewels, the things she had once set such store by, gone up in smoke. All of it, dust and ashes. None of it meant a damned thing, in the end.

But she couldn't say it. It choked her, every time she thought about Toby and his miserable death. And she looked at her third husband and suddenly the thought was there: *He wanted Toby's clubs. He wanted me. He kills without a second thought.*

Clara felt all the blood drain from her face. She stepped back from his embrace, folded her arms around her middle. He'd hurt her with that stupid gift. She felt sad, angry, near to tears. *That* was what he thought of her. And she . . . oh shit, she really was in love with him.

She'd been in love with him ever since he'd shown up at Frank's funeral, it had hit her right then, unexpectedly. And him? He'd married her to get her clubs, and her body. That was all. And worse – he might even have killed Toby to do it.

Life had played a massive, sick joke on her. She couldn't believe it. She'd stumbled into exactly the same trap Mum had – she'd fallen in love, given herself body and soul to a man, left herself wide open to harm. And by tricking him into this marriage, she'd given Marcus more than enough cause to hate her. She'd been all kinds of a fool, she could see that now.

'Just leave me alone,' she said sharply, turning away before he could see how hurt and bewildered she was.

'Glad to,' said Marcus, and left the room. He didn't even pause to pick up the box.

98

Next day Clara scooped up one of the bouncers on the door of the Oak and went to the fourth-floor flat off Regent Street that her sister Bernie shared with her friend Sasha. Bernie let her in while Liam and the pit bull stayed outside the door.

'Where's Sasha?' asked Clara, sitting down on one dusty throw-covered sofa.

'She stayed over at Colin's – her boyfriend's.' Bernie was chewing on a hangnail as she spoke.

'Right.'

'What do you want, Clara?'

'That's a fine greeting from one sister to another,' said Clara lightly.

'I don't *have* a sister any more.'

'Bernie, for God's sake . . . '

'No! Just say what you've got to say and bugger off, all right?'

'All right. I want Henry's address, if you've got it.'

Bernie slumped down onto the sofa opposite Clara and stared at her. 'What would you want that for? You never had any time for Henry.'

'He knew a friend of mine,' said Clara carefully. 'I want to talk to him about her.'

'Knew? As in, he doesn't know her any more?'

'She's dead.'

'Wait, I don't get this. If the woman's dead, what's to talk about?'

'She was murdered, Bernie.'

Bernie sat up sharply. '*What?*'

'Yeah. And I want to talk to Henry because he knew her, and he might know something about what happened to her.'

Bernie gave a sour smile at this. 'Still trying to control the whole world and everything in it, aren't you, Clara?'

'I don't know what you mean.'

'The Bill will sort it. Why go poking into things like that?'

'The Bill don't give a shit about people like Sal. They've had months to sort it and they've done fuck-all. So you won't give me his address?' Clara stood up. She was determined to do something for Sal, to let her rest in peace as she should. Her killing could have been random, committed by any thug off the street, or it could have been closer to home.

She thought of Yasta Frate, buck-naked as he mounted Sal in those pictures, flaunting his bull-like body as he abused little boys in those other ghastly images. She'd felt sick just looking at them. Then she thought of Sears, and of Henry. Most of all, she thought of Henry; and her thoughts horrified her.

As if making a decision, Bernie stood up. She went over to the mantelpiece. Grabbed a pencil and pad, jotted something down, then tore off a sheet of paper and handed it to Clara, moving twitchily, like she always did.

'There you go,' she said. 'But trust me – Henry won't be any more pleased to see you than I am. Now, if there's nothing else . . . ?'

There wasn't. Clara took the address and left.

99

One thing that really pissed off Fulton Sears was hiring a geezer to do a job and then finding out that he'd been screwed over the deal.

'So where the fuck is he then?' he asked his boys.

They shrugged. Dutch Dave had taken the commission to top Clara Redmayne a week ago. They knew about the near-miss outside the Oak – which had in Sears's opinion been fucking careless – but Dave had said not to worry, it was in hand. And then the cunt had disappeared off the face of the earth.

'He's got half a grand of my money, up front.'

His boys shrugged again, uneasy. They were glad that Ivan Sears had shown up, because Fulton was losing it big-style, muttering about the place about that *bitch*, that *cunt*.

'Paulie? He was supposed to touch base with you, that right?'

Paulie nodded. 'But he hasn't, boss. Not a word, not a call, nothing.'

Sears's boxer dog sniffed around his feet, hungry and hoping for a titbit. Sears kicked the dog away. It yelped, and sloped off to lie down on the other side of the room.

'Calm down,' said Ivan, perturbed to see his brother in such a state. This rate, they'd *never* get back up to Manchester to wave Ma a not-so-fond farewell. He was going to have to take this situation in hand, he could see it.

'Somebody find him,' said Fulton, fumbling to light a fag with his shaking bandaged hands. A couple of months on from what she had done to him, and his wounds were healing. But his heart wasn't. He'd loved her. Truly, deeply. But now that love was gone, turned to bitter hatred, he was stoked up on puff and coke and he wanted her *dead*.

'Somebody do it, *right now*.'

100

You were only as good as your last envelope, the boys had told Henry when he'd first started working for Fulton Sears, and it was true. He did the milk round, collected cash from stalls and restaurants that paid protection, and every time you had to come back with a nice thick wedge of loot in the envelope, or you were in big trouble.

Fortunately, Henry had a talent for collecting cash.

'You got the money?' he would ask when he first started on the job. Of course they would try it on, test his mettle.

He always thought of it like that when the fucks wouldn't pay up, or they said they'd have it next week, or they said they only had part of it and the rest would follow: they were 'testing his mettle', seeing how far they could push it.

Not very far at all was the answer to that. Henry had a straight choice, it seemed to him: either he got the cash, or he got a kicking from Sears. So he had to get the cash, and get it he did.

'You got the money?' he asked now, talking to a big fat Italian who ran a profitable trattoria off Queen Street, all decked out in red, green and white like the Italian flag, his two sons flipping pizzas out the back room with the scent of garlic and fried tomatoes wafting out into the restaurant, the whole family working away front of house and back, and

Sears skimming a good bit off the top so that they never got any trouble.

Of course, fail to pay Fulton Sears and there would be trouble, big-style. Bloke was about as stable as sweating gelignite, and he was getting worse by the day. Word on the street was that Clara had given Fulton Sears his marching orders from the club doors; some people were even saying that Fulton Sears had come on to Clara, gone up to her office with a full set of fingers and come back down with most of them missing and his balls damned near kicked into orbit. But he couldn't believe *that*. Now big brother Ivan had shown up, and the whole thing looked like it was about to blow.

The man paid up straight away and Henry moved on to his next target, a brand-new dry-cleaning business, so the new owners were Soho virgins and of course they had no idea how this thing worked. Henry walked into the store and the bell over the door dinged. He was assailed by chemical odours.

'Stinks in these places,' he said to the blond guy behind the counter, who was taking a soiled brown garment from a customer for cleaning.

'That's the perc,' said the blond.

'The what?' asked Henry, not that he gave a fuck.

'Perchloroethylene,' said the man. 'Otherwise known as tetrachloethydene.'

Henry was looking around at all the big plastic-coated wedding dresses and full-length curtains hanging around the sides of the shop. He could see the back of the shop through an open doorway. There was a whoosh of steam as garments were pressed and finished. Several people were working back there, filling machines, operating dryers, including a dark-haired woman who glanced at Henry with suspicion.

'Got my money?' asked Henry when the customer had departed, clutching her ticket.

'Ah!' The guy was all big smiles; he was fresh-faced as a school kid. 'Well, here's part of it,' he said, and whipped open the till and handed Henry an envelope. Henry opened it, counted it; fifty pounds short.

'I'll have the rest by Friday,' he was rattling on, smiling.

'No, this afternoon,' said Henry, pocketing the envelope.

'Well, as I said—'

'No.' Henry held up a hand, stopping the flow of words. 'I want my money and I want it by two o'clock. All right?'

The smile was still in place. 'As I tried to explain—'

'I'll be back at two,' said Henry, and left.

The blond guy was still smiling, silly cunt.

Henry called back in at two o'clock and he had Joey with him – six feet of uncomplicated muscle.

The blond guy with the professional happy smile came to the counter again.

'The money?' asked Henry.

'As I told you—' said the blond guy.

He didn't have time to get another word out. Joey pulled him over the counter and whacked him on the jaw. He went down in front of the counter like a sack of shit, knocking over a display of multicoloured cotton reels and assorted shoe dyes and brushes. Both Henry and Joey waded in to give him the kicking he deserved. Shrieks and shouts went up from the back room, and the dark-haired woman ran out to the front of the shop and yelled: 'I'll call the police!'

By then they were finished with the guy, who lay groaning and blood-covered on the floor.

Henry pointed a finger at him as he lay there, wincing, clutching his bruised stomach, blinking up at his attackers in stark terror, pain and amazement.

'Half an hour, arsehole. We'll be back and you'd better have it.'

Henry and Joey left to the merry tinkling accompaniment of the shop bell.

Half an hour later, they were back. The dark-haired woman hadn't phoned the police. The blond man was propped behind the till on a stool, white-faced, bloodstained and not smiling any more. When he saw Henry and Joey come back in, he opened the till straight away with a shaking hand, and gave Henry another envelope with the fifty pounds inside.

'Now, why the fuck couldn't you do that in the first place?' asked Henry, pocketing the cash.

'Bloody *arseholes*,' said the blond man, trembling with anger. 'You *bastards*.'

'You better remember that,' said Henry. Then he and Joey moved on to their next venue.

Before they could get there, Clara came up to them in the street, Liam dragging his knuckles along the pavement by her side. She'd tried to catch Henry at home, but his landlady had said he was out at work. She'd looked for him around the area, and here he was, coming out of the dry cleaners while stuffing something in his pocket. He saw her there, turned to Joey and said: 'Wait in the car.'

'That's *her*, yeah?' said Joey.

'Wait in the car,' said Henry more sharply.

Joey went. Henry looked into his sister's face. 'What's up, you got a death wish or something?' he asked her.

'I want to talk,' said Clara.

'You're crazy.'

'About Sal,' said Clara.

Henry exhaled. 'Who?'

'Sal Dryden. A worker of mine. The woman was killed. But you and she were close for a while.'

'OK,' he said. 'So talk.'

397

101

They walked in Soho Square, skirting the statue and coming to a halt beside the little Tudor-style summer house. The venerable old Windmill was a few steps away in Great Windmill Street, the Oak was on the corner opposite, and Raymond's Revue Bar was at Walker's Court with its massive sign, just a stone's throw away. This – the Square Mile of Vice – was her homeland now. Soho, with its seedy alleyways, its strip joints and its teeming mass of humanity, had become a part of her; it was in her blood.

'Fulton Sears is after you,' said Henry.

'I know.' Clara indicated Liam, skulking not three feet away. 'Look, I brought reinforcements.'

'He got a hit ordered on you, but word is the guy's gone AWOL. Don't know why you ain't dead right now, frankly.'

Clara knew. The hitman was dead – not her. Marcus had seen to that. But Sears would catch up. Once he realized his hired gun was done for, no doubt he'd come at her with another one, or with something different, something worse.

She'd learned a lot in life, but what she'd learned most clearly was that she'd spent nearly ten years chasing after security of one sort or another, only to discover that there was no security to be had anywhere, except in yourself, in your own strength.

So she wasn't running away from her fears any more: she

was running *toward* them, determined to crush them, once and for all.

'What you want to talk to me for?' asked Henry.

'Someone told me you had a thing going with Sal.'

'Yeah. For a while last year.'

'Didn't it worry you? Going where Yasta Frate went first?'

'I knew about that.' Henry frowned. 'I knew what happened. That Frate came over on the boat and leeched off Sal. She told me. It was no big secret. Besides, it was over. He was her landlord and she wasn't happy about that, but there you go.'

'It wasn't *that* over. She had some porno pics taken with him last summer. Him and an assortment of kids, I might add.'

Henry was watching her face. 'I heard something about that,' he said. 'The Bill questioned him. Got nowhere, of course. Big surprise.'

Clara returned his look with a stony glare. 'Maybe you wanted to pay Sal back for getting involved with Frate again.'

Clara had no illusions about her brother. He'd been bad all his life, and she couldn't think that he would have changed now, not when he was mixing with lowlife like Sears and his boys.

'So what happened? You have a fight over those pictures, lose it, kill her?' asked Clara.

Henry stopped walking and stared at her. '*What?* Hey—'

'Come on, Henry. You've done things. Terrible things. I don't think you'd draw the line at this. I don't think you even know where the line is.'

Henry was shaking his head. 'I was sorry as hell over what happened to Sal.'

'So you're saying you had no part in it?' Clara stared at

him. He was wearing the same obdurate expression that he'd worn when questioned at twelve years old, and at fifteen. Now he was seventeen, a young man, and she still didn't trust him an inch. 'What about the house fire, Henry?'

'Now what you on about?'

'My house burned down. Toby was killed. Didn't you like the thought of me doing well at last? Did you really hate me that much?'

Henry was still shaking his head. 'Jesus, you don't change. Anything that happened, it was always my fault, wasn't it? And it still is.'

'Well, you said it. Remember the money you stole? And the dog? That poor bloody tutor, how you battered him? Now I guess you've moved on to bigger things. Like Sal. Like Toby.'

Henry was silent for a beat, biting his lip. Then he said: 'You seriously think I did Sal? And Toby Cotton? Fuck's sake! I didn't even know the guy.'

'Yeah, but I know you, Henry. Remember?'

Henry looked her full in the face. 'You're wrong,' he said.

Clara's expression hardened. 'I just said it, Henry. I know you, better than anyone else.'

'Better than Bernie?'

'Yeah. Even her.'

'I dunno why you're concerning yourself with all this shit,' said Henry. 'You got enough problems. You got Fulton Sears on your back and now his big brother Ivan's come down from Manchester to help out. Ivan's the head of the clan, you don't want to get on the wrong side of *that* bastard, believe me.'

'You enjoy working for that pig?'

'It's a job. It's a living. Better than working for you, I bet. You got to fix everybody's lives up for them, ain't you,

Clara? You got to be in control. Poor fucking Bernie couldn't even marry that pitiful bastard photographer of hers, because he didn't come up to scratch in your eyes.'

'He *didn't* come up to scratch, you got that right. He was the one who took the pictures. Frate paid big money for them, big enough to get David started in business.'

'Yeah? Well, maybe he is a bad apple, but it was her choice, not yours. And *she* ain't all that, anyway. Thank fuck I got out from under your little dictatorship years ago. I'm not sorry about that.'

Clara frowned. What did *that* mean? 'Henry—'

'No. The answer is no. I didn't do Sal and I didn't torch your house. You can believe that or not, I don't give a shit either way, all right?' He turned away from her. Then he paused, turned back. 'You think it was all *me*, don't you? Always, it was *me*. I was the bad one, the one who did wrong.'

'What are you talking about?'

'The fucking dog, Clara. Think about it. I wasn't the only person in that house. Yeah, I stepped up and took it on the chin because I was only a kid and I was scared shitless of the consequences. Like they say, sis: *The truth will out.*'

Clara was so shocked that she could only stare at him. She could feel the sun, beating down on her skin, could hear the traffic, could see people moving around them, but she felt stilled, trapped in time, caught in a bubble of sick awareness where the only focus was Henry's words.

'What are you saying?' she gasped out at last. 'What the hell are you *saying*?'

He shook his head at that. 'Nah, I've said enough. Look – don't come near me again. Joey's seen us talking and that's gonna be hard enough to explain away. I don't want Sears getting any doubts about whose side I'm on in this little war we got going on here. You understand me?'

'You're on *his* side,' said Clara. Jesus, *what* was that he'd said?

'Remember that,' said Henry.

'Oh God,' she murmured. 'Oh no . . . '

Into her mind then came Jasper, saying he'd passed Bernie in the hall on the night of Toby's death, at ten o'clock. And now it came to Clara that Bernie had appeared in front of her hours after that, when the fire was raging. She'd assumed that Bernie had just come home then.

'Oh, please, no,' said Clara. But she knew the truth now; she knew it. 'I have to talk to her.'

'Do yourself a favour,' said Henry. 'Don't. Not about this.'

'I have to,' said Clara. 'Right now.'

Henry shrugged. 'Well, on your own head be it.'

102

Sasha opened the door to the fourth-floor flat off Regent Street when Clara knocked on it not an hour after her talk with Henry.

'Oh, it's you,' she said. Her eyes slipped past Clara and fastened on Liam.

'She in?' asked Clara.

Sasha shook her head.

'I'll wait then,' said Clara, and pushed past her into the room with the dusty couches and the dream-catchers and the faint sickly sweet lingering smell of pot in the stuffy air. There was a new telephone on a side table. She sat down on one of the couches, Liam remained outside the door.

'She could be ages,' said Sasha.

'Doesn't matter,' said Clara.

'You want some herbal tea or something?'

'No. Thanks.'

'Is it urgent then?' she asked.

Clara gave her a steady-eyed stare. 'It's private,' she said, and Sasha gave up all attempts at social intercourse and went off to her room.

Bernie came in over an hour later. She looked surprised to find Clara waiting for her, and not particularly pleased about it either.

'Blimey, what brings you here again?' she asked, coming in and decanting a bag of groceries onto a side table. 'Did you find Henry?'

Clara opened her mouth to speak and Sasha's bedroom door opened. Sasha came out, pulling on a pink-and-blue patchwork coat.

'Going out,' she said to the room at large, and left, pushing past Liam outside the flat door.

'OK,' said Bernie, flopping down on the couch opposite Clara. 'Did you find him?' she repeated.

'Yeah. I did.'

'And?'

Clara swallowed hard and looked at her sister. Sweet, gentle, jittery little Bernie. 'He told me a couple of things. Things I couldn't quite make sense of.'

'Oh? What?' Bernie fished in her handbag, pulled out a packet of Capstan cigarettes and a silver lighter. She took out a cigarette, lit it, and inhaled luxuriously. 'God, that's better,' she sighed. She held out the packet. 'Want one?'

'No thanks.'

'So what were these things he told you?'

Bernie inhaled again, then blew out a dragon's-breath of blue smoke through her nostrils.

'About Frank's dog. And the pound note he was supposed to have stolen, remember that?' asked Clara.

Bernie's eyes narrowed as she squinted against the smoke. 'Yeah, of course I do. Why?'

'Henry said he wasn't the only person in the house. And he was right, of course. There was also me. And you.'

Bernie's gaze flickered down and to the left, fastening upon something on the couch. She picked off a speck of lint, dropped it onto the carpet. Then she twitched and gave a little laugh. 'What, he's trying to say he didn't do those things? Come on!'

'That's what he's saying, yes. And I know *I* didn't. I wasn't even in the house at the time when Attila was killed. Which only leaves you, Bernie. Only you.'

Bernie was nodding slowly. She took another deep drag of the cigarette and then rested her head against the high back of the couch, blowing out smoke in a leisurely stream from her open mouth as her eyes rested on the ceiling.

'You got nothing to say about it?' asked Clara, as the silence lengthened.

Bernie's head tilted forward again and her eyes fastened on Clara's. She smiled, but it was a smile without warmth.

'I got plenty to say,' she said. 'But trust me – you won't want to hear it.'

'Try me,' said Clara.

Bernie crossed her legs and watched Clara, saying nothing. Then she took another drag of her cigarette and said: 'OK. Settle in, Clara. You sitting comfortably? Then I'll tell you a story. Only it's not a story at all, not a made-up one. This one is *real*.'

103

Henry sent Joey back to Sears's place with the car, hoping he'd say nothing about seeing him with his sister. Then, making sure he was unobserved, he walked quickly over to the Oak and told the bouncer on the door that he wanted to talk to Redmayne.

'You're Sears's boy,' said the bouncer, looking at Henry with unfriendly eyes.

'Yeah. But I want to talk to Redmayne. It's urgent.'

'Got a message from Sears then?'

'No, it's a message from *me*. I'm Redmayne's brother-in-law, you know.'

'No, you're fucking not. You're Sears's boy,' repeated the bouncer, and hauled Henry inside and frisked him. Meanwhile, he called one of the bar staff and had them dial through to upstairs, tell Marcus he had a visitor.

Satisfied Henry wasn't carrying anything he shouldn't, the bouncer pushed him into the bar.

'Sit there,' he said, and shoved Henry down onto a bar stool. The staff moved around, watching Henry curiously while cleaning glasses and restocking the optics.

Marcus came down within five minutes and stopped when he saw who was there.

'You wanted to speak to me?' he asked, coming over to where Henry sat.

'Not really,' said Henry. He was furious with himself for coming here, for weakening. Clara was his enemy, she had been against him all his life. Blaming him, sending him away, everything *his* fault, always *his* fault.

But . . . she was also his sister. And blood was blood, after all. He had a strong feeling that she was walking into things that she couldn't begin to deal with. That opening a can of worms about all the shit they'd lived with could be a bad move. A *terrible* move. Push a rat into a corner and it would fly at your throat. Cornered, accused, he had a queasy feeling that Bernie might react the same way.

He hated that he was worried about Clara. But it was a fact; he was. She was, despite it all, despite *everything*, his blood. And she had tried to do her best for him, he knew that. So he'd had to come here, against his own better judgement.

'What is it?' asked Marcus, watching Henry closely.

'It's Clara,' said Henry. 'There's something you should know . . . '

104

For a long time Bernie said nothing. Then slowly, quietly, she began to speak.

'You got yourself married off to Frank to get us out of that place owned by Lenny Lynch, you remember?' said Bernie.

Clara nodded. How could she forget? She could remember even now how miserable, how trapped, how desperate she had felt back then. But she had made a choice; the only possible choice, in the circumstances.

'The coppers were coming, weren't they? The doctor knew you were under age and we – me and Henry – were going to get taken into care. Probably you too, I suppose. Turns out, that would have been better, but what did any of us know? Talk about Babes in the Wood. And you took charge, didn't you, Clara. Like always.'

'I did what I thought was best, Bernie. For all of us.' She had, too. Allied herself to an old man, submitted herself to a sham marriage, she'd done all that to make sure the family stayed together and had food on the table. She'd done more than her best, she'd done *everything* for them.

'So off we ran to Frank's place, Frank who used to collect the rent from us with that dog, that fucking thing, alongside him. I couldn't believe you'd done that at first, because I'd always been so terrified of his rap at the door.'

Clara thought back. Bernie had always cringed at the sight of Frank at the door, Frank wearing his old brown leather coat, the snarling dog at his side.

'Show me a brown leather coat to this day and I still feel pretty much the same,' said Bernie.

'You weren't frightened of Frank once you got used to him, though – were you?' asked Clara, perturbed. She had always thought it was the *dog* that frightened Bernie. Not Frank himself. The thought made her anxious and uneasy.

'Frightened? No. I got used to it.' Bernie stubbed out the remains of her cigarette and quickly lit another, inhaling deeply before continuing. 'But you know what I think? I think something *died* in me the day we moved in there.'

'I don't know what you mean,' said Clara.

'You remember that first night we got there? When he was drunk and he tried to get in the bedroom door?'

'Yes, of course I do.'

'Well, that set the scene for me.'

What Clara was thinking now was too horrible to give voice to.

Bernie's face was sneering as she stared at her sister. 'No one ever fucked with Clara, did they? You were always the tough one. I know you marked Frank's card for him the very next morning. Made the boundaries very clear. Only they were just *your* boundaries. They didn't apply to me.'

I'll be your wife, Clara remembered saying to him in the kitchen, when she'd slashed him with the carving knife.

But . . . oh shit, now Clara was starting to feel bile rising in her throat . . . had the lines between her and Bernie been blurred in Frank's eyes? He'd taken on Clara, Henry and Bernie. They were part of a package, never to be split apart.

Clara swallowed hard. Then again. Finally she was able to get the words out. 'Did . . . are you saying that Frank interfered with you? Is that what you're saying, Bernie?'

Bernie looked at her with expressionless eyes. 'Whenever you weren't around, there he'd be. Waiting to pounce on me. On poor innocent little Bernie, so sweet-tempered, so accommodating.' Bitterness laced her voice now. She let out a harsh, tremulous laugh. 'Jesus, I was so glad when he died. If he'd lived any longer, you know what? I'd have *poisoned* the bastard.'

105

After that, Clara had to excuse herself. She asked for the loo, and Bernie directed her out along the hall. Liam looked at her white, waxen face curiously, but said nothing as she passed him by. Once in the toilet with the door securely locked, Clara lifted the lid on the stained and reeking communal toilet and vomited hard into the pan. She retched until only clear bile came up, thinking all the time *Oh God, Bernie . . . oh, Frank, you fucking shit.*

She had done everything for her family but in the end it turned out she had not done anywhere near enough. She had not saved Bernie from an elderly man's depredations, in fact she had done worse: she had delivered her to his door. She had placed her in harm's way.

God forgive me, I didn't know. How could I know . . . ?

Composing herself, empty of sickness, Clara flushed the chain and turned to the sink. No soap. She rinsed her mouth, splashed her face with cold refreshing water. Looking around for a towel, she found none and so she wiped her face and hands on her dress. There was no mirror in there and she felt glad about that; she must look a fright.

She unlocked the door, went back along the hall, past Liam, and into the overheated, pot-stinking room again. Bernie was still sitting on the couch; she was on her third cigarette now. Chain-smoking – when had she started doing that?

Clara took her place opposite Bernie again and looked at her steadily. Clara's heart was still racing, her stomach screwed up with tension, and her mind was turning it all over, thinking *Could I have seen the signs? Did I miss anything that would have told me what was happening?*

But she remembered nothing. Whatever Frank had done, he had done in secret, stealthily, creepy as a spider, waiting for her back to turn and then leaping in.

'The pound note. You said you found it in Henry's bed,' said Clara.

'I lied.'

'*Why?*'

'Because I wanted to cause someone else as much pain as I was feeling. I wanted to hurt someone, something, it didn't matter who or what. Poor little Henry was such an obvious target. And so were you.'

'I thought it was all Henry, but he said it was you. God, Bernie, why? *Why?*'

'He said he'd never tell,' said Bernie.

Clara's heart seemed to twist in her chest. That was the cry of a child, of the dear sweet Bernie she had always known. Not some monster who could steal from her own sister, burn an animal to death, and let her innocent brother take the blame.

'I pushed him into it,' said Clara. 'Don't blame Henry.'

'I don't. Not at all. I blame *you*.' Suddenly Bernie's tone was vicious. She pushed back her long sleeve. 'Look at this, Clara. Look at what you've done to me.'

Clara looked and felt her stomach turn over with horror. There were countless red weals on Bernie's arm. They looked like slash marks from a razor or a knife.

Bernie always wore long sleeves.

How long had she been doing this to herself? Months? Years? Forever?

'Sometimes it helps,' said Bernie with a crazy laugh. 'If I cut myself, sometimes it just feels better, takes the pressure off, you know? That's how it felt when I burned the dog.'

'Frank's dog,' said Clara, aware that her voice was shaking.

'Oh, I enjoyed that. That fucking thing. I hated it.'

'And you let Henry take the blame. You let me think the worst of him.'

'He knew I did it. He caught me in the act. And I told him that if he gave me away, if he didn't take the blame, then I would be put away in jail and it would all be his fault.'

'So he covered for you.' Clara could see how this would happen: Henry, dragged from pillar to post all his childhood, had craved stability. Bernie's actions had threatened that. And he would have wanted to protect his sister, to smooth these awful incidents over . . . yes, he would have covered for her. Of course he would.

'Jesus, Bernie, I'm sorry,' said Clara, her voice breaking.

But Bernie only shrugged. 'You will be,' she said flatly, and it sounded like a threat.

106

Clara was staring at her sister, at this hostile *stranger*, searching for some remnant of Bernie, the real Bernie, the kind and gentle girl she had once been.

Or pretended to be.

Because, for much of her life, that's all Bernie had been: a pretence. Deep down she had been wounded, hurt beyond belief. Dragged into a situation in which she felt powerless. Clara's heart bled for her, but at the same time she felt a shiver of complete revulsion. Who could do those things that Bernie had done? Who but a cold-blooded person, someone without any human feelings.

'You said something died in you when we moved in with Frank,' said Clara, trying to connect, trying to build some sort of bridge between herself and this woman she realized she barely knew.

'Oh now, that's the truth,' said Bernie. She took up the cigarette packet but it was empty and she flung it aside, started chewing her lip. 'I make the right noises though, don't I? I watch the news and pretend to care. I talk to friends – I do have friends – and make out I give a shit for their troubles. Which I don't. I tried . . . ' Bernie clutched at her head at this point and gave a rueful smile . . . 'I really tried with David. To get into it, into a proper relationship with a man, but somehow I couldn't. I was frigid. Sexually.

And maybe emotionally too. He wanted to marry me, of course. And of course it would have been a fucking disaster because he would have seen in the end that I was only pretending, only *trying* to be normal, and he would have wanted kids and I don't think I could have faced that – but who knows? I wanted to make it work. But you stepped in, didn't you, fixing it so I found those pictures, showing what he was *really* into.'

'To be fair,' said Clara, 'I think he only did it for the money.'

'As if that helps!'

'*You* could get help,' said Clara.

'What, with what goes on in my brain? I suppose I could, yes.' Bernie was staring at her sister. 'You did all right out of it all, though, didn't you? I doubt poor tubby old Frank bothered *you* very much. You wouldn't let him, would you? Tough, that's you. Always in charge, always in control. And now you've got that Redmayne bloke eating out of your hand.'

'I don't think Marcus Redmayne eats out of anyone's hand,' said Clara. 'He'd bite, I promise you. Right through to the bone.'

'D'you love him then? D'you feel all *tingly*,' said Bernie mockingly, 'when you see him?'

Shit, I do. I really do.

But Clara wasn't about to share that with the wider world. Not even with her sister. Suddenly she felt tired, drained to nothing. All her life, she'd had the knives out for Henry. And she'd been so wrong, so completely and utterly sucked in by Bernie's deception. It was *Bernie* who should have been her focus, her concern, not him.

And now . . .

Clara had to swallow hard to form the words. 'Bernie . . . about Sal. The murdered girl, the one in the pictures.'

415

'Oh, you mean the whore. David had a fling with her, you know. Not too big a surprise, when you consider what they were up to together. I expect he found her a lot more accommodating in bed than I was. I bet she'd do the oral stuff and everything. I even struggled with the missionary.'

Clara felt as if someone had punched all the wind out of her. She felt disgusted, sick to her stomach. 'Tell me you didn't. Please. Just tell me it isn't true, and you'll never hear another word about it from me.'

Bernie's eyes were wild and bright in her pixie face. 'And if I don't?' she asked.

'Then . . . I don't know. I suppose I'll have to go to the police. Or something.'

'Oh shit, Clara. Of course I didn't kill that bitch Sal Dryden. But you know what? I *did* kill your precious Toby. I set his house alight and him in it after you ruined my chances with David. Why should *you* be happy, and not me? Huh?'

Clara could only stare. Toby had died because of Bernie's bitterness toward her, Clara. Where was Bernie, where was her sweet ever-moving, jittery sister?

Now Clara was remembering that night, the awful night when she had lost Toby.

'Jasper said he passed you in the hall as he was leaving. You came home at ten o'clock,' she said, dry-mouthed with horror and revulsion and a chilling fear. Bernie sounded mad, unhinged, capable of anything.

'Was that the blond bit of fluff? But *you* saw me coming in at two, didn't you,' said Bernie. 'Well, I did come back at ten. But to make it all look convincing, I went out the back later and reappeared at the front gate at two, when I knew you'd get home after the clubs shut. Not that any of it matters now.'

There was a heavy knock against the door, raised voices.

A man shouted. Then there was a dull, reverberating *thump* against it, a muffled groan, and then silence.

'Oh, and now we have visitors,' said Bernie, hopping to her feet almost gaily. 'I made a call, you just wait and see . . . '

Clara lurched to her feet, all her senses alert, her heartbeat accelerating. She knocked into the coffee table, sending it flying as Bernie shot past her to the door. Whatever was coming through it, Clara knew it wasn't good news.

And she was right.

Bernie threw the door open wide. And there, standing on the threshold was Fulton Sears, but unbandaged, undamaged. Clara stared at him in horrified disbelief and then she remembered what Henry had said: Big brother Ivan had come down from Manchester.

This wasn't Fulton.

This was *Ivan*, the head of the Sears clan.

And he'd come for her.

107

'What have you done?' Clara turned to Bernie.

'Nothing much. Sold you down the river, that's all,' said Bernie, her face twisted. She was sweating, hopping from foot to foot.

Jesus, she almost looks possessed, thought Clara, and felt a fresh stab of fear catch her midriff.

'All these years, and you didn't know how much I truly hated you for what you put me through with that vile old man. Now, here's my revenge. At last.'

Ivan Sears was lumbering into the room. Beyond him, Clara could see Liam on the floor, groaning, out of it, his face bloody.

She was on her own here.

Her heart was beating so hard it felt like it was going to burst straight out through her chest wall. She was on her own here. She could barely breathe, she was practically choking on fear as she stared at Sears walking toward her.

She had no razored lapels today. Nothing.

Move, she thought. *Come on, for fuck's sake. Move!*

Her feet seemed glued to the floor, she was paralysed with fear.

Move!

Somehow she got her legs going, and she went in the only direction she could. Sears was blocking her path to the door and he would grab her, kill her, if she tried to pass him. Bernie, her face alight with almost demonic malice, was in front of the other door and would slow her down, stop her passing. There was no handy little kitchenette in here that she could raid for a knife, for anything to use as a weapon.

Ivan Sears was only four feet away from her now.

'So *you're* the cunt who's got my little bro wound up like a corkscrew. You're the one with the dirty tricks, the copper's nark, yeah?'

Christ, I'm going to die, she thought.

Clara moved, breaking into a run from a standing start. She ran straight at Bernie, saw surprise on Bernie's face. Summoning all her strength, Clara shoved her sister aside and lunged through the door to one of the bedrooms, hearing Bernie's yell of shock as she did so. There was a lock inside – a miracle! – so she turned that, locking herself in and them out. She heard Sears's weight pound against the other side of the door and staggered back from it, the air whooping down into her chest in panicky gasps.

Clara glanced around her. The bed. It was a single, she could move it. She ran over, dragged and shoved and pushed the thing until it was across the doorway. Again Sears lunged at the door, making it quiver in its frame, and he let out a roar of frustration.

One good kick and he'll be through, thought Clara. Then he'll get the bed out of the way and kill me.

She looked around again. There was the window, and there was a fire escape beyond it. Behind the door she could hear Bernie – Christ, *Bernie!* – shouting 'Get her! Go on!'

Clara flung herself across the room, yanked up the sash window and scrambled out onto the fire escape. As she did so, she heard Ivan Sears kick the door in and then come crashing through, shoving the bed back so hard that it tipped over.

108

Marcus drove them in the borrowed Hillman Super Minx while Henry directed him through the traffic-packed streets. Marcus pulled up in front of Bernie's building with a screech of brakes and both men flew out of the car.

'Which floor?' Marcus snapped as they ran to the front of the building.

Henry told him.

'You stay at the front, I'm going round the back and up the fire escape,' said Marcus.

'OK,' said Henry.

Marcus took off at a run.

Hearing Sears coming behind her, Clara slipped in panic and fell, hitting the hard metal of the fire escape. The sharp impact pounded into her hips, her knees, her shoulder. All the breath left her in one loud *whoosh*.

She tried to haul herself to her feet, stumbled on un-steady legs and fell down the first zigzagging flight of stairs and landed with another crash that shook every bone in her body. Agony erupted in a dozen places but she struggled upright and staggered down the next half-flight of jagged rusted stairs, and lay there for a second, winded, terrified, thinking, *Oh God, help me.*

Ivan Sears was coming after her.

She crawled upright, lurched and stumbled down another flight and, oh shit, *there*, she could hear him now, pounding down the steps, she could feel the whole structure trembling beneath his weight and the quick heavy tread of his steps as he flung himself after her.

She glanced back and she could see him, thundering and cursing as he chased her down.

Horribly, she saw Bernie not far behind him, looking down too.

Something hardened in Clara at that moment and she told herself: *No, they won't beat me. I won't let them beat me.*

She hurled herself further on down the escape, and prayed. Because Sears was faster than her. And Sears was furious, vengeful and determined.

He's going to catch me, she thought as he pounded on downward, shaking the whole structure under her feet.

I can't outrun him.

He's going to kill me.

109

'There! Up there, look!' Henry shouted.

Henry hadn't stayed at the front; he'd followed Marcus round to the back of the building where there was a road full of parked cars, some rubbish bins, no pedestrians. Marcus looked up the huge black iron structure of the fire escape and there was Clara, running down, Sears coming after her. Sears was so close behind her that if he reached out right now, he would touch her, grab her, finish her off, throw her the rest of the way down to the ground.

'Fuck!' muttered Marcus, and started up at a run.

Clara could hear Sears's grunting breaths as he hauled his bulk down the fire escape after her. He was *that* close. Too close. She tried to run faster, but her legs felt like cotton wool, she was shaking with shock and fear. Down below she could see Henry and then she spotted Marcus, on the fire escape below her, but Sears was *so* close, she couldn't outrun him and in a moment he was going to grab her.

She'd bought herself a little time by running, that was all. Because now, *right now* he was reaching out, his huge bulk crashing and thumping on the metal stairs, and . . .

It was all too late, too late.

Sears grabbed her arm, yanked her to a staggering halt.

Clara screamed and turned, raking her nails over his face,

but he was *grinning*, the bastard was grinning. He'd got her.

Blood sprang from the scratches but he didn't even seem to notice, far less care. Clara's body hit the front of his and she was enveloped in his heat, his hatred. He pulled one huge fist back—

Here it comes

—and there was nothing she could do, she couldn't run, couldn't escape, she was finished. She sagged, helpless, out of strength, out of hope.

His fist moved, angling toward her jaw. He would knock her unconscious, throw her over the edge, break her to bits on the road below. Marcus was too far down to help even if he wanted to.

I'm dead, she thought.

110

Wincing, panting, frozen with horror, Clara waited for the blow to fall, the one that would knock her unconscious before she took a long downward plunge into the next world.

But Sears was hesitating. His arm was raised, his fist pulled back, but he was still, frozen mid-action.

Clara stood there, gasping, almost moaning with fear, but he didn't move.

Relishing the moment, she thought. *He's got me and he's going to draw this out, enjoy it to the full.*

Sears was standing there like a statue. His muddy eyes were wide open, staring.

And then he started to topple forward onto Clara. She let out a cry as his whole weight leaned upon her. And as he fell forward, she saw there was a large kitchen knife protruding from between his shoulder blades, buried up to the hilt in his flesh.

And she saw Bernie, standing right behind him.

Their eyes met.

'Shit! I couldn't . . . I bloody couldn't do it . . . ' moaned Bernie.

Clare stepped to one side, and Ivan Sears crashed down onto the escape, dead.

Clara was too shocked to think, or even speak. Bernie had saved her. Marcus was running up, he'd soon be here.

'I couldn't do it,' said Bernie, and she was sobbing crazily now. 'It's all your fault, *everything* is your fault, and I wanted to do it, but I couldn't.'

Clara's legs couldn't hold her up for a second longer. She collapsed onto the fire escape and closed her eyes.

There was a heavy tread on the metal and then Marcus came up onto their level. 'Clara?' he said.

Clara opened her eyes and looked up at him. Marcus took hold of her hands and pulled her to her feet, pulled her into his arms. She clung to him helplessly.

Marcus eyed Bernie over his wife's shoulder.

Bernie had stopped crying. Her face was wet with tears but she was smiling and there was something manic, something *terrible*, in that smile. 'You ought to watch yourself with her,' she said, nodding to Clara. 'She's a dangerous woman.'

And then Bernie spread her arms as if she was about to fly.

'*No!*' Clara turned, reaching out desperately, and Marcus moved too, but they were both too late.

Bernie leaned her waist into the edge of the fire escape, arms still spread, and overbalanced. She fell without a sound, without the merest suggestion of a scream.

'Bernie . . . ' said Clara, bursting into tears.

And then Bernie hit the ground far below.

111

It all came out over the next few horrible days. Numb with grief, Clara sat in the police station with Marcus beside her – no Henry. Henry had vanished after Bernie had committed suicide, without a word to his older sister.

They gave statements. Told the Bill that Sears had a grudge against Clara because his younger brother had become obsessed with her, that Ivan Sears had followed her to Bernie's flat and it was there that he'd chased her out onto the fire escape; and it was there that her sister had saved her, knifed Sears to death, then flung herself from the fire escape in a paroxysm of guilt.

Clara knew the true explanation was nowhere near as simple as that, but it would do.

There were endless questions, it took hours: but finally they left the cop shop and went home to the Calypso.

'I need a bath,' said Clara vaguely, and she locked herself in the bathroom and ran a bath, stripped and sat in the hot water and cried bitter tears over the loss of Bernie. She'd been so stupid, so blind, not seeing what torment Bernie was going through, and blaming it all on Henry – who was totally innocent. No wonder he hated her, when she had treated him so badly, misunderstood him so completely.

Oh Christ. Bernie.

Her poor sister. In the end, the pain had all been too

much for her. Trapped inside her own tormented head, she had done the only possible thing: she had set herself free.

Clara could see it all over again: Bernie taking flight from the fire escape, falling end over end to her death. The chilling, God-awful *smack* of her body hitting the pavement. They had all run down after that, as if they could do anything. Ridiculous, really. Pitiful.

Bernie had been lying on her back, her neck twisted, blood pooling out from the back of her head. Her eyes were open, staring up at the sky. She was dead, of *course* she was dead, what did they think, that they could reassemble her or something?

Henry, white-faced, had gone to a phone box, called the police.

They'd reported it. They had to. People had come out from neighbouring properties at the back of the building, there were witnesses.

And now it was over. Still so hard to believe that Bernie had done all that she did. Killed Toby, Toby who had been so kind to her, because of Clara objecting to her relationship with David Bennett.

David Bennett.

She thought of him, and Sal, and Yasta Frate. Yes, she believed Henry when he said he didn't kill Sal – but she *had* to know who did.

She stood up and dried herself and put on Marcus's towelling robe that was far too big for her. Then she went back into the sitting room. Marcus was there. He poured her a gin and tonic, himself a whisky. Handed her the drink as she sat down.

'You OK?' he asked. He knew she wasn't.

Clara nodded. Sipped at the gin, put her glass aside. He sat down beside her and she cuddled in against him. He put his arm around her shivering shoulders.

'I'm bloody sorry,' he said.

'I know,' she said in a small voice.

'Anything I can do?'

Clara looked up into those black eyes. 'Right now? Just hold me, will you? And later . . . '

'Yeah? What?'

'I have to go and see someone. And I want you with me.'

'OK,' he said, and held her, stroked his hand over her hair.

At last, she had someone she could depend on. He wasn't Frank. He wasn't Toby. Maybe he *had* married her for Toby's clubs, but right now she didn't care. Agonized over Bernie, she could only be glad that he was here with her.

Bernie was over.

No more pain for her, no more torment. Clara closed her eyes and wept and hoped that somewhere, somehow, her sister was finally at peace.

112

There was only one way Clara felt she could stop herself from going completely mad over Bernie's death, and that was to distract herself. So within a couple of days she was up and dressed and wanting to make some visits. There would be a funeral soon to sort out, and they had already been to the registrar's to register the death. It was all too awful to even think about.

So she didn't.

Instead, she took Marcus with her to pay another visit to Yasta Frate.

'Shit! Not you two again,' said Frate when they came into his cellar club one evening, jazz pounding out, everyone hurling themselves around on the dance floor, the whole place reeking of cigarettes, the atmosphere thick with smoke and the scent of sweat and hard liquor.

There he was at one of the candlelit tables, elegantly dressed in his pony-skin coat. Clara wondered, didn't he sweat to death in that thing in here? There was no air. But she guessed he wore it like armour, that coat and the rakishly tilted Stetson hat – he liked to make an impression.

He was certainly making an impression on Clara: she thought he was a nasty piece of shit.

'Yeah, us two,' said Marcus, and there were four of his

boys with them tonight, white boys in black territory. They were getting a lot of hostile stares.

'So what you want this time?' asked Frate. He was puffing on a Havana cigar, sending out perfect circles of smoke into the fuggy air.

'How about a confession?' said Clara. One of the boys pulled out a chair for her, and she sat down. Marcus and the others remained standing.

'To *what*?' Frate asked.

'Sal Dryden. You were her landlord last year, weren't you. And you like to collect your rents in person because you don't trust anyone else enough to have them do it for you. That right?'

'So what?' He blew a smoke ring in her face.

'*So*: Sal lay there dead for quite a while. When a colleague of mine went there to check on her, the door was closed. When we went back later and found Sal dead, it was ajar. So *someone* had been in there. And I think that someone was you. Because the rent man would certainly have called during that time. Or the landlord, in this case, and that's you. *You* called in that time, and you killed her.'

Yasta Frate gave a big beaming grin and picked a fleck of cigar leaf out of his teeth. 'Imaginative! I like that. And you're putting this together how? Because I had a little something going with the girl for a while? Because we had our pictures taken together?'

Clara's eyes hardened. 'No. Because you were her landlord. And you *must* have been there. Collected the rent. You always collect your own rent, don't you. Or you tried to. Forget the pictures.'

'That Bennett guy, he's clever with that camera.' Yasta grinned and waggled his eyebrows. 'Gets the angle *just* right, yeah? Shows off a man's finer parts. He's not so smart when it comes to the money side, I heard though. Amazin' what a man will do, when some hard cash is involved, don't you think?'

'I said forget the pictures. The Bill obviously have. Kind of them.'

Clara glared at him while he smiled complacently back at her. The coppers were in his pay – *deep* in, they must be, to let it all pass the way they had. She cleared her throat. She felt physically sick, just talking to him.

'Were you jealous when she took up with Henry Dolan last year?' she asked him.

Yasta shrugged. 'What's that to me? We done. Strictly business after that. Hey, you know what? Maybe it's that *Henry* you should be questioning, girl. There's a bad buzz around that fella. Heard all sorts.'

'Like what?' Clara's heart was thumping.

'He's a bad motherfucker. Things back in his past, I heard. Word is, he was killin' stuff when he was in short drawers. That's what I heard. Now that ain't right. And you come round here askin' me about it? You're lookin' in the wrong place.'

Clara looked up at Marcus. He raised an eyebrow, shook his head.

'You *must* have been there,' she insisted. The pounding of the music, the mad swirling of the dancers, the smoke, talking to this piece of scum, all of it was giving her a headache.

Yasta leaned his elbows on the table. 'You want the truth?' He stubbed the cigar out in an ashtray.

'That's all I came for,' said Clara.

'Truth? Honey, the truth is, I *was* there.'

Clara went very still. 'What?'

'I was there. I went to collect the rent and the door was open. I looked in and there she was, laid out dead, slit right open.'

'And you didn't report it.'

'You kiddin' me? She was dead, what could I do?'

'So what did you do?' Clara looked at his face, sheened with sweat. Was he lying?

'I took the money out of her purse – it was there on the table by the door. Truth was, I was shaken up. *Nasty* in there, she was *ripe*. I think I dropped a few coins on the floor, chucked the purse back down, and I vamoosed.'

Her brain was spinning. Sal. Toby. Bernie. Her whole world had crashed around her and she felt bereft, bewildered. And now he was saying *this*. Making her think *Oh God, Henry, did you? Could you?* If Bernie hadn't killed Sal, then *had* Henry done it?

She stood up. She had to get out of here, get some air.

'Hey, don't I even get a thank you for helping?' shouted Yasta Frate after her departing back.

Clara didn't turn around. She walked out of the club with Marcus and the boys and stood panting in the night air outside, gasping in each breath, trying not to pass out.

'Come on,' said Marcus, taking her arm. 'Let's go home.'

113

Clara felt ill, drawn, a ghost of herself. The nightmares were back, and she was finding it hard to go on. But she had to. What else was there to do? She lay in bed at nights beside a slumbering Marcus and thought, *Could Henry have done that?* For so long she had believed the worst of her brother, but all that Bernie had confessed to her showed that she'd been horribly mistaken.

Maybe it's just bad blood, she thought.

That was possible. Their dad had fiddled the accounts, run out on them. Bernie . . . *ah Jesus, Bernie!* . . . had been twisted, wrecked by all that had happened to her. And Henry . . . Henry was the enigma. Misread all his life. Capable of strong-arm stuff on the streets now. More than capable.

But was he capable of murdering Sal?

Frate's last words to her about his visit to Sal had the ring of truth to them. Poor old Sal, always desperate for money, desperate enough to sell herself, sell her soul, and yet never managing to hold on to the cash she craved so much. But Frate was a practised liar, was he *really* telling the truth? Was Clara mistaken? She'd been mistaken about so much in her life.

In the gloom of the night, she watched the dim outline of Marcus, sleeping. Her husband. Who didn't love her, but wanted her in bed with him. Who kept a mistress in luxury.

Was he keeping her still?

She thought of Paulette and ground her teeth and wished . . . for what? That he was in love with *her*. That he would commit himself to *her*, not some tart. Because she knew she was in love with him, and it was a reckless love, a complete love, like . . . like Bernie had felt for David Bennett.

She rolled onto her back and stared into the darkness and thought about Bennett. She wished so much that Bernie had never met him, then she would not have intervened, and the whole train wreck that had become their lives would not have happened.

Too late for that now, though.

Bennett had been the thing Bernie fastened upon in a bid to save her sanity. Clara saw that now. A man who had a talent but was poor and also devious. Who couldn't keep money and never made much and could put his scruples aside when it suited him. Who had to crawl to filth like Frate to scratch a living. Who'd been there on the spot when she'd found poor butchered Sal, who had been flush with extra cash before she died . . .

'Marcus?' she whispered. Dawn was creeping through the curtains, lighting the room with an ambient glow.

'Hmm?' he rolled over, threw his arm around her. 'What?' he mumbled.

'Wake up.'

114

David Bennett was there at the desk, stamping the backs of small prints, each with a corner cut off. He looked up as they came in, her, Marcus and two of the boys – not Liam, he was off resting up. Ivan Sears had hurt him, but he would be OK.

'Fuck! You again,' said Bennett irritably when he saw her.

'Yeah, me again,' said Clara. Raw as she felt with pain over Bernie, she had to do this. 'I wanted to talk to you about Sal.'

'There's nothing to say. It's a pity, what happened to her. That's all.'

'Oh, I think there's a bit more than *that*. Where do you keep your bank statements?' asked Clara.

'You *what*?' Bennett half-laughed.

'I want to see your bank statements.'

'Fuck off!' snapped Bennett, and stood up.

Marcus shoved him back down. 'Where are they?' he asked, his black eyes boring into Bennett's.

'What the f— what the hell would you want to see them for?'

'Where are they?' repeated Marcus.

'None of your fucking business,' said Bennett.

Marcus's gaze was stony. He cocked his head, and the heavies went to the desk, started rifling through the drawers.

'Hey . . . ' Bennett protested.

They carried on. Then straightened, shook their heads.

'Where?' asked Marcus again.

'I don't think—'

Marcus hit him. Then he hit him again. Blood spattered all over the prints and Bennett let out a yell of protest.

'*Where?*' said Marcus again. 'You've got three seconds to answer or you'll get another one.'

'I don't see—'

'One.'

'Why do you—'

'Two.'

'All right, for God's sake! All right! They're in there, down in the darkroom.' With a shaking hand he clutched at his bleeding mouth and indicated the door on his right.

'Is it locked?'

'Of course it bloody is.' Bennett opened the top drawer, took out a key, gave it to one of the heavies.

The two men went to the door, opened it to darkness. Flicked on the light. They went down a shallow set of steps. Clara followed. At the bottom was another door. One of the men pushed it open. Inside was a gloomy red-lit square box of a room, with prints pegged up on a small line, and red, white and grey dishes lined up. There was a strong whiff of chemicals down here. And there, in the far corner, was the file cabinet.

Clara took the key and went over and opened it. David Bennett was pretty organized for an artistic type. Things were neatly labelled. CAR and INSURANCE and NEGA-TIVES 1-250, all set out. Not alphabetical, but neat nevertheless. BANK STATEMENTS was easy to find. Clara pulled out the file and took it back up to the reception area with her. Marcus's two goons followed.

Marcus was still at the desk, and David Bennett was still

in his chair, a reddening handkerchief clamped to his mouth. He went both wide-eyed and pale as Clara laid the file out on the desk, opened it up, took out his statements for the last year.

'My friend Jan told me something very interesting and I've only just remembered it,' she said to Bennett. 'She said that Sal Dryden had been flush with more cash than usual before her death. Bragging about her bank book and how much dosh she had in it. And . . . ' Clara hesitated, looking down the lines of figures . . . 'Dear me, you're a bit hard up, aren't you? Especially here, in the months before Sal died.'

'Look . . . ' he said.

But Clara went on.

'There were some big sums going into the account now and again . . . I guess that was Yasta Frate's input for the porno pictures, yes? Not many of those. But there was a regular payment going out, five hundred pounds every month. That's a big amount, wouldn't you say? And I would also guess that if the police were to check Sal's old bank book – *if* they cared enough to bother – they would find that same amount going *in* every month. Looking at these statements, those payments stopped when Sal died. Isn't that funny?' She looked into his eyes. 'No, not funny at all, actually. She was going to tell Bernie, my sister, your sweet little fiancée, what you were really like, unless you paid up. Sal was blackmailing you. Wasn't she?'

115

'All right!' Bennett's voice was muffled beneath the hankie. He glared up at Marcus. 'Christ, you knocked out my fucking tooth.'

'Sal was blackmailing you. She was always desperate for cash and she knew you wouldn't want Bernie finding out about those porno shots you took. So she hatched a plan. She'd fleece you,' said Clara.

'All right, it's true,' he burst out. 'She was crippling me, that cow. She said she'd tell Bernie everything, but what the hell does any of it matter now anyway? *You* made sure Bernie knew all about me.'

'And now Bernie's dead,' said Clara quietly.

'She . . . *what*?'

'She committed suicide.'

'Christ.' He looked genuinely shocked. Maybe he *had* loved her, in his twisted way.

'Go on about Sal,' prompted Clara.

'What? Well . . . I had to stop her,' he shrugged helplessly. 'She was cleaning me out. I didn't know which way to turn. So I went there. Asked her to stop, but she just laughed. She laughed in my face! I got so mad. *Furious*. And I did it.'

'They always say murderers like to revisit the scene,' said Clara. 'Is that what you were doing, the day we met outside her flat?'

He was nodding now. He let out a shaky breath. 'You know what? It's a relief to admit it. It's been tormenting me, all this. I kept going back there. Not just the day I saw you, but before that. It . . . haunted me. I'm not a violent man, you know. I'm not a bad man. I went back there . . . and it was horrible. I couldn't believe what I'd done, but she *forced* me to do it.'

Clara exchanged a long look with Marcus. Then she looked again at David Bennett, the object of her sister's love. If Bernie had lived . . . this would have *destroyed* her. But Bernie was already gone. She wouldn't suffer any more.

'Now what?' asked Bennett as silence fell.

'Now,' said Clara, 'we go down the nick with you and these statements. And you confess. You tell them you killed Sal Dryden.'

'Wait . . . ' He was shaking his head, seeing his whole world falling apart in front of him.

Clara looked at him and her eyes were hard. 'Or you vanish. We can make people vanish, you know. Quite easily. A long stretch inside – or a quick exit. You choose.'

116

A few days after Bernie had taken her dive off the fire escape, Henry dragged himself out of bed. Depression sapped him, made him feel weak. Bernie's death, Bernie's tormented life that had impacted so viciously on his own, kept running through his head. Clara, turning her back on him for all that time. He hadn't deserved that. He'd been wounded by it, and had put up a thick defensive shell around himself because of it.

He washed, dressed, ate some toast, drank some tea, and wondered what the fuck he was going to do with the rest of his life.

He was finished with working for that nutjob Fulton Sears, he knew that for certain. Maybe he could carve out a chunk of the action for himself, who knew? Right now, he didn't have the energy, but life went on. Life *always* went on, and soon he knew he would start to feel himself again. He was tough, resilient; he'd had to be. So maybe Clara had even done him a favour. Maybe Bernie had, too. Who knew?

He went to Sears's flat and knocked on the door. None of the other boys were about outside, and that surprised him. But then, really? Rats always deserted a sinking ship, and Fulton Sears was sunk all right.

One of the boys – it was Joey, dim, faithful, strong in the arm and weak in the head – opened the door, let him in.

'Sears in?' asked Henry.

Joey shrugged, his face unhappy. Henry followed him into the lounge and there was Fulton Sears sitting in the corner on the carpet. There was a smashed table beside him, and bits and pieces around him – a comb, a broken watch, a hankie. Sears's eyes were wandering around the room, not fastening on anything. His trousers were wet where he'd pissed himself, and he was muttering something under his breath.

'Holy shit,' said Henry.

Sears's boxer dog whined and nudged at Henry's leg, looking up at him with pitiful eyes. The dog looked emaciated. Wasn't anybody feeding the damned thing? Certainly not Sears. He was out of it. Henry stepped closer to the man on the floor.

'Fulton? Mr Sears?' he said.

Sears didn't even look at him, didn't seem able to focus. And now that Henry was closer he could hear that Sears was saying over and over again *cunt bitch whore cunt bitch whore.*

He turned. 'Joey, we . . . ' he started, and then he realized he was talking to thin air. Joey was gone. And would not return; he could see there was nothing to come back for. Sears had once been a power on the streets of Soho, but that time was past.

Henry let out a sigh.

Then he turned and left the flat, the dog trailing at his heels. He went to the phone box, dialled 999, and asked for an ambulance.

He came out of the box. The dog was sitting there, waiting. What was the mutt's name? Charlie?

'Hey, Charlie,' he said.

The dog wagged its stumpy tail, gave a little grin.

Henry sighed again. 'Come the fuck on then,' he said. 'Let's go.'

117

Milly Sears was *seriously* pissed off with her husband. She was sitting in the hospital beside his mother's bed, and *Christ* the old girl was taking her time over shuffling off the old mortal coil. He was the one who should be here, seeing to all this shit, not her. And where was he? Living it up down in London.

Oh, she knew Ivan. He'd be shagging other women down there for sure. And drinking too much; that beer belly of his was getting out of control, she kept telling him. But did he listen? He did not.

And when she'd done all this, when the old girl finally kicked the bucket, who was going to be left sorting out that disgusting pest-hole bungalow? *Her*, that's who. Muggins.

She heaved a sigh and looked at his mother. That old cow had never liked her. Milly had red hair, and his mother always said you could never trust a woman with red hair, she would be fiery and she'd like sex too much.

Like it or not, I'm certainly not getting much of it, thought Milly bitterly.

Ivan wasn't interested in her any more. She suspected that new secretary at the car sales place; he always looked in the other direction a bit too carefully whenever *that* little bint was about.

'Mrs Sears?'

The nurse was standing there on the other side of the bed, staring at her. Milly snapped back to the here and now.

'I'm afraid she's gone,' said the nurse.

Milly looked at her mother-in-law's face, at the sagging jaw and half-open eyes. The old bitch had died, and she hadn't even noticed.

'Oh!' Milly sprang to her feet. 'Oh God.' She'd been sitting here beside a corpse, all unaware. The nurse was looking at her, so she fished out her hankie and puckered her face, dabbed at her eyes. 'Oh dear,' she said.

The nurse pulled the sheet up over the old woman's face.

'There will be some forms to fill in, if you'd like to come into the office?' asked the nurse.

Milly nodded, and followed as the nurse led the way.

When Milly finally got home in the small hours of the morning, it was to find the police on her doorstep.

Christ, what's he been and done now? she wondered as her taxi drove away.

Ivan was always half a step away from being banged up. He took risks, liked the dodgy deals. She wished to Christ he wouldn't do that. They'd be getting the cash from the bungalow soon, it wasn't like he had to worry about money.

'Mrs Sears? Millicent Sears?' asked one of the Bill.

'Yes. That's me,' she said.

'Can we go inside?' asked the other one.

She was shagged out from all the hospital nonsense. And now *this*. Bloody Ivan, when would he ever learn to play things straight?

'What's this about?' she asked nervously.

'I'm afraid we've some bad news.'

So she went inside with them, sat them down in the lounge, and that was when Milly Sears found out that her husband Ivan had been murdered while in London, and she was a widow.

This time, she didn't have to force the tears.

This time, they were real.

118

Clara was finding things different as she went around the Soho streets. Surprisingly different. People were nodding their heads to her, even *smiling* at her, where before they had been spitting at her and calling her a nark.

Marcus had his red E-type Jag back again, the clubs were ticking over, everything was right with the world – except she was crippled with grief over Bernie. Wishing she could have spotted the signs, could have been more sensitive, could have *known* what was going on with her little sister.

But how could she?

And Henry! She felt so bad about Henry, the way she'd misjudged him, even when he was only a child. Bernie had deceived her, it was true, but shouldn't she have been more aware, shouldn't she have somehow *seen* what was happening?

She couldn't even bring herself to make the arrangements for Bernie's funeral, she felt too numb, too sad. It was Henry who picked up the slack, stepped in, did what was necessary. Henry, who was virtually a stranger to her because she had pushed him away all his life, Henry with that skinny chestnut-and-white boxer dog trailing around at his heels.

'You're a heroine now,' said Marcus when she mentioned

the attention she was getting on the streets. 'You got the man who killed Sal Dryden.'

'Some heroine,' said Clara gloomily. 'My sister was in bits. And I didn't even notice.'

'She hid it from you.'

'I'll never forgive myself.'

'Yeah,' said Marcus. 'You will.'

119

Life went on. Clara toured around the clubs the way she always had, and landed up at the Heart of Oak to find little Jan in her long black evening gown, sitting on a bar stool before the start of evening's trade while the barman polished glasses and restocked the mixers.

'Hiya, Clar!' Her face lit up when she saw Clara come in.

'Jan,' said Clara, sitting down. She'd given up telling Jan not to call her Clar. It never did sink in.

Then Jan's face sobered. 'I heard about your sister. I'm sorry, Clar. It's awful.'

'Thanks.' The pain lanced her again, the grief, the awful finality of what Bernie had done. She would never see her again, and it killed her to know that, to acknowledge the truth of it.

'I never had a sister,' said Jan, her eyes anxious as they rested on Clara's face.

'No?' Clara really didn't want to talk about this. She was afraid she'd begin to cry and never be able to stop.

'No. I was an only child. Wasn't even wanted.'

Clara looked at Jan. No sisters or brothers. No friends, only Sal. And Sal was gone. She felt a sudden wave of warmth for poor tubby awkward little Jan.

'We can be sisters,' said Clara after a moment's thought. 'You and me. Not *blood*, but as good as. How about that?'

Jan's face flushed and her eyes filled with tears. 'Really?' she gasped.

'Yeah, really.'

Jan flung herself off her stool and hugged Clara hard. 'Shit, that's wonderful!' she giggled, laughing and crying at the same time.

'Don't mark the dress,' said Clara, smiling.

'No! OK.' Jan sniffed and reassembled herself, heaved herself back up onto her bar stool. She swiped at her eyes. 'Sisters!' she laughed.

'Yeah. Sisters.'

'Clar?'

'Yeah, Jan?'

'Do you think Gordon likes me?'

No, thought Clara. Then she looked at Jan's hopeful bright-eyed face and said: 'I think he does. Maybe. He's shy, that's all.'

'Honest? You think he does?'

'Honest. I do.'

Jan was beaming again. She looked almost beautiful when she smiled like that, and Clara thought that if Gordon could learn to like her, he'd be getting a good deal. Then Jan's face fell.

'About Sal . . . ' she started.

'It's sorted,' said Clara. 'Let it rest now.'

'They're saying you found out who did it,' said Jan.

'It's done, Jan. Shut the fuck up about it, will you? She's at peace.'

'Yeah.' Jan sighed. 'She is. She never had much peace when she was alive, always grubbing around after money like she did, so let's hope she's got some peace now, eh?'

'Yeah,' said Clara. 'Let's hope.'

120

It was a secure unit, Victorian, with high red-brick walls topped with barbed wire. Marcus met up with Colin Drewmore – who was a psychiatric assistant and an old mate of an old mate who could give Marcus the inside dirt on what was going on – a hundred yards away from the guarded main gate.

Colin was a fit-looking man in his forties with a hawkish face, a bald head and sharp grey eyes, dressed in white tunic and trousers. Marcus guessed that you'd need to be fit in there, handle whatever crap happened to erupt with the inmates. And you'd need those sharp eyes to look out for all those *very* sharp objects.

They wandered off along the road and Marcus got straight down to it.

'So – what's the word?' he asked as they strolled in the sunshine, the high walls on their right. He thought of all those poor bastards closeted inside, some of them clean off their heads and dreaming they were Edward the Seventh, others heavily tranquillized because they had dangerous impulses. Marcus guessed that he knew which category Fulton Sears would fit into.

Colin shrugged. 'He's sedated a lot of the time.'

'Right.'

'He talks a lot. Mumbles. You know. A lot of them do.'

'And says what?'

'Talks about a woman. A bitch, he calls her. Laughing at him. Says he's going to kill her.'

Marcus stopped walking, turned and looked full in Colin's face. Colin gulped. Those black eyes seemed to bore straight through him.

'What I want to know is,' said Marcus slowly, 'is there any chance he'll be let out?'

Colin shrugged again. 'You know these bleeding-heart liberal types we get coming in here sometimes, sympathizing with the bastards, saying it's inhuman to lock them up. Bollocks, I say. One geezer ripped his old lady's eyes out – you saying he shouldn't be locked up after that? I should say so. But you see what we get? Soft upper-crust twerps who think these people can be healed, reformed, made better.'

'And can they? Can *he*?' asked Marcus.

'Not a fucking chance. But whether or not he'll smarm his way around one of these nice well-educated middle-aged frumps who come in here, convince them he's as sane as you or me, who knows?'

'So he could get out. Next year, the year after, who knows?'

'That he could.'

Marcus pulled out his wallet, counted out five hundred. Thought of Clara. And Pistol Pete's head and hands on his desk. He slipped the money into Colin's palm. Looked into Colin's eyes. 'Right then,' he said.

Colin nodded, and pocketed the cash.

121

From the unit where Fulton Sears was being detained, Marcus drove over to the flat to see Paulette. She was surprised to see him. He hadn't been anywhere near her since his wedding day.

'Oh! It's you,' she said, scooping up her apricot toy poodle into her arms and looking at Marcus with hostile eyes.

'Yeah, me again. You OK?'

'Do you *give* a shit?'

'I'm still paying the rent on this place, aren't I?'

'Yeah. You are. But I guess you're getting your jollies off little wifey now, aren't you? Well, when marriage palls, you can come back to me, I don't mind.'

Paulette was doing her pouty Brigitte Bardot thing, looking at him with smoky eyes. Then she gave a sudden, brilliant smile and put the poodle down and slipped her arms up around Marcus's neck. Marcus gently took hold of her arms and disengaged them. Paulette's smile slipped.

'Paulette,' said Marcus.

'Yeah? What?'

'It's done. You and me.'

Paulette's jaw dropped. '*What?*'

'The rent's paid up to the end of the month and I have this for you.' He handed her a brown envelope. Paulette looked inside. It was stuffed with fivers. 'That will give you time to find something else, make other arrangements. OK?'

Paulette's mouth was moving, she was gulping for air like a fish yanked from a river.

'But, I . . . for fuck's sake! I've been with you for *ten years*! You *bastard*!'

The poodle yapped at Marcus, sensing its mistress's mood.

'If that thing bites me, I'm going to kick its arse,' warned Marcus.

Paulette snatched the poodle back up.

'Poor baby, poor Binky, you're frightening him,' she snapped. 'What, you got someone else lined up to be your girl around town then? You got someone else on the side that wifey don't know about, you *arsehole*?'

'Yeah, that's right,' said Marcus, and turned away from her. Let her think that, if she wanted. It was a damned sight less complicated than the truth.

'*Motherfucker!*' screamed Paulette as Marcus walked out the door.

122

Clara had to go back, just one last time. There was something eating at her, eating into her soul, and she couldn't rest until it was done. It was late in the evening, not long after Bernie's death, not long after Clara had realized, painfully, that they had all been living a lie, and she was in the Blue Bird nightclub and the Everly brothers were filling the act's break with 'Crying in the Rain'. Marcus was over at the Blue Heaven seeing Gordon about something or other. Counting the money again, she supposed.

'Liam?' Clara went to the big man who had accompanied her to Bernie's on that fateful day. Liam was built like a tank, in his thirties, with keen brown eyes and a mop of dark curly hair. He seemed none the worse for the pasting Ivan Sears had given him.

'Yeah, Mrs Redmayne?'

'Call me Clara, for God's sake. I need to go out and do something.'

'I'll drive you,' said Liam, as Clara had known he would.

'Just need to pick up something first,' said Clara, and she went to the table Marcus always occupied when he was in, the prime table at the front near the stage; from underneath it she took what he kept concealed there: the hammer.

She left the spiked knuckledusters.

She wouldn't need those.

123

Ted Hagan had been verger at St James's church for fifteen years, and he loved his job. The vicar was a sweet man, mildly eccentric, but that didn't matter. Every day was full of joy for Ted because he could work in and around the church grounds, making them perfect, keeping everything running as smoothly as an oiled clock.

Whistling, he walked up the path in the sun, happy to be going in to work. He had the surplices to send off to the laundry, the prayer books to straighten, the hymns for today's christening to be put up on the board, and Mrs Milner would be in soon to do the flowers; her husband grew red hollyhocks and deep blue delphiniums, they would look so nice.

And then he stopped walking.

He stared.

His mouth fell open.

'Jesus!' he burst out. And then clapped a hand over his mouth, asking forgiveness for taking the Lord's name in vain.

Then he stood there, his happy mood disintegrating as he saw what some vandal had done in the night. He strode over to the place and stared again. Where once there had been a headstone, beautifully carved and lovingly inscribed, there was now nothing but a pile of rubble, jagged bits of stone that had been pulverized by some unthinking, uncaring *shit*.

Oh God, he mustn't curse and swear, not even in his thoughts, it was bad.

But *this* was bad too.

This was awful.

He bent and picked up a chunk of wrecked masonry. There was just the remnant of a name there. FRANK.

He bent again, picked up another piece and read it: HATTON.

Frank Hatton.

Poor soul, his grave had been destroyed. Ted looked around him. All the other graves were untouched. He let out a sigh at the wickedness of the human race. He was going to have to tell the vicar about this, *right now*.

124

'Oh. Hi! It's you,' said Sonya when she opened the door of her flat over the sweet shop and found Paulette standing there.

'Yeah, hi!' Paulette air-kissed Sonya's cheeks, thinking that the Russian or Yugoslavian or whatever the fuck Sonya might be was looking very chic today. She was obviously about to head out the door, dressed in a chocolate mink coat, high heels and dark glasses. Rings glinted on her fingers. Big gold earrings glittered when she flicked back her white-blonde hair.

Paulette hadn't brought Binky out with her today; she'd left her precious little man yapping his head off in the flat. She had things to do, Sonya to visit in particular, and she was worried that Sonya might not like dogs. Time was moving on, and soon Marcus's largesse would be coming to an end. She still kept a horse in livery, she still had her personal grooming to keep up to the required standard. She was a party girl, and she had to carry on looking the business, even if she had lost her meal ticket.

'Did you want something?' prompted Sonya. Paulette had never visited her before, although she had always known where she lived. Paulette in fact had always made it a point to look down her nose at Sonya, to be bitchy and unkind because she was the head man's girl and not just the kept girl of his second-in-command. So why the social call now?

'Um . . . well, yes. This is a little awkward, if I could come in . . . ?'

Sonya stepped back, let Paulette into the flat.

'Have a seat,' she said, and glanced at her watch.

'I won't keep you. I only wanted to say that I was so sorry over what happened to Pete,' said Paulette.

'Oh! Well, that's kind of you,' said Sonya.

'Not at all. It was a tragedy. Awful.' Paulette swallowed delicately. 'Do you have someone else in your life now?'

Sonya heaved a sigh. 'Marcus gave me a job in one of the clubs. Hat-check girl, bit of a come-down. I hated it, and the pay was shit. But a girl has to live, and I've got used to a certain lifestyle,' she said. 'So yes, I do have someone, he's . . . nice.'

The MP who now kept Sonya *was* nice. Flamboyant and elegant, he liked living rich and high. He wasn't Pistol Pete, but beggars could not be choosers.

'Marcus and I have split,' said Paulette. 'It was a mutual thing.'

'Oh.'

'Yeah, it was all wearing a little thin. On both sides.' Paulette gave a vivid smile. 'So I'm back on the market again. Free and single. And I wondered . . . I just thought, if you have any contacts who might be interested . . . '

So that's why she's here, thought Sonya. She'd heard the word going around and knew that Paulette wasn't telling the truth. Marcus had dumped her, and everyone was saying it was because he was – of all crazy things – in love with his wife. Sonya wondered if that was true. Maybe. Maybe not. He'd certainly done well out of Black Clara's clubs, that was for sure.

Sonya looked at Paulette sitting there, her honey-blonde

hair carefully curled, her grape-green eyes so hopeful. Paulette had never been nice to her, but Sonya had been taught good manners and kindness at her mother's knee, so it was Paulette's lucky day.

'Actually,' said Sonya in that charmingly accented lilt of hers, 'there's a party tonight. They have asked me to bring along some friends, so if you'd like . . . ?'

'I'd love it!' gushed Paulette.

When they got to the posh address in Belgravia, each of them done up to the nines, Sonya knocked on the door. They could hear music seeping out through the walls of the place, could hear laughter and the clink of champagne glasses.

The level of noise shot up dramatically as the door was opened by a tall narrow-hipped blond man wearing nothing at all. His large erection was jutting out from a haze of mouse-coloured curls. Paulette thought she'd seen him somewhere, and then she realized: it was in the papers, and he was a well-respected Cabinet Minister. He smiled at them and his cock bobbed an exuberant welcome.

Behind him, she could see a pale-skinned nude woman with dark hair bent over a semi-circular table, her tiny breasts swinging as a portly man entered her energetically from behind. He looked round at the door at the new arrivals but he didn't stop what he was doing.

'Come in, come in,' he called. 'The more the merrier!'

Sonya didn't even blink; neither did Paulette. *Off with the old, on with the new*, she thought. Sonya had been forced to settle for this, and now she was too.

It was going to be *that* sort of evening.

But what the hell.

They were both used to it.

125

Fulton Sears wasn't exactly sure where he was. There had been the flat, the dog, the altar. One moment everything had been fine, and then things had sort of . . . *disintegrated*. People had passed through the flat, talked to him, but he wasn't too clear about what they were saying or even who they were.

Her brother. Henry. He remembered Henry, standing there looking at him.

Clara's brother.

Oh, Clara.

All her stuff, someone had smashed it, pulverized her watch. The table was broken. Her comb, still with her hair attached to it. Her handkerchief, still holding her scent. But . . . she was a bitch, a whore, she'd laughed at him and he was going to kill her very soon.

You promise? the hopeful voice in his head asked him.

Very soon, he promised.

They had brought him here – wherever *here* was – and now he was in a small pink-painted room. They had dressed him in pale blue trousers and a tunic. They spoke to him gently. Fed him. Helped him take a bath. Soon, they told him, he would start to feel better, just take your medication, Fulton, be a good boy.

So he'd worked this much out: all he had to do was be

calm, cooperate, fool them. Stop the muttering; he could do that. He could do anything if he set his mind to it, and one day very soon he was going to walk out of here a free man, and then he was going to kill that cow Clara.

'All right, Fulton? How are we today then, eh?'

Colin was the orderly who looked after him. Sometimes – when he lost it a bit – *sometimes*, not often, there had to be another man in the room too, when they had to hold him down, force the plastic thing between his teeth so he didn't bite clean through his tongue. But those episodes – Colin called them episodes – didn't last long.

Fulton merely grunted and carried on muttering under his breath about Clara, that bitch, that cow. He was having trouble stopping the muttering, and that was annoying, but he was OK. He didn't know precisely where he *was*, but he was safe and warm and plotting his revenge, so he didn't much care. Colin led him along to the bathroom, where the tub was already filled, ready and waiting for him. Like a hotel, this place. Almost cosy. And Colin was nice, with his fox-face and his sharp grey eyes. He smiled, and helped Fulton strip, helped him get in the bath.

The warm water soothed him, it was luxurious. He sighed with pleasure.

'Won't be a mo', Fulton,' said Colin, and left the room.

Fulton closed his eyes and dreamed of her, of Clara, of how surprised she was going to be when he turned up at her door again. Nothing would save her this time, nothing at all. He couldn't wait, he just had to stop this mumbling, which would be hard, but he could do it, convince them he was OK. They'd let him go, and then watch out.

He heard Colin come back into the room and was starting to open his eyes when hands suddenly grabbed his shoulders and pushed him down under the water. He opened his eyes in shock, gasped for air and took in bath water instead. Above him, he could see Colin, and another one.

Fulton thrashed and wriggled like an eel, kicking, his arms flailing, but they were big men, *strong* men; they had to be in this job.

Desperate, he surged upward, got his head above water, whooped air into his starving lungs.

'Shit! No! Fuck me, don't . . . ' he managed to get out, and then they forced him under again.

He couldn't breathe, couldn't draw a single breath. He struggled, he fought, he lashed out, and water cascaded everywhere, all over the floor, the two men were slipping and sliding about but they were holding him down . . .

And all at once it seemed very peaceful; he just inhaled the water, let it all go. Fulton grew still. The air bubbles rising from his mouth and drifting to the surface of the bath water grew slower until finally they stopped.

The men still held him down under the water. Made sure.

Colin looked down at the bug-eyed gaze and the open mouth of the late Fulton Sears for several long minutes, then he nodded to his colleague and together they let go.

'All done,' he said.

126

Henry had organized Bernie's funeral beautifully. There was a butter-yellow yew-wood coffin for her, and a vast floral arrangement of flowers in soft whites, pinks and pale powder blues decorated the top of it. 'Abide with Me' was sung by the small congregation, and the sermon spoke of the afterlife, of Bernie's release from the pains of this world to enjoy the glories of heaven.

God, I really hope so, thought Clara as she stood there in the church, Marcus on one side of her, Henry on the other. She'd barely spoken to Henry in the days after Bernie's tragic death, and she didn't know what to say to him now. She felt she could say sorry forever, and it would never be enough to make up for all he'd been through.

Jan and some of the other girls and boys from the clubs were there, and Sasha, Bernie's friend; but much as the vicar wanted to say it was all fine, that Bernie was in a better place, Clara's mood was still bleak.

She was glad when it was finally over, and they went out to the graveside and the vicar said the words and it was finished; Bernie's coffin was lowered into the ground. Clara threw a pink rose in on top of it. Touchingly, little Jan came up to her, squeezed her hand, hugged her, and she remembered their conversation.

Jan was her only sister now.

'Chin up,' Jan whispered in her ear, and then it was all done and everyone was going back to the Oak for the wake.

Marcus moved away, talking to someone in the crowd, and Jan did too. Clara stood alone for a moment with Henry. They exchanged a look. Then Clara said: 'I don't know what to say to you.'

'There's nothing to say,' said Henry.

'Yes there is! I didn't *know*, Henry. I thought you were vile, the things you did. I didn't know it wasn't you. You should have come to me. Told me the truth.'

Henry shrugged. 'I was a kid, Clar. I was scared to death.'

Clara looked at him, her 'little' brother with his copper-brown hair and his blue-grey eyes. Henry had grown up so handsome, with a solid, unflinching air about him. Bernie's manipulations and Clara's own harshness had taught him a toughness, a self-reliance, that she could only admire.

'I'm sorry I misjudged you, Henry. Really I am.' Clara shook her head, blinked back tears as she looked at the open grave. 'I didn't know how damaged she was. I didn't know what was happening to her. Those things she did, and blamed them on you. And then Toby! Henry, she burned him to death . . . ' Clara's voice choked. 'She admitted it.'

Henry was silent. They both stood there and stared at their sister's grave.

'We've come a hell of a long way, haven't we?' said Clara. 'We've come so far – but now we've lost Bernie.'

Henry nodded. They'd come a very long way indeed. Clara in particular – from riches to rags and then back to riches again.

'Clara – we were always going to lose Bernie. She was running out of time fast, from the minute she first drew breath,' he said.

Clara looked at his face. Thought of all they'd been

through, the whole wild merry-go-round that had been their lives so far.

'Do you think he'll ever come back, Henry?' she asked.

'Who?'

'Dad. Do you think he ever will?'

'Seriously?' Henry let out a gusting sigh. 'I can hardly even remember what he looked like. But come back? No. I doubt it. We're on our own, Clar. Just like always.'

Clara took a breath and tentatively linked her arm through his. He didn't shrug it away.

'We'll have to bloody well manage then, won't we?' she said.

'Yeah,' he said, with the ghost of a smile. 'We will.'

127

A few days after Bernie's funeral, Marcus drove over to Bond Street to make a purchase and then to his mum's place. *Quite* some place, it was, all paid for by him. And he knocked at the door, but no one answered. His mother *never* went out. Frail and elderly now, she was practically a recluse.

Marcus went down the side alley and out to the back. Knocked there, too. No answer.

'Ma?' he shouted, peering in through the glassed top half of the door, wondering where she'd got to.

No answer.

Marcus broke the glass with his elbow, reached in, popped the door open. Then he stepped into the kitchen, which was neat as a new pin; well, of course it was. He paid for the cleaner, too.

'Ma?' he called again, moving down the hallway and into her sitting room. He stopped just inside the door, and there she was.

The fire had burned down to ashes and he thought she must have been sitting there in her usual station beside it since yesterday. She looked the same as always; immaculately turned out, skinny, made-up, her hair neat.

'Ma?' he said more quietly.

She didn't stir. He walked over to her chair, took a closer

look. Her eyes were closed. She was dozing. He reached out, touched her shoulder. No movement. Then he laid his hand against her cheek and he saw that she was dead.

'Fuck it. Ma,' he said softly.

He felt a bit shaky so he sat down in the chair on the other side of the hearth. He had a blue Tiffany box in his hand, tied with white ribbon; another gift that she would have put aside. And now he was looking at the little table beside her chair, and at the built-in cupboard behind that.

She's dead, he thought, and wondered why he didn't feel anything.

It's because you hated her, right?

All his life she'd been cold to him and he'd never understood why. And now . . . now he could see that he never would. After a long while he took a deep, shaky breath, then he stood up and edged around behind her chair to undo the little clasp on the cupboard. He thought he knew what he would find. He opened the door, pulled it wide.

It was full of pale blue boxes tied with white ribbon.

She hadn't opened even one of his gifts, not *one*.

He gulped and shook his head and felt tears spring into his eyes. Christ, when had he last shed actual tears? When they'd been bombed out and she hadn't bothered to look for him? Maybe then. Since then, nothing. And he wasn't going to shed any now, he decided. She wasn't even worth it.

He drew in a shuddering breath and went back along the hall and out of the kitchen door.

EPILOGUE

Three weeks later, Clara got home late from touring the clubs. Home was now the Calypso, the largest of Marcus's clubs; they had a very nice furnished flat above it. She went up the stairs, kicking off her shoes, tugging off her earrings, and there he was, sprawled out asleep on the couch in black slacks and a white shirt, her gorgeous husband, his black hair dishevelled, his whole body relaxed. There was a tumbler of whisky on the table beside him. The stereo was on, and Ketty Lester was singing 'Love Letters'.

Clara passed by the couch, thinking that his mother's death didn't seem to have touched him at all. He hadn't shed a single tear at her funeral. But maybe that was a front. They all put on a front at times, her, Henry, Marcus, *everyone*. It got you through, when life was hard.

Marcus grabbed her wrist. His eyes opened and stared up into hers.

'Thought you were asleep,' said Clara.

'Nah. I was waiting up. For you.'

'That's nice.'

'Listen to that,' said Marcus.

'What?'

'That song. We danced to that at our wedding, remember?'

'I remember you were so mad at me you nearly snapped my spine in half,' said Clara.

Marcus yanked her down so that she fell onto him. Clara let out a yell of protest, then laughed.

'That could be our song,' said Marcus.

'It could,' agreed Clara.

He stared at her with those black, black eyes of his. 'You're fucking beautiful,' he said.

'You think so?'

'I do.'

'As beautiful as – for instance – Paulette?'

'Paulette's history,' said Marcus.

Clara narrowed her eyes at him. Her heart had picked up pace because this had been tormenting her ever since they got married; that he was still keeping Paulette, still seeing her, that she was and would remain his mistress.

'Is that the truth?' asked Clara, smoothing her hands over his chest.

'It's the truth.'

'Marcus,' said Clara. What the hell. Why not say it? 'I love you.'

Now he was staring at her from inches away. 'Not just my money?'

'Not just that, no.' Even if he was a pauper, she knew it wouldn't matter to her. She must be going mad, *insane*, but it was true.

'Clara.'

'Hm?'

'What the hell happened to you? Really?'

Clara sighed. He'd asked her this before, but maybe now she could give an answer.

'You mean, what made me a money-grubbing gold-digger?' Her smile was ironic. 'How long have you got?'

'As long as it takes. Tell me.'

So she told him. About losing everything she'd once held dear, and the slums, and her mother and the birth of the dead baby; and then marrying Frank Hatton to keep her family together, and all that she had believed about Henry, and all that she had missed going on with Bernie, then Toby and his death. By the time she got to that, she was weeping, hard cleansing tears of sorrow and regret.

He stretched and put his arms around her and pulled her closer. When she finally stopped crying he said: 'My turn now. I fell in love with you when I saw you looking so happy at Frank Hatton's funeral. Didn't even recognize the feeling, because you know what? I have never once been in love before. I thought, what a bitch, she's pleased he's dead. And then I thought,' he gave a grin, '*Wow! Look at the tits on that!*'

Clara thumped his chest and had to laugh. Then she gazed at him and felt a hard lump in her throat. 'You don't just love me for my money? For the clubs? For all that?'

'Money is the root of all evil, don't they say that? I like *acquiring* the clubs, the thrill of the chase . . . but money? I've got enough, even without yours. You know that.'

Clara thought of how hurt she had been when she saw him and Gordon in the office, counting out the cash from her clubs. 'My body then,' she said.

'Oh yeah, that.' Marcus's hands slid between them and he grabbed a double handful. 'That's a bonus, got to admit it.'

'Marcus.'

'What?'

'Just shut up and kiss me.'

And as Ketty Lester sang on, Marcus happily obeyed.